MEMOIRS OF A SPORTSMAN

MEMOIRS OF A SPORTSMAN

BY

IVÁN TURGÉNIEFF

TRANSLATED FROM THE RUSSIAN BY
ISABEL F. HAPGOOD

Short Story Index Reprint Series

BOOKS FOR LIBRARIES PRESS
FREEPORT, NEW YORK

First Published 1904
Reprinted 1969

STANDARD BOOK NUMBER:
8369-3211-0

LIBRARY OF CONGRESS CATALOG CARD NUMBER:
75-101823

MANUFACTURED BY
HALLMARK LITHOGRAPHERS, INC.
IN THE U.S.A.

CONTENTS

I

MEMOIRS OF A SPORTSMAN

I

KHOR AND KALÍNITCH

ANY one who has had occasion to pass from the Bolkhóff district to the Zhízdrin district, has, in all probability, been struck by the sharp difference between the races of people in the Governments of Orel [1] and Kalúga. The Orel peasant is small of stature, round-shouldered, surly, gazes askance from beneath his brows, lives in miserable huts of ash lumber, discharges husbandry-service for the lord of the manor, does not occupy himself with trading, eats bad food, and wears plaited slippers of linden bark; the Kalúga peasant, who pays the lord of the manor a quit-rent in lieu of personal husbandry-service, is tall of stature, his gaze is bold and merry, he is clean and white of face, he deals in butter and tar, and wears boots on festival days. An Orel village (we are speaking of the eastern part of the Orel Government) is generally situated in the midst of tilled fields, near a ravine somehow converted into a filthy pond. With

[1] Pronounced: Aryól.—TRANSLATOR.

the exception of a few willow-trees, which are always ready for service, and two or three puny birches, you will not see a tree for a verst round about; cottage clings close to cottage, the roofs are covered with rotten straw. . . . . A Kalúga village, on the contrary, is generally surrounded by a forest; the cottages stand further apart and more upright, and are covered with boards; the gates are fast locked, and the wattled fence round the back yard is not broken down, nor does it bulge outward, inviting a visit from every passing pig. . . . . . . And things are better for the huntsman, also, in the Kalúga Government. In the Orel Government, the forests and squares [1] will disappear within the next five years, and there is not a sign of a marsh; in the Kalúga Government, on the contrary, the clearings covered with a growth of bushes extend for hundreds, the marshes for scores, of versts,[2] and that noble game-bird the black-cock has not been exterminated, the amiable snipe abounds, and that busybody the partridge gladdens and startles both gunner and dog with its abrupt flight.

While visiting the Zhízdrin district, in the capacity of a sportsman, I met in the fields, and

[1] "Squares," in the Government of Orel, is the designation for vast, flat masses of bushes; the dialect of Orel is distinguished, as a whole, by a multitude of peculiar, sometimes very well-aimed, sometimes decidedly uncouth, words and turns of speech.—AUTHOR.

[2] A verst is two-thirds of a mile.—TRANSLATOR.

struck up an acquaintance with, a petty landed proprietor of Kalúga, Polutýkin, who was passionately fond of hunting and was, consequently, a splendid fellow. He had a few weaknesses, it is true: for example, he was in the habit of offering himself in marriage to all the wealthy marriageable girls in the Government, and when his hand and house were declined, with shattered heart he confided his grief to all his friends and acquaintances, but continued to send sour peaches and other unripe products of his garden to the parents of the marriageable girls; he was fond of repeating the selfsame anecdote over and over again, which, notwithstanding Mr. Polutýkin's reverence for its qualities, absolutely never made a single person laugh; he was in the habit of lauding the writings of Akím Nakhímoff and the novel "Pinna"; he stuttered; he called his dog Astronomer; he said *odnátche* instead of *odnáko* (but), and had set up in his house a French system of cookery, the secret whereof, according to his cook's understanding of the matter, consisted in completely altering the taste of every viand: meat, from the hands of this skilful artist, smacked of fish, fish tasted like mushrooms, macaroni like gunpowder; on the other hand, not a single carrot ever got into the soup, without having assumed the shape of a lozenge or a trapezium. But, with the exception of these few and insignificant failings, Mr.

Polutýkin was, as I have already said, a splendid fellow.

On the first day of my acquaintance with Mr. Polutýkin, he invited me to spend the night with him.

" It is about five versts to my house,"—he added:—" 't is a long way to trudge afoot; let us drop in first at Khor's." (The reader will excuse me if I do not reproduce his stuttering.)

" And who is Khor? "

" Why, a peasant of mine. . . . . He lives not far from here."

We wended our way thither. In the middle of the forest, in a cleared and cultivated glade, Khor's isolated farmstead was erected. It consisted of several edifices of pine logs, connected by fences; in front of the principal cottage stretched a penthouse, supported by slender posts. We entered. We were greeted by a young lad, twenty years of age, tall and handsome.

"Ah, Fédya! Is Khor at home? "—Mr. Polutýkin asked him.

" No. Khor has gone to town,"—replied the young fellow, displaying a row of snow-white teeth. " Is it your order that I harness up the little cart? "

" Yes, brother. And fetch us some kvas." [1]

[1] A sort of small beer, made by pouring water on the crusts of the sour, black, rye bread (or on rye meal) and fermenting it. I leave the friendly, simple " brother " in literal translation, here

KHOR AND KALÍNITCH

We entered the cottage. Not a single Súzdal [1] picture was pasted upon the neat timber walls; in the corner, in front of a heavy, holy picture in a silver setting, burned a shrine-lamp; the linden-wood table had been recently planed off and washed; no lively cockroaches [2] were roaming between the planks and over the frames of the windows, neither were any meditative black beetles concealed there. The young man speedily made his appearance with a large white jug filled with good kvas, a huge hunk of wheaten bread, and a dozen salted cucumbers in a wooden bowl. He placed all these eatables on the table, leaned against the door, and began to gaze at us with a smile. Before we had had time to finish our refreshments, the cart rumbled up in front of the porch. We went out. A boy of fifteen, curly-haired and rosy-cheeked, was sitting in the driver's place, and with difficulty holding in a well-fed piebald stallion. Round about the cart stood six young giants, all of whom bore a strong resemblance both to each other and to Fédya. "All young Polecats!" [3] remarked Polutýkin. "All young Polecats,"—chimed in Fédya, who had followed us out to the porch:

as elsewhere, instead of using "my dear fellow," "my boy," "my lad," or the like.—Translator.

[1] A kind of cheap lithograph made in the town named.—Translator.

[2] "Prussians," literally.—Translator.

[3] Khor', a polecat; Khor'ki, young polecats, or Khor's sons.—Translator.

" and this is not all, either: Potáp is in the forest, and Sídor has gone to town with old Khor. . . . See here, Vásya," he went on, addressing the driver:—" go like the wind: thou art driving the master. Only, look out, and slow down at the jolting-places: otherwise thou wilt spoil the cart and disturb the master's belly!" The remaining young Khors grinned at Fédya's sallies.— " Help Astronomer in!" exclaimed Mr. Polutýkin, solemnly. Fédya, not without satisfaction, lifted the dog, which was smiling in a forced way, into the air, and deposited him on the bottom of the cart. Vásya gave the horse his head. We drove off. " That 's my counting-house yonder," said Mr. Polutýkin suddenly to me, pointing at a small, low house:—" would you like to go in? "— " With pleasure."—" It is abolished now," he remarked, as he alighted:—" but it 's worth inspection, all the same."—The office consisted of two empty rooms. The watchman, a crooked old man, ran in from the back yard.—" Good day, Minyáitch," said Mr. Polutýkin: " But where 's the water? "—The crooked old man vanished, and immediately returned with a bottle of water and two glasses. " Try it," said Polutýkin to me: " It 's good spring water." We drank a glass apiece, whereupon the old man made us a reverence to the girdle.—" Well, now, I think we can drive on," remarked my new friend. " In this office I sold to merchant Allelúieff four desyatínas [1] of forest, at a good price."—We seated ourselves in the cart, and half an hour later we drove into the yard of the manor-house.

" Tell me, please," I asked Polutýkin at supper:—" why does your Khor live apart from your other peasants? "

" This is why: he 's a clever peasant. Five and twenty years ago, his cottage burned down; so then he came to my late father, and said: ' Permit me, Nikolái Kúzmitch, to settle in your forest, on the marsh. I 'll pay you a good quit-rent there.'—' But why dost thou wish to settle on the marsh? '—' Well, because I do: only, dear little father, Nikolái Kúzmitch, be so good as not to use me for work any more, but impose whatever quit-rent you see fit.'—' Fifty rubles a year! '—' All right.'—' And look out, I won't tolerate any arrears! '—' Of course, there shall be no arrears.' . . . . . And so he settled on the marsh. Since that time, the people have nicknamed him The Polecat (Khor)."

" Well, and has he grown rich? "

" Yes. Now he pays me a hundred rubles quit-rent, and I 'm thinking of raising it again. More than once I have said to him: ' Buy thy freedom! Khor, take my advice, buy thy freedom!' . . . . But he, the beast, assures me that he can't afford to; he has n't any money, he says. . . . But, of course, he has! "

[1] A desyatína is 2.70 acres.—TRANSLATOR.

On the following day, we went off hunting again as soon as we had drunk tea. As we were passing through the village, Mr. Polutýkin ordered the coachman to halt at a low-roofed cottage, and shouted loudly: " Kalínitch! "—" Immediately, master, I 'll be there immediately,"— rang out a voice from the yard:—" I 'm tying on my linden-bark slippers."—We drove at a footpace; outside of the village we were overtaken by a man of forty, tall of stature, gaunt, with a small head which was bent backward. This was Kalínitch. His good-natured, swarthy face, pitted here and there with pock-marks, pleased me at the first glance. Kalínitch (as I afterward learned) went hunting with his master every day, carried his game-bag, sometimes his gun also, spied out where the bird alighted, fetched water, picked strawberries, erected huts of shelter, ran behind the drozhky; Mr. Polutýkin could not take a step without him. Kalínitch was a man of the merriest, gentlest possible nature, was incessantly humming to himself, casting care-free glances in all directions, spoke somewhat through his nose, smilingly screwed up his bright-blue eyes, and frequently clasped his thin, wedge-shaped beard in his hand. He walked in a leisurely way, but with huge strides, leaning lightly on a long, slender staff. In the whole course of the day, he never addressed me once, served me without servility, but looked

10

after his master as he would after a child. When
the intolerable sultriness of midday made us seek
a shelter, he led us to his bee-farm, in the depths
of the forest. Kalínitch threw open to us the
tiny cottage, draped with trusses of dry, sweet-
smelling grass, made us a bed on the fresh hay,
and putting on his head a sort of sack with a net,
took a knife, a pot, and a fire-brand, and betook
himself to his beehives, to cut out some honey
for us. We drank the warm, transparent honey
like spring-water, and fell asleep to the monotonous humming of the bees and the chattering
rustle of the leaves. A light gust of wind
awakened me. . . . . . I opened my eyes, and
saw Kalínitch: he was sitting on the threshold of
the half-open door, and carving a spoon with his
knife. For a long time I admired his face, gentle and clear as the sky at eventide. Mr. Polutýkin also awoke. We did not rise at once. It
is pleasant, after a long tramp and a deep sleep,
to lie motionless on the hay: the body luxuriates
and languishes, the face is flushed with a faint
heat, sweet languor closes the eyelids. At last
we rose, and went out to roam about until the
evening. At supper I began to talk again about
Khor and also about Kalínitch.—" Kalínitch is
a good peasant,"—said Mr. Polutýkin to me:—
" a zealous and obliging peasant; but he cannot
keep his domestic affairs in order: I am always
taking him away. Every day he goes hunting

with me. . . What sort of farm-management is possible under the circumstances—you can judge for yourself."—I agreed with him, and we went to bed.

On the following day, Mr. Polutýkin was obliged to go to town on business connected with his neighbour Pitchukóff. His neighbour Pitchukóff tilled some of his land, and on the land thus tilled had whipped one of his peasant women. I went hunting alone, and toward evening dropped in at Khor's. On the threshold of the cottage an old man received me,—a bald old man, low of stature, broad-shouldered, and thick-set—the Polecat himself. I gazed with curiosity at this Khor. The cut of his countenance reminded me of Socrates: there was the same lofty, knobby brow, the same small eyes, the same snub nose. We entered the cottage together. The same Fédya brought me milk and black bread. Khor seated himself on the bench, and stroking his curly beard with the utmost composure, entered into conversation with me. He felt his dignity, apparently, and moved and spoke slowly, occasionally smiling beneath his long moustache.

We chatted together about the seed-planting and the harvest, about the life of the peasants. . . . He seemed to agree thoroughly with me; only, afterward, I became ashamed, and felt that I had not been saying the right thing. . . . Somehow, it turned out so strangely. Khor sometimes expressed himself queerly, out of wariness, it must have been. . . . Here is a sample of our conversation:

" See here, Khor," I said to him: " why dost not thou buy thy freedom from thy master? "

" And why should I buy my freedom? As it is, I know my master, and I know what quit-rent I have to pay. . . . we have a good master."

" But it is better to be free, nevertheless,"—I remarked.

Khor gazed askance at me.

" Of course," said he.

" Well, then, why dost not thou buy thyself free? "

Khor twisted his head around.

" Wherewith wouldst thou have me buy my freedom, dear little father? "

" Come now, enough of that, old man. . . . ."

" If Khor were to become a freeman," he went on in an undertone, as though speaking to himself:—" any one who lives without a beard would be Khor's superior."

" But shave off thy beard."

" What 's the beard? the beard is grass: it can be mown."

" Well, what then? "

" Why, you know, Khor will fall straightway among the merchants; the merchants lead a comfortable life, and they wear beards."

"What then, thou art engaged in trade also, art thou not?"—I asked him.

"We do a little trade in butter and tar. . . . . Dost thou command us to harness up the light cart, dear little father?"

"Thou keepest a tight rein on thy tongue, and art a man who knows his own mind," I thought. "No," I said aloud:—"I don't want the cart; I shall be roaming in the vicinity of thy farm to-morrow, and, with thy permission, I will stop and pass the night in thy hay-barn."

"Pray do. But wilt thou be comfortable in the barn? I will order the women to spread a sheet and place a pillow for thee. Hey there, women!"—he shouted, rising from his seat:— "hither, women! . . . . And do thou go with him, Fédya. For women are a stupid lot.

A quarter of an hour later, Fédya escorted me to the barn with a lantern. I threw myself down on the fragrant hay; my dog curled himself up at my feet; Fédya bade me good night, the door squeaked and slammed. It was a good while before I could get to sleep. A cow came to the door, and breathed hard a couple of times; my dog growled at her with dignity; a pig passed by, grunting meditatively; a horse somewhere near at hand began to chew hay and snort . . . . at last I fell asleep.

At dawn Fédya waked me. That merry, dashing young fellow pleased me greatly; and, so far as I had been able to observe, he was a favourite with old Khor also. The two bantered each other very amiably. The old man came out to meet me. Whether it was because I had passed the night under his roof, or for some other reason, at all events, Khor treated me much more graciously than on the preceding evening.

" The samovár is ready for thee,"—he said to me, with a smile:—" let us go and drink tea."

We seated ourselves around the table. A robust peasant woman, one of his daughters-in-law, brought a pot of milk. All his sons entered the cottage in turn. " What a tall family thou hast!"—I remarked to the old man.

" Yes," he said, biting off a tiny morsel of sugar:—" they have, apparently, no complaints to make against me or against my old woman."

" And do they all live with thee? "

" Yes. They want to, themselves, so here they live."

" And are all of them married? "

" That one yonder, the scamp, won't marry," —he replied, pointing at Fédya, who, as before, was leaning against the door.—" Váska is too young, he must wait a while."

" But why should I marry? " retorted Fédya: " I 'm comfortable as I am. What do I want with a wife? For the sake of snarling at each other, pray? "

"Oh, get out! . . . I know thee! thou wearest a silver ring.[1] . . . . . Thou wouldst like to be sniffing around the women among the house-serfs. . . . 'Stop that, you impudent thing!'" went on the old man, imitating the house-maids. "I know thee thoroughly, thou lazy creature!"

"And what is there good about a woman?"

"A woman is a worker,"—remarked Khor, impressively. "A woman is a man's servant."

"But what do I want with a worker?"

"That's exactly the point, thou art fond of picking up the hot coals by making a catspaw of other people. We know all about fellows of your stamp."

"Well, marry me off, then, if that's the case. Hey? What dost thou say to that? Why art thou silent?"

"Come, that will do, that will do, jester. Dost thou not see that we are bothering the gentleman. I'll marry thee off, never fear. . . And be not angry, dear little father: the child is little as yet, seest thou, and hasn't succeeded in acquiring sense."

Fédya shook his head. . . . . .

"Is Khor at home?"—resounded a familiar voice outside the door,—and Kalínitch entered the cottage with a bunch of wild strawberries in his hand, which he had plucked for his friend

[1] That is, he was getting foppish and so showing an interest.—TRANSLATOR.

KHOR AND KALÍNITCH

Khor. The old man gave him a cordial greeting. I stared in amazement at Kalínitch: I must confess, that I had not expected such "sentimentality" from a peasant.

On that day, I set out on my hunt four hours later than usual, and spent the three following days with Khor. My new acquaintances interested me. I do not know how I won their confidence, but they talked unreservedly with me. I listened to them and watched them with pleasure. The two friends did not resemble each other in the least. Khor was a decisive, practical man with an administrative head, a rationalist; Kalínitch, on the contrary, belonged to the class of idealists, romanticists, exalted and dreamy people. Khor understood reality, that is to say: he had established himself comfortably, he had amassed a little money, he got along well with his master, and with the other authorities; Kalínitch wore linden-bark slippers, and worried along as best he might. Khor had bred a large family, obedient and harmonious; Kalínitch had had a wife, once upon a time, of whom he had been afraid, and had never had any children at all. Khor saw through Mr. Polutýkin; Kalínitch worshipped his master. Khor loved Kalínitch, and afforded him his protection; Kalínitch loved and respected Khor. Khor talked little, laughed and reasoned to himself; Kalínitch expressed himself with fervour, although he could

not gabble as fluently[1] as a dashing factory hand.
. . . But Kalínitch was endowed with preroga-
tives which Khor himself recognised; for example: he could conjure blood,[2] fear, madness, and
expel worms; he was successful with bees, he had
a light hand. Khor, in my presence, requested
him to lead a newly bought horse into the stable,
and Kalínitch, with conscientious pompousness,[3]
complied with the old sceptic's request. Kalínitch stood closer to nature; but Khor to people,
to society; Kalínitch did not like to reason, and
believed everything blindly; Khor rose even to
the ironical point of view on life. He had seen
a great deal, he knew a great deal, and I learned
much from him. For instance: from his narra-
tives I learned that every summer, before the
mowing, a small peasant cart of a peculiar aspect makes its appearances in the villages. In
this cart sits a man in a kaftan, and sells scythes.
For cash, he charges a ruble and twenty-five
kopéks in coin, or a ruble and fifty kopéks in
bank-bills; on credit, he asks three paper rubles
and a silver ruble. All the peasants buy on
credit, of course. Two or three weeks later, he
makes his appearance again, and demands his
money. The peasant's oats are just reaped, so he
has the wherewithal to pay, he goes with the merchant to the dram-shop, and there he discharges

[1] Russian: " Sing like a nightingale."—TRANSLATOR.
[2] Stop the flow, as in nosebleed.—TRANSLATOR.
[3] Because he had " the lucky hand."—TRANSLATOR.

18

his debt. Some landed proprietors conceived the idea of buying the scythes themselves, for cash, and distributing them, on credit, to the peasants, at the same price; but the peasants proved to be dissatisfied, and even fell into a state of dejection; they had been deprived of the satisfaction of tapping the scythe and listening to the ring of it, of turning it about in their hands, and asking the crafty merchant from the petty burgher class, twenty times in succession: " See here, young fellow, that is n't such a very good scythe, is it? "—The same tricks take place also over the purchase of reaping-hooks, with merely this difference, that in this case the women take a hand in the matter, and sometimes force the pedlar to thrash them, for their own benefit. But the women are the greatest sufferers in any case. The men who contract to supply material for the paper-mills entrust the purchase of rags of a special sort to men who, in some districts, are called " eagles." An " eagle " of this sort receives from the merchant a couple of hundred rubles in bank-bills, and sets forth in quest of booty. But, in contrast to the noble bird from whom he has received his name, he does not swoop down openly and boldly,—quite the reverse: the " eagle " resorts to craft and wiles. He leaves his little cart somewhere or other in the bushes near the village, and sets forth along the back yards and back doors, just as though he were some passing stranger, or simply a roving vagrant. The women divine his approach by instinct, and steal forth to meet him. The trading compact is completed in haste. For a few copper farthings the peasant woman delivers to the " eagle " not only every useless rag, but frequently her husband's shirt and her own gown. Of late, the women have found it profitable to steal from themselves, and rid themselves in this manner of the hemp, especially of hemp-yarn,— an important extension and improvement of the " eagles' " industry! On the other hand, the peasant men have grown alert, and at the slightest suspicion, at the mere distant rumour, of the appearance of an " eagle," they proceed swiftly and vivaciously to corrective and precautionary measures. And, as a matter of fact, is it not an outrage? Selling the hemp is their business,—and they really do sell it—not in town,—they would have to trudge to the town,— but to travelling dealers, who, for the lack of scales, reckon forty handfuls as a pud,[1]—and you know what sort of a fist and what sort of a palm the Russian man possesses, especially when he " waxes zealous "! Of such tales I, an inexperienced man, and a " resident " in the country (as we say in our government of Orel), heard aplenty. But Khor did not tell stories all the time; he questioned me about many things.

[1] A trifle over thirty-six pounds, English.—TRANSLATOR.

KHOR AND KALÍNITCH

He learned that I had been abroad, and his curiosity was inflamed. . . . Kalínitch kept pace with him; but Kalínitch was more affected by descriptions of nature, of mountains, waterfalls, remarkable buildings, great towns; administrative and governmental questions interested Khor. He inquired into everything in turn:—" Do they have everything yonder just as we have, or is it different? . . Come, tell me, dear little father, how is it? . . . . " Ah! Akh! O Lord, Thy will be done!"—Kalínitch would exclaim in the course of my narrative; Khor maintained silence, contracted his thick eyebrows in a frown, and merely remarked, from time to time, " That would n't suit us, but it 's good—it 's right."—I cannot transmit to you all his queries, and there is no reason that I should; but I carried away from our conversations one conviction, which, in all probability, will be utterly unexpected to my readers,—the conviction that Peter the Great was pre-eminently a Russian man—Russian, to wit, in his reforms. The Russian man is so convinced of his strength and vigour that he is not averse to making a violent effort: he takes little interest in his past, and looks boldly ahead. What is good pleases him, what is sensible he wants to have given to him, and whence it comes is a matter of perfect indifference to him. His healthy mind is fond of jeering at the lean German brain; but the Germans, in Khor's words, are an interesting little race, and he was ready to learn of them. Thanks to the exclusive nature of his situation, of his practical independence, Khor talked to me about many things which you could n't pry out of any other man with a crowbar,—as the peasants say, grind out with a millstone. He really understood his position. In chatting with Khor, I heard, for the first time, the simple, clever speech of the Russian peasant. His knowledge was tolerably extensive, of its kind, but he did not know how to read; Kalínitch did. "Reading and writing came easy to that blockhead," remarked Khor:—"and his bees have never died when they swarmed."—"But thou hast had thy children taught to read and write?"—Khor remained silent for a while.—"Fédya knows how."—"And the others?"—"The others don't."—"Why not?"—The old man made no reply, and changed the conversation. Moreover, sensible as he was, he had a great many prejudices and bigoted ideas. For example, he despised women from the bottom of his soul, and when he was in merry mood he jeered at and ridiculed them. His wife, aged and waspish, never descended from the oven all day long, and grumbled and scolded incessantly; her sons paid no attention to her, but she kept her daughters-in-law in the fear of God,—under her thumb. Not without reason does the husband's mother sing in Russian ballads: "What sort of a son art thou to me, what sort of a family man! thou beatest not thy wife, thou beatest not the young woman. . . . . ." I once took it into my head to stand up for the daughters-in-law, I tried to arouse Khor's compassion; but he calmly replied to me, " Why do you bother yourself with such . . . . . trifles,—let the women wrangle; . . . . if they are interfered with 't will be all the worse, and it is n't worth while to soil one's hands." Sometimes the ill-tempered old woman crawled down from the oven, called the watch-dog in from the anteroom, saying: " Come here, come here, doggy! " and beat it on its gaunt back with the oven-fork, or took up her stand under the penthouse and " yowled," as Khor expressed it, at all the passers-by. But she feared her husband, and, at his command, she took herself off to her place on the oven. But the most curious thing of all was to listen to a dispute between Khor and Kalínitch, when Mr. Polutýkin was in question.—" Don't touch him, Khor,"—said Kalínitch.—" But why does n't he have some boots made for thee? " retorted the other.—" Eka, boots! . . . . what do I want of boots? I 'm a serf." . . . . " Well, and here am I a serf too, but see here—" . . . . At this word, Khor elevated his leg, and showed Kalínitch his boot, carved, probably, out of mammoth hide.— " Ekh, but art thou one of us? " replied Kalínitch.—" Well, he might, at least, give thee some

bark slippers: for thou goest a-hunting with him;
thou must wear out a pair a day, I should think."
—"He does give me money for slippers."—
"Yes, and last year he presented thee with a ten-
kopék piece."—Kalínitch turned away in vexation, but Khor burst out laughing, whereat his
little eyes completely disappeared.

Kalínitch sang quite agreeably, and played on
the *balaláika*.[1] Khor would listen and listen to
him, then suddenly loll his head on one side, and
begin to chime in, in a mournful voice. He was
especially fond of the song: "Oh, thou my Fate,
my Fate!" Fédya omitted no opportunity to
banter his father. "What has moved thee to
pity, old man?" But Khor propped his cheek on
his hand, shut his eyes, and continued to bewail
his fate. . . . . On the other hand, there was
no more active man than he at any other time;
he was eternally busy about something or other
—mending a cart, propping up the fence, looking over the harness. He did not, however, affect any special degree of cleanliness, and in reply to my comments he once said that "the
cottage must smell as though it were inhabited."

"But just see,"—I retorted:—"how clean
everything is at Kalínitch's bee-farm."

"The bees would n't live otherwise,"—he said
with a sigh.

"And hast thou a hereditary estate of thine

[1] A triangular, three-stringed guitar.—TRANSLATOR.

own?"—he asked me on another occasion.—
"Yes."—"Is it far from here?"—"About a
hundred versts."—"And dost thou live on thy
estate, dear little father?"—"Yes, I do."—"And
thou amusest thyself chiefly with thy gun, I suppose?"—"I must confess that I do."—"And a
good thing it is, too, dear little father; shoot as
many black-cock as thou wilt, and change thy
steward as often as possible."

On the fourth day, at evening, Mr. Polutýkin
sent for me. I was sorry to part from the old
man. In company with Kalínitch, I seated myself in the cart. "Well, good-bye, Khor; may
health be thine!" I said. . . . . "Good-bye,
Fédya."—"Good-bye, dear little father, good-
bye; don't forget us." We drove off; the sunset
had just begun to blaze out.—"The weather will
be splendid to-morrow," I said, glancing at the
clear sky.—"No, there will be rain,"—Kalínitch
replied:—"the ducks yonder are splashing, and
the grass smells awfully strong."—We drove
among the bushes. Kalínitch began to sing in
a low tone, as he bounced about on the driver's
seat, and kept staring, staring at the sunset
glow. . . . .

On the following day, I quitted Mr. Polutýkin's hospitable roof.

II

ERMOLÁI AND THE MILLER'S WIFE

In the evening, Ermolái and I set off to the
" stand-shooting." . . . . But, possibly, not all
my readers know what that is. Listen then, gentlemen.

A quarter of an hour before sunset, in spring,
you enter the woods with your gun, and without
your dog. You search out for yourself a spot
somewhere close to the border of the woods, scan
your surroundings, look to your percussion-cap,
exchange winks with your companion. A quarter of an hour has elapsed. The sun has set, but
it is still light in the forest; the air is pure and
limpid; the birds are chirping volubly; the young
grass gleams with the gay shimmer of an emerald
. . . you wait. The interior of the forest gradually grows dark; the scarlet light of the evening
sky glides slowly along the roots and boles of
the trees, rises ever higher and higher, passes
from the lower, almost bare boughs, to the motionless crests of the trees, which are falling
asleep. . . . And lo, now the crests also have
grown dim; the crimson heaven turns blue. The
odour of the forest is intensified, a warm moisture

is lightly wafted abroad; the fleeting breeze dies away around you. The birds sink to sleep—not all at once—but according to their species: now the chaffinches have fallen silent, in a few moments the hedge-sparrows will do the same, and after them the greenfinches. In the forest, everything grows darker and darker. The trees flow together in huge, blackish masses; the first tiny stars peer out timidly in the blue sky. All the birds are asleep. The redtails, the little woodpeckers, alone are still chirping sleepily. . . . And now they, also, have grown silent. Once more the resonant voice of the pewit has rung out overhead; an oriole has uttered a mournful cry somewhere or other; the nightingale has trilled for the first time. Your heart is languishing with anticipation, and all of a sudden—but only sportsmen will understand me—all of a sudden, athwart the profound silence, a peculiar sort of croaking and hissing rings out, the measured sweep of rapid wings becomes audible,—and a woodcock, his long beak handsomely bent on one side, flies swimmingly from behind a dark birch-tree to meet your shot.

That is what " stand-shooting " means.

So, as I was saying, Ermolái and I set out for the stand-shooting; but pardon me, gentlemen; I must first make you acquainted with Ermolái.

Picture to yourselves a man five and forty years of age, tall, gaunt, with a long, thin nose, a narrow forehead, small grey eyes, dishevelled hair, and broad, mocking lips. This man went about, winter and summer, in a yellowish nankeen kaftan, of German cut, but girt with a belt; he wore blue, full trousers, and a cap with a lamb-skin border, presented to him by a ruined landed proprietor in a merry mood. To his girdle were attached two bags, one in front, artfully twisted into two halves, for powder and shot,—the other behind, for game; but the wads Ermolái procured from his own, seemingly inexhaustible, cap. He might easily have bought himself a cartridge-box and a game-bag out of the money paid to him for the game he sold, but he never once even so much as thought of such a purchase, and continued to load his gun as before, excit-ing the amazement of spectators by the art wherewith he avoided the danger of spilling or mixing the powder and shot. His gun was sin-gle-barrelled, with a flint lock, addicted, more-over, to the bad habit of " kicking " viciously, the result of which was, that Ermolái's right cheek was always plumper than the left. How he could hit anything with that gun was more than even a clever man could divine; but hit he did. He had a setter dog, Valétka,[1] a very re-markable creature. Ermolái never fed him. " As if I were going to feed a dog,"—he argued: —" moreover, a dog is a clever animal, it will

[1] Little knave or valet; also, knave at cards.—TRANSLATOR.

find food for itself." And, in fact, although Valétka astonished even the indifferent passer-by
with his emaciation, still he lived, and lived long;
and even, in spite of his wretched condition, he
never once got lost, nor exhibited a desire to abandon his master. Once upon a time, during his
youthful years, he absented himself for a couple
of days, led astray by love; but that folly speedily broke away from him. Valétka's most remarkable quality was his incomprehensible indifference to everything on earth. . . . . If I
were not speaking of a dog, I would use the
word disenchantment. He generally sat with
his bob-tail tucked up under him, scowled, shiv-
ered, now and then, and never smiled. (Every-
one knows that dogs have the power of smiling,
and even of smiling very prettily.) He was
extremely ill-favoured, and not a single idle
house-serf omitted an opportunity to jeer spitefully at his appearance; but Valétka endured all
these jeers and even blows with remarkable coolness. He afforded particular satisfaction to the
cooks, who immediately tore themselves from
their work, and set out in pursuit of him with hue
and cry, when he, in consequence of a weakness
not confined to dogs alone, thrust his hungry
snout through the half-open door of the seduc-
tively warm and sweet-smelling kitchen. On a
hunt, he distinguished himself by indefatigabil-
ity, and he had a very respectable scent; but if

he accidentally overtook a wounded hare, he promptly devoured every bit of him, to the very last little bone, with great gusto, somewhere in the cool shade, at a respectful distance from Ermolái, who swore in all known and unknown dialects.

Ermolái belonged to one of my neighbours, a country squire of the ancient sort. These old-fashioned landed proprietors do not like " snipe," and stick to domestic fowls. It is only on exceptional occasions—on birth-days, saints' days, and election days [1]—that the cooks of squires of the ancient cut undertake to prepare the long-billed birds, and, waxing furious, as a Russian is wont to do when he himself does not quite understand what he is about, they invent for them such complicated sauces, that most of the guests survey with curiosity and attention the viands placed before them, but cannot possibly bring themselves to taste them. Ermolái had orders to furnish his master's table, once a month, with a couple of brace of black-cock and partridges, and, for the rest, was permitted to live where and how he pleased. He was discarded, as a man who was fit for no work whatsoever,—" a ne'er do well," as we say in the Government of Orel. They did not furnish him with powder and shot, as a matter of course, in consonance with the self-same principle on which he did not feed his dog.

[1] For Marshal of the Nobility.—TRANSLATOR.

THE MILLER'S WIFE

Ermolái was a man of a very singular nature; care-free as a bird, decidedly loquacious, absent-minded, and clumsy in appearance; he was extremely fond of drink, never lived long in one place, shuffled his feet as he walked, and swayed from side to side,—and with all his shuffling and swaying to and fro, he would cover a distance of fifty versts in twenty-four hours. He exposed himself to the most varied experiences; he would pass the night in the marshes, in trees, on roofs, under bridges, more than once he sat locked up in garrets, cellars, and barns, lost his gun, his dog, his most indispensable garments, was thrashed long and violently,—and, notwithstanding, after a while, he would return home clothed, with his gun and his dog. It was impossible to call him a jolly man, although he was almost always in a fairly cheerful mood; his general aspect was that of a droll fellow. Ermolái was fond of chatting with a nice man, especially over a glass of liquor, but even that not for long at a time; he would rise and walk off.—"But where the devil art thou going? Night is falling."—"Why, to Tcháplino."—"But what hast thou got to trudge to Tcháplino for—ten versts away?"—"Why, to spend the night there with peasant Sofrón."—"Come, spend the night here."—"No, I can't."—And off would go Ermolái, with his Valétka, into the dark night, through the bushes and the ravines, and, as likely as not, the poor peasant

31

Sofrón would not let him into the house, and, in all probability, would pummel his back for him to boot: " Don't go bothering honest folks." On the other hand, there was no one who could be compared with Ermolái in the art of catching fish at flood-water in spring, of getting crawfish with his hands, of searching out game by instinct, of decoying woodcock, of training hawks, of enticing nightingales with the " forest pipes," with " cuckoo call." [1] . . . . One thing he could not do: train dogs; he had not the patience. He had a wife. He went to see her once a week. She dwelt in a miserable, half-ruined little hut, scraped along somehow or other, and often did not know at night whether she would have enough to eat on the morrow or not, and, in general, her lot was a bitter one. Ermolái, that carefree, good-natured man, treated her harshly and roughly, assuming at home a threatening and surly aspect,—and his poor wife did not know how to please him, trembled at his glance, bought him liquor with her last farthing, and servilely covered him with her sheepskin coat when he, stretching himself out majestically on the oven, fell into a heroic slumber. More than once I had occasion to observe in him the involuntary manifestations of a certain surly ferocity. I did not like the expression of his face when

---

[1] Hunters for nightingales are familiar with these terms: they designate the best " passages " in the nightingale's song.—AUTHOR.

he bit the neck of a wounded bird. But Ermolái
never remained at home for more than one day;
and, away from home, he was again transformed
into " Ermólka," as he was called for a hundred
versts round about, and as he occasionally called
himself.[1] The meanest house-serf was conscious
of his superiority over this vagabond,—and, possibly for that very reason, treated him in a
friendly manner; while the peasants first gladly
pursued and caught him, like a hare in the field,
but afterward released him and bade him Godspeed, and having once recognised the fact that
he was a queer fish, they did not touch him again,
but even gave him bread, and entered into conversation with him. . . . . This was the man
whom I took with me as a hunter, and with him
I set out for " stand-shooting " in a large birch
grove on the bank of the Ísta.

Many Russian rivers have one hilly shore and
the other in level plains, like the Volga; so has
the Ísta. This little river winds about in an extremely capricious way, writhing like a snake,
never flows straight for a single half-verst, and,
in some places, from the crest of a steep hill,
about ten versts of it are visible, with dams and
ponds, mills, vegetable-plots enclosed with willows, and dense gardens. The Ísta abounds
in fish, especially in mullet (the peasants catch

---

[1] The diminutive form conveys the idea of an amiable, good fellow. Ermólka may also mean the skull-cap.—TRANSLATOR.

them, with their hands, in the heat of the day, under the bushes). Small sandpipers fly whistling along the rocky shores, dotted with cold, bright springs; wild ducks swim out into the centre of the ponds, and gaze cautiously about; herons stand out prominently in the shadow, in the bays, under the precipices. . . . . We had been standing at " stand-shooting " for about an hour, and had killed a couple of brace of woodcock; and, being desirous of trying our luck once more before sunrise (one can also go stand-shooting early in the morning), we decided to pass the night in the nearest mill. We emerged from the grove, and descended the hill. The river was flowing on in dark-blue waves; the air had grown thick, burdened with the nocturnal moisture. We knocked at the gate. The dogs began to bark in the yard. " Who 's there? "—rang out a hoarse, sleepy voice.—" Sportsmen: let us in to pass the night."—There was no answer.—" We will pay."—" I 'll go and tell the master. . . Shut up, you damned beasts! . . . . Ekh, I 'd like to murder you! "—We heard the labourer enter the cottage; he speedily returned to the gate.—" No," he said, " the master does not command me to admit you."—" Why not? " —" Why, he 's afraid: you are hunters; the first thing anybody knows, you 'll be setting the mill afire; you see, you have that sort of ammunition." —" What nonsense! "—" Anyhow, our mill was

burned down the year before last: some cattle-
drovers spent the night here, and, you know,
probably they set it ablaze."—" But, brother, we
can't spend the night out of doors, of course! "—
" As you please." . . . . He went off, clumping
with his boots.

Ermolái wished him divers unpleasant things.
" Let's go to the village,"—he ejaculated, at
last, with a sigh. But it was two versts to the
village. . . . " Let's pass the night here,"—said
I:—" it is warm out of doors; the miller will
send us out some straw, if we pay for it."
—Ermolái agreed, without making any difficulties.—Again we began to thump on the gate.—
" What do you want now? "—rang out the voice
of the hired man again:—" I told you, you
couldn't."—We explained to him what we
wanted. He went to consult his master, and
came back accompanied by the latter. The
wicket screeched. The miller made his appearance, a man of lofty stature, with a fat face, a
bull neck, and a huge, round belly. He assented
to my proposal. A hundred paces from the mill
there was a tiny shed, open on all sides. Thither
they brought us straw and hay; the workman
placed the samovár on the grass beside the
stream, and squatting down on his heels, began
zealously to blow into the pipe. . . . . The coals
flared up brilliantly, illuminating his youthful
face. The miller ran to arouse his wife, and, at

last, himself suggested to me that we should
spend the night in his cottage; but I preferred
to remain in the open air. The miller's wife
brought us milk, eggs, potatoes, and bread. The
samovár soon began to hiss, and we set to drinking tea. Vapours rose from the river; there was
no wind; the corncrakes were calling all around
us; faint noises resounded near the mill-wheels:
now the drops dripped from the blades, again
the water trickled through the bars of the sluice-
gate. We built a small bonfire. While Ermolái
was roasting the potatoes in the ashes, I managed
to fall into a doze. . . . . A faint, repressed whispering aroused me. I raised my head: before
the fire, on an overturned cask, sat the miller's
wife, chatting with my huntsman. I had already, from her garb, her movements, and her
mode of speech, divined that she was of the
house-serf class—not a peasant woman, and not
a petty burgheress; but only now did I scan her
face well. Apparently, she was about thirty
years of age; her thin, pale face still preserved
traces of remarkable beauty; I was particularly
pleased by her eyes, which were large and mournful. She had her elbows propped on her knees,
and her face rested on her hands. Ermolái was
sitting with his back toward me, and feeding the
fire with chips.

"There's murrain in Zheltúkhino again,"—
said the miller's wife:—"both of Father Iván's

cows are down with it. . . . . Lord have mercy!"

" And how are your pigs?"—inquired Ermolái, after a pause.

" They 're alive."

" You might, at least, give me a sucking-pig."

The miller's wife remained silent for a while, then sighed.

" Who 's this you 're with?"—she asked.

" With a gentleman—the gentleman from Kostomárovsk."

Ermolái flung several fir-branches on the fire; the branches immediately began to crackle vigorously, the thick, white smoke puffed out straight in his face.

" Why would n't your husband let us into the cottage?"

" He 's afraid."

" What a fat-belly! . . . . My dear little dove, Arína Timofyéevna, do thou fetch me out a little glass of liquor!"

The miller's wife rose, and disappeared into the gloom. Ermolái began to sing in an undertone:

> " When to my loved one I did go,
> All my boots I quite wore out."

Arína returned with a small caraffe and a glass. Ermolái half rose to his feet, crossed himself, and tossed off a glassful at a gulp. " I love it! " he added.

Again the miller's wife seated herself on the cask.

" Well, how goes it, Arína Timofyéevna,— thou art still ailing, I suppose? "

" Yes, I am."

" What 's the matter? "

" My cough torments me at night."

" The gentleman has fallen asleep, apparently,"—said Ermolái, after a brief silence.— " Don't go to the doctor, Arína: 't will be the worse for thee."

" I 'm not going, as it is."

" But do thou come and stay with me."

Arína bowed her head.

" I 'll drive my own wife away, in that case," —went on Ermolái. . . " I really will, ma'am."

" You 'd better wake up your master, Ermolái Petróvitch; the potatoes are roasted enough, you see."

" Why, let him go on with his nap,"—remarked my faithful servant, indifferently,—" he has run his legs off, so he is sleepy."

I turned over on the hay. Ermolái rose, and came over to me.—" The potatoes are ready, sir, please eat."

I emerged from beneath the shed-roof; the miller's wife rose from the cask, and started to go away. I entered into conversation with her.

" Is it long since you took over this mill? "

" Our second year began on Trinity-day." [1]

" Where does thy husband come from? "

Aría did not understand my question.

" Whence comes thy husband? " [2]—repeated Ermolái, raising his voice.

" From Byelyóff. He is a burgher of Byelyóff."

" And art thou also from Byelyóff? "

" No, I 'm a serf. . . . I was a serf."

" Whose? "

" Mr. Zvyérkoff's. Now I 'm a free woman."

" Of what Zvyérkoff? "

" Alexander Sílitch."

" Wert not thou his wife's maid? "

" And how do you know that?—Yes, I was."

I gazed at Aría with redoubled curiosity and sympathy.

" I know thy master,"—I went on.

" Do you? "—she replied, in a low voice,—and dropped her eyes.

I must tell the reader why I gazed upon Aría with so much sympathy. During my sojourn in Petersburg, I had accidentally made the acquaintance of Mr. Zvyérkoff.[3] He occupied a

---

[1] In the Eastern Church this is Whitsunday, or Pentecost. The following day, which is an equally great feast, is " the Day of the Descent of the Holy Spirit." But the grand Pentecost celebration is on Trinity-day.—TRANSLATOR.

[2] The gentleman says, correctly, " otkúda " (whence); Ermolái says, incorrectly, " otkéleva."—TRANSLATOR.

[3] Zvyérkoff is derived from *Zvyer,* a wild beast.—TRANSLATOR.

rather important post, and bore the reputation of being a clever and active man. He had a wife, plump, sensitive, tearful, and ill-tempered, a heavy, commonplace creature; he had also a son, a regular little squire's son of the old-fashioned type, spoiled and stupid. Mr. Zvyérkoff's personal appearance did not predispose one much in his favour: tiny, mouse-like eyes gazed craftily out of a broad, almost square face, a large, sharp-pointed nose, with flaring nostrils, projected from it; closely-clipped grey hair reared itself in a brush above a furrowed brow, thin lips twitched and smiled incessantly. Mr. Zvyérkoff generally stood with his legs straddled far apart, and his thick little hands thrust into his pockets. It once fell to my lot to drive out of town in the same carriage with him. We fell into conversation. Being an experienced, energetic man, Mr. Zvyérkoff began to instruct me in the "way of truth."

"Permit me to remark to you,"—he squeaked, at last:—"all you young men reason and talk about everything at random: you know very little about your own fatherland; Russia is an unknown country to you, gentlemen,—that's what it is! . . . . You never read anything but German books. Here, for example, you are telling me this, that, and the other, about . . . well, that is to say, about house-serfs. . . . Very good, I don't deny it, that's all very good; but you don't

know them, you don't know what sort of folks
they are." Mr. Zvyérkoff blew his nose loudly,
and took a pinch of snuff. " Allow me to relate
to you, as an example, one little anecdote: you
may find it interesting." (Mr. Zvyérkoff cleared
his throat). " You know, I suppose, what sort
of a wife I have: apparently, it would be difficult
to find a kinder woman than she, you must
agree to that. Her maids never have any hard-
ships—their life is simply paradise visibly realised. . . . . But my wife has laid it down as
a rule for herself: not to keep married maids.
Really, it 's not the thing to do: children will arrive,—and this, and that,—well, and how is a
maid to look after her mistress then, as she
should, and attend to her ways: she no longer
cares for that, she 's no longer thinking of that.
One must reason humanely. So, sir, we were
once driving through our village, it must be—I
want to tell you accurately, not to lie—fifteen
years ago. We saw that the Elder had a little girl,
a daughter, a very pretty creature; there was
even, you know, something obsequious about her
manners. My wife says to me: ' Kokò,'—that is
to say, you understand, that 's what she calls
me,—' let 's take this young girl to Petersburg;
she pleases me, Kokò.' . . . ' We 'll take her,
with pleasure,' says I. The Elder, of course,
fell at our feet; he could not have expected such
luck, you understand. . . . . . Well, of course,

the girl wept, out of folly. Now, it really is rather painful, at first: the parental house . . . . in general . . . . it's not in the least surprising. But she soon got used to us; at first we put her in the maids' room; they taught her, of course. And what do you think? . . . . The girl made astonishing progress; my wife simply took a violent fancy to her, and at last appointed her as her personal maid, over the head of the other maids . . . . . observe! . . . And I must do her the justice to say, that my wife had never before had such a maid,—positively, never; obliging, modest, obedient—simply, everything that is required. On the other hand, I must admit that my wife petted her too much: she dressed her capitally, fed her from our own table,[1] gave her tea to drink . . . . well, and every sort of thing you can imagine! So, after this fashion, she served my wife for ten years. All of a sudden, one fine morning, just fancy, Arína comes in—her name was Arína—comes into my study, without being announced,—and, flop! she goes at my feet. . . . I will tell you frankly, that I cannot endure that sort of thing. A man should never forget his dignity, is n't that so? "—' What dost thou want? '—' Dear little father, Alexander Sílitch, I crave a favour.'—' What is it? '— ' Permit me to marry.'—I must confess to you

[1] Russian servants always used to have, and generally have still, their own cook and special food, such as cabbage soup, buckwheat groats, and sour, black rye bread.—TRANSLATOR.

that I was amazed.—'But dost not thou know,
fool, that thy mistress has no other maid?'—'I
will serve the mistress as usual.'—'Nonsense!
Nonsense! thy mistress does not keep married
maids.'—'Malánya can take my place.'—'I beg
that thou wilt not argue!'—'As you will.'.....
I must admit, that I was dumfounded. I tell
you this is the sort of man I am: nothing so
offends me, I venture to assert, so violently offends me, as ingratitude. . . . . For there is no
need of my telling you—you know what sort of
a wife I have: an angel in the flesh, kindness inexpressible. . . . . . It seems as though even a
malefactor would have pity on her. I ordered
Arína out of the room. Perhaps she 'll recover
her senses, I thought; one does n't wish, you
know, to believe evil, black ingratitude in a person. But what do you think? Six months later,
she is good enough to apply to me again, with the
same request. Then I drove her away in wrath,
I admit it, and threatened her, promised to tell
my wife. I was upset. . . . . But conceive my
surprise: a little while later, my wife comes to
me, in tears, so agitated that I was fairly frightened.—'What has happened?'—'Arína . . . . .
You understand. . . . I am ashamed to speak
out.'—'It cannot be! . . . . who is it?'—'Petrúshka, the footman.' I flew into a rage.
That 's the kind of man I am . . . . don't like
half-measures! . . . . . Petrúshka . . . . is not to

blame. We can punish him; but, in my opinion, he is not to blame. Arína . . . . well, what is there . . . . well, well, what more is there to be said?' Of course, I immediately gave orders to have her hair cut off short, to clothe her in striped ticking, and to exile her to the country. My wife was deprived of an excellent maid, but there was no help for it: one cannot tolerate disorder in the household. It is better to amputate an ailing member at one blow. . . . . . Well, well, and now, judge for yourself,—well, now, you know what my wife is, you see, you see, she 's, she 's, she 's . . . . an angel, in short! . . . . She had got attached to Arína, you see,—and Arína knew it, and was not ashamed. . . . . . Hey? No, tell me . . . hey? But what 's the use of discussing it! In any case, there was nothing else to be done. And that girl's ingratitude pained me, me myself, for a long time. Say what you will . . . . . you need not look for heart, for feeling in those creatures! You may feed a wolf as you will, he always has his eye on the forest. . . . . Forward march, science! But I merely wished to prove to you . . . . ."

And, without finishing his sentence, Mr. Zvyérkoff turned away his head, and wrapped himself more closely in his cloak, manfully stifling his involuntary emotion.

The reader now understands, probably, why I gazed at Arína with sympathy.

" Hast thou been married long to the miller? "
—I asked her, at last.

" Two years."

" But is it possible that thy master permitted it? "

" My freedom was purchased."

" By whom? "

" Savély Alexyéevitch."

" Who is he? "

" My husband." (Ermolái smiled to himself.)
" But did my master talk to you about me? "—
added Arína, after a brief silence.

I did not know what reply to make to her question. " Arína! " shouted the miller from afar.
She rose and went away.

" Is her husband a good man? "—I asked
Ermolái.

" So-so."

" And have they any children? "

" They had one, but it died."

" How did it come about—did the miller take
a liking to her? Did he pay a large ransom for
her? "

" I don't know. She knows how to read and
write; in his business it . . . . . that sort of
thing . . . . is an advantage. Consequently,
he must have taken a fancy to her."

" And hast thou known her long? "

" Yes. I used to go to her master's formerly.
Their manor is not far from here."

" And dost thou know Petrúshka the foot-man? "

" Piótr Vasílievitch? Of course I know him."

" Where is he now? "

" He has become a soldier."

We fell silent.

" She appears to be ill? "—I asked Ermolái, at last.

" Ill? I should say so! . . . . I think the stand-shooting will be good to-morrow. It would n't be a bad thing for you to get some sleep now."

A flock of wild ducks dashed whistling over our heads, and we heard them drop down on the river, not far from us. It was completely dark now, and beginning to grow cold; a nightingale was trilling loudly in the grove. We buried ourselves in the hay, and went to sleep.

III

THE RASPBERRY WATER

THE heat often becomes unbearable at the beginning of August. At that time, between twelve and three o'clock, the most resolute and concentrated man is in no condition to go hunting, and the most devoted dog begins " to clean the sportsman's spurs," that is to say, trots behind him at a foot-pace, with his eyes painfully screwed up, and his tongue lolling out in an exaggerated manner; and, in reply to his master's reproaches, he meekly wags his tail, and expresses confusion on his countenance, but does not advance. Precisely on such a day I chanced to be out on a hunt. For a long time, I resisted the temptation to lie down somewhere in the shade, if only for a moment; for a long time, my indefatigable dog continued to rummage among the bushes, although, evidently, he did not expect any rational result from his feverish activity. At last, the stifling sultriness compelled me to think of saving my last strength and faculties. I managed to drag myself to the little river Ísta, already familiar to my indulgent readers, lowered myself from a crag, and strolled along the damp,

47

yellow sand in the direction of a spring known throughout the whole neighbourhood as " The Raspberry Water." This spring wells forth from a crevice in the bank, which gradually is converted into a small but deep ravine, and twenty paces thence it falls into the river with a merry, babbling sound. Oak bushes have overgrown the slopes of the ravine; around the spring, soft, velvety grass gleams green; the sun's rays hardly ever touch its cold, silvery waters. I reached the spring; on the grass lay a birch-bark dipper, left behind by some passing peasant for public use. I took a drink, lay down in the shade, and cast a glance around me. At the bay formed by the spring's entrance into the river, and for that reason always covered with a faint ripple, sat two old men, with their backs toward me. One of them, rather thickset and lofty of stature, in a neat, dark-green kaftan and a flat felt cap, was catching fish,—the other, a thin, small man in a patched seersucker short coat, and without a cap, was holding the pot of worms on his lap, and now and then passing his hand over his small grey head, as though desirous of protecting it from the sun. I looked more intently at him, and recognised in him Styópushka from Shumíkhino. I beg the reader's permission to introduce this man to him.

A few versts distant from my hamlet, lies the large village Shumíkhino, with a stone church, erected in the name of Saints Kozmá and Damián. Opposite this church, a spacious manor-house of a landed proprietor formerly flaunted itself, surrounded by various outbuildings,— offices, work-shops, bath-houses, and temporary kitchens, detached wings for visitors and stewards, hot-houses for flowers, swings for the retainers, and other more or less useful structures.

In this mansion dwelt wealthy landed gentry, and everything was proceeding in an orderly manner with them,—when, all of a sudden, one fine morning, this whole blessed establishment[1] was burned to the ground. The gentry removed to another nest; the farm sank into a state of desolation. The vast heap of ashes where the manor had stood was converted into a vegetable-garden, encumbered here and there by piles of bricks, the remnants of the former foundations. A tiny hut had hastily been constructed from the surviving beams, covered with barge-planks,[2] which had been purchased ten years previously for the erection of a pavilion in the Gothic style; and the gardener, Mitrofán, with his wife, Aksínya, and their seven children were established therein. Mitrofán received orders to supply the master's table, one hundred and fifty versts dis-

---

[1] In the original, *blagodát,* blessing.—TRANSLATOR.

[2] The barges used on Russian rivers to transport firewood and so forth are riveted together with huge wooden pegs only, and are broken up at the end of the voyage. The lavishly perforated planks sell for a very low price.—TRANSLATOR.

tant, with fresh herbs and vegetables; to Aksínya was entrusted the oversight of the Tyrolean cow, which had been purchased at a high price in Moscow, but was unfortunately deprived of all possibility of reproduction, and, consequently, had never given any milk since she had been acquired; into her hands was given also a crested, smoke-coloured drake, the "quality's" sole fowl; no duties were assigned to the children, on account of their tender age, which, nevertheless, did not, in the least, prevent their becoming thoroughly lazy. I chanced to pass the night, on a couple of occasions, with this gardener,—I was in the habit of getting cucumbers from him in passing, which cucumbers, heaven knows why, were characterised even in summer by their size, their worthless, watery flavour, and their thick, yellow skin. It was at his house that I had seen Styópushka for the first time. With the exception of Mitrofán and his family, and of the deaf, old churchwarden, Gerásim, who lived as a charity in a tiny chamber at the house of the one-eyed soldier's widow, not a single house-serf remained in Shumíkhino, for it was not possible to regard Styópushka, whom I intend to introduce to the reader, either as a man in general, or as a house-serf in particular.

Every individual has at least some sort of position in society, some connection or other; every house-serf receives, if not wages, at least the so-

THE RASPBERRY WATER

called " allowance ": Styópushka received absolutely no aid, was related to no one, no one knew
of his existence. This man had not even a past;
no one mentioned him; it is hardly probable that
he was even included in the revision-lists.[1]   Ob-
scure rumours were in circulation, to the effect
that, once upon a time, he had been valet to some
one; but who he was, whence he came, whose son
he was, how he had got into the number of the
Shumíkhino subjects, in what manner he had
acquired the seersucker kaftan which he had
worn from time immemorial, where he lived,
what he lived on,—as to these points positively
no one had the slightest idea, and, to tell the
truth, no one bothered himself about these questions. Grandpa Trofímitch, who knew the gene-
alogy of all the house-serfs in an ascending line
back to the fourth generation, once said merely,
that Stepán was related to a Turkish woman,
whom the late master, Brigadier[2] Alexyéi Ro-
mánitch, had been pleased to bring back with him
from a campaign, in his baggage-train.   And
it even happened that, on festival days, days
of universal gifts and hospitable entertainment,
with buckwheat patties and green wine, after the
ancient Russian custom,—even on such days,

[1] The revised lists of male serfs, made at intervals of years, in
the pre-emancipation days, as a basis of taxation.—TRANSLATOR.
[2] A military rank between Colonel and Lieutenant-General,
instituted by Peter the Great, and abolished under Paul I.—
TRANSLATOR.

51

Styópushka was not wont to present himself at
the tables set forth or at the casks of liquor, did
not make his reverence, did not kiss the master's
hand, did not drain off at a draught a glass under
the master's eye and to the master's health, a
glass filled by the fat hand of the superintendent,—perchance, some kind soul, in passing,
would bestow upon the poor fellow the bit of
patty which he had not been able to finish off.
At Easter, people exchanged the kiss of greeting
with him, but he did not tuck up his greasy sleeve,
he did not pull a red egg out of his rear pocket,
he did not present it, panting and blinking, to the
young master, or even to the gentlewoman, the
mistress herself. In summer, he lived in a pen
behind the chicken-coop, and in winter, in the
anteroom of the bath-house; in extremely cold
weather he spent the night in the hay-loft.
People got used to seeing him about, they even
gave him a kick sometimes, but no one entered
into conversation with him, and he himself, apparently, had never opened his mouth since he
was born. After the conflagration, this forsaken
man took refuge with the gardener, Mitrofán.
The gardener let him alone, he did not say to
him, " Live with me," but he did not turn him out
of doors. And Styópushka did not live with the
gardener: he lodged in, he hovered about, the
vegetable-garden. He walked and moved without making a sound; he sneezed and coughed

into his hand, not without terror; he was eternally bustling about and making himself busy, like an ant; and all for his food, for his food alone. And, as a matter of fact, had he not worried about his nourishment from morning until night, —my Styópushka would have died of hunger. 'T is a bad thing not to know in the morning what you will have had to eat by nightfall! Now, Styópushka would be sitting under the hedge, gnawing at a radish, or sucking at a carrot, or crushing a dirty head of cabbage beneath him; again, he would be carrying a bucket of water somewhere or other, and grunting over it; and again, he would light a tiny fire under a pot, and fling some black morsels, drawn from the breast of his shirt, into the pot; or he would be pounding away at his own place in the store-room with a billet of wood, driving in a nail, or putting up a small shelf for his bread. And all this he did in silence, as though from around a corner: cast a glance, and he had already vanished. And then, all of a sudden, he would absent himself for a couple of days; of course, no one noticed his absence. . . . . And the first you knew, there he was again, somewhere near the hedge, placing chips stealthily under the tripod. His face was small, his eyes were yellowish, his hair grew clear down to his eyebrows, he had a small, pointed nose, very large ears, transparent like those of a bat, a beard which looked as apparently of a fort-

night's growth, never any more of it, never any
less. This was the Styópushka whom I encountered on the bank of the Ísta, in the company of
another old man.

I went up to him, bade him good morning,
and seated myself by his side. In Styópushka's
companion I recognised another acquaintance:
he was a man who had belonged to Count Piótr
Ílitch * * *, and had been set at liberty by
him, Mikhaílo Savélitch, nicknamed The Fog
(Tumán). He lived with the consumptive petty
burgher of Bolkhóff who kept the posting-house,
where I stopped quite frequently. The young
officials and other persons of leisure who traverse
the Orel highway (the merchants, laden with
their striped feather-beds,[1] care not for it) can
still see, at a short distance from the big, church-
village of Tróitzkoe (Trinity), a huge, wooden,
two-storied house utterly deserted, with roof falling to ruin, and windows tightly nailed up, which
stands on the very verge of the road. At midday, in clear, sunny weather, nothing more melancholy can be imagined than this ruin. Here
once dwelt Count Piótr Ílitch, famous for his
hospitality, a wealthy grandee of the olden days.
All the government used to assemble at his house,
and dance and amuse themselves gloriously, to
the deafening thunder of a home-trained orches-

[1] Even now, in some parts of Russia, mattresses, sheets, and
towels must be carried by the traveller; and down-pillows, also, are
very generally carried.—TRANSLATOR.

tra, the crash of rockets and Roman candles; and, in all probability, more than one old woman, who now passes the deserted mansion of the gentry, sighs and recalls the days gone by, and her vanished youth. Long did the Count hold wassail, long did he stroll about, with a courteous smile, among the throng of his obsequious guests; but, unhappily, his estate did not hold out to the end of his life. Completely ruined, he betook himself to Petersburg, sought a place in the service, and died in a hotel chamber, before he had received an answer. The Fog had served as his butler, and had received his emancipation papers during the Count's lifetime. He was a man of sixty, with a regular and agreeable countenance. He smiled almost constantly, as only people of Katherine the Second's time do smile nowadays, good-naturedly and majestically; when he talked, he slowly thrust forward and compressed his lips, caressingly screwed up his eyes, and uttered his words somewhat through his nose. He blew his nose and took snuff in a leisurely way also, as though he were engaged in serious business.

" Well, how goes it, Mikhaílo Savélitch,"—I began:—" hast thou caught any fish? "

" Why, please to look in the basket yonder: I 've caught two perch, and five small mullet. . . . Show them, Styópka."

Styópushka held the wicker basket toward me.

"How art thou getting on, Stepán?"—I asked him.

"L . . . . i . . . . i . . . a-a . . . . so-so-o, dear little father, pretty well,"—replied Stepán, stammering as though a pud weight were hung on his tongue.

"And is Mitrofán well?"

"Yes, o-o-of . . . . . course, dear little father."

The poor fellow turned away.

"The fish are n't biting well, somehow,"—remarked The Fog:—"it 's awfully hot; the fish have all hidden themselves under the bushes, and gone to sleep. . . . . . Bait the hook with a worm, Styópa." (Styópushka got a worm, laid it on his palm, gave it a couple of whacks, put it on the hook, spat on it, and gave it to The Fog.)

"Thanks, Styópa. . . . And you, dear little father,"—he went on, turning to me:—" you are pleased to go a-hunting?"

"As you see."

"Just so, sir. . . . . And what 's that hound of yours, English or some sort of Kurland animal?"

The old man was fond of showing off: as much as to say, "We 've seen the world also!"

"I don't know of what breed he is, but he 's a good one."

"Just so, sir. . . . And are you pleased to travel with dogs?"

"I have a couple of leashes."

THE RASPBERRY WATER

The Fog smiled, and shook his head.

"That's exactly the way: one man is fond of dogs, and another would n't take them as a gift. What I think, according to my simple judgment, is: that dogs should be kept more for the dignity of the thing, so to speak. . . . . And that everything should be kept in style: and that the horses should be in style, as is proper, and everything in style. The late Count—may the kingdom of heaven be his!—was not a sportsman by nature, I must admit; but he kept dogs, and was pleased to go out with them a couple of times a year. The whippers-in would assemble in the courtyard, in scarlet kaftans trimmed with galloon, and blow blasts on their horns; his Illustriousness would condescend to come out, and his Illustriousness's horse would be led up; his Illustriousness would mount, and the head huntsman would put his feet into the stirrups, take off his cap, and present the reins to him in it. His Illustriousness would deign to crack his hunting-crop, and the whippers-in would begin to halloo, and move away from the courtyard. A groom would ride behind his Illustriousness, and lead the master's two favourite hounds in a leash, with his own hands, and would so keep a watch, you know. . . . . And he sits high aloft, the groom does, on a kazák saddle,[1] such a rosy-cheeked fellow he was, and rolls his little eyes

[1] The kazák saddle has a fat down-cushion, between a high pommel and high back.—TRANSLATOR.

around. . . . . Well, and of course there were
guests on this occasion. And amusement and
honour were observed. . . . Akh, he has broken
loose, the Asiatic! "—he suddenly added, pulling
out his hook.

" They say that the Count led a pretty lively
life in his day—how was that? "—I asked.

The old man spat on the worm, and flung in his
hook.

" He was a very lordly man, everybody knew,
sir. The leading persons from Petersburg, as
one may say, used to come to visit him. They
used to sit at table and eat in their blue ribbons.
Well, and he was a master-hand at entertaining
them. He would summon me to him: ' Fog,'
says he, ' I require some live sterlet to-morrow;
order them to be procured, dost thou hear? '—
' I obey, your Illustriousness.' He used to im-
port embroidered coats, wigs, canes, perfumes,
ladekolon [1] snuff-boxes, such huge pictures, of
the best quality, from Paris itself. He would
give a banquet,—O Lord and Sovereign Master
of my life! [2] what fireworks and pleasure-drives
there would be! They would even fire off can-
non. There were forty musicians alone on hand.
He kept a German bandmaster; and the German
was awfully conceited: he wanted to eat at the
same table with the gentlemen and ladies; so his

[1] Eau de Cologne.—TRANSLATOR.
[2] A quotation from a familiar prayer, by St. Ephraim of
Syria, used during the Great Fast (Lent).—TRANSLATOR.

THE RASPBERRY WATER

Illustriousness gave orders that he should be turned out of doors, and bidden godspeed: ' My musicians understand their business without him,' says he. You know how it was: the master had the power to do as he liked. They would set to dancing, and dance until dawn, and chiefly the lakosez-matradura . . . . .[1] eh . . . . . eh . . . . . eh . . . . . . thou art caught, brother! " . . . . (The old man pulled a small perch out of the water.) "Take it, Styópa.—He was the right sort of a master, the master was,"—pursued the old man, throwing his line again:—" and he was a kind soul too! He 'd thrash you, on occasion— and the first you knew, he 'd have forgotten all about it. Okh, those mistresses, Lord forgive! 'T was they that ruined him. And, you see, he chose them chiefly from the lower classes. You 'd suppose that they could n't want for anything more. But no,—you must give them the most costly thing in the whole of Europe! And I must say: why not live at ease,—that 's the proper thing for a gentleman . . . . . but as for ruining yourself, that 's not right. There was one in particular: her name was Akulína; she 's dead now,—the kingdom of heaven be hers! She was a simple wench, the daughter of the village policeman of Sitóvo, and such a termagant! She used to slap the Count's cheeks. She bewitched him utterly. She shaved the brow of my

[1] L'écossais.—TRANSLATOR.

nephew: [1] he had spilled chocolate on her new gown . . . . and he was not the only one whose brow she shaved. Yes. . . . . And nevertheless, it was a good little time! "—added the old man, with a deep sigh, as he dropped his eyes and relapsed into silence.

" But you had a severe master, I see,"—I began, after a brief pause.

" That was the taste then, dear little father," —returned the old man, shaking his head.

" That is no longer done now,"—I remarked, without removing my eyes from him.

He surveyed me with a sidelong glance.

" Now, things are better, certainly,"—he muttered—and flung his line far out.

We were sitting in the shade; but even in the shade it was stifling. The heavy, sultry air seemed to have died down; the burning face sought the breeze with anguish, but there was no breeze. The sun fairly beat from the blue, darkling sky; directly in front of us, on the other shore, a field of oats gleamed yellow, overgrown here and there with wormwood, and not a single ear of the grain stirred. A little lower down, a peasant's horse was standing in the river up to his knees, and lazily swishing himself with his wet tail; now and then, a large fish swam up under an overhanging bush, emitted a bubble,

[1] That is, had him made a soldier for the long term then obligatory. The hair was shaved to mark the man and prevent desertion.—TRANSLATOR.

and gently sank to the bottom, leaving behind him a faint surge. The grasshoppers were shrilling in the rusty grass; the quails were calling in a reluctant sort of way; hawks floated above the fields, and frequently came to a standstill, swiftly fluttering their wings, and spreading out their tails like a fan. We sat motionless, overwhelmed with the heat. All at once, behind us, in the ravine, a noise resounded: some one was descending to the spring. I looked round, and beheld a peasant about fifty years of age, dusty, in shirt and bark-slippers, with a plaited birch-bark wallet and a long coat thrown over his shoulders. He approached the spring, drank eagerly, and rose to his feet.

" Eh, Vlas? "—cried The Fog, taking a look at him:—" good day, brother. Whence has God brought thee? "

" Good day, Mikhaílo Savélitch,"—said the peasant, advancing toward us,—" from afar."

" Where hast thou been? "—The Fog asked him.

" I have been to Moscow, to the master."

" Why? "

" I went to petition him."

" To petition him about what? "

" Why, that he would reduce my quit-rent, or put me on husbandry-service, or send me for settlement elsewhere, perhaps. . . . My son is dead —so I can't manage it now alone."

" Is thy son dead? "

" Yes. The deceased,"—added the peasant, after a brief silence:—" lived in Moscow, as a cabman; I must confess that he paid my quit-rent."

" But is it possible that thou art on quit-rent now? "

" Yes."

" What did thy master say? "

" What did the master say? He drove me off! ' How darest thou come straight to me,' says he; ' thou art bound to report first to the steward . . . . and where am I to transfer thee for settlement? Do thou first,' says he, ' pay up thine arrears.' He was thoroughly angry."

" Well, and so thou hast come back? "

" So I have come home. I should have liked to find out whether the deceased had left any goods behind him, but I could n't get a straight answer. I says to his employer, says I: ' I 'm Philip's father; ' and he says to me: ' How do I know that?—And thy son left nothing,' says he; ' he 's in debt to me, to boot.' Well, and so I went my way."

The peasant told us all this with a grin, as though it were a question of some one else; but a tear welled up in his small, puckered-up eyes, and his lips quivered.

" Art thou going home now? "

" Why, where else should I be going? Of

course, I 'm going home. My wife must be whistling into her fist now with hunger, I think."

" But thou mightest . . . knowest thou . . ." began Styópushka suddenly,—then grew confused, stopped short, and began to rummage in the pot.

" And shalt thou go to the steward? "—went on The Fog, glancing at Styópa not without surprise.

" Why should I go to him? . . . . I 'm in arrears, anyway. My son was ailing for about a year before he died, so that he did not pay even his own quit-rent. . . . And I don't care: there is nothing to be got from me. . . . Be as crafty as you will here, brother,—'t is in vain: my head is not responsible!" The peasant broke into a laugh. " Kintilyán Semyónitch may worry over it as he will . . . . but . . . ."

Again Vlas laughed.

" Well, that 's bad, brother Vlas,"—articulated The Fog, pausing between his words.

" How is it bad? No. . . . ." Vlas's voice broke. " How hot it is! "—he went on, mopping his brow with his sleeve.

" Who is your master? "—I inquired.

" Count * * *, Valerián Petróvitch."

" The son of Piótr Ílitch? "

" Yes, the son of Piótr Ílitch,"—replied The Fog. " The deceased Piótr Ílitch allotted Vlas's village to him during his lifetime."

" Is the Count well? "

"Yes, thank God,"—responded Vlas.—
"Handsome as steel, his face is as though it
were stuffed with fat."

"See there, dear little father,"—continued
The Fog, turning to me:—"it would be all right
near Moscow, but he has put him on quit-rent
here."

"But at how much a household?"

"Ninety-five rubles a household,"—muttered
Vlas.

"Well, there now, you see; and there's only
the littlest bit of ground, because 't is all the
master's forest."

"And they say he has sold that,"—remarked
the peasant.

"Well, there now, you see . . . . Styópa, give
me a worm. . . . . Hey, Styópa? What's the
matter with thee? hast thou fallen asleep?"

Styópushka started. The peasant sat down
beside us. Again we maintained silence for
a while. On the other shore, some one started up
a song, and such a mournful one! . . . My poor
Vlas grew dejected. . . . . .

Half an hour later we parted company.

IV

ONE day, in autumn, on my way home from the distant fields, I caught cold, and was taken ill. Fortunately, the fever overtook me in the county-town, in the hotel. I sent for the doctor. Half an hour later, the district physician made his appearance, a man of short stature, thin and black-haired. He prescribed for me the customary sudorific, ordered the application of mustard-plasters, very deftly tucked my five-ruble bank-note under his cuff,—but emitted a dry cough and glanced aside as he did so,—and was on the very verge of going off about his own affairs, but somehow got to talking and remained. The fever oppressed me; I foresaw a sleepless night, and was glad to chat with the kindly man. Tea was served. My doctor began to talk. He was far from a stupid young fellow, and expressed himself vigorously and quite entertainingly. Strange things happen in the world: you may live a long time, and on friendly terms, with one man, and never once speak frankly from your soul with him; with another you hardly manage to make acquaintance—and behold:

65

either you have blurted out to him your most secret thoughts, as though you were at confession, or he has blurted out his to you. I know not how I won the confidence of my new friend,—only, without rhyme or reason, as the saying is, he " took " and told me about a rather remarkable occurrence; and now I am going to impart his narrative to the indulgent reader. I shall endeavour to express myself in the physician's words.

" You are not acquainted,"—he began, in a weak and quavering voice (such is the effect of unadulterated Beryózoff snuff) :—" you are not acquainted with the judge here, Pável Lúkitch Mýloff, are you? . . . . . You are not? . . . . . Well, never mind." (He cleared his throat and wiped his eyes.) " Well, then, please to observe that the affair happened—to be accurate—during the Great Fast, in the very height of the thaw. I was sitting with him at his house, our judge's, and playing preference. Our judge is a nice man, and fond of playing preference. All of a sudden " (my doctor frequently employed that expression: " all of a sudden ") " I am told: ' A man is asking for you.' ' What does he want? '—said I. They tell me: ' He has brought a note—it must be from a sick person.' —' Give me the note,'—said I. And so it proved to be from a sick person. . . . . . Well, very good,—that 's our bread and butter, you un-

derstand. . . . . . And this was what was the
matter: the person who wrote to me was a
landed proprietress, a widow; she says: ' My
daughter is dying, come for the sake of our Lord
God, and horses have been sent for you.' Well,
and all that is of no consequence. . . . . But she
lives twenty versts from town, night is falling,
and the roads are such, that—faugh! And she
herself was the poorest of the poor, I could n't
expect to receive more than two rubles,[1] and even
that much was doubtful; and, in all probability,
I should be obliged to take a bolt of crash-linen
and some scraps or other. However, you understand, duty before everything. All of a sudden,
I hand over my cards to Kalliópin, and set off
homeward. I look: a wretched little peasant-
cart is standing in front of my porch; peasant-
horses,—pot-bellied, extremely pot-bellied,—the
hair on them a regular matted felt; and the
coachman is sitting hatless, by way of respect.
Well, thinks I to myself: evidently, brother, thy
masters don't eat off gold. . . . . You are
pleased to laugh, but I can tell you a poor man,
like myself, takes everything into consideration.
. . . . If the coachman sits like a prince, and
does n't doff his cap, and grins in his beard to

[1] The doctor's fee, as fixed by law, in Russia, is absurdly small.
Every one, therefore, gives what he sees fit—certain prices being
only tacitly understood as proper for certain men. The doctor
is supposed to accept what is offered, and it is contrary to eti-
quette for him to remonstrate against the sum.—TRANSLATOR.

boot, and waggles his whip, you may bet boldly
on getting a couple of bank-bills! But, in this
case, I see that the matter does not smack of that.
However, thought I to myself, it can't be helped:
duty before everything. I catch up the most indispensable remedies, and set out. Will you believe it, we barely managed to drag ourselves
to our goal. The road was hellish: brooks, snow,
mud, water-washed gullies; for, all of a sudden,
a dam had burst—alas! Notwithstanding, I got
there. The house is tiny, with a straw-thatched
roof. The windows are illuminated: which signifies, that they are expecting me. An old
woman comes out to receive me,—such a dignified
old woman, in a mob-cap; ' Save her,' says she,
' she is dying.' 'Pray don't worry,' I say to
her. . . . . . . ' Where is the patient?'—
' Here, please come this way.'—I look: 't is a
neat little room, in the corner a shrine-lamp, on
the bed a girl of twenty years, unconscious. She
is fairly burning with heat, she breathes heavily:
—'t is fever. There are two other young girls
present, her sisters,—thoroughly frightened, in
tears.—' See there,' say they, ' yesterday she was
perfectly well, and ate with appetite: this morning she complained of her head, and toward
evening, all of a sudden, she got into this condition.' . . . . I said again: ' Pray don't worry,'
—you know, the doctor is bound to say that,—
and set to work. I let blood, ordered the appli-

cation of mustard-plasters, prescribed a potion. In the meantime, I looked and looked at her, and do you know:—well, upon my word, I never before had seen such a face . . . . a beauty, in one word! I fairly go to pieces with compassion. Such pleasing features, eyes . . . . . Well, thank God, she quieted down; the perspiration broke out, she seemed to regain consciousness, cast a glance around her, smiled, passed her hand over her face. . . . . Her sisters bent over her, and inquired: 'What ails thee?'—'Nothing,'—says she, and turned away. . . . . I look . . and lo, she has fallen asleep. 'Well,' I say, 'now the patient must be left in peace.' So we all went out of the room on tiptoe; only the maid remained, in case she should be needed. And in the drawing-room, the samovár was already standing on the table, and there was Jamaica rum also: in our business, we cannot get along without it. They gave me tea, and begged me to spend the night there. . . . I consented: what was the use of going away now! The old woman kept moaning. 'What's the matter with you?' said I: 'she'll live, pray do not feel uneasy, and the best thing you can do is to get some rest yourself: it's two o'clock.'—'But will you give orders that I am to be awakened, if anything should happen?'—'I will, I will.'—The old woman went off, and the girls also betook themselves to their own room; they made up a bed for me in the drawing-room. So I lay down,—but I could n't get to sleep,—and no wonder! I seemed to be fretting over something. I could n't get my sick girl out of my mind. At last, I could endure it no longer, and all of a sudden, I got up: I thought: ' I 'll go and see how the patient is getting along.' Her bedroom adjoined the drawing-room. Well, I rose, and opened the door softly,—and my heart began to beat violently. I took a look: the maid was fast asleep, with her mouth open, and even snoring, the beast! and the sick girl was lying with her face toward me, and throwing her arms about, the poor thing! I went up to her. . . All of a sudden, she opened her eyes, and fixed them on me! . . . . . ' Who is this? Who is this?'—I was disconcerted.—'Don't be alarmed, madam,' said I: ' I 'm the doctor, I have come to see how you are feeling.'—' You are the doctor?'—' Yes, the doctor. . . . . Your mamma sent to the town for me; we have bled you, madam; now, please to lie quiet, and in a couple of days, God willing, we 'll have you on your feet again.'—' Akh, yes, yes, doctor, don't let me die . . . . please, please don't!'—' What makes you say that, God bless you!'—' Her fever is starting up again,' I thought to myself. I felt her pulse: it was the fever, sure enough. She looked at me,—then, all of a sudden, she seized my hand.—' I 'll tell you why I don't want to die, I 'll tell you, I 'll tell you . . . . now we are alone; only, if you please, you must n't let anybody know . . . . listen!' . . . . I bent down; she brought her lips to my very ear, her hair swept my cheek,—I confess that my head reeled, —and began to whisper. . . . . . I could understand nothing. . . . . . . Akh, why, she was delirious. . . . . She whispered and whispered, and very rapidly at that, and not in Russian, finished, shuddered, dropped her head back on the pillow, and menaced me with her finger.—' See that you tell no one, doctor.' . . . Somehow or other, I contrived to soothe her, gave her a drink, waked up the maid, and left the room."

Here the doctor took snuff frantically, and grew torpid for a moment.

"But, contrary to my expectation,"—he went on,—"the patient was no better on the following day. I cogitated, and cogitated, and all of a sudden, I decided to remain, although other patients were expecting me. . . . But, you know, that cannot be neglected: your practice suffers from it. But, in the first place, the sick girl was, really, in a desperate condition; and, in the second place, I must tell the truth, I felt strongly attracted to her. Moreover, the whole family pleased me. Although they were not wealthy people, yet their culture was, I may say, rare. . . . . Their father had been a learned man, a writer; he had died in poverty, of course, but had managed to impart a splendid education

to his children; he had also left behind him
many books. Whether it was because I worked
so zealously over the sick girl, or for other
reasons, at all events, I venture to assert that
they became as fond of me as though I had
been a relative. . . . . In the meantime, the
thaw had reduced the roads to a frightful condition: all communications were, so to speak, utterly cut off. . . . The sick girl did not get well
. . . day after day, day after day. . . . But so,
sir . . . . then, sir . . . ." (The doctor paused
for a while).—" Really, I do not know how to
state it to you, sir . . ." (Again he took snuff,
grunted, and swallowed a mouthful of tea.) " I
will tell you, without circumlocution,—my patient . . . . anyhow . . . . well, either she fell in
love with me . . . . . . or, no, she did n't exactly fall in love with me . . . but, anyway . . .
really, how shall I put it? . . ." (The doctor
dropped his eyes, and flushed crimson.)

" No,"—he went on with vivacity:—" she
did n't fall in love with me! One must, after all,
estimate one's self at one's true value. She was a
cultivated girl, clever, well-read, and I had forgotten even my Latin, completely, I may say.
So far as my figure is concerned " (the doctor
surveyed himself with a smile), " also, I have
nothing to boast of, apparently. But the Lord
God did n't distort me into a fool, either: I won't
call white black; I understand a thing or two

myself. For example, I understood very well indeed that Alexandra Andréevna—her name was Alexandra Andréevna—did not feel love for me, but, so to speak, a friendly inclination, respect, something of that sort. Although she herself, possibly, was mistaken on that point, yet her condition was such, as you can judge for yourself . . . . . However,"—added the doctor, who had uttered all these disjointed speeches without stopping to take breath, and with obvious embarrassment:—" I have strayed from the subject a bit, I think. . . . So you will not understand anything . . . . . but here now, with your permission, I 'll tell you the whole story in due order."

He finished his glass of tea, and began to talk in a more composed voice.

" Well, then, to proceed, sir. My patient grew constantly worse, and worse, and worse. You are not a medical man, my dear sir; you cannot comprehend what takes place in the soul of a fellow-being, especially when he first begins to divine that his malady is conquering him. What becomes of his self-confidence! All of a sudden, you grow inexpressibly timid. It seems to you, that you have forgotten everything you ever knew, and that the patient does not trust you and that others are beginning to observe that you have lost your wits, and communicate the symptoms to you unwillingly, gaze askance at you, whisper together . . . . . . eh, 't is an evil plight! But there certainly must be a remedy for this malady, you think, if you could only find it. Here now, is n't this it? You try it—no, that 's not it! You don't give the medicine time to act properly . . . . now you grasp at this, now at that. You take your prescription-book, —it certainly must be there, you think. To tell the truth, you sometimes open it at haphazard: perchance Fate, you think to yourself . . . . . But, in the meanwhile, the person is dying; and some other physician might have saved him. A consultation is necessary, you say: ' I will not assume the responsibility.' And what a fool you seem under such circumstances! Well, and you 'll learn to bear it patiently, in course of time you won't mind it. The man dies—it is no fault of yours: you have followed the rules. But there 's another torturing thing about it: you behold blind confidence in you, and you yourself feel that you are not capable of helping. Well then, that was precisely the sort of confidence that Alexandra Andréevna's whole family had in me:—and they forgot to think that their daughter was in danger. I, also, on my side, assured them that it was all right, while my soul sank into my heels. To crown the calamity, the thaw and breaking up of the roads were so bad, that the coachman would travel whole days at a time in quest of medicine. And I never left

the sick-chamber, I could n't tear myself away,
you know, I related ridiculous little anecdotes,
and played cards with her. I sat up all night.
My old woman thanked me with tears; but I
thought to myself: 'I don't deserve your gratitude.' I will confess to you frankly,—there's
no reason why I should dissimulate now,—I had
fallen in love with my patient. And Alexandra
Andréevna had become attached to me: she
would let no one but me enter the room. She
would begin to chat with me, and would interrogate me—where I had studied, how I lived, who
were my parents, whom did I visit? And I felt
that she ought not to talk, but as for prohibiting
her, positively, you know, I could n't do it. I
would clutch my head:—'What art thou doing,
thou villain?'—But then, she would take my
hand, and hold it, and gaze at me, gaze long, very
long, turn away, sigh, and say: 'How kind you
are!' Her hands were so hot, her eyes were big
and languishing.—'Yes,' she would say,—'you
are a good man, you are not like our neighbours
. . . no, you are not that sort. . . . How is
it that I have never known you until now!'
—'Calm yourself, Alexandra Andréevna,'—I
would say. . . . 'I assure you, I feel I do not
know how I have merited . . . . only, compose
yourself, for God's sake . . . . everything will
be all right, you will get well.'—And yet, I must
confess to you," added the doctor, bending for-

MEMOIRS OF A SPORTSMAN

ward, and elevating his eyebrows:—" that they had very little to do with the neighbours, because the lower sort were not their equals, and pride prevented their becoming acquainted with the rich ones. As I have told you, it was an extremely cultured family:—and, so, you know, I felt flattered. She would take her medicine from no hands but mine . . . she would sit up half-way, the poor girl, with my assistance, take it, and look at me . . . . and my heart would fairly throb. But, in the meantime, she grew worse and worse: ' She will die,' I thought, ' she will infallibly die.' Will you believe it, I felt like lying down in the grave myself: but her mother and sisters were watching, and looking me in the eye . . . . and their confidence disappeared.

" ' What is it? What is the matter?'—' Nothing, ma'am; 't is all right, ma'am!'—but it was n't all right, I had merely lost my head! Well, sir, one night I was sitting alone once more, beside the sick girl. The maid was sitting in the room also, and snoring with all her might. . . . Well, there was no use in being hard on the unfortunate maid: she was harassed enough. Alexandra Andréevna had been feeling very badly all the evening; she was tortured by the fever. She kept tossing herself about clear up to midnight; at last, she seemed to fall asleep; at all events, she did not stir, but lay quietly. The shrine-lamp was burning in front of the holy picture in the corner. I was sitting, you know, with drooping head, and dozing also. All of a sudden, I felt exactly as though some one had nudged me in the ribs. I turned round. . . O Lord, my God! Alexandra Andréevna was staring at me with all her eyes . . . . . her lips parted, her cheeks fairly blazing.—'What is the matter with you?'—'Doctor, surely I am dying?'—'God forbid!'—'No, doctor, no; please don't tell me that I shall recover . . . . don't tell me . . . if you only knew . . . listen, for God's sake, don't conceal my condition from me!'—and she breathed very fast.—'If I know for certain that I must die . . . . I will tell you everything, everything!'—'For heaven's sake, Alexandra Andréevna!'—'Listen, I have n't been asleep at all, you see; I've been watching you this long while . . . . for God's sake . . . I believe in you, you are a kind man, you are an honest man; I adjure you, by all that is holy on earth—tell me the truth! If you only knew how important it is to me. . . Doctor, tell me, for God's sake, am I in danger?'—'What shall I say to you, Alexandra Andréevna, for mercy's sake!'—'For God's sake, I beseech you!'—'I cannot conceal from you, Alexandra Andréevna, the fact that you really are in danger, but God is merciful . . . . . .'—'I shall die, I shall die!' . . . . And she seemed to be glad, her face became so cheerful; I was frightened.—'But don't be afraid,

don't be afraid, death does not terrify me in the
least.'—All of a sudden, she raised herself up,
and propped herself on her elbow.—' Now . . . .
well, now I can tell you that I am grateful to
you with all my soul, that you are a kind, good
man, that I love you.' . . . . I stared at her like
a crazy man; dread fell upon me, you know. . .
' Do you hear?—I love you!' . . . . ' Alexandra
Andréevna, how have I deserved this!'—' No,
no, you don't understand me . . . . thou dost
not understand me.' . . . . And all of a sudden,
she stretched out her arms, clasped my head, and
kissed me. . . . Will you believe it, I came near
shrieking aloud. . . . . I flung myself on my
knees, and hid my head in the pillow. She was
silent; her fingers trembled on my hair; I heard
her weeping. I began to comfort her, to reassure
her . . . . to tell the truth, I really do not know
what I said to her.—' You will waken the maid,
Alexandra Andréevna,' I said to her. . . ' I
thank you . . . . believe me . . . . calm yourself.'—' Yes, enough, enough,' she repeated.
' God be with them all; well, they will wake; well,
they will come—it makes no difference: for I
shall die. . . . . But why art thou timid, what
dost thou fear? raise thy head. . . . Can it be
myself? . . . . in that case, forgive me,'—' Alexandra Andréevna, what are you saying? . . . .
I love you, Alexandra Andréevna.'—She looked
me straight in the eye, and opened her arms.

—' Then embrace me.' . . I will tell you frankly: I don't understand why I did not go crazy that night. I was conscious that my patient was killing herself; I saw that she was not quite clear in her head; I understood, also, that had she not thought herself on the brink of death, she would not have thought of me; for, you may say what you like, 't is a terrible thing, all the same, to die at the age of twenty, without having loved any one: that is what was tormenting her, you see; that is why she, in her despair, clutched even at me,—do you understand now? But she did not release me from her arms.—' Spare me, Alexandra Andréevna, and spare yourself also,' I said. —' Why should I?' she said. ' For I must die, you know.' . . . She kept repeating this incessantly.—' See here, now; if I knew that I would recover, and become an honest young lady again, I should be ashamed, actually ashamed . . . . but as it is, what does it matter?'—' But who told you that you were going to die?'—' Eh, no, enough of that, thou canst not deceive me, thou dost not know how to lie; look at thyself.'—' You will live, Alexandra Andréevna; I will cure you. We will ask your mother's blessing on our marriage. . . . We will unite ourselves in the bonds. . . We shall be happy.'—' No, no, I have taken your word for it, I must die . . . . thou hast promised me . . . thou hast told me so.' . . . This was bitter to me, bitter for many reasons. And yoᴜ

can judge for yourself, what trifling things happen: they seem to be nothing, yet they hurt. She
took it into her head to ask me what my name
was,—not my surname, but my baptismal name.
My ill-luck decreed that it should be Trífon.
Yes, sir, yes, sir; Trífon, Trífon Ivánovitch.
Everybody in the house addressed me as doctor.
There was no help for it, I said: ' Trífon, madam.' She narrowed her eyes, shook her head, and
whispered something in French,—okh, yes, and
it was something bad, and then she laughed, and
in an ugly way too. Well, and I spent the
greater part of the night with her in that manner. In the morning, I left the room, as though
I had been a madman; I went into her room
again by daylight, after tea. My God, my God!
She was unrecognisable: corpses have more colour when they are laid in their coffins. I swear
to you, by my honour, I do not understand now,
I positively do not understand, how I survived
that torture. Three days, three nights more did
my patient linger on . . . . and what nights
they were! What was there that she did not say
to me! . . . . And, on the last night, just imagine,—I was sitting beside her, and beseeching
one thing only of God: ' Take her to Thyself,
as speedily as may be, and me along with her.'
. . . All of a sudden, the old mother bursts into
the room. . . . . I had already told her, on the
preceding day, that there was but little hope, that

the girl was in a bad way, and that it would not be out of place to send for the priest. As soon as the sick girl beheld her mother, she said:— 'Well, now, 't is a good thing thou hast come . . . look at us, we love each other, we have given each other our promise.'—'What does she mean, doctor, what does she mean?'—I turned deathly pale.—'She's delirious, ma'am,' said I; ''t is the fever heat.' . . But the girl said: 'Enough of that, enough of that, thou hast just said something entirely different to me, and hast accepted a ring from me. . . . . Why dost thou dissimulate? My mother is kind, she will forgive, she will understand; but I am dying—I have no object in lying; give me thy hand.' . . . . I sprang up and fled from the room. The old woman, of course, guessed how things stood.

"But I will not weary you, and I must admit that it is painful to me to recall all this. My patient died on the following day. The kingdom of heaven be hers!" added the doctor hastily, with a sigh. "Before she died, she asked her family to leave the room, and leave me alone with her.—'Forgive me,'—she said,—'perhaps I am culpable in your sight . . . . . my illness . . . but, believe me, I have never loved any one more than I have loved you . . . . do not forget me . . . . take care of my ring.' . . . . ."

The doctor turned away; I took his hand.

"Ekh,"—he said,—"let's talk of something

else, or would n't you like to play preference for a while? Men like us, you know, ought not to yield to such lofty sentiments. All we fellows have to think of is: how to keep the children from squalling, and our wives from scolding. For since then, you see, I have managed to contract a legal marriage, as the saying is. . . Of course . . . . I took a merchant's daughter: she had seven thousand rubles of dowry. Her name is Akulína; just a match for Trífon. She 's a vixen, I must tell you; but, luckily, she sleeps all day. . . But how about that game of preference? "

We sat down to play preference, for kopék stakes. Trífon Ivánitch won two rubles and a half from me—and went away late, greatly elated with his victory.

V

MY NEIGHBOUR RADÍLOFF

In autumn, the woodcock frequently take up their stand in ancient linden parks. We have a good many such parks in the Government of Orel. Our great-grandfathers, in selecting residence sites, invariably laid out a couple of desyatínas of good land in a fruit-orchard, with alleys of linden-trees. During the last fifty—at the most, seventy—years, these farms, these "noblemen's nests," have been gradually disappearing from the face of the earth; their manors have rotted away or have been sold for removal, the stone offices have become converted into heaps of ruins, the apple-trees have died out and gone for firewood, the fences and wattled hedges have been annihilated. Only the lindens have thriven gloriously as of yore, and now, surrounded by tilled fields, proclaim to our volatile race "our fathers and brethren departed this life."[1] A most beautiful tree is such an aged linden.

[1] A quotation from the "augmented litany" in the services of the Eastern Catholic Church: "Furthermore, we pray for . . . . all our devout fathers and brethren departed this life before us, Orthodox believers, who here, and in all the world, lie asleep in the Lord."—TRANSLATOR.

. . . . . Even the ruthless axe of the Russian peasant spares it. Its leaves are small, its mighty boughs spread out widely in all directions, beneath them reigns eternal shadow.

One day, as I was roving with Ermolái over the fields in quest of partridges, I espied on one side an abandoned park, and directed my footsteps thither. No sooner had I entered the edge of the grove than a woodcock rose with a whir from the bushes. I fired, and at the same moment a cry rang out a few paces from me: the frightened face of a young girl peered forth from behind the trees, and immediately vanished. Ermolái rushed up to me.—" Why do you shoot here? A landed proprietor lives here."

Before I could answer him, before my dog, with noble dignity, could fetch me the bird I had killed, hasty footsteps made themselves audible, and a man of lofty stature, with moustaches, emerged from the grove, and halted in front of me, with an aspect of displeasure. I made my excuses as best I might, mentioned my name, and offered him the bird which had been shot on his domain.

" Very well,"—he said to me, with a smile, " I will accept your game, but only on one condition: that you will stay to dinner with us."

I must confess that I was not greatly pleased at his suggestion, but it was impossible to refuse.

" I am the proprietor who lives here, and your

neighbour, Radíloff; perhaps you have heard of me,"—went on my new acquaintance:—" this is Sunday, and my dinner ought to be fairly decent, otherwise I would not have invited you."

I made the sort of reply which is customary on such occasions, and started to follow him. The recently cleaned path soon led us out of the linden grove; we entered the kitchen-garden. Among the aged apple-trees and overgrown gooseberry bushes gleamed round, pale-green heads of cabbage; hop-vines garlanded the tall poles in festoons; dark-brown sticks rose in dense array from the beds, entangled with dried pea-vines; huge, flat squashes seemed to be wallowing on the ground; cucumbers gleamed yellow from beneath their dusty, angular leaves; along the wattled fence tall nettles rocked to and fro; in two or three places Tatár honeysuckle, elder-trees, and sweet-briar grew in masses,—the remains of bygone " flower-plots." By the side of a small fish-pond, filled with reddish and slimy water, a well was visible, surrounded by puddles. Ducks were busily splashing and waddling in these puddles; a dog, trembling all over and with eyes screwed up, was gnawing a bone in the open glade; a piebald cow was nipping idly at the grass there, now and then flirting her tail over her gaunt back. The path swerved aside; from behind thick willows and birches, there peeped forth at us a small, aged grey house, with a board

roof and a crooked porch. Radíloff halted.—
" By the way,"—he said good-naturedly, looking me square in the face:—" Now I come to
think of it; perhaps you don't want to enter my
house at all; in that case . . . . ."

I did not give him an opportunity to finish,
and assured him that, on the contrary, it would
give me great pleasure to dine with him.

" Well, as you like."

We entered the house. A young fellow in a
long kaftan of heavy blue cloth met us on the
porch. Radíloff immediately ordered him to
give Ermolái some vódka; my huntsman made
a respectful obeisance to the back of the magnanimous giver. From the anteroom, papered
with divers motley-hued pictures and hung
around with cages, we entered a small room—
Radíloff's study. I took off my hunting accou-
trements, and set my gun in one corner; the
young fellow in the long-tailed kaftan brushed
me off with alacrity.

" Come, now let us go into the drawing-room,"
—said Radíloff, cordially:—" I will introduce
you to my mother."

I followed him. In the drawing-room, on the
central divan, sat an old lady of short stature, in
a light-brown gown and a white mob-cap, with
a kindly, emaciated face, a timid and mournful
gaze.

" Here, mother, let me introduce our neighbour, * * *."

The old lady half-rose, and bowed to me, without letting go her hold on a coarse worsted reticule in the shape of a bag.

" Have you been long in our parts? "—she asked, in a weak and gentle voice, blinking her eyes.

" No, madam, not long."

" Do you intend to stay here long? "

" Until winter, I think."

The old lady relapsed into silence.

" And here,"—joined in Radíloff, pointing to a tall, thin man, whom I had not noticed on entering the drawing-room:—" this is Feódor Mikhyéitch. . . . Come on, Fédya, show the visitor thine art. Why hast thou tucked thyself into a corner? "

Feódor Mikhyéitch immediately rose from his chair, picked up from the window-sill a miserable fiddle, grasped his bow—not by the end, as is the proper way, but by the middle, leaned the fiddle against his breast, shut his eyes, and began to dance, singing a song and sawing away on the strings. Judging from his appearance, he was seventy years old; a long nankeen coat dangled mournfully against his thin, bony limbs. He danced; now he shook his small, bald head in a dashing way, again he twisted it about, stretched out his sinewy neck, stamped his feet up and down on one spot, and sometimes, with evident difficulty, he bent his knees. His toothless mouth emitted a decrepit voice. Radíloff must have divined, from the expression of my face, that Fédya's " art " did not afford me much pleasure.

" Come, very good, old man, that will do,"— he said:—" thou mayest go and reward thyself."

Feódor Mikhyéitch immediately laid the fiddle on the window-sill, bowed first to me, as visitor, then to the old lady, then to Radíloff, and left the room.

" He was once a landed proprietor also,"— pursued my new friend:—" and a rich one, but he ruined himself—so now he lives with me . . . . but in his day he was regarded as the leading gay rake in the government; he carried two wives away from their husbands, he kept singers, he himself danced and sang in a masterly manner. . . . But would n't you like some vodka? for dinner is already on the table."

A young girl, the one of whom I had caught a glimpse in the garden, entered the room.

" Ah, here 's Olya too! "—remarked Radíloff, slightly turning away his head:—" I beg that you will love and favour her. . . . Well, let 's go to dinner."

We betook ourselves to the dining-room, and seated ourselves. While we were walking from the drawing-room and taking our seats, Feódor Mikhyéitch, whose eyes had begun to beam and his nose to flush a little red from his " reward," sang: " Let the thunder of victory resound!" A special place was set for him in one corner, at a little table without a cloth. The poor old man could not boast of cleanliness, and therefore he was always kept at a certain distance from the company. He crossed himself, sighed, and began to eat like a shark. The dinner really was far from bad, and, in its quality of a Sunday dinner, did not lack quivering jelly and Spanish breezes (patties). At table, Radíloff, who had served for ten years in an army infantry regiment, and had been in Turkey, began to tell stories. I listened to him attentively, and stealthily watched Olga. She was not very pretty; but the calm and decided expression of her face, her broad, white brow, thick hair, and, in particular, her brown eyes, small but sensible, clear and vivacious, would have struck any one else in my place. She seemed to watch Radíloff's every word; it was not interest but passionate attention which was depicted on her countenance. Radíloff, as to years, might have been her father; he called her " thou," but I instantly divined that she was not his daughter. In the course of the conversation he mentioned his deceased wife— " her sister," he added, indicating Olga. She blushed swiftly, and dropped her eyes. Radíloff paused for a while, and changed the subject. The old lady never uttered a word throughout the dinner, ate hardly anything herself, and did not press anything on me. Her features exhaled a sort of timorous and hopeless expecta-

MEMOIRS OF A SPORTSMAN

tion, that sadness of old age which makes the onlooker's heart contract painfully. Toward the end of the dinner Feódor Mikhyéitch undertook to "glorify" [1] the hosts and the guest, but Radíloff, after a glance at me, requested him to hold his tongue; the old man passed his hand across his mouth, blinked his eyes, bowed and sat down again, but this time on the very edge of his chair. After dinner, Radíloff and I betook ourselves to his study.

In people who are powerfully and constantly occupied by a single thought or a single passion, there is perceptible something common to them all, a certain external resemblance in demeanour, however different, nevertheless, may be their qualities, capacities, positions in the world, and

[1] The "Glory" is reckoned among the Christmas songs, or carols, and in its dignified form relates, like many other folk-songs, to the harvest. In this form, extracts or adaptations of it are used in connection with solemn occasions—a fragment of it appeared as part of the miniature decoration of the menu for the present Emperor's coronation banquet, for instance. In another form, it is one of the Twelfth-Night songs among young people, and used like the divining games common to All-Hallowe'en. In this latter form, Ostróvsky has utilized it in his play, "Poverty is not a Sin," Act II, Scene v. The form referred to above is the stately one, and runs somewhat as follows: "Glory to God in heaven, *Glory!*—To our Lord on this earth, *Glory!*—May our Lord (the word used is *gosudár,* which, with a capital, means the Emperor), never grow old, *Glory!*—May his bright robes never be spoiled, *Glory!*—May his good steeds never be worn out, *Glory!*—May his trusty servants never falter, *Glory!*—May the right throughout Russia, *Glory!*—Be fairer than the bright Sun, *Glory!*—May the Tzar's golden treasury, *Glory!*—Be for ever full to the brim, *Glory!*—May the great rivers, *Glory!*—Bear their renown to the sea, *Glory!*—The little streams to the mill, *Glory!*"—Obviously, this can easily be adapted to any circumstances.—TRANSLATOR.

90

education. The more I observed Radíloff, the
more did it seem to me that he belonged to the
category of such people. He talked about farming, about the harvest, the mowing, about the
war, about the county gossip and the approaching elections,[1] talked without constraint, even
with interest, but suddenly he heaved a sigh,
dropped into an arm-chair, like a man who is
exhausted with heavy toil, and passed his hand
over his face. His whole soul, kind and warm,
seemed to be permeated through and through,
saturated with one feeling. I had already been
struck by the fact that I could not discern in him
a passion either for eating, or for liquor, or for
hunting, or for Kursk nightingales,[2] or for
pigeons afflicted with epilepsy, or for Russian
literature, or for pacers, or for hussar jackets,
or for card-playing or billiards, or for dancing
parties, or for paper-mills and beet-sugar fac-
tories, or for embellished arbours, or for tea, or
for trace-horses trained to the degree of perver-
sion,[3] or for fat coachmen girt directly under
the armpits, for those magnificent coachmen,
whose eyes—God knows why—twist asquint and

[1] For Marshal of Nobility; for the Government or district.—TRANS-
LATOR.
[2] The nightingales from the Kursk Government are reputed the
finest in the country, and have several extra " turns " to their song.
—TRANSLATOR.
[3] Meaning—the side horses in the tróïka or three-horse team,
trained to gallop spread out like a fan from the central trotter, with
heads held down and backwards, so that those in the equipage can see
their eyes and nostrils—this in extremes.—TRANSLATOR.

fairly pop out of their heads at every movement of their necks. . . . " What sort of a country squire is he, I 'd like to know! " I thought.
And in the meantime, he put on no airs of being
a gloomy man, and discontented with his lot; on
the contrary, he fairly reeked with an atmosphere of unfastidious good-will, cordiality, and
almost offensive readiness to be hail-fellow-well-
met with every one who came along, without discrimination.   It is true that, at the same time,
you felt that he could not make friends, really
become intimate, with any one whomsoever, and
that he could not, not because he had no need of
other people in general, but because his whole
life had, for the time being, turned inward.   As
I intently observed Radíloff, I could not possibly imagine him to myself as happy, either now
or at any other time.   He was not a beauty,
either; but in his glance, in his smile, in his whole
being there was concealed something extremely
attractive,—precisely that: concealed.   So, apparently, one would have liked to know him
better, to love him.   Of course, the country
squire, the steppe-dweller, was apparent in him
at times; but, notwithstanding, he was a splendid
fellow.

We had just begun to discuss the new Marshal
of the Nobility for the district, when, all of a
sudden, Olga's voice resounded at the door:
" Tea is ready."   We went to the drawing-room.

MY NEIGHBOUR RADÍLOFF

Feódor Mikhyéitch was sitting, as before, in his nook between the small window and the door, with his feet modestly tucked up. Radíloff's mother was knitting a stocking. Through the windows open toward the garden there wafted in the chill of autumn and a scent of apples. Olga was busily pouring out tea. I surveyed her now with greater attention than at dinner. She spoke very little, like all country maidens in general, but in her, at least, I did not observe any desire to say something fine, together with a torturing sense of emptiness and impotence; she did not sigh, as though from a superabundance of inexpressible sentiments, did not roll up her eyes, did not smile dreamily and indefinitely. Her gaze was calm and indifferent, like that of a person who is resting after a great happiness, or a great anxiety. Her walk, her movements, were decided and unconstrained. She pleased me greatly.

Radíloff and I got to talking again. I cannot now recall how we arrived at the familiar remark: how frequently the most insignificant things produce a greater impression than the most important.

" Yes,"—said Radíloff:—" I have had that experience myself. I have been married, as you know. Not long . . . . three years; my wife died in childbed. I thought that I should not survive her; I was frightfully afflicted, overwhelmed, but I could not weep—I went about like a madman. They dressed her, in the usual way, and placed her on the table—here, in this room. The priest came; the chanters came, and they began to sing, to pray, to cense with incense; I made reverences to the earth, but not a tear did I shed. My heart seemed to have turned to stone, and my head also,—and I had grown heavy all over. Thus passed the first day. On the following morning I went to my wife,—it was in summer, the sun illumined her from head to feet, and so brilliantly.—All at once I saw . . . ." Here Radíloff involuntarily shuddered. . . " what do you think? One of her eyes was not quite closed, and on that eye a fly was walking. . . . I fell to the floor in a heap, unconscious, and when I recovered my senses, I began to weep, to weep,—I could not stop. . . ."

Radíloff relapsed into silence. I looked at him, then at Olga. . . . I shall never forget the expression of her face as long as I live. The old lady dropped the stocking on her knees, pulled a handkerchief from her reticule, and stealthily wiped away a tear. Feódor Mikhyéitch suddenly rose to his feet, seized his fiddle, and started a song in a hoarse, wild voice. He probably wished to cheer us up; but we all shuddered at his first sound, and Radíloff requested him to be quiet.

" However,"—he went on:—" what has happened, has happened; the past cannot be recalled, and, after all . . . . everything is for the best in this world, as Voltaire—I think it was—once said," he added hastily.

"Yes,"—I returned:—"of course. Besides, every misfortune may be borne, and there is no situation so bad, but that one can escape from it."

"Do you think so?"—remarked Radíloff.— "Well, perhaps you are right. I remember lying half-dead in the hospital in Turkey: I had putrid fever. Well, our quarters were nothing to brag of—of course, it was war-time,—and we thanked God for even that much! All of a sudden, more patients were brought to us,—where were they to be put? The doctor rushed hither and thither: there was no room. At last he came up to me, and asked the assistant: 'Is he alive?' The man answered: 'He was this morning.' The doctor bent over me, listening: I was breathing. My friend lost patience. 'Well, he has got a stupid sort of nature,'—said he:—'why, the man will die, he will infallibly die, and he keeps creaking on, dragging along; he merely takes up space, and interferes with others.' Well, I thought to myself, thou art in a bad way, Mikhaílo Mikhaílitch. . . . And behold, I got well and am alive at the present moment, as you may see. So, you must be right."

"I am right, in any case,"—I replied:—"even

if you had died, you would have escaped from your evil state."

" Of course, of course,"—he added,—dealing the table a heavy blow with his hand. . . . " All that is required, is to make up one's mind. . . . . What 's the sense of enduring a bad situation? . . . . Why delay, drag matters out? . . ."

Olga rose swiftly and went out into the garden.

" Come, now, Fédya, a dance-tune,"—exclaimed Radíloff.

Fédya leaped to his feet, strode about the room with that peculiar dandified gait wherewith the familiar " goat " treads around the tame bear, and struck up: " When at our gate . . . ."

The rumble of a racing-gig resounded at the entrance, and a few moments later there came into the room an old man of lofty stature, broadshouldered and heavily-built, freeholder Ovsyánikoff. . . . But Ovsyánikoff is so remarkable and original a person, that, with the reader's permission, we will discuss him in another excerpt. But now, I will merely add, on my account, that on the following day Ermolái and I set off a-hunting as soon as it was light, and from the hunt went home; . . . that a week later, I ran in to see Radíloff, but found neither him nor Olga at home, and two weeks afterward learned that he had suddenly disappeared, abandoned his mother, and gone off somewhere or other with his sister-in-law. The whole government was in commotion, and gossiping about this occurrence, and only then, at last, did I understand the expression of Olga's face during Radíloff's story. It had not breathed forth compassion alone then: it had also flamed with jealousy.

Before my departure from the country I called on old Mme. Radíloff. I found her in the drawing-room; she was playing " fool " with Feódor Mikhyéitch.

" Have you any news from your son? "—I asked her at last.

The old lady began to weep. I questioned her no further about Radíloff.[1]

---

[1] Marriage with a sister-in-law is prohibited in the Eastern Catholic Church. Two brothers may not even wed two sisters.— TRANSLATOR.

VI

FREEHOLDER OVSYÁNIKOFF [1]

PICTURE to yourselves, dear readers, a stout, tall man, seventy years of age, with a face somewhat suggestive of that of Krylóff,[2] with a clear and intelligent gaze, beneath overhanging eyebrows: with a stately mien, deliberate speech, slow gait; there is Ovsyánikoff for you. He wore a capacious blue surtout with long sleeves, a lilac silk kerchief round his neck, brightly-polished boots with tassels, and, altogether, resembled a well-to-do merchant. His hands were very handsome, soft and white; in the course of conversation, he frequently fingered a button of his coat. Ovsyánikoff, by his dignity and impassiveness, his intelligence and laziness, his straightforwardness and stubbornness, reminded me of the Russian

---

[1] The "freeholders" constitute a peculiar intermediate class, neither gentry nor peasants. They are: 1. Settlers who regard themselves of noble lineage, and, in some cases, fórmerly owned serfs. 2. Descendants of nobles of the court service and of military men who were colonised in the Ukráina (Border-Marches) in the XVIIth century. They are found chiefly in the governments of Tambóff, Vorónezh, and neighbouring governments, once the Border-Marches.—TRANSLATOR.

[2] Iván Andréevitch Krylóff (1763–1844), the famous Russian fabulist.—TRANSLATOR.

boyárs of the times anterior to Peter the Great:
. . . . the féryaz [1] would have suited his style.
He was one of the last survivors of the olden
days. All his neighbours respected him extremely, and regarded it as an honour to know
him. His brother freeholders all but said their
prayers to him, doffed their caps to him from
afar, were proud of him. Generally speaking,
to this day, we find it difficult to distinguish a
freeholder from a peasant: his farming-opera-
tions are almost worse than those of a peasant,
his calves are forever in the buckwheat fields, his
horses are barely alive, his harness is of ropes.
Ovsyánikoff was an exception to the general
rule, although he was not reputed to be wealthy.
He lived alone with his wife, in a snug, neat little
house, kept only a small staff of servants, clothed
his people in Russian style, and called them labourers. And they really tilled his land. He did
not claim to be a nobleman, he did not pretend
to be a landed proprietor, he never, as the saying
is, " forgot himself," he did not seat himself at
the first invitation, and at the entrance of a new
visitor he invariably rose from his seat, but with
so much dignity, with so much majestic courtesy,
that the visitor involuntarily saluted him the
more profoundly. Ovsyánikoff held to ancient
customs not out of superstition (he had a fairly

[1] An ancient, long-skirted coat, with long sleeves, no collar,
and no defined waist-line.—TRANSLATOR.

liberal soul), but from habit. For example, he did not like equipages with springs, because he did not find them comfortable, and drove about either in a racing-gig, or in a small, handsome cart with a leather cushion, and himself held the reins over a good bay trotter. (He kept only bay horses.) The coachman, a rosy-cheeked young fellow, with his hair cut in a bowl-shaped crop, clad in a bluish long coat and a low sheep-skin cap, and with a strap for a girdle, sat respectfully by his side. Ovsyánikoff always slept after dinner, went to the bath on Saturdays, read only religious books (on which occasions he pompously set a pair of silver-mounted spectacles astride of his nose), rose and went to bed early. But he shaved off his beard, and wore his hair in foreign fashion. He welcomed visitors with much affection and cordiality, but did not bow to their girdles, did not fuss, did not treat them to all sorts of dried and salted viands.— " Wife! " he would say deliberately, without rising from his seat, and turning his head slightly in her direction:—" Fetch the gentlemen some dainty morsel or other." He regarded it as a sin to sell grain, the gift of God, and in the year 1840, at a time of general famine and frightfully high prices, he distributed his entire store to the neighbouring landed proprietors and peasants; in the following year, they repaid their debt to him in kind, with gratitude. The neighbours frequently resorted to Ovsyánikoff with appeals to arbitrate, to effect reconciliations between them, and almost always submitted to his decree, obeyed his advice. Many, thanks to him, got the boundaries of their land definitely settled. . . . . . But after two or three skirmishes with landed proprietresses, he announced that he declined any sort of intervention between persons of the female sex. He could not endure haste, agitated precipitation, women's chatter and "fussiness." Once it happened that his house caught fire. A labourer rushed precipitately to him, yelling: "Fire! Fire!"—"Well, what art thou yelling for?" said Ovsyánikoff, calmly:—"Give me my hat and staff."—He was fond of breaking in his horses for himself. One day, a mettlesome Bitiúk [1] dashed headlong down-hill with him, toward a precipice. "Come, that will do, that will do, thou green colt,—thou wilt kill thyself," Ovsyánikoff remarked good-naturedly to him, and a moment later flew over the precipice, along with his racing-drozhky, the small lad who was sitting behind, and the horse. Luckily, the sand lay in heaps at the bottom of the ravine. No one was injured, but the Bitiúk dislocated his leg.—"Well, there, thou seest,"— went on Ovsyánikoff in a calm voice, as he rose

[1] "Bitiúks"—horses from Bitiúk; a special race, which were reared in the Government of Vorónezh, near the well-known "Khryenovóy" (the former stud-farm of Count Orlóff).—Trans-lator.

from the ground:—" I told thee so."—And he had found himself a wife to match him. Tatyána Ilínitchna Ovsyánikoff was a woman of lofty stature, dignified and taciturn, with a cinnamon-brown silk kerchief forever bound about her head. She exhaled a chilly atmosphere, although not only did no one accuse her of being severe, but, on the contrary, many poor wretches called her "dear little mother" and "benefactress." Regular features, large, dark eyes, thin lips, still bore witness to her formerly renowned beauty. Ovsyánikoff had no children.

I made his acquaintance, as the reader already is aware, at Radíloff's, and a couple of days later I went to see him. I found him at home. He was sitting in a large leathern arm-chair, and reading the Tchetyá-Mináya.[1] A grey cat was purring on his shoulder. He welcomed me, according to his wont, caressingly and in stately wise. We entered into conversation.

" But pray tell me truly, Luká Petróvitch,"— I said, among other things;—" Things were better formerly, in your time, were n't they?"

" Some things really were better, I will tell you,"—returned Ovsyánikoff:—" We lived more peacefully; there was greater ease, really. . . . But, nevertheless, things are better now; and they will be better still for our children, God willing."

[1] "The Martyrology," or Lives of the Saints.—TRANSLATOR.

" But I expected, Luká Petróvitch, that you would laud the olden days to me."

" No, I have no special cause to laud the olden times. Here, now, to give an instance, you are a landed proprietor at the present day, just such a landed proprietor as your deceased grandfather was before you, but you will never have the power he had! and you are not the same sort of a man, either. Other gentlemen oppress us nowadays; but, evidently, that cannot be dispensed with. You can't make an omelette without breaking eggs. No, I no longer see what I used to wonder at in my youth."

" And what was that, for example? "

" Why, take this now, for instance, I will refer to your grandfather once more. He was an overbearing man! he wronged folks like me. Now, perhaps you know—and how can you help knowing about your land?—that wedge which runs from Tcheplýgino to Malínino; . . . . . . You have it planted to oats now. . . . Well, that's ours, you know,—every bit of it ours. Your grandfather took it away from us; he rode out on horseback, pointed it out with his hand, said: " My property,"—and took possession of it. My father, now dead (the kingdom of heaven be his!), was a just man, but he was also a hot-tempered man, and he would not put up with that,—and who does like to lose his property? —and he appealed to the court of law. One

judge gave it to him, but the others did not agree,
—they were afraid. So they reported to your
grandfather to the effect that ' Piótr Ovsyánikoff is making a complaint against you; he says
you have been pleased to deprive him of his land.'
. . . . Your grandfather immediately sent his
huntsman Bausch to us, with a squad. . . . So
they took my father and carried him off to your
hereditary estate. I was a little lad then, and ran
after them, barefooted. What next? . . . . They
took him to your house, and flogged him in front
of the windows. And your grandfather stood
on the balcony, and looked on; and your grand-
mother sat at the window and looked on also.
My father shouts: ' Dear little mother, Márya
Vasílievna, intercede! Do you, at least, spare
me!' But all she did was to keep rising up, now
and then, and taking a look. So then they made
my father promise to retire from the land, and
they ordered him to return thanks, to boot, that
they had let him go alive. And so it has remained
in your possession. Just go and ask your own
peasants: ' What is that land called?' The land
of the oaken cudgel [1] it is called, because it was
taken away by an oaken cudgel. And that is
why it is impossible for us, the petty people, very
greatly to regret the ancient order of things."

I did not know what reply to make to Ovsyánikoff, and did not dare to look him in the face.

[1] *Dubovshstchína,* in Russian.—TRANSLATOR.

FREEHOLDER OVSYÁNIKOFF

" And then take another of our neighbours, who made his nest among us in those days,—Kómoff, Stepán Niktopoliónitch. He tormented my father to death: if not with biting, with scratching. He was a drunken fellow, and fond of standing treat, and when he had taken a glass too much, he would say in French, ' C'est bon,' and carry on so, that it was enough to make one want to take the holy pictures out of the room, with shame! He would send and invite all the neighbours to favour him with their company. He had tróïkas standing ready harnessed; and if you did n't come, he 'd drop down on you himself. . . . And such a strange man as he was! When he was sober, he did not lie; but as soon as he began to drink he would begin to relate that in Peter [1] he had three houses on the Fontánka: one red, with one chimney; another yellow, with two chimneys; and the third blue, with no chimney,—and three sons (but he was not married) : one in the infantry, one in the cavalry, and the third a gentleman of leisure. . . . And, he said, that in each of his houses dwelt one of his sons; that admirals came to visit the eldest, generals to visit the second, and nothing but Englishmen to visit the third! Well, and he would rise to his feet and say: ' To the health of my eldest son, he 's the most respectful!'—and begin to weep. And woe be

[1] Petersburg.—TRANSLATOR.

to the man who undertook to refuse! ' I 'll shoot him,'—he would say: ' and I won't allow him to be buried!' . . . . Or he would spring up and begin to shout: ' Dance, ye people of God, for your own amusement and my consolation!' Well, you 'd dance, though you might die for it, you 'd dance. He utterly wore out his serf girls. They used to sing in chorus all night long until the morning, and the one who raised her voice the highest got a reward. And if they began to tire, he would drop his head on his hands, and begin to grieve: ' Okh, an orphaned orphan am I! they are abandoning me, the dear little doves!' Then the stablemen would immediately administer a little encouragement to the girls. He took a fancy to my father: how could one help that? He almost drove my father into his grave, you know; and he really would have driven him into it, had he not died himself, thank the Lord: he tumbled headlong from the pigeon-house, in a drunken fit. . . . So that 's the sort of nice neighbours we used to have! "

" How times have changed! "—I remarked.

" Yes, yes,"—assented Ovsyánikoff. . . . " Well, and there 's this to be said: in the olden days, the nobles really lived more sumptuously. Not to mention the grandees: I had a chance to admire them in Moscow. 'T is said they have now died out there also."

" Have you been in Moscow? "

106

" Yes, long ago, very long ago. I'm now in my seventy-third year, and I travelled to Moscow when I was sixteen."

Ovsyánikoff heaved a sigh.

" And whom did you see there? "

" Why, I saw a great many grandees—and everybody saw them: they lived openly, gloriously, and amazingly. Only, not one of them equalled Count Alexyéi Grigórievitch Orlóff-Tchesménsky.[1] I used to see Alexyéi Grigórievitch frequently: my uncle served him as major-domo. The Count deigned to live at the Kalúga Gate, on Sháblovka street. There was a grandee for you! It is impossible to imagine to one's self such an imposing carriage, such gracious courtesy, and impossible to describe it. What was not his stature alone worth, his strength, his glance! Until you knew him, you would n't enter his house—you'd be afraid, regularly intimidated; but if you did go in, you felt as though the sun were warming you, and you'd get cheerful all through. He admitted every one to his presence, and was fond of everything. At races he drove himself, and would race with anybody; and he would never overtake them all at once, he would n't hurt their feelings, he would n't cut

---

[1] One of Katherine II's favourites, who won his title of " Tchesménsky " by his victory over the Turkish fleet at Tchesmé in 1769. A silver dinner-plate which he twisted into a roll with his fingers is preserved in the Hermitage Museum, St. Petersburg.—TRANSLATOR.

them off short, but probably he would pass
them just at the end; and he was so caressing,
—he would comfort his adversary, praise his
horse. He kept first-class tumbler pigeons. He
used to come out into the courtyard, seat himself
in an arm-chair, and order them to set the pigeons
flying; and all around, on the roofs, stood men
with guns, to ward off the hawks. A big silver
vase of water was placed at the Count's feet; and
he would look into the water and watch the
pigeons. The poor and the needy lived on his
bread by the hundred . . . and how much money
he gave away! But when he got angry, it was
like the thunder roaring. A great alarm, but
nothing to cry about: the first you knew,—he
would be smiling. He would give a feast,—and
furnish drink for all Moscow! . . . . and what
a clever man he was! he conquered the Turk, you
know. He was fond of wrestling, too; they
brought strong men to him from Túla, from
Khárkoff, from Tambóff, from everywhere. If
he overcame a man, he would reward him; but
if any one conquered him, he would load that
man with gifts, and kiss him on the lips. . . .
And during my stay in Moscow, he organised
such a hare-hunt as never was seen in Russia; he
invited all the sportsmen in the whole empire to
be his guests, and appointed a day three months
ahead. Well, and so they assembled. They
brought dogs, huntsmen,—well, an army arrived,

a regular army! First they feasted, as was proper, and then they set off for the barrier. An innumerable throng of people had collected. . . . . And what do you think? . . . . Why, your grandfather's dog outran them all."

"Was n't it Milovídka?"[1] I asked.

"Yes, Milovídka. . . . So, the Count began to entreat him: ' Sell me thy dog,' says he: ' ask what price thou wilt.'—' No, Count,' says he, ' I 'm not a merchant: I don't sell useless rags, and for the sake of honour, I 'm even willing to surrender my wife, only not Milovídka. . . . . . I 'll surrender myself as a prisoner first.' And Alexyéi Grigórievitch praised him: ' I like that,' says he. And he drove your grandfather back in his own carriage; and when Milovídka died, they buried her in the garden with music,—they buried the bitch, and placed a stone with an inscription on it over the bitch's grave."

"Why, so Alexyéi Grigórievitch really never did offend any one,"—I remarked.

"Yes, he was always like that: the man who is sailing in shallow water himself is the one who picks quarrels."

"And what sort of a man was that Bausch?" —I asked, after a brief pause.

"How is it that you have heard about Milovídka, and not about Bausch? . . . . He was the head huntsman and whipper-in of your

<hr>

[1] From *míliy,* pretty, and *vid,* aspect.—TRANSLATOR.

grandfather. Your grandfather loved him no
less than he did Milovídka. He was a desperado,
and no matter what your grandfather ordered,
he executed it in the twinkling of an eye, even
if it was to hurl himself on a knife. . . . . And
when he halloed on the hounds, it was as though
a groan filled the forest. And all of a sudden,
he would get a fit of obstinacy, and alight from
his horse, and lie down. . . . And just as soon
as the hounds ceased to hear his voice, it was all
over! They would abandon a hot scent, they
would n't continue the chase, on any terms whatsoever. I-ikh, how angry your grandfather used
to get! ' I 'll turn thee wrong side out, thou
antichrist! I 'll pull thy heels out through thy
throat, thou soul-ruiner!' And it would end in
his sending to inquire what he wanted, why he
was not uttering the halloo! And in such cases,
Bausch would generally demand liquor, would
drink it off, get up, and begin to whoop again
magnificently."

"You seem to be fond of hunting also, Luká
Petróvitch?"

"I would have liked it . . . . that 's a fact,
but not now: now my day is over,—but in my
youth . . . . and, you know, it 's awkward, because of my rank. It is n't proper for the like
of me to try to imitate the nobles. That 's the
truth of it: one man of our class—a drunkard
and incapable—used to tag on to the gentry . . . .

but what pleasure is there in that! You only put
yourself to shame. They gave him a miserable,
stumbling horse; and they kept picking off his
cap and flinging it on the ground; they would
strike him with their hunting-whips, as though
he were a horse; and he would laugh all the while
himself, and make the others laugh. No, I tell
you: the smaller the rank, the more rigidly must
you behave, otherwise, the first thing you know,
you will be disgracing yourself."

" Yes,"—pursued Ovsyánikoff, with a sigh,—
" much water has flowed past since I have lived
in the world: other days have arrived. Especially in the nobles do I perceive a great change.
The petty gentry have all either entered the government service, or else they don't stay still in
one place; and as for the greater estate-owners,
they are unrecognisable. I have had a good look
at them, at the big men, in connection with the
delimitation of boundaries. And I must tell
you, my heart rejoices as I look at them:
they are affable, polite. Only this is what sur-
prises me: they have all studied the sciences,
they talk so fluently that your soul is moved
within you, but they don't understand real business, they are n't even awake to their own advantage: why, a serf, their manager, can drive them
whithersoever he pleases, like a slave. Here
now, for example, perhaps you are acquainted
with Korolyóff, Alexander Vladímirovitch,—

is n't he a regular noble? A beauty, rich, educated at the ' 'niversity,' I believe, and has been
abroad, talks fluently, modestly, shakes hands
with all of us. You do know him? . . . . well,
then hearken to me. Last week, we assembled
at Beryózovka, on the invitation of the arbitrator,
Nikifór Ilitch. And the arbitrator, Nikifór
Ilitch, says to us: ' Gentlemen, we must fix the
boundaries; 't is a shame that our section has
lagged behind all the rest; let 's get to work.'
So we set to work. Discussions and disputes
began, as is usual; our attorney began to put
on airs. But Porfíry Ovtchínnikoff was the first
to make a row. . . . And on what ground does
the man make a row? He does n't own an inch
of land himself: he manages it on behalf of his
brother. He shouts: ' No! you can't cheat me!
no, you 've got hold of the wrong man! hand over
the plans, give me the surveyor, the seller of
Christ, hand him over to me!'—' But what is
your claim? '—' So you think you 've caught a
fool, forsooth! have n't I just announced my demands to you? . . . no, you just hand over those
plans,—so there now! ' And he is thwacking the
plans with his hand the while. He dealt a deadly
insult to Márfa Dmítrievna. She shrieks: ' How
dare you sully my reputation? '—' I,'—says he,
' would n't want my brown mare to have your
reputation.' They administered some madeira
to him by force. They got him quieted down,

—and others began to make a rumpus. Alexánder Vladímiritch Korolyóff, my dear little dove, sits in a corner, nibbling at the knob of his cane, and merely shaking his head. I felt ashamed, 't was more than I could endure, I wanted to flee from the room. ' What does the man think of us? ' I said to myself. And behold, my Alexánder Vladímiritch rises, shows that he wishes to speak. The arbitrator begins to fuss, says: ' Gentlemen, gentlemen, Alexánder Vladímiritch wants to speak.' And one can't help praising the nobles: all of them immediately became silent. So Alexánder Vladímiritch began and said: 'We appear to have forgotten the object for which we have come together; although the delimitation of boundaries is, indisputably, advantageous for the proprietors, yet in reality, it is established for what purpose?—it is for the purpose of making things easier for the peasant, so that he can toil and discharge his obligations the more conveniently; but as things stand now, he does not know even which land is his, and not infrequently has to travel five versts to till the soil, —and he cannot be held to account.' Then Alexánder Vladímiritch said that it was a sin for a landed proprietor not to look out for the welfare of the peasants; that, in short, the sensible way of viewing the matter was, that their advantage and our advantage are identical: if they are well off, we are well off, if they are in evil plight, so are we; . . . . and that, consequently, 't is a sin and foolish to fail of agreement because of trifles. . . . And he went on, and on. . . . And how he did talk! It fairly gripped your soul. . . . And all the nobles hung their heads, I myself was on the very verge of melting into tears. 'T is a fact, that there are no such speeches in the ancient books. . . . And what came of it? He himself would n't surrender four desyatínas of moss-bog, and would n't sell it either. Says he: ' I 'll have my men drain that swamp, and I 'll set up—I 'll set up a cloth-mill on it, with improvements. I,' says he, ' have already selected that location: I have my own calculations on that score. . . And if it had only been just! But the simple facts in the case were,—that Alexánder Vladímiritch's neighbour, Antón Karásikoff, had been too stingy to bribe Alexánder Vladímiritch's manager with a hundred rubles. So we parted without having accomplished any business. And Alexánder Vladímiritch considers himself to be in the right up to the present time, and keeps babbling idly about a cloth-mill, but he does n't set about draining the bog."

"And how does he manage his estate? "

" He is all the time introducing new-fangled notions. The peasants don't approve of them, —but there 's no use in paying any attention to them. Alexánder Vladímiritch is acting rightly."

"How so, Luká Petróvitch? I thought you clung to the old ways."

"I—am quite a different matter. I'm not a noble, you see, nor a landed proprietor. What does my farming amount to? . . . . And I don't know any different way, either. I try to act according to justice and the law,—and that's all a man can do. The young gentlemen don't like the former ways: I applaud them. . .'T is time to use their brains. Only, there's this sad point about it: the young gentlemen are awfully subtle. They treat the peasants as though they were dolls: turn them this way and that, break them and cast them aside. And the manager, a serf, or the steward, of German parentage, gets the peasants into his claws again. And if one of the young gentlemen would only set an example, would demonstrate: 'This is the way things should be managed!' . . . . But what is to be the end of it? Is it possible that I shall die without having beheld the new order of things? . . . Why is it? the old has died out, and the new does not prosper!"

I did not know how to answer Ovsyánikoff. He cast a glance about, moved closer to me, and continued, in an undertone:

"Have you heard about Vasíly Nikoláitch Liubozvónoff?"

"No, I have not."

"Please to explain to me what sort of marvels

are these. I am utterly at a loss to understand. Why, his own peasants told the tale, but I will not take their speeches into account. He's a young man, you know, who came into his inheritance not long ago, at his mother's death. Well, and he comes to his patrimonial estate. The peasants have assembled to have a look at their master. Vasíly Nikoláitch comes out to them. The peasants look, and—amazing to relate!—the master is wearing velveteen trousers as though he were a coachman, and has donned short boots with fancy tops; he has put on a red shirt, and a coachman's kaftan also; he has let his beard grow, and has such a queer little cap on his head, and his face is queer too,—not precisely drunk, but as though he were out of his wits. ' Good day, my lads!' [1] says he: ' Good luck to you!' [2] The peasants make him a reverence to the girdle, —but in silence: they had got frightened, you know. And he himself seemed to be timid. He began to make a speech:

" ' I 'm a Russian,' says he, 'and you are Russians too; I love everything Russian. . . . . I have a Russian soul,' says he, ' and my blood is Russian also.' . . . . And all of a sudden, as though it were a command: ' Come now, my

---

[1] Literally: " Health, my lads! " The official greeting of an officer to his soldiers, to which there is an official reply.—TRANSLATOR.

[2] Literally: " God be your helper." The customary greeting to any peasant one may meet.—TRANSLATOR.

children, sing a Russian folk-song!' The peasants' hamstrings began to tremble; they turned utterly stupid. One bold lad tried to strike up a tune, but immediately squatted down on the ground, hid himself behind the rest. . . . . And there was cause for amazement: there used to be among us landed proprietors, desperate fellows, arrant rakes, to tell the truth: they dressed almost like coachmen, and danced themselves,[1] played on the guitar, sang and drank with the worthless house-serfs, feasted with the peasants; but this Vasíly Nikoláitch, you see, is just like a handsome girl: he's always reading books, or writing, when he isn't declaiming verses aloud,—he never converses with any one, he holds himself aloof, he's forever strolling in the garden, as though he were bored or sad. The former manager was thoroughly intimidated, at first; before the arrival of Vasíly Nikoláitch, he made the rounds of all the peasants' houses, made obeisance to everybody,—evidently, the cat knew whose meat he had eaten,—that he was in fault! And the peasants cherished hopes; they thought: ' Fiddlesticks, brother!—thou wilt soon be called to account, dear little dove; thou wilt soon be weeping thy fill, thou extortioner!' . . . . But it turned out instead,—how shall I announce it to you!

[1] The view taken of dancing, in olden days, in Russia was— that it was derogatory to the dignity of gentlefolks; something to be performed for them by their serfs, or paid inferiors.— TRANSLATOR.

117

The Lord Himself could n't make head or tail of what happened! Vasíly Nikoláitch summoned him to his presence, and says to him, flushing scarlet himself the while, and breathing fast—so, you know: ' Be just, don't oppress any one on my estate,—dost thou hear?' And from that day forth, he has never ordered him to appear before him! He lives on his own paternal estate, as though he were a stranger. Well, and the overseer breathed freely and enjoyed himself; but the peasants don't dare to approach Vasíly Nikoláitch: they're afraid. And, you see, here's another thing which is deserving of surprise: the master bows to them, and looks courteous,—but their bellies fairly ache with fright. Now, what sort of queer goings-on do you say these are, dear little father? . . . . Either I have become stupid, or grown old,—but I don't understand."

I answered Ovsyánikoff, that, in all probability, Mr. Liubozvónoff was ill.

" Ill, indeed! He's thicker through than I am, and his face, God be with him, is very big around, in spite of his youth. . . . However, the Lord knows!" (And Ovsyánikoff heaved a deep sigh.)

" Well, setting aside the nobles,"—I began: —" What have you to say to me about the freeholders, Luká Petróvitch?"

" No, you must excuse me from that,"—he

said hastily:—" really . . . I would tell you . . . but what's the use! " (Ovsyánikoff waved the subject aside with his hand.) "We'd better drink tea. . . . Peasants, downright peasants; nevertheless, to tell the truth, what are we to do? "

He fell silent. Tea was served. Tatyána Ilínitchna rose from her place and seated herself nearer to us. During the course of the evening, she had noiselessly left the room several times, and as noiselessly returned. Silence reigned in the room. Ovsyánikoff drank cup after cup, in a slow and stately way.

" Mítya was here to-day,"—remarked Tatyána Ilínitchna in an undertone.

Ovsyánikoff frowned.

" What does he want? "

" He came to ask forgiveness."

Ovsyánikoff shook his head.

" Now, just look at that,"—he continued, addressing me:—" what ought a man to do about his relatives? 'T is impossible to renounce them. . . Here now, God has rewarded me with a nephew. He's a young fellow with brains, a dashing young fellow, there's no disputing that; he studied well, only, I can't expect to get any good of him. . . He was in the government service—he abandoned the service: you see, he had no chance of promotion. . . . Was he a noble? And even nobles don't get to be generals instantaneously. And so, now he is living in idleness.

. . . And that might pass,—but he has turned into a pettifogger! He composes petitions for the peasants, writes reports, teaches the rural policemen, shows up the surveyors for what they are, lounges about the dram-shops, picks up acquaintance at the posting-houses with petty burghers from the town, and with yard-porters. Is n't a catastrophe imminent? And the captain and commissary of the rural police have already threatened him. But he, luckily, knows how to jest, he makes them laugh, and then, afterward, he 'll stir up a mess for them. . . . Come now, is n't he sitting in thy chamber?" . . he added, turning to his wife:—" I know thy ways: thou art such a tender-hearted creature,—thou showest him thy protection."

Tatyána Ilínitchna dropped her eyes and blushed.

" Come, that 's how it is,"—went on Ovsyáni-koff. . . . " Okh, thou spoiler! Well, order him to come in,—so be it, for the sake of our dear guest, I will forgive the stupid fellow. . . Come, order him in, order him in. . . . ."

Tatyána Ilínitchna went to the door and called out: " Mítya!"

Mítya, a young fellow of eight and twenty years, tall, finely built, and curly-haired, entered the room, and, catching sight of me, halted on the threshold. His clothing was of foreign cut, but the unnatural size of the puffs on the shoulders were sufficient proof in themselves that it had been made not only by a Russian tailor, but by a Russian of the Russians.

" Well, come on, come on,"—said the old man: " of what art thou ashamed? Thank thy aunt: thou art forgiven. . . Here, dear little father, let me introduce him,"—he went on, pointing to Mítya:—" he's my own blood nephew, but I shall never be able to get on with him. The end of the world has come!" (We bowed to each other.) " Come, speak up, what sort of a scrape hast thou got into yonder? What are they complaining about thee for! Tell us? "

Mítya, evidently, did not wish to explain and defend himself before me.

" Afterward, uncle,"—he muttered.

" No, not afterward, but now,"—went on the old man. . . . " I know that thou art ashamed before the noble squire: so much the better, punish thyself. Pray, be so good as to speak out. . . . We are listening."

" I have no reason to feel ashamed,"—began Mítya, with vivacity, and shook his head.— " Pray judge for yourself, dear uncle. The Ryeshetílovo freeholders come to me and say: ' Defend us, brother.'—' What do you want? '— ' Why, this: our grain warehouses are in accurate order,—that is to say, nothing could be better; all at once, an official comes in: " I have orders to inspect the warehouses." He inspected them, and says: " Your warehouses are in disorder, there are important omissions, I am bound to report to the authorities."—" Why, wherein consist the omissions? "—" I know what they are," says he. . . . . We came together, and decided to thank the official in proper fashion,—but old Prokhóritch interfered; says he: " In that way, you 'll only whet his appetite for more. Well, really now, haven't we any rights? "—So we heeded the old man, but the official flew into a rage, and made a complaint, wrote a report."—' But were your warehouses really in proper order? ' I asked.—' As God sees me, they were in order and we have the legal quantity of grain. . . .' ' Well,' said I, ' then there 's no cause for you to fear,' and I wrote the document for them. . . . . And no one yet knows in whose favour it will be decided. . . . And as for people having complained to you about me in this connection,— that is easy to understand: everybody looks out for number one."

" Everybody else,—only, evidently, not thou," —said the old man in an undertone. . . . . . " And what sort of intrigues hast thou been engaging in, with the Shutolómovo peasants? "

" How do you know about that? "

" I do know.

" I was in the right there also,—please judge for yourself again. Bezpándin, a neighbour of the Shutolómovo peasants, ploughed four desya-

tínas of land. ' The land is mine,' said he. The
Shutolómovo men are on quit-rent, their squire
has gone abroad,—judge for yourself,—who is
there to stand up for them? But the land is
theirs, indisputably, has belonged to the serfs
since time immemorial. So they come to me, and
say: ' Write a petition.' And I wrote it. But
Bezpándin heard about it, and began to make
threats: ' I'll pull that Mítka's shoulder-blades
out of their sockets,' says he, ' if I don't tear his
head clean off his shoulders. . . .' Let's see
how he'll tear it off: it's whole up to the present
moment."

" Well, don't boast; thy head's of no use to
thee,"—remarked the old man:—" thou art a
downright crazy man!"

" But, uncle, was n't it you yourself who said
to me . . . . . "

" I know, I know what thou art going to say to
me,"—Ovsyánikoff interrupted him;—" exactly
so: a man should live according to justice, and
is bound to aid his neighbour. There are times
when he should not even spare himself. . . But
dost thou always act in that manner? Don't folks
lead thee to the dram-shop? don't they treat thee
to drinks? don't they pay thee respect? ' Dmítry
Alexyéitch, dear little father,' say they, ' help
us, and we will show thee our gratitude,'—and
thrust a ruble or a blue bank-note into thy
hand under their coat-tails? Hey? Is n't that

what happens? Tell me, is n't that the way of it? "

" In that respect, I really am guilty,"—replied Mítya, dropping his eyes,—" but I take nothing from the poor, and don't act against my conscience."

" Thou dost not take now, but when thou findest thyself in evil state,—thou wilt take. Thou dost not act against thy conscience . . . . ekh, shame on thee! Thou always upholdest saints, that means!—But hast thou forgotten Bórka [1] Perekhódoff? . . . Who bustled about on his behalf? Who lent him protection? Hey? "

" Perekhódoff suffered through his own fault, 't is true." . . .

" He spent the government money. . . . A nice joke that! "

" But just consider, dear uncle: poverty, a family. . . . ."

" Poverty, poverty. . . He 's a drinking man, a hard drinker; . . . that 's what he is! "

" He took to drink from misery,"—remarked Mítya, lowering his voice.

" From misery! Well, thou mightest have helped him, if thy heart is so warm, but thou mightest have refrained from sitting in the dramshop with a drunken man thyself. That he talks eloquently,—much of a rarity that is, forsooth! "

" He 's the kindest man possible. . . . ."

" Everybody 's kind, according to thee. . . . . .

[1] The disrespectful diminutive of Borís.—Translator.

Anyhow,"—continued Ovsyánikoff, addressing his wife:—" they have sent him off . . . . well, yonder, thou knowest whither." . . . .

Tatyána Ilínitchna nodded her head.

"Where hast thou disappeared to these days?"—began the old man again.

"I have been in the town."

"I suppose thou hast been playing billiards all the while, and guzzling tea, and twanging on the guitar, and slipping stealthily through the public offices, concocting petitions in back rooms, and showing thyself off in great style with the young merchants? That's so, isn't it? . . . . Tell me!"

"Probably it is,"—said Mítya, with a smile. . . "Akh, yes! I came near forgetting: Fúntikoff, Antón Parfénitch, invites you to dine with him on Sunday."

"I won't go to that big-bellied fellow's house. He'll serve us with fish worth a hundred rubles, and prepared with tainted butter. I'll have nothing whatever to do with him!"

"By the way, I met Fedósya Mikhaílovna."

"What Fedósya is that?"

"Why, the one who belongs to Squire Garpéntchenko, you know, who bought Mikúlino at *suction*.[1] Fedósya is from Mikúlino. She lives in Moscow as a seamstress, and paid quit-rent, one hundred and eighty-two rubles a year. . . . And she knows her business: she received fine

[1] Auction.—TRANSLATOR.

orders in Moscow. But now, Garpéntchenko
has ordered her back, and is keeping her here
idle, and assigns her no duties. She is ready
to purchase her freedom, and has told her master
so, but he announces no decision. You are
acquainted with Garpéntchenko, uncle,—so
could n't you speak just a little word to him?
And Fedósya will pay a good ransom."

"Not out of thy money, is it? Well, well, all
right, all right, I 'll speak to him. Only, I don't
know,"—went on the old man, with a displeased
countenance:—" that Garpéntchenko,[1] Lord forgive him, is an extortioner: he buys in notes, lends
at usurious interest, acquires estates under the
hammer. . . . . And who brought him to our
parts? Okh, how I detest these newcomers! It
won't be a short matter to get any satisfaction
from him;—however, we shall see."

"Use your efforts, uncle."

"Good! I will. Only, see here now, mind
what I say! Come, come, don't defend thyself.
. . . God bless thee, God bless thee! . . . Only,
hereafter, look out, or, by heaven, Mítya, 't will
be the worse for thee,—thou wilt come to grief,
by heaven, thou wilt! . . . I can't carry thee on
my shoulders forever. . . . I 'm not an influen-
tial man myself. Now go, with God's blessing."

[1] Evidently, from his name, ending in *enko,* the man was a
Little Russian, whose compatriots bear in Russia the reputation
of being as " canny " as the Scotch in England, or as " sharp "
as the Yankees in America.—TRANSLATOR.

FREEHOLDER OVSYÁNIKOFF

Mítya left the room. Tatyána Ilínitchna followed him.

"Give him some tea, thou child-spoiler,"—shouted Ovsyánikoff after her. . . . . . "He's not a stupid young fellow," he went on:—" and he has a kind soul, only, I'm afraid for him. . . . But pardon me, for having taken up so much of your time with trifles."

The door into the anteroom opened. There entered a short, greyish-haired man, in a velvet coat.

"Ah, Franz Ivánitch!"—exclaimed Ovsyáni-koff:—" good morning, what mercies does God show to you?"

Permit me, amiable reader, to make you acquainted with this gentleman also.

Franz Ivánitch Lejeune, my neighbour and a landed proprietor of Orel, attained to the honourable rank of a Russian noble in manner not entirely usual. He was born in Orléans, of French parents, and set off in company with Napoleon to conquer Russia, in the capacity of a drummer. At first, everything went as though on oiled wheels, and our Frenchman entered Moscow with head erect. But on the return journey poor M—r. Lejeune, half frozen and without his drum, fell into the hands of the Smolénsk peasants. The Smolénsk peasants locked him up for the night in an empty fulling-mill, and on the following morning led him to a hole in the ice, close to the dam, and began to entreat the drummer " de la grrrrande armée," to do them a favour, that is, to dive under the ice. M—r. Lejeune could not assent to their proposal, and, in return, he began to try to prevail upon the Smolénsk peasants, in the French dialect, to set him free to return to Orléans. " There, messieurs," said he, " dwells my mother, *une tendre mère*." But the peasants, probably in consequence of their ignorance as to the geographical situation of Orléans, continued to propose to him a trip under the ice, with the downward current of the winding little river Gnilotyórka, and had already begun to encourage him with gentle thrusts in the vertebræ of his neck and back, when, all of a sudden, to the indescribable joy of Lejeune, the sound of a small bell rang out, and on to the dam drove a huge sledge with a gay-hued rug on the exaggeratedly elevated foot-board behind, and drawn by a team of three roan-horses. In the sledge sat a fat, red-faced landed proprietor in a wolf-skin coat.

" What are you doing there? "—he asked the peasants.

" Why, we 're drowning a Frenchman, dear little father."

" Ah! "—returned the squire, indifferently, and turned away.

" Monsieur! Monsieur! "—shrieked the poor man.

" Ah, ah! "—remarked the wolf-skin coat, re-provingly:—" he has come to Russia with the twelve nations,[1] has burned Moscow,—the accursed one!—has torn the cross from Iván Velíky,[2] and now 't is ' Musieu, Musieu! ' and now he has tucked his tail between his legs! The thief ought to suffer torture. . . . . Drive on, Fílka! "

The horses started.

" Ah, stop, though! "—added the squire. . . . " hey, thou, Musieu, dost understand music? "

" *Sauvez-moi, sauvez-moi, mon bon monsieur!* "—repeated Lejeune.

" Did any one ever see such a race! and not one of them knows a single word of Russian! *Musique, musique, savez musique vous?*—on piano *jouez savez?* "

Lejeune understood, at last, what the landed proprietor was driving at, and nodded his head affirmatively.

" *Oui, monsieur, oui, oui, je suis musicien; je joue tous les instruments possibles! Oui, monsieur . . . . . Sauvez-moi, monsieur!* "

" Well, thou hast had a narrow escape,"—retorted the squire. . . " Release him, my lads: here 's a twenty-kopék piece for you, for liquor."

---

[1] In the grand Te Deum which is celebrated always on Christmas Day, in commemoration of the delivery of Russia, in 1812, the French and their allies are called " the Gauls and the Twelve Nations "—the word employed for nation being the one which is derived from the same root as the word heathen.—TRANSLATOR.

The great belfry of the Kremlin.—TRANSLATOR.

" Thanks, dear little father, thanks. Please take him."

They seated Lejeune in the sledge. He was choking with joy, he wept, trembled, made obeisance, thanked the squire, the coachman, the peasants. He wore a green under-jacket with pink ribbons, and the weather was gloriously cold. The squire cast a silent glance at his blue and benumbed limbs, wrapped the unhappy man in his fur cloak, and carried him home. The servants flocked together. They hastily warmed, fed, and clothed the Frenchman. The squire conducted him to his daughters.

" Here, children,"—he said to them:—" I 've found a teacher for you. You have kept pestering me, ' Teach us music and the French dialect ': so here 's a Frenchman for you, and he plays on the piano too. . . . Come on, Musieu,"—he continued, pointing to the miserable little piano, which he had purchased five years previously from a Jew, who, however, peddled Cologne water:—" show us your skill: *jouez!* "

Lejeune, with sinking heart, seated himself on the stool: he had never laid finger on a piano since he was born.

" Come, *jouez, jouez!* "—repeated the squire.

In desperation, the poor fellow banged on the keys as though they had been a drum, and played at haphazard. . . . . " I really thought," he said, as he told the story afterward, " that my rescuer would seize me by the collar, and fling me out of the house." But, to the intense amazement of the involuntary improvisatore, the landed proprietor, after a while, slapped him approvingly on the shoulder. " Good, good,"— said he, " I see that thou knowest how; go now, and rest."

A couple of weeks later, Lejeune was transferred from this landed proprietor to another, a wealthy and cultivated man, became a favourite with him through his cheerful and gentle disposition, married his pupil, entered the government service, married his daughter to landed proprietor Lobysányeff of the Orel government, a retired dragoon and poet, and himself removed his residence to Orel.

And it was this same Lejeune, or, as he was now called, Franz Ivánitch, who entered the room of Ovsyánikoff, with whom he was on friendly terms. . . . .

But, perhaps, the reader is already tired of sitting with me at Freeholder Ovsyánikoff's, and therefore I will preserve an eloquent silence.

VII

" LET's go to Lgoff,"—said Ermolái, who is already known to the reader, to me one day;— " we can shoot a lot of ducks there."

Although a wild duck offers nothing particularly attractive for a genuine sportsman, still, in the temporary absence of other game (it was the beginning of September; the woodcock had not yet arrived, and I had got tired of tramping over the fields after partridges), I gave heed to my huntsman, and set off for Lgoff.

Lgoff is a large village on the steppe, with an extremely ancient stone church of one cupola, and two mills, on the marshy little river Rosóta. Five versts from Lgoff this little stream becomes a broad pond, overgrown along the edges and here and there in the middle with dense reeds. On this pond, in the bays or stagnant spots amid the reeds, there bred and dwelt an innumerable mass of ducks of all possible varieties: widgeon, semi-widgeon, pintails, teals, mergansers, and so

[1] The soft sign between the *l* and the *g* renders the former soft: so that this is pronounced almost as though spelled L[i]goff.— TRANSLATOR.

132

forth. Small coveys were constantly flying to and fro, hovering over the water, and a shot started up such clouds of them, that the sportsman involuntarily clapped one hand to his cap and emitted a prolonged: " Phe-e-ew!"—Ermolái and I started to walk along the edge of the pond, but, in the first place, the duck, which is a wary bird, does not take up its stand on the shore itself; in the second place, even if any laggard and inexperienced teal had succumbed to our shots and lost its life, our dogs would not have been able to retrieve it in the dense reedgrowth: in spite of the most noble self-sacrifice, they could neither have swum, nor walked on the bottom, and would have cut their precious noses against the sharp edges of the reeds all in vain.

" No,"—said Ermolái at last:—" this won't do: we must get a boat. . . . Let's return to Lgoff."

We set off. We had taken only a few steps when from behind a thick willow, a decidedly wretched setter ran forth to meet us, and in its wake a man made his appearance—a man of medium stature, in a blue, very threadbare coat, a yellowish waistcoat, trousers of the tint known as *gris-de-laine* or *bleu-d'amour*, hastily tucked into boots full of holes, with a red kerchief on his neck, and a single-barrelled gun on his shoulder. While our dogs, with the Chinese ceremonial habitual to their race, sniffed at the unfamiliar individual, who was evidently intimidated, tucked his tail between his legs, dropped his ears, and briskly wriggled all over without bending his knees and showing his teeth the while,—the stranger came up to us, and made a very polite obeisance. Judging by his appearance, he was about five and twenty years of age; his long, light chestnut hair, strongly impregnated with kvas, stuck out in motionless little pig-tails,—his small brown eyes blinked amiably,—his whole face, bound up with a black kerchief, as though he were suffering from the toothache, beamed voluptuously.

"Allow me to introduce myself,"—he began, in a soft, insinuating voice:—"I 'm the huntsman here, Vladímir. . . . . On hearing of your arrival, and learning that you had deigned to direct your steps to the shores of our pond, I have decided, if it will not be disagreeable to you, to offer you my services."

Huntsman Vladímir talked precisely like a young provincial actor who plays the parts of the leading lovers. I accepted his proposal, and before we reached Lgoff I had succeeded in learning his history. He was a house-serf who had been set at liberty; in his tender youth, he had studied music, then had served as valet, knew how to read and write, had read a few little books, so far as I could make out, and while now existing, as many do exist in Russia, without a far-

thing in cash, without any fixed occupation, subsisted on something pretty near akin to heavenly
manna. He expressed himself with remarkable
elegance and obviously took a foppish pride in his
manners; he must have been a frightful dangler
after the women, too, and, in all probability, enjoyed successes in that line: Russian maidens love
eloquence. Among other things, he directed my
attention to the fact, that he sometimes called on
the neighbouring landed proprietors, and went
to town to visit, and played preference, and was
acquainted with people in the county capital.
He smiled in a masterly manner, and with extreme diversity; the modest, reserved smile
which played over his lips when he was listening
to the remarks of other people, was particularly
becoming to him. He would listen to you, and
agree with you perfectly, but nevertheless he did
not lose the sense of his own dignity, and seemed
to be desirous of giving you to understand that,
on occasion, he might put forth an opinion of his
own. Ermolái, being a man of not too much education, and not in the least " subtle," undertook
to address him as " thou." You ought to have
seen the grin with which Vladímir addressed him
as " you-sir." . . . .

" Why are you wearing that kerchief-band-
age? "—I asked him.—" Have you the toothache? "

" No, sir,"—he replied:—" it is, rather, the

noxious result of imprudence. I had a friend, a fine man, sir, not a huntsman at all, as that sometimes happens, sir. Well, sir, one day he says to me: ' My dear friend, take me a-hunting: I feel curious to know what diversion there is in that.' Naturally, I did not wish to refuse my comrade; I furnished him with a gun, sir, for my part, and took him a-hunting, sir. Well, sir, we hunted our fill, as was proper; and, at last, we took it into our heads to rest, sir. I sat down under a tree; but he, on his side, on the contrary, began to play pranks with his gun, sir, and took aim at me. I requested him to stop it, but, in his inexperience, he did not heed me, sir. The gun went off, and I lost my chin and the forefinger of my right hand. . . . . . "

We reached Lgoff. But Vladímir and Ermolái had decided that it was impossible to hunt without a boat.

" Sutchók has a barge-plank punt," [1]—remarked Vladímir:—" but I don't know where he has hidden it. I must run to him."

" To whom? " I asked.

" Why, a man lives here whose nickname is Sutchók " (The Twig).

Vladímir, with Ermolái, set off in quest of The Twig. I told them that I would wait for them at the church. As I inspected the tombstones in the churchyard, I hit upon a blackened, quadrangular urn, with the following inscrip-

---

[1] A flat boat knocked together from old barge planks.

tions: on one side, in French characters: " Ci-gît
Théophile-Henri, Vicomte de Blangy; " on another: " Beneath this stone is interred the body
of Count Blangy, French subject; born 1737,
died 1799, at the age of 62; " on the third side:
" Peace to his ashes; " on the fourth side:

Beneath this stone lies a French emigrant:
He had birth distinguished and talent.
By the massacre of wife and family distressed,
He abandoned his fatherland by the tyrant oppressed;
The shores of the Russian land having attained,
In his old age a hospitable roof-tree he gained;
The children he taught, the parents consoled. . . . .
Here the Almighty Judge has given rest to his soul.

The arrival of Ermolái, Vladímir, and the man
with the strange nickname, The Twig, interrupted my meditations.

Barefooted, tattered, and dishevelled, The
Twig seemed, from his appearance, to be a retired house-serf, about sixty years of age.

" Hast thou a boat? "—I asked.

" I have,"—he replied, in a dull and cracked
voice:—" but it 's very bad."

" How so? "

" It 's coming apart; and the plugs have fallen
out of the holes." [1]

" A great misfortune that," put in Ermolái:
" but we can stuff in tow."

[1] See note on page 21.—TRANSLATOR.

"Of course, that is possible,"—assented The Twig.

"But who art thou?"

"The squire's fisherman."

"How canst thou be a fisherman, and have thy boat in such disrepair?"

"Why, there are no fish in our river."

"Fish don't like rusty swamp-water,"—remarked my huntsman, pompously.

"Well,"—I said to Ermolái:—"go, get some tow, and repair the boat for us, and be quick about it."

Ermolái departed.

"Well, I suppose we shall go to the bottom, anyway?"—I said to Vladímir.

"God is merciful,"—he replied. "In any case, we are bound to suppose that the pond is not deep."

"No, it isn't deep,"—remarked The Twig, who talked in a curious manner, as though half asleep:—"and there is slime and grass on the bottom, and it's all overgrown with grass. However, there are pit-holes too."

"But if the grass is so strong,"—remarked Vladímir:—"it will be impossible to row."

"Why, but who does row a punt? It must be shoved with a pole; I have a pole yonder,—or a shovel will do."

"A shovel is clumsy, I don't suppose one could touch bottom with it in some places,"—said Vladímir.

" That 's true, it is awkward."

I sat down on a grave to wait for Ermolái. Vladímir went off a little way, from a sense of propriety, and sat down also. The Twig continued to stand in the same spot, with drooping head, and hands folded behind his back, out of old habit.

" Tell me, please,"—I began:—" hast thou been a fisherman here long? "

" This is the seventh year,"—he replied, with a start.

" And what was thy previous occupation? "

" Formerly I was a coachman."

" Who discharged thee from the post of coachman? "

" Why, the new mistress."

" What mistress? "

" Why, the one who has bought us. You don't know her: Alyóna [Eléna] Timofyéevna, such a fat woman . . . . and not young."

" What made her take it into her head to promote thee to be the fisherman? "

" God knows. . She came to us from her estate, from Tambóff, ordered all the house-serfs to assemble, and came out to us. First of all, we went and kissed her hand, and she made no objection: she was not angry. . . And then she began to question us, one after the other: what did each do, what duties did he perform? My turn came; so she asks: ' What hast thou been? ' I say: ' A coachman! '—' A coachman? Well, a

pretty sort of coachman thou art; just look at
thyself: a coachman, forsooth! 'T is not fit that
thou shouldst be a coachman: thou shalt be my
fisherman, and thou must shave off thy beard.
When I come hither, thou art to supply fish for
my table, dost hear?' . . . So from that time
forth, I have been reckoned a fisherman. And
it is my business, you see, to keep the pond in
order. . . . . But how is it to be kept in order? "

" To whom did you formerly belong? "

" Why, to Sergyéi Sergyéitch Pékhteroff.
We came to him through inheritance. But he
did not own us long,—six years in all. And I
served as coachman to him . . . but not in town
—there he had others, but in the country."

" And wert thou always a coachman, from thy
youth up? "

" A coachman, indeed! I became a coachman
under Sergyéi Sergyéitch, but before that I was
the cook,—but not in town, but thus, in the country."

" And whose cook wert thou? "

" Why, my former master's, Afanásy Nefyóditch, uncle to Sergyéi Sergyéitch. He bought
Lgoff, Afanásy Nefyóditch bought it, and Sergyéi Sergyéitch inherited the estate."

" From whom did he buy it? "

" Why, from Tatyána Vasílievna! "

" From what Tatyána Vasílievna? "

" Why, the one yonder, who died year before

last, near Bolkhóff . . . . I mean to say, near
Karátchevo,—a spinster. . . . . And she was
never married. Don't you know her? We came
to her from her father, from Vasíly Semyónitch.
She owned us a pretty long time . . . . about
twenty years."

" Well, and so thou wert her cook? "

" At first, in fact, I was a cook, and then I became kofischenk."

" What? "

" Kofischenk."

" What sort of an employment is that? "

" Why, I don't know, dear little father. I
was attached to the butler's pantry, and my
name was Antón, and not Kuzmá. Those were
the mistress's orders."

" Is thy real name Kuzmá? "

" Yes."

" And wert thou kofischenk all the time? "

" No, not all the time: I was also an actor."

" Is it possible? "

" Of course I was. . . . I played in the
keatre. Our mistress set up a keatre in her
house."

" What parts didst thou play? "

" What were you pleased to ask, sir? "

" What didst thou do in the theatre? "

" Why, don't you know? Well, they would
take and dress me up; and I would walk about
decked out, or stand, or sit, as the case might be.

They would tell me: ' This is what thou must say '—and I would say it. Once I represented a blind man. . . They put a pea under each of my eyelids. . . So they did! "

" And after that, what wert thou? "

" After that, I became a cook again."

" Why did they degrade thee to the position of cook? "

" Why, my brother ran away."

" Well, and what wert thou with the father of thy first mistress? "

" Why, I discharged various duties: first I was a page, a falet, a shoemaker, and also a whipper-in."

" A whipper-in? . . . . And didst thou ride to hounds? "

" I did, and injured myself: I fell from my horse, and hurt the horse. Our old master was very severe; he ordered me to be flogged, and to be apprenticed to a shoemaker in Moscow."

" What dost thou mean by apprenticeship? I don't suppose thou wert a whipper-in while thou wert a child? "

" I was over twenty."

" And what sort of instruction could there be at twenty? "

" Of course, if the master ordered, there was no help. But, luckily, he died soon after,—and they brought me back to the village."

" But when didst thou learn the art of cookery? "

The Twig raised his thin, sallow face a little, and laughed aloud.

" Why, does one learn that?—But even the peasant women can cook! "

" Well," said I:—" thou hast seen sights in thy day, Kuzmá! And what dost thou do now, as fisherman, if there are no fish on thy mistress's estate? "

" Why, dear little father, I have nothing to complain of. And thank God that I was made the fisherman. For the mistress ordered just such another old fellow as me—Andréi Pupýr— to the paper-mill as water-carrier. ' 'T is sinful,' says she, ' to eat the bread of idleness.' . . . . And Pupýr was counting on favour: his first cousin's son is clerk in the mistress's office, and he had promised to report about him to the mistress, to remind her of him. Much he reminded her! . . . And Pupýr, before my very eyes, bowed down to his cousin-nephew's feet."

" Hast thou any family? Hast thou been married? "

" No, dear little father. The late Tatyána Vasílievna—the kingdom of heaven be hers!—permitted no one to marry. God forbid! She used to say: ' I live unwedded, as you see. What self-indulgence! who needs it? ' "

" On what dost thou live now? Dost thou receive wages? "

" Wages, indeed, dear little father! . . . They give me my victuals—and thanks to Thee, O Lord, for that same! I 'm well satisfied. May God prolong our mistress's life! "

Ermolái returned.

" The boat is repaired,"—he said surlily.— " Go fetch thy pole—thou! " The Twig ran for his pole. During the whole time of my conversation with the poor old man, Vladímir the huntsman had stared at him with a scornful smile.

" A stupid man, sir,"—he said, when the latter went away:—" an entirely uneducated man, a peasant, sir, nothing more, sir. He cannot be called a house-serf, sir . . . he was just bragging all the time, sir. . . . Just judge for yourself, sir, how could he be an actor, sir? You have deigned to bother yourself unnecessarily, you have condescended to chat with him, sir! "

A quarter of an hour later, we were seated in the punt. (We had left the dog in the cottage, under the oversight of the coachman Iegudiíl.) We were not very comfortable, but hunters are not extremely fastidious folks. The Twig stood at the blunt-pointed stern, and " shoved." Vladímir and I sat on the cross-seats of the boat. Ermolái placed himself in front, at the very bow. In spite of the tow, water speedily made its appearance under our feet. Fortunately, the weather was calm, and the pond was as quiet as though asleep.

We floated on rather slowly. The old man with difficulty pulled his long pole out of the ooze, all wound about with the green threads of the submarine sedges; the thick, circular pads of the marsh lilies also impeded the progress of our boat. At last we reached the reeds, and the fun began. The ducks rose noisily, " tore themselves " from the pond, frightened by our unexpected appearance in their domain, shots followed them thick and fast, and it was diverting to see those bob-tailed birds turn somersaults in the air and flop down heavily on the water. As a matter of course, we did not retrieve all the ducks we shot: the slightly wounded dived; some, killed outright, fell into such dense clumps of reeds that even Ermolái's carroty-hued little eyes could not detect them; but, nevertheless, by dinner-time our boat was filled to overflowing with game.

Vladímir, to the great amazement of Ermolái, proved to be very far from a good shot, and after each unsuccessful discharge felt surprised, inspected and blew into his gun, was puzzled, and, at last, explained to us the reason why he had missed his aim. Ermolái shot, as usual, with triumphant success; I, quite badly, according to my wont. The Twig gazed at us with the eyes of a man who has been in the service of the gen-

try from his youth up, shouted now and then
" Yonder, yonder is another duck!"—and kep
incessantly scratching his back—not with his
hands, but with his shoulders, which he set in mo
tion. The weather was magnificent: round
white clouds floated high and softly over ou
heads, and were clearly reflected in the water; the
reeds whispered around us; the pond, in spots
glittered like steel in the sunlight. We were pre
paring to return to the village, when, all of a
sudden, a decidedly unpleasant accident hap
pened to us.

We had long since noticed that the water had
been gradually but constantly gathering in ou
punt. Vladímir was commissioned to bail it out
by means of a dipper, which my provident hunts
man had abstracted, in case of need, from a peas
ant woman who was not watching. Things wen
on as they should, until Vladímir forgot his duty
But toward the end of the hunt, as though by way
of farewell, the ducks began to rise in such flocks
that we hardly had time to load our guns. In
the smoke of the firing, we paid no attention to
the condition of our punt,—and suddenly, at a
violent motion on the part of Ermolái (he was
trying to secure a duck which had been killed
and was bearing his full weight against the gun
wale), our decrepit vessel careened, filled with
water, and triumphantly went to the bottom,—
fortunately, at a spot where the water was not

deep. We cried out, but it was already too late: a moment later, we were standing up to our necks in the water, surrounded by the floating carcasses of the dead ducks. I cannot now recall without laughter the frightened, pallid countenances of my companions (probably, my own face was not distinguished by its high colour at the time, either); but at that moment, I must confess, it never entered my head to laugh. Each of us held his gun over his head, and The Twig, probably owing to his habit of imitating his superiors, elevated his pole on high also. Ermolái was the first to break the silence.

"Whew, damn it!"—he muttered, spitting into the water: "here's a pretty mess! And it's all thy fault, thou old devil!"—he added angrily, turning to The Twig:—"what sort of a boat dost thou call that?"

"Forgive me!"—faltered the old man.

"Yes, and thou art a nice one too,"—went on my huntsman, turning his head in the direction of Vladímir:—"why wert not thou on the look-out? why didst thou not bail? thou, thou, thou . . . ."

But Vladímir was already past retorting; he was trembling like a leaf, his teeth were chattering, and he was smiling in a wholly senseless way. What had become of his fine language, his sense of delicate propriety, and his own dignity!

The accursed punt rocked weakly under our feet. . . . At the moment of our ship-wreck, the water had seemed to us extremely cold, but we soon got used to it. When the first alarm subsided, I glanced about me: all around, at a distance of ten paces from us, grew reeds; far away, over their tops, the shore was visible. "We 're in a bad plight!" I thought.

"What are we to do?"—I asked Ermolái.

"Why, here now, let 's see; we can't spend the night here,"—he replied.—"Here now, hold my gun,"—he said to Vladímir.

Vladímir submissively obeyed.

"I 'll go and search out a ford,"—went on Ermolái, with confidence, as though in every pond there must, infallibly, exist a ford,—took the pole from The Twig, and set off in the direction of the shore, cautiously probing the bottom.

"But canst thou swim?"—I asked him.

"No, I can't,"—rang out his voice, from behind the reeds.

"Well, then he 'll drown,"—indifferently remarked The Twig, who had at first been frightened, not at the danger, but at our wrath, and now, with perfect composure, merely drew a long breath from time to time, and, apparently, felt no imperative necessity to alter his situation.

"And he 'll perish quite uselessly, sir,"—added Vladímir, plaintively.

Ermolái did not return for more than an hour.

That hour seemed an eternity to us. At first we
exchanged shouts with him very assiduously; then
he began to answer our calls more infrequently,
and at last he fell silent altogether. In the village the bells began to ring for vespers. We did
not talk with each other, we even tried not to look
at each other. The ducks hovered over our
heads; some prepared to alight beside us, but
suddenly soared aloft, "like a shot," as the saying is, and flew quacking away. We began to
grow numb. The Twig blinked his eyes, as
though he were inclined to be sleepy.

At last, to our indescribable joy, Ermolái returned.

" Well, what now? "

" I have been to the shore; I have found a
ford."

" Let us go."

We wanted to set off on the instant; but first
he drew a rope from his pocket under water,
tied the dead ducks by their legs, took both
ends in his teeth, and strode on in front; Vladímir followed him, I followed Vladímir, and The
Twig closed the procession. It was about two
hundred paces to the shore. Ermolái walked
onward boldly, and without a halt (so well had
he taken note of the road), only calling out,
from time to time: " More to the left,—there 's
a sink-hole on the right!" or: " To the right,—
there on the left you 'll stick fast." . . . . At

times the water reached our throats, and twice
the poor Twig, being lower of stature than the
rest of us, choked and emitted bubbles.—" Come,
come, come! "—shouted Ermolái menacingly at
him,—and The Twig scrambled, floundered
about with his feet, hopped, and, somehow or
other, reached a shallower spot; but, even in ex-
tremity, he could not bring himself to clutch the
tail of my coat. Worn out, dirty, soaked, we
reached the shore at last.

Two hours later, we were all sitting, dried so
far as that was possible, in a large hay-shed, and
preparing to sup. Iegudiíl, extremely slow to
start, disinclined to move, sagacious and sleepy,
stood at the gate, and assiduously regaled The
Twig with snuff. (I have noticed that coachmen
in Russia speedily strike up friendship.) The
Twig snuffed it up furiously to the point of
nausea: spat, coughed, and, to all appearances
experienced great satisfaction. Vladímir as
sumed a languid air, lolled his head on one
side, and said little. The dogs wagged their
tails with exaggerated briskness, in anticipation
of oatmeal porridge; the horses were stamping
and neighing under the shed. . . . . The sun
had set; its last rays dispersed in crimson streaks;
little golden clouds spread over the sky, grow
ing ever thinner and thinner, like a fleece washed
and combed. . . . . Songs resounded in
the village.

VIII

T was a magnificent July day, one of those
days which come only when the weather has been
fair for a long time. From the very earliest
dawn the sky is clear; the morning glow does not
flame like a conflagration: it pours itself forth
in a gentle flush. The sun, not fiery, not red-hot,
as in the season of sultry drought, not of a dull
crimson, as before a tempest, but bright, and
agreeably radiant, glides up peacefully under
a long, narrow cloudlet, beams freshly, and
plunges into its lilac mist. The thin upper edges
of the outstretched cloudlet begin to flash like
darting serpents; their gleam resembles the
gleam of hammered silver. . . . But now the
sportive rays have burst forth once more,—and
the mighty luminary rises merrily and majestically, as though flying. In the neighbourhood of
midday, a multitude of round, high-hanging
clouds make their appearance, of a golden-grey
hue, with tender white rims. Like islands, scattered upon a river which has overflowed to an
endless extent, and streams around them in pro-
foundly-transparent branches of level azure, they

151

hardly stir from their places. Further away,
toward the horizon, they move to meet each other,
press close upon one another, and there is no azure
to be seen between them, but they themselves are
as blue as the sky: they are all permeated,
through and through, with light and warmth.
The colour of the horizon, a light, pale lilac, does
not undergo any change all day long, and is the
same all the way round; nowhere does it grow
darker, nowhere is a thunder-storm brewing;
here and there, perhaps, bluish streaks run downward from above, or a barely perceptible shower
sprinkles down. Toward evening, these clouds
vanish; the last of them, blackish and undefined
in form, like smoke, lie in rosy, curling wreaths
over against the setting sun; at the place where
it has gone down as tranquilly as it rose in the
sky, a scarlet aureole stands, for a little while
above the darkening earth, and, flickering softly
like a carefully carried taper, the evening star
kindles in it. On such days, the colours are all
softened, bright but not gaudy; over everything
rests the imprint of a certain touching gentleness. On such days the heat is sometimes very
great; sometimes, even, it is " stewing hot " on
the slopes of the fields; but the breeze chases
away, disperses the accumulated sultriness, cir
cling wind-gusts—an unfailing sign of settled
weather—wander in tall white columns of dus
along the roads across the tilled land. The dry

ure air is redolent of wormwood, crushed rye,
buckwheat; even an hour before nightfall, you
will feel no dampness. This is the sort of
weather which the farmer craves for harvesting
his grain.

On precisely such a day, I was once hunting
partridges in the Tchyórnoye district of the Túla
government. I had found and shot quite a lot
of game; my well-filled game-bag was cutting
pitilessly into my shoulder; but the evening glow
had already died out, and in the air, which was
still light, although no longer illuminated by the
rays of the setting sun, the chilly shadows were
beginning to thicken and spread abroad when, at
last, I decided to return home. With swift
strides I traversed a long " square " of second-
growth bushes, climbed a hill, and, instead of the
familiar level stretch with its oak copse, which
I had expected to see on my right, and the low-
browed white church in the distance, I beheld an
entirely different set of places, with which I was
not acquainted. At my feet stretched a narrow
vale; directly opposite, a dense grove of aspen
trees rose in a steep wall. I halted in bewilderment, and glanced about me. . . . . . " Oho! " I
thought: " why, I have lost my way completely:
I have kept too much to the right," and, amazed
at my mistake, I briskly descended the hill. I
was immediately beset by a disagreeable, motionless dampness, as though I had entered a cellar:

the thick, tall grass on the floor of the vale, a
wet through, gleamed like a smooth, white table
cloth; somehow, one felt uneasy about steppin
on it. I scrambled up the opposite slope a
alertly as possible, keeping to the left, along th
aspen grove. Bats were already flitting above it
slumbering crests, mysteriously circling and quiv
ering against the confusedly-clear sky; a belate
hawk flew past smartly and directly upward
hurrying to its nest. " Now, as soon as I tur
yonder corner," I thought to myself, " I sha
immediately strike the road;—but I have mad
a loop of a verst! "

At last, I reached the corner of the forest, bu
there was no road: some low-growing, unfelle
bushes spread out broadly in front of me, an
beyond them, far, far away, a stretch of wast
land was visible. Again I came to a standstil
" What 's the meaning of this? . . . Why, whei
am I? "—I began to recall how and where I ha
roamed during the course of the day. . . " El
why, these are the Parákhinsko bushes!" I ex
claimed at last: " that 's it exactly! that must l
the Sindyéevo copse yonder. . . But how in tl
world did I get here? So far? . . . . 'T
strange! Now I must keep to the right again

I went to the right, through the bushes. In tl
meantime night was drawing on, and growin
like a thunder-cloud; it seemed as though, alon
with the nocturnal exhalations, the darkness ros

rom all directions, and even streamed down
rom on high. I hit upon an unbeaten, overgrown path; I advanced along it, attentively
gazing ahead. Everything around was swiftly
growing black and silent,—only the quails ut-
ered a call from time to time. A small night
bird, darting inaudibly and low on its soft wings,
lmost came into collision with me, and dived
side in affright. I emerged upon the edge of
he bush-growth, and wended my way along the
boundary strip of sward between two fields. Al-
eady I could make out distant objects only with
lifficulty: the field gleamed dimly white around
ne; beyond it, moving nearer with every passing
moment in huge masses, surged up the grim
gloom. My footsteps resounded dully in the
hilly air. The sky, which had paled, began to
urn blue again,—but it was the nocturnal blue
low. Tiny stars began to twinkle, to stir in it.

That which I had been on the point of taking
or a grove, turned out to be a dark, round
hillock. "But where am I, then?" I repeated,
once more, aloud, halted for the third time, and
tared inquiringly at my English, yellow-spotted
hound, Dianka, positively the cleverest of all
our-footed creatures. But the cleverest of
quadrupeds only wagged her tail, blinked her
weary eyes dolefully, and gave me no practical
dvice. I felt ashamed in her presence, and
ushed desperately onward, as though I had sud-

denly divined whither I ought to go, skirted
the hillock, and found myself in a shallow de-
pression, tilled all around. A strange feeling immediately took possession of me. This hollow
had almost the form of a regular kettle, with
sloping sides; on its bottom several large, white
boulders reared themselves on end,—they seemed
to have crawled down there to hold a secret con-
ference, and the place was so deaf and dumb, the
sky hung over it so flatly, so dejectedly, that my
heart contracted within me. Some sort of a
small, wild animal was whining weakly and pitifully among the boulders. I made haste to retreat behind the hillock. Up to this moment, I
had not yet lost hope of finding my way home
but now I became definitively convinced that I
was completely lost, and without making the
slightest further effort to recognise my surroundings, which were almost entirely drowned
in the mist, I walked straight ahead, guided by
the stars, at random. . . . I continued to walk
thus for about half an hour, with difficulty put
ting one foot before the other. It seemed to me
that, never since I was born, had I been in such
desert places: not a single light twinkled any
where, not a sound was audible. One sloping hill
succeeded another, fields stretched out after
fields in endless succession, bushes seemed fairly
to spring out of the earth in front of my very
nose. I kept walking on and on, and was already

making ready to lie down somewhere until the morning, when, suddenly, I found myself on the brink of a frightful abyss.

I hastily drew back my foot, which was thrust forward, and athwart the barely penetrable gloom of night I descried, far down beneath me, a vast ravine. A broad river swept around it in a semicircle which swerved away from me; steely gleams of water, flashing forth rarely and dimly, designated its course. The hill on which I found myself descended in an almost perpendicular precipice; its huge outlines stood out, darkling, against the bluish aërial waste, and directly beneath me, in the angle formed by the precipice and the level plain, beside the river, which, at that point, stood like a dark, motionless mirror, beneath the very steep face of the hill, burned and smoked, side by side, two fires. Around them people were swarming, shadows were flickering, the front half of a small, curly head was at times brilliantly illuminated. . .

I recognised, at last, whither I had come. This meadow is renowned in our vicinity under the name of the Byézhin Meadow. . . . . . . But there was no possibility of getting home, especially by night; my legs were giving way beneath me with weariness. I made up my mind to approach the fires, and, in the company of the people, whom I took for drovers, to await the dawn. I made a successful descent, but before I

could release from my hand the last bough I had
clutched, two large, white, shaggy dogs flew at
me, barking viciously. Ringing childish voices
resounded around the fires; two or three little
boys rose hastily from the ground. They ran
toward me, called off the dogs, who had been
particularly surprised by the appearance of my
Dianka, and I approached them.

I had made a mistake in taking the persons
who were sitting round those fires for drovers.
They were simply peasant children from the
neighbouring village, who were herding the
horses. In our parts, during the hot summer
weather, the horses are driven out to graze in the
fields at night: by day, the flies and gadflies
would give them no peace. It is a great treat for
the peasant lads to drive the herd out at eventide
and drive them home at dawn. Seated, capless,
and in old half-coats, on the most restive nags,
they dash on with merry whoops and shouts, with
dangling arms and legs, bouncing high aloft,
with ringing laughter. The light dust rises in a
column and blows along the road; far away, the
vigorous trampling of hoofs is borne on the air,
the horses race onward, pricking up their ears;
in front of all, flirting its tail, and incessantly
changing foot, gallops a shaggy reddish-yellow
beast, with burdock burs in its tangled mane.

I told the little lads that I had lost my way,
and sat down with them. They asked me

whence I had come, fell silent, drew aside. We
chatted a little. I lay down under a gnawed
bush, and began to look about me. It was a wonderful picture; around the fires quivered, and, as
it were, flickered, resting against the darkness, a
round, reddish reflection; the flame, flashing up
now and then, cast swift gleams beyond the limit
of that circle; a thin tongue of light would lick
the bare boughs of the scrub-willows and instantly vanish;—long, sharp-pointed shadows,
breaking forth, for a moment, in their turn,
rushed up to the very fires: the gloom wrestled
with the light. Sometimes, when the flame
burned more feebly, and the circle of light contracted, a horse's head would suddenly thrust
itself forward out of the invading gloom,—a
brown horse, with a sinuous white mark on the
forehead, or all white,—and gaze attentively and
dully at us, briskly chewing a long tuft of grass
the while, and, lowering again, immediately disappear. All that was audible was, that it continued to chew and snort. From the illuminated
place, it was difficult to discern what was going
on in the darkness, and, consequently, everything
near at hand seemed enveloped in an almost black
curtain; but further away, toward the horizon,
hills and forests could be dimly descried, in long
splashes. The dark, pure sky stood solemnly and
boundlessly high above us, with all its mysterious
majesty. The breast felt sweet oppression as it

inhaled that peculiar, fresh and enervating fragrance—the fragrance of a Russian summer night. Hardly a sound was audible round about. . . . Only now and then, in the near-by river, a large fish would splash with sudden sonorousness, and the reeds upon the banks would rustle faintly, barely rocked by a truant wave. . . . The fires alone crackled softly.

The little boys sat around them; there, also, sat the two dogs, who would have liked to devour me. For a long time, they could not reconcile themselves to my presence, and, sleepily screwing up their eyes, and casting sidelong glances at the fire, they growled, now and then, with the consciousness of their own dignity; first they growled, and then whined faintly, as though they regretted the impossibility of fulfilling their desire. There were five lads in all: Fédya, Pavlúsha, Iliúsha, Kóstya, and Ványa. (I learned their names from their conversation, and intend to introduce them at once to the reader.)

You would have said that the first, the oldest of them all, Fédya, was fourteen. He was a graceful lad, with handsome, delicate, and rather small features, curly fair hair, light eyes, and a constant, half-merry, half-abstracted smile. He belonged, by all the tokens, to a rich family, and went out thus into the fields, not through necessity, but because he wished it, for amusement. He wore a gay print shirt with a yellow border;

a small, new peasant's long-coat, hanging from his shoulders, the sleeves unused, hardly held in place on his narrow shoulders; from his sky-blue girdle hung a small comb. His boots, with narrow leg-pieces, were really his boots—not his father's. The second lad, Pavlúsha, had tangled, black hair, grey eyes, broad cheek-bones, a pale, pockmarked face, a large, but regular mouth; his whole head was huge as a beer-kettle, as the expression is, his body stubby, uncouth. He was a homely little fellow,—there's no denying that! —but, nevertheless, he pleased me: his gaze was very sensible and direct, and power resounded in his voice. His garments were nothing to boast of: they consisted of a plain hemp-cloth shirt and patched trousers. The face of the third, Iliúsha, was rather insignificant; hook-nosed, long, mole-eyed, it expressed a sort of stupid, sickly anxiety; his tightly compressed lips did not move, his knitted brows did not unbend,—he seemed to be always screening his eyes from the fire. His yellow, almost white hair stuck out in pointed tufts from beneath a low-crowned, felt cap, which he was incessantly pulling down over his ears with both hands. He wore new linden-bark slippers and leg-cloths; a thick cord, wound thrice around his body, carefully confined his neat, black coat. He and Pavlúsha were, apparently, not over twelve years of age. The fourth, Kóstya, a little lad of ten, excited my curiosity by his thoughtful and melancholy gaze. His whole face was small, thin, freckled, pointed below, like that of a squirrel; his lips were hardly discernible; but his large, black eyes, shining with a liquid gleam, produced a strange impression: they seemed to want to express something for which the tongue—his tongue, at all events—had no words. He was short of stature, of fragile build, and dressed quite poorly. At first, I came near not noticing the last one, Ványa: he was lying on the ground, peaceably curled up under an angular rug, and only now and then did he thrust out from beneath it his curly chestnut head. This boy was, at most, seven years of age.

So I lay there under a bush, apart, and surveyed the little lads. A small kettle hung over one of the fires: in it they were boiling " 'taties." Pavlúsha was watching it, and, kneeling, thrust a chip into the frothing water. Fédya was lying propped on his elbow, with the tails of his coat spread apart. Iliúsha was sitting beside Kóstya, and also screwing up his eyes intently. Kóstya had dropped his head a little, and was gazing off somewhere into the distance. Ványa did not stir under his rug. I pretended to be asleep. Gradually, the boys began to talk again.

At first they prattled about one thing and another, about the toils of the morrow, about the horses; but, all of a sudden, Fédya turned to

Iliúsha and, as though renewing an interrupted conversation, asked him:

" Well, and what wert thou saying—hast thou seen the domovóy? "[1]

" No, I have not seen him, and it is n't possible to see him,"—replied Iliúsha, in a hoarse, weak voice, whose sound precisely matched the expression of his face. " I heard him. . . . . And I was n't the only one."

" And whereabouts on your premises does he haunt? "—inquired Pavlúsha.

" In the old stuff-chest room."[2]

" But do you go to the mill? "

" Of course we do. My brother Avdiúshka and I are plater-boys."

" See there, now—you are mill-hands! " . . . .

" Well, and how didst thou come to hear him? "—asked Fédya.

" Why, this way. It happened that brother Avdiúshka and I, along with Feódor Mikhyéevsky and the squint-eyed Iváshka, and another Iváshka, who is from the Red Hills, and still another Iváshka Sukhorúkoff, and other boys also; there were ten of us lads in all,—the whole gang, that is to say; well, and it happened that we had to pass the night in the stuff-chest room,—that is to say, it did n't happen so, but Nazároff, the

---

[1] House-sprite, like the banshee.—TRANSLATOR.
[2] The building, in paper-mills, where the paper is bailed out of the stuff-chests. It is close to the dam, under the wheel.

overseer, forbade us to go home: says he:
' What 's the good,' says he, ' of you boys trudg-
ing home; there 's a lot of work for to-morrow,
so don't you go home, my lads.' And so we
stayed, and all lay down together, and Avdiúshka says, ' Well, boys, and what if the domovóy should come?' . . . . And before he, Avdyéi
that is, had finished speaking, some one suddenly
walked across over our heads; but we were lying
down-stairs, and he was walking up-stairs, by
the wheel. We hear him walking, and the
boards fairly bend under him, and crack; now
he has passed over our heads; the water suddenly
begins to roar and roar against the wheel; the
wheel begins to bang and bang, and to turn; but
the sluice-gate is shut. We wonder:—who can
have raised it, so that the water comes through?
But the wheel went on turning and turning, and
then stopped. Then that person went to the door
up-stairs again, and began to descend the stairs,
and came down as though he were in no hurry;
the steps fairly groaned beneath him. . . . . Well,
the person came to our door, waited, waited,—
and suddenly the door flew wide open. We
started up in terror, we looked—nothing! . . . .
All of a sudden, behold, the mould at one of the
stuff-chests began to move, rose up, tipped, and
floated, floated like that, through the air, as
though some one were rinsing with it, and then
went back to its place. Then, at another chest,

the hook was taken from the nail, and put back on the nail again; then some one seemed to go to the door, and suddenly began to cough and hawk, like some sort of sheep, and so noisily. . . . . We all tumbled together in a heap, and crawled under one another. . . . . How scared we were that time!"

"You don't say so!"—remarked Pável.—"What made him cough?"

"I don't know; the dampness, perhaps."

All relapsed into silence.

"Well,"—inquired Fédya:—"are the 'taties done?"

Pavlúsha felt of them.

"No, they're still raw. . . . . Whew, what a splash,"—he added, turning his face in the direction of the river:—"it must be a pike . . . . and yonder is a shooting star."

"See here, fellows, I'll tell you something,"—began Kóstya, in a thin little voice:—"Listen to what daddy told me the other day."

"Come on, we're listening,"—said Fédya, with a patronising mien.

"Of course, you know Gavrílo, the village carpenter?"

"Well, yes; we do."

"But do you know why he is always such a melancholy man: always silent, you know? This is why he is so melancholy: Once on a time, fellows, says my daddy, he went to the forest for nuts. So he went to the forest for nuts, and got lost; God knows where he came out. So he walked and walked, fellows,—but no! he could n't find the road! and night was already at hand. So he sat down under a tree; ' I 'll just wait until morning,' says he to himself,—so he sat down, and fell into a doze. And while he was sleeping, he suddenly heard some one calling him. He looks—no one. Again he fell asleep, —again came the call. Again he looks and looks around: and in front of him, on a bough, sits a water-nymph; she rocks to and fro, and calls him to her, while she herself is dying with laughter. And she laughs so! . . . .And the moon was shining strongly,—so strongly, clearly is the moon shining, that everything is visible, my boys. So she calls him, and sits there on the bough, all brilliant, and white, just like a roach or a gudgeon,—or a carp, also, is whitish and silvery like that. . . . . Gavrílo the carpenter fairly fell back in a swoon, fellows; but she, you know, shrieked with laughter, and kept beckoning him to her with her hand, like this. Gavrílo tried to rise, tried to obey the water-nymph, fellows, but, you see, the Lord suggested something to him: he just made the sign of the cross over himself. . . . And how hard he found it to make that sign of the cross, fellows! He says: ' My hand was simply like stone, it would n't move. . . . Akh, thou wicked nymph, ah! '—So, fellows, when he

made the sign of the cross, that water-sprite
ceased to laugh, and suddenly began to weep, as
it were. . . . She weeps, fellows, and wipes her
eyes with her hair, and her hair is as green as thy
hemp. So Gavrílo stared and stared at her, and
began to question her: ' Why weepest thou, thou
imp of the forest?' But the water-sprite says to
him: ' Thou shouldst not have crossed thyself, O
man,' says she; ' thou mightest have lived with
me to the end of thy days; and I am weeping, I
am pining away, because thou hast crossed thyself; and 't is not I alone, who shall pine: pine
thou, also, until the end of thy days.' Then she
vanished, fellows, and Gavrílo immediately understood how he was to get out of the forest. . . .
Only, from that time forth, he goes about always
in that melancholy way."

" Ekha! "—remarked Fédya, after a brief silence:—" but how can such a wicked forest
demon spoil a Christian soul,—he ought n't to
have listened to her!"

" Oh, go along with you! "—said Kóstya.—
" And Gavrílo said she had such a thin, wailing
voice, like a toad's."

" Did thy dad narrate that himself? "—went
on Fédya.

" Yes, he did. I was lying on the platform
over the oven, and heard everything."

" A wonderful affair! Why should he be
melancholy? . . . . Why, you know, if she

called him, 't was because ' she had taken a fancy
to him.' "

" Yes, she had taken a fancy to him! "—put in
Iliúsha.—" Of course, she wanted to tickle him,
—that 's what she wanted. That 's what they do,
those water-nymphs."

" Why, and there must be water-nymphs here,
too,"—remarked Fédya.

" No,"—replied Kóstya:—" this is a clean
place, a free place; for one thing, the river is
hard by."

All fell silent. Suddenly, somewhere in the
far distance, there rang out a long-drawn, sonorous, almost moaning sound, one of those incomprehensible nocturnal noises, which sometimes
well up in the midst of profound stillness, rise
aloft, hang suspended in the air, and slowly dis-
perse, at last, as though they died away. You
strain your ear,—and it seems as though there
were nothing, yet it is tinkling. It seemed as
though some one had shouted for a long, long
time, at the very horizon, and some one else had
answered his shout from the forest with a thin,
shrill laugh, and a weak, hissing whistle flew
with lightning speed along the river. The little
lads exchanged glances, and shuddered.

" The power of the cross be with us! "—whispered Ilyá.

" Ekh, you simpletons! "—cried Pável: " what
are you frightened at? Look here, the 'taties are

boiled soft." (They moved up round the little kettle, and began to eat the smoking-hot potatoes; Ványa alone did not stir.) "What's the matter with thee?"—said Pável.

But he did not crawl forth from under his linden-bast rug. The little kettle was speedily emptied completely.

"But have you heard, my lads,"—began Iliúsha:—"what happened the other day at Varnávitzy?"

"On the dam, thou meanest?"—asked Fédya.

"Yes, yes, on the dam, the broken dam. 'T is an unhallowed place, you know, so unhallowed, and so God-forsaken. Everywhere around there are such ravines and precipices, and down the precipices snakes breed."

"Well, what happened? Go ahead and tell us."

"Why, this is what happened. Perhaps thou dost not know it, Fédya, but we have a drowned man buried there, and he was drowned long, long ago, when the pond was still deep; only his grave is still visible, and even that is barely visible: 't is just a tiny mound. . . . . Well, the other day, the manager calls up Ermíl the dog-keeper; says he: ' Go to the post-office, Ermíl.' Ermíl always does ride to the post-office: he has starved off all his dogs: that's why they don't live with him, and they never did live with him, anyway, but he's a fine whipper-in, he has all the gifts. So Ermíl rode off for the mail, and he lagged in the town, and he was drunk when he started to ride back. And the night was a bright night: the moon was shining. . . . So Ermíl is riding across the dam: his road lay that way. And as he is riding along, huntsman Ermíl sees, on the drowned man's grave, a young ram strolling about,—such a white, curly, pretty little ram. So Ermíl thinks to himself: ' I 'll catch him,—why should he be wasted like this? '—so he slipped off his horse, and took him in his hands. . . . But the ram did n't mind it at all. So Ermíl goes to his horse, but the horse opens his eyes wide and stares, and neighs and tosses his head; but he untied it, mounted, and the ram with him, and started off again: he held the young ram in front of him. He looked at it, and the ram just stared him straight in the eye. He began to feel uneasy, did Ermíl the huntsman: ' I don't remember ever to have heard,' says he, ' that rams stared folks in the eye in this fashion; ' however, he did n't mind; he began to stroke its fur,—and says he: ' Ba-a, ba-a! ' And all of a sudden, the ram showed his teeth, and says to him the same: ' Ba-a, ba-a! . . . ' "

Before the narrator could utter this last word, the two dogs suddenly rose with one impulse, rushed away from the fire, barking convulsively, and vanished into the darkness. All the boys were thoroughly frightened. Ványa jumped out from under his mat. Pavlúshka flew after the dogs with a yell. Their barking swiftly retreated into the distance. . . . The uneasy running to and fro of the startled herd of horses was audible. Pavlúsha shouted loudly: " Grey! Beetle! " . . . . . In a few moments, the barking ceased; Pável's voice was already wafted to us from afar. . . . . A little more time elapsed; the boys exchanged glances of bewilderment, as though anticipating that something was about to happen. . . . Suddenly the hoof-beats of a galloping horse became audible; it stopped abruptly at the very fire, and Pavlúsha, who had been clinging to its mane, leaped from its back. The two dogs also sprang into the circle of light, and immediately sat down, lolling out their red tongues.

" What was it yonder? What was the matter? "—asked the boys.

" Nothing," — replied Pável, waving his hand toward the horse:—" 't was just that the dogs scented something. I thought it was a wolf,"—he added in an indifferent voice, breathing fast, with the full capacity of his chest.

I involuntarily admired Pavlúsha. He was very handsome at that moment. His ugly face, animated by the swift ride, blazed with dashing gallantry and firm resolution. Without even a switch in his hand, he had darted off alone, by night, without the slightest hesitation, to en-

counter a wolf. . . . . "What a splendid boy!"
I thought, as I gazed at him.

"And have you seen them,—the wolves, I
mean?"—asked cowardly Kóstya.

"There are always a lot of them here,"—replied Pável:—"but they are uneasy only in
winter."

Again he curled up in front of the fire. As
he seated himself on the ground, he dropped his
hand on the shaggy neck of one of the dogs, and
for a long time the delighted animal did not
turn its head, as it gazed sidelong, with grateful
pride, at Pavlúsha.

Ványa cuddled up under his mat again.

"What were those horrors thou wert narrat-
ing to us, Iliúsha?"—began Fédya, to whose lot,
as the son of a wealthy peasant, it fell to act the
part of leader (he himself said very little, as
though he were afraid of lowering his dignity).
—"And 't was the Evil One who prompted the
dogs to set up that barking. . . . But, in fact,
I have heard that that locality of yours is unhallowed."

"Varnávitzy? . . . . I should say so! unhallowed the worst way! The old master has been
seen there more than once, they say—the deceased master. He wears a long-skirted dressing-gown, they say, and keeps sighing all the
while, as though he were hunting for something
on the ground. Grandaddy Trofímitch met him

once.—' What is it, dear little father, Iván Ivánitch,' says he, ' that thou art searching for on the
ground?' "

" He asked him that? "—interrupted the astounded Fédya.

" Yes, he asked him."

" Well, Trofímitch is a gallant fellow to do
that. . . . Well, and what happened? "

" ' I 'm looking for the saxifrage,' says he.
And he talks in such a dull, dull voice:—' The
saxifrage.' [1]—' And what dost thou want of
saxifrage, dear little father, Iván Ivánítch? '—
' My grave is crushing me, crushing me, Trofímitch; I want to get out, to get out. . . . . . ' "

" What a fellow! "—remarked Fédya;—
" Probably he had n't lived long enough."

" What a marvel! " said Kóstya:—" I thought
dead folks could be seen only on Relatives' Saturday." [2]

" Dead folks can be seen at any hour,"—con-
fidently put in Iliúsha, who, so far as I was able
to observe, was better acquainted than the rest
with all the rural superstitions. . . . . " But on

[1] Literally, rend-rock—the rock-splitting plant.—TRANSLATOR.
[2] Certain Saturdays in the year, on which requiem services are
held for dead relatives. One such Saturday occurs in Lent; another in the autumn, called " Dmítry's Day," when dead ancestors
in general, and in particular those who fell on that day in the
battle of Kulikovo, 1380, under Prince Dmítry ' Donskóy ' (of the
Don), which broke the Tatár yoke, are commemorated. But the
one particularly referred to here is that which precedes Pentecost
(Trinity Sunday and the Day of the Spirit, Monday).—TRANS-
LATOR.

Relatives' Saturday you can also see the living person whose turn it is to die that year. All you have to do is to sit on the church porch, and keep staring at the road; and those who are destined to die that year will pass by. Peasant-wife Uliyána, of our village, went and sat on the church porch last year."

"Well, and did she see any one?"—inquired Kóstya, with interest.

"Of course she did. At first, she sat there a long, long time, without seeing or hearing anybody . . . . but a dog seemed to keep barking and barking somewhere or other. . . . . All at once, she looks, and a little boy, with nothing on but his shirt, comes walking along the path. She looked closely—'t was Iváshka Feodósyeff . . ."

"The one who died last spring?"—interrupted Fédya.

"The very same. He was walking along, without raising his little head. . . . And Uliyána recognised him. . . But then she looked again, and a woman was coming along. She stared and stared,—akh, O Lord!—'t was she herself, Uliyána herself, who was coming along the road."

"Was it really she herself?"—asked Fédya.

"God is my witness, it was."

"Well, what of it?—she is n't dead yet, you know."

"But the year is n't over yet. Just take a look at her: she 's on the point of death."

All relapsed into silence again. Pável flung a handful of dry twigs on the fire. They turned sharply black with the suddenly upflaring flame, crackled, began to smoke, and set to writhing, thrusting upward their singed tips. The reflection of the fire darted out in all directions, with abrupt flickerings, especially upward. All at once, from somewhere or other, a white pigeon flew straight into this reflection, circled with affright in one spot, all flooded with the hot glare, and disappeared, with flapping wings.

" It must have escaped from home,"—remarked Pável.—" Now it will fly until it hits against something, and it will spend the night, until daybreak, on whatever it hits against."

" See here, Pavlúsha,"—said Kóstya:—" is n't it true, that it was a spirit flying to heaven, hey? "

Pável tossed another handful of twigs on the fire.

" Perhaps so,"—he said at last.

" But tell me, please, Pavlúsha,"—began Fédya:—" was the heavenly vision [1] visible also with you in Shalámovo? "

" When the sun was invisible? Certainly."

" You must have been frightened too, I think? "

" Well, we were n't the only ones. Our master, although he had explained to us beforehand that we should see a vision, was so scared himself, they say, when it began to grow dark, that he

[1] That is what our peasants call an eclipse of the sun.

was beside himself with fear. And in the house-serfs' cottage, the peasant-wife cook, just as soon as it began to grow dark, I hear, took and smashed all the pots in the oven with the oven-fork. ' Who wants to eat now? ' says she: ' the day of judgment has come.' And such rumours were circulating in our village, brother,—to the effect that white wolves would overrun the earth, and eat up the people, a bird of prey would swoop down, and then Tríshka himself would be seen." [1]

" What is that Tríshka? "—asked Kóstya.

" Dost not thou know? "—put in Iliúsha hotly:—" well, brother, whence comest thou that thou dost not know about Tríshka? You 're great stay-at-homes in your village, that's what you are! Tríshka will be a wonderful man who will come, and he will be such a wonderful man that it will be impossible to catch him, and no one will be able to do anything to him: so wonderful will the man be. The peasants will want to seize him, for example: they will go out against him with cudgels, they will surround him, but he will avert their eyes,—he will avert their eyes in such a way, that they will slay each other. They will put him in prison, for example,—he will ask for a drink of water in a dipper: they will fetch him the dipper, and he will dive down into it, and that 's the last they will ever see of him. They

---

[1] The belief in " Tríshka " is, probably, a reflection of the legend about Antichrist.

will put chains on him, but he will shake his hands and they will fall off him. Well, and that Tríshka will go through the villages and the towns; and that Tríshka, the cunning fellow, will lead astray the Christian race . . . . well, and they will not be able to do anything to him. . . . . He will be such a wonderful, such a crafty man."

" Well, yes,"—went on Pavlúsha, in his drawling voice:—" that 's the man. They 've been expecting him in our village too. The old folks said, that as soon as the heavenly vision began, Tríshka would come. So the vision began. All the people scattered out into the street, into the fields, to wait and see what would happen. And we have a conspicuous, extensive site, you know. They are gazing when, suddenly, down-hill from the town, comes some man or other, such a peculiar man, with such a wonderful head . . . they all shout out at once: ' Óï, Tríshka 's coming! óï, Tríshka 's coming!' but 't was nothing of the sort. Our elder crawled into the ditch; his wife got stuck fast in the board at the bottom of the gate, and yelled at the top of her voice; she scared her watch-dog so that it broke loose from its chain, and leaped over the wattled hedge, and fled off to the forest; and Kúzka's father, Dorofyéitch, sprang into the oats, and squatted down, and set to piping like a quail: he thought, perhaps, the enemy, the soul-spoiler, would have mercy on a mere bird. So they all set up a rumpus! . . . . But the man who was coming was our cooper, Vavíla; he had bought himself a new tub with handles, and had put the empty tub on his head.''

All the boys burst out laughing, and again became silent for a moment, as it often happens with people who are conversing in the open air. I cast a glance around: the night reigned, sovereign, triumphant; the damp chill of late evening had given way to the dry warmth of midnight, and it still had long to lie like a soft coverlet over the slumbering fields; a long time still remained before the first lisp, the first fine dews of dawn. There was no moon in the sky: at that time it rose late. Innumerable golden stars seemed all to have glided softly, twinkling in emulation of one another, in the direction of the Milky Way, and, in truth, as you gazed at them, you yourself began to feel the headlong, uninterrupted onward flight of the earth. . . A strange, sharp, wailing cry suddenly rang out twice in succession over the river, and, after the lapse of a few seconds, was repeated farther away. . . .

Kóstya shuddered: . . . . . " What 's that?''

"That 's a heron screaming,"—returned Pável, composedly.

" A heron,"—repeated Kóstya. . . . " But what was it, Pavlúsha, that I heard last night,'' —he added, after a short silence:—" perhaps thou knowest . . . . .''

" What didst thou hear? "

" Why, this is what I heard. I was going from Kámennaya-Grýada [Stone-Ridge] to Sháshkino. First I kept altogether in our hazel-copse, and then went by the pool—thou knowest, at the place where it makes a sharp turn into the cliff,— there's a deep pit there, you see, made by the spring freshets, which never dries up; it's still all overgrown with reeds, you know; so, as I was walking past that water-hole, boys, somebody began to groan from that same hole, and so pitifully, so pitifully . . 'Oo-oo . . . oo-oo . . oo-oo!' I was seized with such terror, my brothers: the hour was late, and the voice was so painful.—What could it have been? hey? "

" Thieves drowned Akím the forester in that pool the year before last,"—remarked Pavlúsha; —" so, perhaps, it was his soul wailing."

" Why, that must have been it, my brothers," —returned Kóstya, opening wide his eyes, which were huge already. . . . " I did n't know that they had drowned Akím in that pool: I would have been scared much worse."

" But they say there are small frogs,"—went on Pavlúsha,—" which cry out in that pitiful way."

" Frogs? well, no, it was n't frogs . . . which made that . . . . ." (The heron screamed again above the river).—" Deuce take it! "—ejaculated Kóstya, involuntarily:—" it shrieks like the forest-demon."

" The forest-demon does n't shriek,—he 's dumb,"—put in Iliúsha:—" he only claps his hands and cracks . . . ."

" And hast thou seen him,—the forest-demon? I 'd like to know,"—Fédya interrupted him, sneeringly.

" No, I have n't, and God forbid that I should see him; but other folks have seen him. The other day now, he tricked a peasant; he led him on and on through the forest, and all the while round one and the self-same meadow. . . . . He barely got home by daylight."

" Well, and did he see him? "

" Yes. He says he stands so big, so big, and dark, and muffled up, behind a tree, as it were, so that you can't get a good look at him, as though he were hiding from the moon, and he stares and stares with his little eyes, and blinks them, and blinks . . . ."

" Do stop that! "—exclaimed Fédya, with a slight shudder, and a twitch of his shoulders:— " Pfu! . . . ."

" And why is this nasty crew distributed over the world? "—remarked Pável:—" really now, why? "

Again a pause ensued.

" Look, look, boys,"—suddenly **rang** out

Ványa's childish voice:—" Look at God's little stars, like bees swarming! "

He poked his fresh little face out from under the mat, propped himself on his little fist, and slowly raised on high his large, tranquil eyes. The eyes of all the little lads were raised to the sky, and were not soon lowered.

" Well, Ványa,"—began Fédya, affectionately:—" how about thy sister Aniútka,—is she well? "

" Yes,"—replied Ványa, with a slight lisp.

" Tell her, we want to know why she does n't come to see us."

" I don't know."

" Tell her that she must come."

" I 'll tell her."

" Tell her that I 'll give her a present."

" And wilt thou give me one too? "

" Yes, I 'll give thee one too."

Ványa sighed.

" Well, no, I don't want it. Better give it to her: she 's such a good girl."

And again Ványa laid his head on the ground. Pável rose, and took the empty kettle in his hand.

" Where art thou going? "—Fédya asked him.

" To the river to dip up some water. I want a drink of water."

The dogs rose and followed him.

" Look out, don't tumble into the river! "— shouted Iliúsha after him.

"Why should he tumble in?"—said Fédya—"He'll take care of himself."

"Yes, so he will. All sorts of things happen he'll stoop down and begin to dip up the water and the water-sprite will grab him by the hand and pull him in to himself. Then people will begin to say: 'The little fellow tumbled into the water. . . .' Much he did! . . . . . Yo-onder he has made his way in among the rushes," he added, listening.

The rushes, in fact, were moving,—"whispering," as they express it among us.

"And is it true,"—asked Kóstya:—"that Akulína the fool has been crazy ever since the time she was in the water?"

"Yes, ever since then. . . Just look at her now! But they say that before that, she used to be a beauty. The water-sprite spoiled her. He did n't expect, you see, that they would pull her out so soon. So he spoiled her, down on the bottom, at his own place."

(I had met that Akulína more than once myself. Covered with rags, frightfully thin, with a face as black as a coal, a confused look, and teeth eternally exposed in a grin, she would stamp up and down for hours in one and the self-same spot, somewhere on the highway, with her bony arms pressed tightly to her breast, and slowly shifting from one foot to the other, like a wild beast in a cage. She understood nothing that

182

was said to her, and only laughed convulsively from time to time.)

"But they say,"—went on Kóstya,—"that Akulína threw herself into the river, because her lover deceived her."

"That's exactly why she did it."

"And dost thou remember Vásya?"—added Kóstya, sadly.

"What Vásya?"—inquired Fédya.

"Why, the one who was drowned,"—replied Kóstya. "What a boy he was! i-ikh, what a boy he was! His mother, Feklísta, how she did love him, that Vásya! And she seemed to have a presentiment, did Feklísta, that water would be his ruin. When Vásya used to go to the river with us boys, to bathe, in summer, she would just quiver all over. The other women did n't mind: they would go past with their wash-troughs themselves, waddling along, but Feklísta would set her trough[1] on the ground and begin to call to him. 'Come back,' says she, 'come back, light of my eyes! okh, come back, my dear little falcon!'—And how he came to get drowned, the Lord knows. He was playing on the shore, and his mother was there also, raking up the hay; all at once, she heard some one making bubbles in the water,—and behold, nothing but Vásya's little cap was floating on the water. Alas, ever

[1] The Russian peasant wash-tub is like a long, shallow trough, or chopping-tray, made of a halved and hollowed log.—TRANS-ATOR.

since then, Feklísta has not been in her right
mind:—she 'll come and lie down on that spot
where he was drowned; she 'll lie there, brothers,
and strike up a song,—you remember, Vásya
always sang the same song,—so she will strike up
that song, and weep, and weep, and complain
bitterly to God . . . . ."

" Yonder comes Pavlúsha,"—said Fédya.

Pavlúsha came up to the fire with a full kettle
in his hand.

" Well, boys,"—he began, after a brief pause:
—" something is wrong."

" Why, what 's the matter? "—asked Kóstya,
hastily.

" I have heard Vásya's voice."

All fairly shuddered.

" What dost thou mean, what dost thou
mean? "—stammered Kóstya.

" God is my witness. No sooner had I begun
to stoop down to the water, than suddenly I
heard myself called by Vásya's little voice, and
from under the water, as it were: ' Pavlúsha,
hey there, Pavlúsha, come hither.' I went away.
But I dipped up the water all the same."

" Akh, O my Lord! akh, O Lord! "—cried the
little lads, crossing themselves.

" That was the water-sprite calling thee, for
sure, Pável,"—added Fédya. . . " And we have
just been talking about him,—about Vásya."

" Akh, 't is a bad omen,"—faltered Iliúsha.

" Come, 't is nothing, drop it! "—said Pável, decisively, and sat down again:—" you can't escape your fate."

The boys subsided into silence. It was evident that Pável's words had produced a profound impression upon them. They began to stretch themselves out in front of the fire, as though preparing to go to sleep.

" What 's that? "—asked Kóstya, suddenly, raising his head.

Pável listened intently.

" 'T is the woodcock flying,—they are whistling."

" But whither are they flying? "

" Away yonder, where, they say, there is no winter."

" And is it possible that there is such a country? "

" There is."

" Is it far away? "

" Yes, far, far away, beyond the warm seas."

Kóstya sighed, and closed his eyes.

More than three hours had already elapsed since I had joined the boys. The moon rose at last: I did not immediately observe it, it was so small and slender. This moonless night, apparently, was as magnificent as before. . . . . . But many stars which had but lately stood high in the heavens, were already sinking toward the dark rim of the earth; everything round about had be-

come perfectly quiet, as things generally do only
toward dawn: everything was sleeping, with the
deep, motionless slumber which precedes the break
of day. The air was no longer so strongly per
fumed,—it seemed to have again become impreg
nated with moisture. . . . Summer nights are
not long! . . . The prattle of the little lads had
died down with the bonfires. . . . The dogs
too, were sleeping; the horses, so far as I was
able to make out by the barely-shining, faintly
spreading light of the stars, were also lying
down, with drooping heads. . . . A light for
getfulness descended upon me; it passed into
slumber.

A fresh current of air blew across my face. I
opened my eyes:—morning was breaking. The
dawn was not, as yet, glowing red anywhere, but
the east was already beginning to grow white.
Everything had become visible, though dimly
visible, all around. The pale-grey sky was light
ing up, turning cold and blue; the stars now
twinkled with a faint light, now disappeared; the
earth had grown damp, the foliage had begun to
sweat; here and there living sounds, voices, were
beginning to resound, and a thin, early breeze
had begun to stray abroad and flutter over the
earth. My body responded to it with a slight
cheerful shiver. I rose briskly to my feet, and
walked toward the little boys. They were all
sleeping like dead men around the smouldering

onfire; Pável alone half-rose, and gazed intently
t me.

I nodded my head to him and went my way,
long the mist-wreathed river. Before I had pro-
eeded two versts, there had streamed forth all
round me over the wide, wet meadow, ahead of
ne, over the hills which were beginning to gleam
reen, from forest to forest, and behind me, over
he long, dusty highway, over the glittering, crim-
on-tinted bushes, and the river, shyly glinting
lue from beneath the dispersing fog—there had
treamed forth first scarlet, then red, then golden
orrents of young, blazing light. . . . . . Every-
hing began to stir, awoke, began to sing, to make
noise, to chatter. Everywhere, like radiant bril-
ants, glowed great dewdrops; the sounds of a
ell were wafted toward me, pure and clear, as
hough they, also, had been washed by the morn-
ig freshness, and, suddenly, the rested herd of
orses dashed headlong past me, driven by the
ids I have mentioned. . . .

Unfortunately, I am bound to add that Pável
ied that same year. He was not drowned; he
as killed by falling from a horse. 'T is a pity,
or he was a splendid young fellow!

IX

I was returning home from the chase in a jolting
peasant cart, and, overwhelmed by the stifling
heat of the sultry, overcast summer's day (every
one knows that, on such days, the heat is some
times even more intolerable than on clear days, es
pecially when there is no breeze), was dozing and
rolling about, with surly impatience surrendering
myself wholly to be devoured by the fine, white
dust, which rose incessantly from the beaten road
from beneath the disjointed and rickety wheels,—
when, all of a sudden, my attention was aroused
by the uneasiness and the agitated movements of
the body of my coachman, who, up to that mo
ment, had been even more sound asleep than my
self. He was jerking at the reins, fidgeting about
on the box, and began to shout at the horses
every now and then casting a glance to one side
I looked round. We were driving over a tilled
plain; low hillocks, also tilled, ran athwart it, in
remarkably steep, wave-like slopes; the eye could
take in, at most, only about five versts of waste

[1] The Metchá is a river of Central Russia to which the epithet
"Fair" is applied as "Dear little mother" (*Mátushka*) is to the
Volga.—Translator.

expanse; far away in the distance, small birch copses alone broke the almost straight line of the horizon with their rounded, yet jagged crests. Narrow paths stretched out through the fields, lost themselves in ravines, wound around swells of the land, and on one of them, which intersected our road about five hundred paces ahead of us, I descried some sort of procession. This was what my coachman was looking at.

It was a funeral. In front, in a peasant cart, drawn by one horse, rode the priest at a foot-pace; the chanter sat beside him and drove; behind the cart, four peasant men, with bared heads, bore the coffin, covered with white linen; two peasant women walked behind the coffin. The shrill, lugubrious voice of one of them reached my ears; I listened: she was wailing. Mournfully did that varying yet monotonous, hopelessly-sorrowful chant resound amid the empty fields. The coachman whipped up his horses: he wanted to get ahead of this procession. 'T is a bad omen to meet a funeral on the road. As a matter of fact, he did succeed in galloping past along the road before the corpse managed to reach it; but we had not proceeded a hundred paces, when, all at once, our cart gave a violent lurch, careened on one side, and almost toppled over. The coachman pulled up his horses, which had started to run away, waved his hand in despair, and spat.

" What 's the matter? "—I asked.

My coachman alighted in silence, and without haste.

" But what 's the matter? "

" The axletree is broken . . . . . burned through,"—he replied gloomily, and suddenly adjusted the breeching on the trace-horse with such indignation that the horse came near going over on its side, but retained its footing, snorted, shook itself, and began very calmly to scratch itself with its teeth below the knee of the right leg.

I alighted, and stood for some time in the road, confusedly absorbed by a feeling of disagreeable surprise. The right wheel was turned almost completely under the cart, and seemed to have elevated its hub on high, in dumb despair.

" What is to be done now? "—I asked, at last.

" Yonder 's the one who is to blame! "—said my coachman, pointing with his whip at the procession, which had already had time to turn into the highway, and was approaching us:—" I 've always noticed it,"—he continued:—" 'T is a sure sign—to meet a corpse. . . . . . Yes."

And again he worried the trace-horse who, perceiving his displeasure and harshness, decided to remain impassive, and only swished its tail modestly from time to time. I walked back and forth for a while, and again came to a halt in front of the wheel.

In the meantime, the corpse had overtaken us.

KASYÁN FROM THE FAIR-METCHA

Turning out peaceably from the road upon the grass, the mournful procession passed our cart. The coachman and I removed our caps, exchanged bows with the priest, and glances with the bearers. They walked with difficulty; their broad chests heaved high. Of the two women who walked behind the coffin, one was very aged and pale; her impassive features, cruelly distorted with grief, retained an expression of strict, rigorous dignity. She walked on in silence, from time to time raising her gaunt hand to her thin, sunken lips. The eyes of the other woman, a young one about five-and-twenty years of age, were red and moist, and her whole face was swollen with weeping; as they came alongside of us, she ceased to wail, and covered her face with her sleeve. . . . . . . But now the corpse had passed us, had turned out again into the highway, and her mournful, soul-breaking chant rang out once more. Having silently gazed after the coffin, as it rocked with regular motion, my coachman turned to me.

" 'T is Martýn the carpenter they 're burying," —said he:—" the one from Ryábaya."

" How dost thou know that? "

" I found it out by the women. The old one is his mother, and the young one is his wife."

" Was he ill? "

" Yes . . . . he had the fever. . . . . The overseer sent for the doctor day before yesterday,

but they did n't find the doctor at home. . . . .
And he was a good carpenter; rather given to
drinking, but a fine carpenter he was. You see
how that woman of his is killing herself. . . . . .
Well, yes, 't is well known: women's tears are
cheap. Women's tears are just the same as water.
. . . . Yes."

And he bent down, crawled under the rein of
the trace-horse, and seized the arch with both
hands.[1]

" But,"—I remarked:—" what are we to do? "

My coachman first braced his knee against the
shoulder of the shaft-horse, shook the arch a
couple of times, adjusted the saddle, then crawled
back again under the rein of the trace-horse, and,
giving it a shove in the muzzle in passing, he
stepped up to the wheel—stepped up to it, and,
without removing his gaze from it, pulled from
beneath the skirts of his coat a birch-bark snuff-
box, slowly tugged at the strap on its cover,
slowly thrust his two thick fingers into the snuff-
box (and it would hardly hold two), kneaded
and kneaded the snuff, puckered up his nose in
advance, inhaled the snuff with pauses between,
accompanying each sniff with a prolonged grunt,
and, screwing up his lids in a painful way, and
blinking his tearful eyes, he plunged into profound meditation.

[1] The arch connecting the shafts, over the neck of the trotter.
The side horses (sometimes only one is used, instead of two) are
very slightly attached by traces.—TRANSLATOR.

" Well, what now? "—I said at last.

My coachman carefully replaced the snuff-box in his pocket, pulled his cap down on his eyebrows, without using his hands, with a movement of his head alone, and thoughtfully climbed upon his box.

" Whither art thou going? "—I asked him, not without surprise.

" Please take your seat,"—he replied calmly, and gathered up the reins.

" But how are we going to drive? "

" We'll drive on all right, sir."

" But the axle. . . ."

" Please take your seat."

" But the axle is broken . . . . ."

" 'T is broken, yes, 't is broken; but we shall manage to get to the settlement . . . . at a walk,—that is to say, yonder, behind the grove, there are dwellings: 't is called Yúdino."

" And dost thou think that we can get there? "

My coachman did not vouchsafe me an answer.

" I would rather go afoot,"—said I.

" As you please, sir. . . . ."

And he flourished his whip. The horses started.

We really did reach the settlement, although the right front wheel hardly held, and revolved in a remarkably strange manner. On one hillock, it came near flying off; but my coachman shouted in a vicious voice, and we made the descent in safety.

The Yúdino hamlet consisted of six tiny, low-roofed cottages, which had already managed to sag down to one side, although, in all probability, they had been erected not long before; not all their yards were enclosed with wattled hedges. As we drove into this settlement, we encountered not a single living soul; there were no hens, nor dogs even, visible in the street; only one black dog, with a bob-tail, sprang out at our appearance, from a completely dried trough, where it must have been driven by thirst, and immediately, without barking, darted headlong under a gate. I entered the first cottage, opened the door into the anteroom, called for the owners,—no one answered me. I shouted a second time: the hungry mewing of a cat resounded on the other side of the door. I pushed it open with my foot; an emaciated cat slipped quickly past me, her green eyes flashing in the dark. I put my head into the room, and looked: it was dark, smoky, and empty. I betook myself to the back yard, and there was no one there, either. . . . A calf was bleating in the paddock; a lame, grey goose was hobbling about a little to one side. I went on to the second cottage,—and there was not a soul in the second cottage. I went to the yard . . . .

In the very middle of the brightly illuminated yard, in the very heart of the heat, as the expression is, there was lying, as it seemed to me, a small boy, face to the ground, his head covered with his long peasant coat. A few paces from him, beside a wretched little cart, stood an emaciated horse in a tattered harness under a thatched shed. The sunlight, falling in streams through the narrow interstices of the rickety penthouse roof, streaked its shaggy, reddish-brown hide with small, bright blotches. There, also, in a lofty bird-house, the starlings were chattering, staring down with calm curiosity from their aërial little dwelling. I went up to the sleeper, and began to rouse him. . . . .

He raised his head, saw me, and immediately sprang to his feet. . . . "What is it, what's wanted? What's the matter?" he muttered, half-awake.

I did not answer him on the instant: so astonished was I by his personal appearance. Picture to yourself a dwarf fifty years of age, with a tiny, swarthy, wrinkled face, a sharp-pointed little nose, small, brown, hardly visible eyes, and thick, curly black hair, which sat on his tiny head like the broad cap on a mushroom.

His whole body was extremely puny and thin, and it is absolutely impossible to convey in words how strange and remarkable was his glance.

"What's wanted?"—he asked me again.

I explained to him the state of the case; he listened to me, never taking his slowly blinking eyes off me.

" Cannot we obtain a new axle? "—I said at last:—" I should be glad to pay for it."

" But who are you? sportsmen? "—he inquired, surveying me from head to foot with a glance.

" Yes."

" You shoot the birds of heaven, I suppose? . . and wild beasts? . . . . And don't you think it is a sin to slay God's birds, to shed innocent blood? "

The queer little old man spoke with great deliberation. The sound of his voice also surprised me. Not only was there nothing infirm audible in it,—it was wonderfully sweet, youthful, and almost effeminately tender.

" I have no axle,"—he added, after a brief pause:—" that one yonder is of no use "—(he pointed at his little cart)—" you have a large cart, I suppose? "

" And cannot one be found in the village? "

" What sort of a village do you call this! . . . No one here has one. . . And there 's no one at home, either: they are all at work. Go your way,"—he said suddenly, and lay down again on the ground.

I had not in the least expected this termination.

" Listen, old man,"—I began, touching his shoulder:—" please to help me."

" Go your way, and God be with you! I 'm

tired: I 've been to the town,"—he said to me, and dragged his coat over his head.

"But please do me the favour,"—I went on:—"I . . . I will pay."

"I don't want thy pay."

"But please, old man . . . ."

He half raised himself, and sat up, with his thin little legs crossed.

"I might guide thee to the place where they are felling timber. Some merchants have bought our grove,—may God judge them, they are carrying off our grove, and have built an office,—may God be their judge! Perhaps thou couldst order an axle of them there, or buy one ready-made."

"Capital!"—I exclaimed joyously. . . "The very thing! . . . let us go."

"An oaken axle, a good one,"—he went on, without rising from his place.

"And is it far to the timber-felling place?"

"Three versts."

"Well, never mind! We can drive there in thy cart."

"But you can't . . . ."

"Come along, let 's start,"—said I.—"Let 's start, old man! My coachman is waiting for us in the street."

The old man rose reluctantly, and followed me to the street. My coachman was in an exasperated state of mind: he had undertaken to water his horses, but there turned out to be extremely little water in the well, and it had a bad flavour, which, so coachmen say, is of prime importance. . . . Nevertheless, at the sight of the old man, he grinned, nodded his head, and exclaimed:

" Ah, Kasyánushka! morning! "

" Morning, Eroféi, upright man! "—replied Kasyán, in a dejected voice.

I immediately communicated his proposition to the coachman; Eroféi expressed his assent, and drove into the yard. While he, with deliberate bustle, unharnessed his horses, the old man stood, with his shoulders leaning against the gate, and stared uncheerfully now at him, now at me. He seemed, somehow, perplexed: he was not over-joyed at our appearance, so far as I could observe.

" And dost thou mean to say that they have sent thee too off here to settle? "—asked Eroféi, suddenly, as he removed the arch from the shaft-horse.

" Me too."

" Ekh! "—said my coachman through his teeth. —" Knowest thou Martýn the carpenter . . . for thou dost know Martýn from Ryábaya, of course? "

" I do."

" Well, he 's dead. We have just met his coffin."

Kasyán shuddered.

" He 's dead? "—he said, and dropped his eyes.

" Yes, he is dead. Why didst not thou cure

him, hey? For they say that thou dost cure, that thou art a healer."

My coachman was, evidently, amusing himself, ridiculing the old man.

" And is this thy cart? "—he added, indicating it with his shoulder.

" Yes."

" Well, what a cart! . . . . d' ye call that a cart? "—he repeated, and taking it by the shafts, he almost turned it upside down. . . . . " A cart! . . . And what are you going to drive to the clearing in? . . . . You can't harness our horse in these shafts: our horses are large,—and what do you call that? "

" I don't know,"—replied Kasyán,—" what you will ride in: perhaps on that little beast yonder,"—he added, with a sigh.

" On that one, dost thou mean? "—put in Eroféi, and stepping up to Kasyán's wretched nag, he poked it disdainfully in the neck with the third finger of his right hand.—" Humph,"—he added reproachfully:—" it 's fast asleep, the idiot! "

I requested Eroféi to harness it to the cart as speedily as possible. I wanted to drive with Kasyán to the clearing: partridges are frequently to be found at such spots. When the cart was quite ready, and I had contrived, somehow or other, to ensconce myself and my dog on its warped, linden-bark bottom, and Kasyán, curling himself up in a ball and with his previous dejected expression on his face, had also taken his seat, on the front rim,—Eroféi approached me, and with a mysterious aspect whispered:

" And well have you done, dear little father, in driving with him. For he 's that sort of a man, he 's a holy fool,[1] and his nickname is—The Flea. I don't know how you managed to understand him. . . . ." I wanted to remark to Eroféi, that, so far, Kasyán had seemed to me to be a very sensible man; but my coachman immediately proceeded, in the same tone:

" Just you keep a sharp watch, to see that he takes you to the right place. And please to pick out the axle yourself: please to get as healthy an axle as possible. . . . .

" How now, Flea,"—he added aloud:—" can a body get a bit of bread from you? "

" Seek: perchance, it may be found,"—replied Kasyán, jerking the reins, and we drove off.

His little horse, to my sincere amazement, went far from badly. During the entire course of our drive, Kasyán preserved an obstinate silence, and to my questions replied abruptly and reluctantly. We soon reached the felling-place, and there betook ourselves to the office, a lofty cottage, which stood isolated above a small ravine that had been hastily spanned by a dam and converted into a

---

[1] These "holy fools," or simple-minded eccentrics, are greatly respected even at the present day in Russia.—TRANSLATOR.

pond. In that office I found two young merchants' clerks, with snow-white teeth, sweet eyes,
sweet, alert speech, and sweetly-wily little smiles,
struck a bargain with them for an axle, and set
off for the clearing. I thought that Kasyán
would remain with the horse, and wait for me;
but he suddenly stepped up to me.

" Art thou going to shoot birds? "—he began:
—" hey? "

" Yes, if I find any."

" I 'll go with thee. . . . May I? "

" Yes, thou mayest."

And he went.—The area which had been
cleared was, altogether, about a verst in extent.
I must confess, that I looked more at Kasyán than
at my dog. Not without reason was he called
The Flea. His black, wholly uncovered head
(moreover, his hair was a fine substitute for any
cap) fairly hopped through the bushes. He
walked with remarkable briskness, and kept constantly skipping, as it were, as he walked, bent
down incessantly, plucked some weeds or other,
thrust them into his bosom, muttered to himself,
and kept looking at me and my dog, with a very
strange, searching glance. In the low bushes, in
the undergrowth, and on clearings there dwell
small grey birds, which are incessantly flitting
from tree to tree and chirping, suddenly swoop-
ing in flight. Kasyán mimicked them, and answered their calls; a young quail flew up, twitter-

ing, from under his very feet,—he twittered back
to it; a lark began to descend above him, fluttering its wings and warbling loudly,—Kasyán
joined in its song. With me he still would not
talk. . .

The weather was magnificent, still finer than
before; but the heat did not abate. Athwart
the clear sky floated infrequent, high-hanging
clouds of a yellowish-white hue, like late-lying
snow in spring, flat and long, like reefed sails.
Their fancifully-patterned edges, light and
downy as cotton, slowly but visibly changed with
every passing moment: they melted away, those
clouds, and no shadow fell from them. Kasyán
and I roamed for a long time about the clearing.
The young shoots, which had not, as yet, managed
to extend themselves longer than an arshín,[1] surrounded with their smooth, slender stems the low,
blackened stumps; round, spongy excrescences
with grey borders, those same punk-growths from
which tinder is made, clung close to the stumps;
the strawberry had sent forth its rosy tendrils
over them; and mushrooms sat there also, close-
crowded in families. One's feet were incessantly
entangled and held fast in the long grass, dried
through and through by the burning sun; everywhere the eyes were dazzled by the sharp, metallic glitter of the young, reddish leaves on the

[1] Twenty-eight inches—the Russian measure corresponding
to the yard.—TRANSLATOR.

trees; all about, the blue clusters of the vetch, the golden chalices of the buttercups, the half-purple half-yellow flowers of John-and-Mary [1] formed a gay-coloured carpet; here and there, alongside the abandoned paths, whereon the traces of wheels were indicated by streaks of a fine, red weed, rose piles of firewood blackened by wind and rain, each containing a cord; a faint shadow was cast by their slanting corners,—there was no other shadow anywhere. A light breeze now woke up, now subsided: it would suddenly blow straight in my face, and frolic, as it were,—rustle merrily, nod and flutter around, gracefully rock the slender tips of the ferns,—and I would rejoice in it . . . but, lo, it has died down, and everything is calm again. Only the grasshoppers shrilled vigorously, as though angry,—and that uninterrupted, harsh, piercing sound is fatiguing. It is suited to the importunate heat of midday; it seems to be born of it, evoked by it, as it were, from the red-hot earth.

At last, without having hit upon a single lair of game, we reached the new clearing. There the recently felled aspens lay sadly on the ground, crushing the grass and the undergrowth; on some, leaves still green, but already dead, hung limply from the motionless boughs; on others, they had already dried and curled up. From the

---

[1] A mint-like plant which has bright-purple leaves and stems and bright-yellow flowers, called " Iván-da-Márya."—TRANSLATOR.

fresh, golden-white chips, which lay in heaps
around the brilliantly moist stumps, there was exhaled an extremely agreeable, bitter odour. Far
away, nearer the grove, the axes were tapping
dully, and, at times, solemnly and quietly, as
though bowing and spreading out its arms, a
curly-foliaged tree sank earthward.

For a long time, I found no game; at last, out
of a spreading oak-bush, through the wormwood
with which it was overgrown, a corncrake flew
forth. I fired; it turned a somersault in the air,
and fell. On hearing the shot, Kasyán swiftly
covered his eyes with his hand, and did not move
until I had reloaded my gun and picked up the
corncrake. But when I started onward, he went
up to the spot where the dead bird had fallen, bent
down to the grass, on which a few drops of blood
were sprinkled, shook his head, cast a frightened
glance at me. . . . . . Afterward, I heard him
whispering: " A sin! . . . . Akh, this is a sin! "

The heat made us, at last, enter the grove. I
threw myself down under a tall hazel-bush, over
which a stately young maple spread finely abroad
its light branches. Kasyán seated himself on the
thick end of a felled birch-tree. I looked at him.
The foliage was swaying faintly up aloft, and its
liquid greenish shadows slipped gently back and
forth over his puny body, wrapped up, after a
fashion, in his dark coat, over his small face. He
did not raise his head. Bored by his taciturnity,

I lay on my back, and began to admire the peaceful play of the tangled leaves against the far-off brilliant sky. 'T is a wonderfully agreeable occupation, to lie on one's back in the forest, and stare upward! It seems to you as though you were gazing into a bottomless sea, that it spreads broadly beneath you, that the trees do not rise out of the earth, but, like the roots of huge plants, descend, hang suspended, in those crystal-clear waves; the leaves on the trees now are of translucent emerald, again thicken into golden, almost black green. Somewhere, far away, terminating a slender branch, a separate leaf stands motionless against the blue patch of transparent sky, and by its side sways another, recalling by its movements the play of a fish's gills, as though the movement proceeded from its own volition, and were not produced by the breeze. The white, round clouds softly float and softly pass, like enchanted submarine islands,—and then, all of a sudden, that whole sea, that radiant atmosphere, those boughs and leaves flooded with sunlight, begin to undulate, to tremble with a fugitive gleam, and a fresh, hurried lisping, resembling the unending, tiny plash of swelling surge, arises. You do not stir —you gaze: and it is impossible to express in words what joy, tranquillity, and sweetness reign in your heart. You gaze:—that deep, pure azure evokes a smile upon your lips, as innocent as itself; as the clouds sail over the sky, and in

MEMOIRS OF A SPORTSMAN

their company, as it were, happy memories pass in garlands through your soul, and it seems to you that your gaze recedes further and further away, and draws you after it, into that calm, beaming abyss, and that it is impossible to tear yourself from that height, from that depth . . . .

" Master, hey there, master! "—said Kasyán, suddenly, in his melodious voice.

I half-rose with amazement; hitherto, he had barely answered my questions, and now he had suddenly begun to speak of his own accord.

" What dost thou want? "—I asked.

" Well, why didst thou kill that bird? "—he began, looking me straight in the face.

" What dost thou mean by ' why ' ? . . . . The corncrake is game: it can be eaten."

" That 's not the reason why thou didst kill it, master: much thou wilt eat it! Thou hast killed it for thine amusement."

" Why, surely, thou thyself, I suppose, dost eat geese and chickens? "

" That is a bird appointed by God for man, but the corncrake is a free bird, a forest bird. And not he alone: there are quantities of them, of all sorts of forest creatures, and creatures of the field, and the river, and the swamp, both up-stream and down-stream,—and 't is a sin to kill them, and they ought to be allowed to live on the earth until their time comes. . . . But another food is appointed to man, a different food and a different drink: grain is God's blessed gift, and the waters of heaven, and tame fowl, from our ancient fathers' day."

I stared in amazement at Kasyán. His words flowed fluently; he did not pause to seek them, he spoke with quiet enthusiasm and gentle dignity, closing his eyes from time to time.

" And so, according to thy view, it is sinful to kill a fish, also? "—I asked.

" A fish has cold blood,"—he returned, with confidence:—" a fish is a dumb brute. It does not fear, it does not rejoice: a fish is a creature without the power of speech. A fish does not feel, the blood in it is not lively. . . Blood,"—he went on, after a pause,—" is a holy thing! Blood does not behold God's dear little sun, blood hides itself from the light . . . 't is a great sin to show blood to the light, a great sin and horror. . . . Okh, very great! "

He sighed, and cast down his eyes. I must admit, that I stared at the strange old man in utter amazement. His speech did not have the ring of a peasant: the common people do not speak like that, neither do fine talkers. This language was thoughtfully-solemn and strange. . . . I had never heard anything like it.

" Tell me, please, Kasyán,"—I began, without taking my eyes from his slightly-flushed face:— " what is thy occupation? "

He did not at once answer my question. His gaze roved uneasily for a moment.

" I live as the Lord commands,"—he said at last,—" and, as for an occupation,—no, I have none. I have n't had much sense since my childhood; I work, as long as my strength lasts, —I 'm a poor workman . . . . how should I be otherwise! I have no health, and my hands are stupid. Well, and in springtime I snare nightingales."

" Thou snarest nightingales?—But didst not thou say, that one should not touch any creature of the forest or the field, and so forth? "

" They must not be killed, that is true; death will take his own, in any case. There 's Martýn the carpenter, for example: Martýn lived and did not live long, and died; now his wife is wasting away with sorrow over her husband and her little children. . . . Neither man nor beast can cheat death. Death does not run, and you cannot run from it; but you must n't aid it. And I don't kill the nightingales,—the Lord forbid! I don't catch them for torture, nor for the destruction of their life, but for man's pleasure, consolation, and delectation."

" Dost thou go to Kursk [1] to catch them? "

" I do go to Kursk, and even further, as it happens. I pass the night in the marshes, and

[1] The nightingales of the Kursk Government are accounted the finest in Russia.—TRANSLATOR.

on the borders of the forest; I spend the night
alone in the fields, in the wilds: there the snipe
whistle, there the hares cry, there the wild drakes
quack.—In the evening I observe, in the morning I listen, at dawn I spread my nets over
the bushes. . . . . Sometimes a nightingale
sings so mournfully, so sweetly . . . . even
mournfully."

" And dost thou sell them? "

" I give them away to good people."

" And what else dost thou do? "

" What do I do? "

" What is thy business? "

The old man remained silent a while.

" I have no business. . . . I'm a bad workman. But I can read and write."

" Thou canst? "

" I can. The Lord, and good people, have
aided me."

" Well, art thou a family man? "

" No, I have no family."

" How is that? . . . Have they all died? "

" No, it just happened so; it did n't chance to
be my luck in life. But that is all under God's
care, we all go under God's care; and a man
must be upright,—so he must! He must please
God, that is to say."

" And hast thou no relatives? "

" I have . . . yes . . . . in a way . . ."

The old man stammered.

209

" Tell me, please,"—I began:—" I heard my coachman ask thee, why thou didst not heal Martýn? Dost thou know how to heal? "

" Thy coachman is an upright man,"—Kasyán answered me, thoughtfully:—" but he is not without sin also. They call me a physician... I a physician, forsooth! .... and who can cure? All that comes from God. But there are . . there are plants, there are flowers: they do help really. Here's the bur-marigold, for example 't is a good weed for man; here's the plantain too; 't is no disgrace to speak of them; they are clean plants—God's plants. Well, but others are not like that: and they help, but 't is a sin; and 't is a sin to speak of them. It might be done with prayer, perhaps. . . . . Well, of course there are words which . . . . And he who believes shall be saved,"—he added, lowering his voice.

" Didst thou not give Martýn anything? "—I asked.

"I heard of it too late,"—replied the old man.—" But what of that!—each one will get what is written in his fate. Martýn was not destined to live long on earth: that's a fact. No, the dear sun does not warm a man who is not fated to live long on earth, as it does other men, and neither does his bread profit him,—'t is as though something summoned him away. . . . Yes; Lord rest his soul! "

" Is it long since they sent you to live in our parts? "—I asked him, after a brief silence.

Kasyán gave a start.

" No, not long: four years. In the old master's time, we always lived in our former place, but the Council of Guardians removed us. Our old master was a gentle soul, a meek man,—the kingdom of heaven be his! Well, the Council of Guardians judged rightly, of course; 't is evident, that so it was right."

" But where did you formerly live? "

" We are from the Fair-Metchá."

" Is that far from here? "

" About a hundred versts."

" And was it better than here? "

" Yes . . . 't was better. There the lands were fertile river-meadows, our nest; but here we have cramped lands, and drought. . . . We are orphaned here. Yonder, at our Fair-Metchá you would climb a hill, and climb—and, O Lord my God, what did you see? hey? River, and meadows, and forest; and there was a church there, and then the meadows began again, you could see far, far away. How far you could see! . . . you gaze and gaze,—akh, truly, you cannot express your feelings! Well, here, to tell the truth, the land is better: clay, good clay, say the peasants; and my grain bears well everywhere."

" Come, old man, tell me the truth: I think thou wouldst like to visit thy native place? "

" Yes, I would like to have a look at it. But
't is good everywhere. I'm a man without a
family, a rover. Well, and that's nothing! can
one sit much at home? But when you walk, when
you walk," he interposed, raising his voice, " your
heart is lighter, in truth. The dear little sun
lights you, and you are more visible to God, and
can sing in better tune. You look to see what
grass is growing; well, you observe it, you pluck
it. The water flows fresh from a spring, for example: holy water; so you drink your fill,—you
note it also. The heavenly birds sing. . . And
then, beyond Kursk lie steppes, such level steppes,
and there is wonder and satisfaction for a man,
there is liberty, there is God's grace! And they
extend, so people say, clear to the warm seas,
where the bird Gamáiun the sweet-voiced dwells,
and the leaves do not fall from the trees in winter,
nor in autumn, and golden apples grow on silver
boughs, and every man lives in abundance and
uprightness. . . For I've been in ever so many
places! I've been to Romyón, and in Simbírsk
the splendid town, and in golden-domed Moscow
too; I've been on our benefactress the Oká
River, and on the Tzna, the darling, and on dear
little mother Volga, and have seen many people,
kind peasants, and have tarried in honourable
towns. . . . Well, I would like to go thither—
and you see . . . . and yet . . . . And I'm not
the only sinful one . . . . many other peasants

wear linden-bark slippers, roam about the world, seek the truth . . . . yes! . . . . But as for home, hey? There's no uprightness in man— that there is n't. . . . ."

These last words Kasyán uttered rapidly, almost unintelligibly; then he said something more, which I could not catch, and his face assumed such a strange expression, that I involuntarily recalled the appellation "holy fool." He cast down his eyes, cleared his throat, and seemed to recover himself.

"What a dear little sun!"—he said in an undertone:—"What grace,—O Lord! what warmth in the forest!"

He shrugged his shoulders, paused for a moment, glanced abstractedly about, and began to sing softly. I could not catch all the words of his drawling song; but I heard the following:

"They call me Kasyán,
Nicknamed The Flea. . . ."

"Eh!"—thought I:—"why, he's improvising." . . . . All at once he started, and stopped short, staring intently into the dense part of the forest. I turned round, and perceived a small peasant maiden, ten years of age, in a little blue sarafán,[1] with a checked kerchief on her head,

[1] The true peasant gown, gathered full on a band, falling in straight folds from the armpits, and supported by cross-bands over the shoulders.—TRANSLATOR.

and a plaited basket in her bare, sunburned hand. She had, probably, not in the least expected to encounter us; she had hit on us, as the expression is, and stood motionless in a green clump of hazel-bushes in a shady little glade, timidly gazing at me with her black eyes. I barely managed to survey her; she immediately ducked behind a tree.

"Ánnushka! Ánnushka! come hither, fear not,"—called the old man, affectionately.

" I 'm afraid,"—resounded a shrill little voice.

" Don't be afraid, come to me."

Ánnushka silently abandoned her ambush, softly made the circuit of it,—her childish foot-steps were hardly audible on the thick grass,— and emerged from the thicket close to the old man. She was not a child of eight, as she had seemed to me at first, from her stunted growth, but of thirteen or fourteeen. Her whole body was small and thin, but very well made and agile, and her pretty little face bore a remarkable re-semblance to that of Kasyán, although Kasyán was not a beauty. There were the same sharp features, the same strange gaze, cunning and con-fiding, thoughtful and piercing, and the move-ments were the same. . . . Kasyán ran his eyes over her; she was standing with her side to him.

" Well, hast thou been gathering mushrooms? " —he asked.

" Yes, mushrooms,"—she replied, with a shy smile.

" Hast thou found many? "

" Yes." (She darted a swift glance at him, and smiled again.)

" And are there any white ones? "

" Yes, some are white."

" Show them, show them." . . . (She lowered the basket from her arm and half-raised a broad burdock leaf, which covered the mushrooms.)— ' Eh!'"—said Kasyán, bending over the basket; 'why, what splendid ones! Good for thee, Ánnushka!"

" Is this thy daughter, Kasyán?"—I asked. (Ánnushka's face flushed faintly.)

"No, just a relative,"—said Kasyán, with feigned carelessness.—" Well, run along, Ánnushka,"—he immediately added:—" run along, and God be with thee. And see here . . . ."

" But why should she go afoot?"—I interrupted him.—" We will drive her with us."

Ánnushka flushed as scarlet as a poppy, seized the handle of the basket with both hands, and cast a glance of trepidation at the old man.

" No, she'll get there, all right,"—he returned, in the same indifferently-drawling tone. —" What is it to her? . . . She'll get there as she is. . . . Run along."

Ánnushka walked off briskly into the forest. Kasyán gazed after her, then cast down his eyes, and smiled. In that prolonged smile, in the few words which he had uttered to Ánnushka, in the very sound of his voice when he spoke to her, there was inexplicable, passionate love and tenderness. He cast another glance in the direction whither she had gone, smiled again, and, mopping his face, shook his head several times.

" Why didst thou send her off so soon? "—I asked him:—" I would have liked to buy her mushrooms. . . . ."

" But you can buy them at home, just as well, whenever you like,"—he answered me, for the first time addressing me as " you."

" Thou hast there a very pretty girl."

" No. . . . The idea! . . . . So-so . . ." he replied, reluctantly, as it were; and, from that moment, relapsed into his former taciturnity.

Perceiving that all my efforts to make him talk again were vain, I wended my way to the clearing. Moreover, the heat had decreased somewhat; but my ill-success continued, and I returned to the settlement with nothing but the one corncrake and a new axle. As we were driving into the yard, Kasyán suddenly turned to me.

" Master, eh, Master,"—said he:—" I am to blame toward thee; for 't was I that drove all the game away from thee."

" How so? "

" Well, that's my secret. And thou hast a trained hound, and a good one, but thou couldst do nothing. When you come to think of it, what are men,—men, hey? Man's a wild beast, but see what has been done with him!"

It would have been useless for me to try to convince Kasyán that it was impossible to "bewitch" the game, therefore I made him no reply. And besides, we immediately turned into the gate.

Ánnushka was not in the cottage; she had managed to get there already and leave her basket of mushrooms. Eroféi fitted the axle in place, after having subjected it preliminarily to severe and unjust criticism; and an hour later, I drove out, having left Kasyán a little money, which, at first, he did not wish to accept; but afterward, when he had reflected and held it in his palm, he thrust it into his bosom. He hardly uttered a single word during the course of that hour; he stood as before, leaning against the gate, made no reply to the reproaches of my coachman, and took an extremely cold leave of me.

As soon as I returned, I observed that my Eroféi was again in a gloomy frame of mind. . . . And, in fact, he had not found a morsel to eat in the village, and the watering facilities for his horses were bad. We drove off. With dissatisfaction expressed even in the nape of his neck, he sat on the box and was frightfully anxious to enter into conversation with me; but, in anticipation of my putting the first question, he confined himself to a low growling under his breath,

and hortatory, sometimes vicious speeches ad
dressed to his horses.—" A village! "—he mut
tered: " A pretty sort of village, forsooth! I
asked for just a little kvas—and there was no
kvas. . . . . Akh, O Lord! And the water,—
simply—phew! " (He spat aloud.) " No cu
cumbers, no kvas,—no nothing. . . . Come now
thou,"—he added in a loud tone, addressing the
right trace-horse:—" I know thee, thou pam
pered beast! Thou 'rt fond of indulging thyself
I think. . . ." (And he lashed it with his whip.)
" The horse has grown thoroughly crafty, but
what a willing beast it used to be! . . . Come
come, look round this way! " [1] . . . . .

" Tell me, please, Eroféi,"—I began:—" what
sort of a man is Kasyán? "

Eroféi did not answer me promptly; he was
in general, a deliberate, leisurely man; but I was
instantly able to divine that my question had
delighted and reassured him.

" The Flea, you mean? "—he said, at last, jerking at the reins:—" he 's a splendid man: a holy
fool, right enough he is; you won't soon find
another such fine man. Now, for example, he 's
point for point, exactly like our roan horse yonder: he 's incorrigible, has got out of hand,—that
is to say, he has struck work. Well, and, after all

---

[1] A well-trained trace-horse (which gallops), in a three-horse
span (a tróïka), is supposed to hold its head lowered and twisted
backward, so that the persons in the carriage can see its eyes and
nostrils.—TRANSLATOR.

what sort of a workman is he, what a wretched body holds his soul,—well, and, all the same . . . . You see, he has been so from his childhood. At first, he used to go with his uncles in the carrying business: he had three of them; well, and then, later on, you know, he got tired of that—he threw it up. He began to live at home, and he would n't even sit still at home: such an uneasy man he was,—a regular flea. Luckily for him, he happened to have a kind master who did n't force him. So, from that time forth, he has been lounging about, like an unconfined sheep. And such a wonderful man he is, God knows: sometimes he 's as silent as a stump, then, all of a sudden, he 'll start to talk,—and what he 'll say, God knows. Is that any way to do? 'T is not. He 's an inconsistent man, so he is. But he sings well. So solemnly—'t is fine, fine."

" And does he really heal? "

" Heal, do you mean? . . . Come, how could he! As if he were that sort of a man! But he cured me of scrofula. . . How could he! He 's a stupid man, so he is,"—he added, after a brief pause.

" Hast thou known him long? "

" Yes. He and I were neighbours in Sytchóvko, on the Fair Metchá."

" And who is that young girl, Ánnushka, who met us in the forest,—is she a relative of his? "

Eroféi glanced at me over his shoulder, and grinned to the full extent of his mouth.

" Eh! . . . . Yes, she 's a relative. She 's an orphan: she has no mother, and no one knows who her mother was. Well, and she must be related to him: she 's awfully like him. . . . Well, and she lives with him. She 's a sharp-witted girl, there 's no denying it: she 's a good girl, and he, the old man, fairly adores her: she is a good girl. And 't is very likely, although you might not believe it, that he has taken it into his head to teach his Ánnushka to read and write. That 's just what you might expect of him: he 's such a peculiar man. So fickle, even ill-balanced, even . . . E-e-eh! " my coachman suddenly interrupted himself, and pulling up his horses, bent over to one side, and began to sniff the air.—" Don't I smell something burning? That I do! I would n't give a rap for these new axles. . . . But, apparently, I greased it all right. I must go and fetch some water: yonder is a pond handy, by the way."

And Eroféi slowly climbed down from his seat, untied the bucket, went to the pond, and, on his return, listened, not without satisfaction, to the hissing of the wheel-box, suddenly gripped by the water. . . . In the space of about ten versts, he was forced to deluge the axle six times, and night had fully closed in when we reached home.

X

THE AGENT

ABOUT fifteen versts from my estate, lives an acquaintance of mine, a young landed proprietor, a retired officer of the Guards, Arkády Pávlitch Pyénotchkin. He has a great deal of game on his estate, his house is built after a plan by a French architect, his servants are dressed in English style, he gives capital dinners, welcomes his guests cordially, and, nevertheless, one is reluctant to go to his house. He is a sagacious, positive man, has received a fine education, as is proper, has been in the service, has mingled with the highest society, and now occupies himself, very successfully, with the administration of his property. Arkády Pávlitch, to use his own words, is stern but just, is deeply concerned for the welfare of his subjects, and chastises them—for their own good. " One must treat them like children," he says, on such occasions: " their ignorance, *mon cher, il faut prendre cela en considération.*" But on the occasions of such so-called sad necessity, he avoids harsh and impetuous movements, and is not fond of raising his voice, but is rather given to poking his finger straight out before him, calmly remarking: " Thou knowest, I requested

221

thee, my dear fellow," or: "What ails thee, my friend? Come to thy senses;" merely compressing his lips a little the while, and twisting his mouth. He is short of stature, elegantly built, very good-looking, keeps his hands and finger-nails with the greatest neatness; his rosy lips and face fairly glow with health. His laugh is resonant and care-free, he screws up his bright brown eyes affably. He dresses extremely well, and with taste; he imports French books, pictures, and newspapers, but is not very fond of reading: he has barely conquered " The Wandering Jew." He plays cards in a masterly manner. Altogether, Arkády Pávlitch is regarded as one of the most cultured noblemen and most enviable matrimonial catches in our government; the ladies are wild over him, and praise his manners in particular. His demeanour is wonderfully good, he is as cautious as a cat, and has never been mixed up in any scandal since he was born, although, on occasion, he is fond of asserting himself and reducing a timid man to confusion. He positively loathes bad company—he is afraid of compromising himself; on the other hand in jovial moments, he announces himself to be a disciple of Epicurus, although, on the whole, he speaks ill of philosophy, calling it " the foggy food of German brains," and sometimes simply " nonsense." He is fond of music, also; at cards, he hums through his teeth, but with feeling; he remembers something from " Lucia " and " Sonnambula," but always gets the pitch rather high. In winter, he goes to Petersburg. His house is in remarkable order; even his coachmen have succumbed to his influence, and every day they not only wipe off the horse-collars and brush their coats, but even wash their own faces. Arkády Pávlitch's house-serfs, 't is true, have a rather sidelong look,—but with us in Russia one cannot distinguish the surly man from the sleepy man. Arkády Pávlitch speaks in a soft and agreeable voice, with pauses, emitting every word with pleasure, as it were, through his handsome, perfumed moustache; he also employs a great many French expressions, such as: " *Mais, c'est impayable!* "—" *Mais, comment donc?* "—and so forth. Nevertheless, I, for one, am not overfond of visiting him, and if it were not for the black-cock and partridges, I should, in all probability, drop his acquaintance entirely. A certain strange uneasiness takes possession of you in his house; even the comfort does not gladden you, and every time that, at evening, the curled valet presents himself before you, in his sky-blue livery with buttons stamped with a coat of arms, and begins obsequiously to pull off your boots, you feel that if, instead of his pale and lean face the wonderfully broad cheek-bones and incredibly-blunt nose of a stalwart young peasant, only just taken from the plough by his master, but who had already contrived to burst in half a score of places, the seams of the nankeen coat recently presented to him, were suddenly to appear before you,—you would be unspeakably delighted, and would willingly subject yourself to the danger of being stripped of your boot and your leg, together, up to the very hip-joint. . . . . In spite of my dislike for Arkády Pávlitch, I once happened to pass the night with him. On the following day, early in the morning, I ordered my calash to be harnessed up, but he would not let me go without breakfast in the English fashion, and conducted me to his study. Along with tea, they served us cutlets, soft-boiled eggs, butter, honey, cheese, and so forth. Two valets, in clean white gloves, swiftly and silently anticipated our slightest wishes. We sat on a Persian divan. Arkády Pávlitch wore full trousers of silk, a black velvet round jacket, a red fez with a blue tassel, and yellow Chinese slippers, without heels. He drank tea, laughed, inspected his finger-nails, smoked, tucked pillows under his ribs, and, altogether, felt in a capital frame of mind. After having breakfasted heartily, and with evident pleasure, Arkády Pávlitch poured himself out a glass of red wine, raised it to his lips, and suddenly contracted his brows in a frown.

" Why has n't the wine been warmed? "—he asked one of the valets in a rather sharp voice.

The valet grew confused, stood stock-still, and turned pale.

"Am not I asking thee a question, my dear fellow?"—went on Arkády Pávlitch, calmly, without taking his eyes off him.

The unhappy valet shifted from foot to foot where he stood, twisted his napkin, and uttered never a word. Arkády Pávlitch lowered his head, and gazed thoughtfully askance at him.

"*Pardon, mon cher,*"—he said, with a pleasant smile, giving my knee a friendly touch with his hand, and again rivetting his eyes on the valet.— "Well, go,"—he added, after a brief silence, elevated his eyebrows, and rang the bell.

There entered a thick-set, swarthy, black-haired man, with a low forehead, and eyes completely buried in fat.

"With regard to Feódor . . . . . take measures,"—said Arkády Pávlitch in an undertone, and with entire self-possession.

"I obey, sir,"—replied the thick-set man, and left the room.

"*Voilà, mon cher, les désagréments de la campagne,*"—remarked Arkády Pávlitch, merrily. "But where are you going? stay, sit with me a while longer."

"No,"—I answered:—"I must go."

"Always hunting! Okh, I have no patience with those sportsmen! But where are you going?"

" To Ryábovo, forty versts from here."

" To Ryábovo? Akh, good heavens, in that case I will go with you. Ryábovo is only five versts from my Shipilóvka, and I have n't been to Shipilóvka for ever so long: I have never managed to make the time. Now it has happened quite opportunely: do you hunt at Ryábovo today, and come to my house in the evening. *Ce sera charmant.* We will sup together,—we will take a cook with us,—you shall spend the night with me. Splendid! splendid! "—he added, without awaiting my reply. *" C'est arrangé. . . .* Hey, who is there? Order the calash to be brought round for us, and be quick about it. You have n't been to Shipilóvka? I should be ashamed to suggest your passing the night in my agent's cottage, were it not that I know you are not fastidious, and would have to pass the night in a hay-barn at Ryábovo. . . . Come on, come on!"

And Arkády Pávlitch began to sing some French romance or other.

" But perhaps you do not know,"—he went on, rocking himself to and fro on both legs:—" my peasants there are on quit-rent. I 'm such a liberal man,—but what are you going to do about it? They pay me their dues promptly, however; I would have put them on husbandry-service long ago, I confess, but there is too little land; and I 'm amazed, as it is, how they make both ends meet. However, *c'est leur affaire.* My

agent there is a fine fellow, *une forte tête,* a statesman! You will see. . . . How conveniently this
has happened, really!"

There was no help for it. Instead of setting
out at ten o'clock in the morning, we set out at
two. Sportsmen will understand my impatience.
Arkády Pávlitch was fond, as he expressed himself, of indulging himself on occasion, and took
with him such an endless mass of linen, provisions,
clothing, perfumes, pillows, and various dressing-
cases, that an economical and self-contained German would have thought there was enough of
these blessings to last him a whole year. Every
time we descended a declivity, Arkády Pávlitch
made a brief but powerful speech to the coachman, from which I was able to deduce the infer-
ence, that my friend was a good deal of a coward.
However, the journey was accomplished with
entire safety; only on one recently-repaired
bridge the cart with the cook tumbled in, and the
hind wheel crushed his stomach.

Arkády Pávlitch, at the sight of the downfall
of his home-bred Karem, became seriously frightened, and immediately gave orders to inquire:
"Were his arms whole?" On receiving an affirma-
tive answer, he immediately regained his composure. Nevertheless, we were a good while on the
way; I rode in the same calash with Arkády Pávlitch, and toward the end of the journey I felt
bored to death, the more so as in the course of

several hours my acquaintance had turned utterly insipid, and had begun to proclaim liberal views. At last, we arrived, only not at Ryábovo but directly at Shipilóvka: somehow, that was the way it turned out. Even without that, I could not have hunted my fill on that day, and therefore, possessing my soul in patience, I submitted to my fate.

The cook had arrived a few minutes in advance of us, and, evidently, had already succeeded in making his arrangements, and notifying the proper persons, for at our very entrance into the boundaries we were met by the elder (the agent's son), a stalwart and red-haired peasant, a good seven feet in height, on horseback and without his cap, in a new peasant-coat wide-open on the chest. " And where is Sofrón? "—Arkády Pávlitch asked him. The elder first sprang alertly from his horse, made an obeisance to the girdle to his master, said: " Good-morning, dear little father, Arkády Pávlitch," then raised his head, shook himself, and announced that Sofrón had gone to Peróff, but that he had already been sent for. —" Well, follow us,"—said Arkády Pávlitch. The elder led his horse aside, out of decorum, sprang on its back, and set off at a trot behind the calash, holding his cap in his hand. We drove through the village. Several peasants in empty carts met us; they were driving from the threshing-floor and singing songs, jouncing about with their whole bodies, and with their legs dangling in the air; but at the sight of our calash and of the elder, they suddenly fell silent, doffed their winter caps (it was summer-time), and half-rose, as though awaiting orders. Arkády Pávlitch graciously saluted them. An alarming agitation had, evidently, spread abroad throughout the village. Women in plaided, home-woven wool petticoats were flinging chips at unsagacious or too zealous dogs, a lame old man with a beard which started just under his eyes jerked his half-watered horse away from the well, smote it in the ribs, for some unknown reason, and then made his obeisance. Dirty little boys, in long shirts, ran howling to the cottages, flung themselves, belly down, on the thresholds, hung their heads, kicked their legs in the air, and in this manner rolled with great agility past the door, into the dark anteroom, whence they did not again emerge. Even the chickens scuttled headlong, in an accelerated trot, under the board at the bottom of the gate; one gallant cock, with a black breast, which resembled a black-satin waistcoat, and a handsome tail, which curled over to his very comb, had intended to remain in the road, and was on the very point of crowing, but suddenly was seized with confusion, and fled also. The agent's cottage stood apart from the rest, in the middle of a thick green hemp-patch. We drew up at the gate. Mr. Pyénotchkin rose, picturesquely

flung aside his cloak, and alighted from the calash, casting courteous glances around him. The
agent's wife received us with low reverences, and
approached to kiss the master's hand. Arkády
Pávlitch allowed her to kiss it to her heart's content, and ascended to the porch. In the anteroom, in a dark corner, stood the elder's wife, and
she also bowed low, but did not venture to kiss
his hand. In the so-called cold cottage,[1] on the
right of the anteroom, two other women were already bustling about: they had carried thence all
sorts of rubbish, empty tubs, sheepskin coats
which had grown stiff as wood, butter-pots, and
a cradle with a pile of rags and a gay-coloured
baby, and had swept up the dirt with a bath-
besom.

Arkády Pávlitch banished them from the
room, and placed himself on the wall-bench,
under the holy pictures. The coachmen began
to bring in trunks, coffers, and other conveni-
ences, using their utmost endeavours to subdue
the clumping of their heavy boots.

In the meantime, Arkády Pávlitch was ques-
tioning the elder about the harvest, the sowing,
and other agricultural subjects. The elder replied satisfactorily, but, somehow, languidly and
awkwardly, as though he were buttoning his kaftan with half-frozen fingers. He stood by the

---

[1] A " cold " cottage, or church, in Russia means one that is not
furnished with the means of heating. — TRANSLATOR.

door, and kept watching and glancing round, every now and then, making way for the alert valet. I managed to catch a glimpse, past his broad shoulders, of the agent's wife silently thrashing some other woman in the anteroom. All at once, a peasant-cart rattled up and halted in front of the porch: the agent entered.

This "statesman," acording to Arkády Pávlitch's words, was short of stature, broad-shouldered, grey-haired, and thick-set, with a red nose, small blue eyes, and a beard in the shape of a fan. We may remark, by the way, that ever since Russia has stood, there has never been an instance in it of a man who has grown corpulent and waxed wealthy, without a wide-spreading beard; a man may have worn a thin, wedge-shaped beard all his life long,—and suddenly, lo and behold, it has encircled his face like a halo,—and where does the hair come from! The agent must have been carousing in Peróff: his face was considerably bloated, and he exhaled an odour of liquor.

"Akh, you, our fathers, our gracious ones,"— he began in a sing-song tone, and with so much emotion depicted on his face, that it seemed as though the tears were on the point of gushing forth;—" at last, you have done us the favour to come to us! . . . . Thy hand, dear little father, thy dear little hand,"—he added, protruding his lips in advance.

Arkády Pávlitch complied with his wish.—
" Well, now then, brother Sofrón, how are thy
affairs thriving? "—he asked, in a caressing
voice.

" Akh, you, our fathers,"—exclaimed Sofrón:
" but how could they go badly, those affairs! For
you, our fathers, our benefactors, you have
deigned to illuminate our wretched little village
with your coming, you have rendered us happy
until the day of our coffins. Glory to Thee,
O Lord, Arkády Pávlitch, glory to Thee, O
Lord! Everything is thriving, thanks to your
mercy. . . ."

Here Sofrón stopped short, darted a glance at
his master, and, as though again carried away by
a transport of feeling (and the liquor was beginning to assert itself, to boot), he again besought
the privilege of kissing his hand, and went on
worse than before.

" Akh, you, our fathers, our benefactors
. . . . . . and . . . . . . what am I saying!
By God, I have gone perfectly mad with joy.
. . . Heaven is my witness, I look, and cannot
believe my eyes. . . . . Akh, you, our fathers! . . . ."

Arkády Pávlitch glanced at me, laughed, and
said: " *N'est-ce pas que c'est touchant!* "

" Yes, dear little father, Arkády Pávlitch,"—
went on the indefatigable agent:—" how could
you do such a thing! you afflict me to the last de-

gree, dear little father: you did not deign to notify me of your coming. And where are you to
spend the night? For the dirt, the rubbish
here . . . . ."

"Never mind, Sofrón, never mind,"—replied
Arkády Pávlitch, with a smile:—" it 's very nice
here."

"Yes, but you, our fathers,—for whom is it
nice? for the likes of us peasants 't is well enough;
but you . . . . akh, you, my fathers, benefactors,
akh, you, my fathers! . . . Forgive me, I 'm a
fool, I 've lost my wits, by God, I 've gone utterly
crazy."

In the meantime, supper was served;—Arkády
Pávlitch began to eat. The old man drove his
son away,—" Thou wilt make the air close," said
he.

"Well, old man, and hast thou settled the
boundaries?"—asked Mr. Pyénotchkin, who,
evidently, was desirous of imitating the peasant
style of speech, and winked at me.[1]

"We have, dear little father: all by thy bounty.
We signed the affidavit day before yesterday.
The Khlýnoff folks were inclined to resist, at first
. . . and they really did kick up a row, father.
They demanded . . . . they demanded . . . .
God only knows what it was they demanded; but
they are a foolish lot, dear little father, a stupid
set of folks. But we, dear little father, by thy

[1] He said *stariná,* instead of *starík,* for " old man."—TRANSLATOR.

mercy, showed our gratitude [1] to Mikolái Miko-
láitch, the middleman; we satisfied him; we acted
entirely according to thy command, dear little
father; as thou wert pleased to command, so we
acted, and everything was done with the knowledge of Yegór Dmítritch."

" Yegór reported to me,"—remarked Arkády
Pávlitch, pompously.

" Of course, dear little father, Yegór Dmítritch did so, of course."

" Well, and I suppose you are satisfied
now? "

This was all that Sofrón was waiting for.—
" Akh, you, our fathers, our benefactors! "—he
began to whine again. . . . " Have mercy on
me! . . . . for don't we pray to the Lord God,
day and night, on behalf of you, our fathers. . . .
There is n't much land, of course. . . . . ."

Pyénotchkin interrupted him.—" Well, all
right, all right, Sofrón; I know thou servest me
zealously. . . . Well, and how about the
threshing? "

Sofrón heaved a sigh.

" Well, you, our fathers, the threshing is n't
very good. And here now, dear little father, Arkády Pávlitch, allow me to announce to you what
sort of a little business has come up." (Here he
came close up to Mr. Pyénotchkin, throwing his
hands apart, bent down, and screwed up one

[1] That is—bribed.—TRANSLATOR.

eye.) "We have found a dead body on our land."

"How did that come about?"

"Why, I myself can't comprehend it, dear little father, you, our fathers,—evidently, the devil made the mess, set the snare. And, luckily, it turned out to be near another man's boundary-line; only, what's the use of concealing the sin? 'T was on our land. I immediately gave orders to have it dragged on to the other man's strip of land,[1] while it was possible, and I set a guard over it, and gave him command: 'Hold thy tongue!' says I. And I explained it to the commissary of police, by way of precaution. 'This was the way of it,' says I; and I treated him to tea, and gratitude. . . . Now, what do you think of it, dear little father? You see, it has been left on the necks of others; for one has to pay two hundred rubles for a dead body,—as surely as one has to pay for a penny roll."

Mr. Pyénotchkin laughed a great deal at his agent's clever ruse, and said to me several times, nodding his head in his direction: *"Quel gaillard, eh?"*

In the meantime, it had grown completely dark out of doors; Arkády Pávlitch ordered the table to be cleared, and hay to be brought. The valet

[1] Endless investigations by the police, and complications, ensue from the finding of a dead body. The person who owns the land is compelled to explain how it came there, and who murdered the victim.—TRANSLATOR.

spread out sheets for us, and laid out pillows; we lay down. Sofrón went to his own quarters, after receiving his orders for the following day. Arkády Pávlitch, while getting to sleep, talked a little more about the capital qualities of the Russian peasant, and then immediately observed to me that, since Sofrón had been in charge, the Shipilóvka serfs had never been a penny in arrears. . . . . The watchman tapped on his board;[1] the baby, who, evidently, had not yet succeeded in becoming thoroughly permeated with a sense of dutiful self-sacrifice, set up a yell somewhere in the cottage. . . We fell asleep.

We rose quite early on the following morning. I was on the point of setting off for Ryábovo, but Arkády Pávlitch wished to show me his estate, and begged me to remain. I was not averse to convincing myself, by actual observation, as to the capital qualities of the statesman Sofrón. The agent presented himself. He wore a blue long-coat, girt with a red belt. He talked much less than on the preceding evening, gazed vigilantly and intently in his master's eyes, replied fluently and in business-like fashion. We went with him to the threshing-floor. Sofrón's son, the seven-foot elder, by all the tokens a very stupid fellow, also followed us, and the village scribe, Fedosyéitch, a former soldier, with a

[1] To prove that he was alert; as with the modern watchman's clock-record. Sometimes the " boards " were sheets of iron. Some such can still be seen beaten into holes in monasteries.—TRANSLATOR.

huge moustache and an extremely strange expression of countenance, joined us: it seemed as though he must have beheld something remarkable very long ago, and had never recovered himself from the sight since. We inspected the threshing-floor, the barns, the grain-ricks, the sheds, the windmill, the cattle-yard, the garden-stuff, the hemp-plots; everything really was in capital order: the dejected faces of the serfs alone caused me some perplexity. In addition to the useful, Sofrón looked after the agreeable: he had planted willows along all the ditches; he had laid out paths and strewn them with sand between the ricks on the threshing-floor; he had constructed a weather-vane on the windmill, in the shape of a bear with gaping jaws, and a red tongue; he had fastened something in the nature of a Greek pediment to the brick cattle-shed, and had written in white-lead, under the pediment: " Bilt in the villige of Shipilofke in onetousan eigh Hundert farty. This catle shet."—Arkády Pávlitch melted completely, took to setting forth to me, in the French language, the advantages of the quit-rent system,—remarking, however, in that connection, that husbandry-service was more profitable for the peasants,—and any quantity of other things! He began to give the agent advice, how to plant potatoes, how to prepare the fodder for the cattle, and so forth. Sofrón listened to his master's remarks with attention, replying now

and then; but he no longer addressed Arkády
Pávlitch either as " father," or as " benefactor,"
and kept insisting that they had very little land,
that it would n't be amiss to buy some more.
" Well then, buy some,"—said Arkády Pávlitch:
—" I 'm not averse to having it bought in my
name."—To these words, Sofrón made no reply,
but merely stroked his beard.—" But it would n't
be a bad idea to go to the forest now,"—remarked
Mr. Pyénotchkin.   Saddle-horses were immediately brought for us; we rode to the forest, or, as
they say in our parts, " the forbidden ground." [1]
In this " forbidden spot " we found an immense
amount of thicket and game, for which Arkády
Pávlitch praised Sofrón, and patted him on the
shoulder. Mr. Pyénotchkin, in the matter of for-
estry, adhered to Russian ideas, and there, on the
spot, he narrated to me what, according to his assertion, was a very amusing incident,—how a
landed proprietor, given to jesting, had taught
his forester a lesson, by plucking out about one-
half of his beard, to demonstrate that the forest
does not grow any thicker for being thinned out.
. . . . However, in other respects, neither Sofrón
nor Arkády Pávlitch avoided innovations. On
our return to the village, the agent led us to in-

---

[1] The peasants have no right to wood from the forests, and no
forest-land was allotted to them after the Emancipation. To prevent their stealing timber (as in "The Wolf," which follows),
broad, deep ditches are often dug across the forest roads by the
proprietors.—Translator.

pect a winnowing-machine, which had recently
been imported from Moscow. The winnowing-
machine really did work well, but if Sofrón had
known what an unpleasant experience was awaiting him and his master during this final stroll,
he would, in all probability, have remained at
home with us.

This is what happened. As we emerged from
the shed, we beheld the following spectacle. A
few paces from the door, beside a filthy puddle,
in which three ducks were carelessly splashing,
stood two serfs: one was an old man of sixty
years, the other a young fellow of twenty, both
in home-made, patched shirts, barefooted, and
girt with ropes. The scribe, Fedosyéitch, was
bustling zealously about them, and would, probably, have succeeded in prevailing upon them to
withdraw, if we had tarried a little longer in the
shed; but, on catching sight of us, he drew himself up in military fashion, fingers on his trous-
ers-seams, and stood stock-still on the spot. The
elder was standing there also, with mouth agape,
and suspended in the act of striking fists. Arkády Pávlitch frowned, bit his lips, and stepped
up to the peasants. Both bowed to his feet, in
silence.

"What do you want? What are you petition-
ing about?"—he asked, in a stern voice, and
somewhat through his nose. (The peasants
glanced at each other and uttered never a word,

but merely screwed up their eyes, as though screening them from the sun, and began to breathe faster.)

" Come now, what is it? "—went on Arkády Pávlitch, and immediately turned to Sofrón:— " from what family are they? "

" From the Tobolyéeff family,"—replied the agent, slowly.

" Come now, what do you want? "—said Mr. Pyénotchkin again:—" Have n't you any tongues, pray? Tell me, thou, what dost thou want? "—he added, nodding his head at the old man.—" And don't be afraid, thou fool."

The old man stretched out his dark-brown, wrinkled neck, opened awry his lips, which had turned blue, ejaculated in a hoarse voice: " Intercede, sir! " and again banged his brow against the ground. The young serf also bowed low. Arkády Pávlitch gazed pompously at the napes of their necks, tossed back his head, and straddled his legs somewhat.—" What 's the matter? Against whom are you complaining? "

" Have mercy, sir! Give us a chance to breathe. . . . . We are tortured to death." (The old man spoke with difficulty.)

" Who has tortured thee? "

" Why, Sofrón Yakóvlevitch, dear little father."

Arkády Pávlitch said nothing for a while.

" What 's thy name? "

" Antíp, dear little father."

" And who is this? "

" My son, dear little father."

Arkády Pávlitch again remained silent for a while, and twitched his moustache.

" Well, and how does he torture thee? "—he began again, glancing at the old man through his moustache.

" Dear little father, he has utterly ruined us. He has given two of my sons as recruits out of their turn, dear little father, and now he is taking away the third one. Yesterday, dear little father, he took my last poor cow from my yard, and thrashed my wife—that's his lordship yonder." (He pointed at the elder.)

" H'm,"—ejaculated Arkády Pávlitch.

" Do not let him utterly ruin me, my benefactor! "

Mr. Pyénotchkin frowned.—" What's the meaning of this? "—he asked the agent in an undertone and with a look of displeasure.

" He's a drunkard, *sir,*"—replied the agent, for the first time employing the " sir ":—" he won't work. He's always in arrears, these last five years, sir."

" Sofrón Yakóvlevitch has paid up my arrears for me, dear little father,"—went on the old man:—" this is the fifth year that he has paid, and how has he paid—he has made me his serf, dear little father, and so . . . . ."

" And how didst thou come to be in arrears? " asked Mr. Pyénotchkin, menacingly. (The old man hung his head.)—" Thou art fond of getting drunk, I think,—of roaming around among the dram-shops? " (The old man tried to open his mouth.)

" I know you,"—went on Arkády Pávlitch with vehemence:—" your business is drinking and lying on the oven; and a good peasant must be responsible for you."

" And he 's an insolent beast, too," the agent interjected into the gentleman's speech.

" Well, that one understands as a matter of course. That is always the case: I have observed it more than once. He leads a dissolute life for a whole year, is insolent, and now flings himself at my feet."

" Dear little father, Arkády Pávlitch,"—said the old man in despair:—" have mercy, defend us,—I 'm not insolent! I speak as I would before the Lord God, 't is more than I can bear. Sofrón Yakóvlevitch has taken a dislike to me,—and for the reason why he has taken the dislike, the Lord be his judge! He is ruining me utterly, dear little father. . . . This is my last son, here . . . and you see . . . . ." (A tear glittered in the old man's yellow, wrinkled eyes.)—" Have mercy, sir, defend us." . . . .

" Yes, and not us alone—" began the young serf. . . . . .

All at once, Arkády Pávlitch flared up:

" And who asked thee, hey? when thou art not asked, hold thy tongue. . . . What's the meaning of this? Hold thy tongue, I tell thee! Hold thy tongue! . . . . . Akh, my God! why, this is simply mutiny! No, brother, I would n't advise any one to mutiny on my estate. . . I have . . . ." (Arkády Pávlitch began to stride back and forth, then, probably, recalled to himself my presence, turned away, and put his hands in his pockets.) . . . . . " *Je vous vous demande bien pardon, mon cher*,"—he said, with a constrained smile, significantly lowering his voice.—" *C'est le mauvais côté de la médaille*. . . . Come, very good, very good,"—he went on, without looking at the peasant men:—" I will give orders . . . good, go your way."—(The peasants did not rise.)—" Well, have n't I told you? . . . it's all right. Go away,—I 'll give orders, I tell you."

Arkády Pávlitch turned his back on them.— " Eternal dissatisfaction,"—he said between his teeth, and walked off homeward with huge strides. Sofrón followed him. The scribe's eyes bulged out, as though he were on the point of making a long leap in some direction. The elder scared the ducks out of the puddle. The petitioners stood a while longer on the same spot, stared at each other, and trudged away whence they came.

A couple of hours later, I was in Ryábovo, and, in company with Anpadíst, a peasant of my acquaintance, was preparing to set off hunt-

ing. Pyénotchkin had sulked at Sofrón up to
the very moment of my departure. I began to
talk with Anpadíst about the Shipilóvka serfs,
about Mr. Pyénotchkin; I asked him, whether he
knew the agent there.

" Sofrón Yakóvlevitch, you mean? . . . .
Oh, don't I just! "

" And what sort of a man is he? "

" He's a dog, and not a man: you won't find
such another dog this side of Kursk."

" But what dost thou mean? "

" Why, Shipilóvka merely stands in the name
of . . . . how do you call him? Pyénkin; he
does n't own it, you see: Sofrón owns it."

" You don't say so? "

" He runs it as his own property. The peasants are up to their ears in debt to him: they
drudge for him like hired men: he sends one off
with the carrier's train, another somewhere else
. . . . . he harries them altogether."

" They have not much land, it seems? "

" Not much? He hires eighty desyatínas from
the Khlínovo folks alone, and from us, one
hundred and twenty; there's a whole hundred
and fifty desyatínas there besides for you. And
land is not the only thing he trades in: he trades
in horses, and cattle, and tar, and butter, and
flax, and a lot of things besides. . . . He's
clever, awfully clever, and rich too, the beast
But this is the bad part of it—he assaults folks

THE AGENT

He 's a wild beast, not a man;—I 've said it: he 's
a dog, a dirty dog, that 's what he is—a dirty dog."

"But why don't the people complain of him?"

"Eksta! What does the master care! What is
it to him, so long as the money is not in arrears?
Yes, just try it,"—he added, after a brief pause:
—"complain. No, he 'll let thee . . . well, just
try it . . . No, he 'll give you to understand . . ." I mentioned Antíp, and related
what I had seen.

"Well,"—said Anpadíst:—"now he 'll devour him alive; he 'll devour that man utterly.
Now the elder will beat him. The poor, unhappy fellow, just think of it! And why is
he suffering? . . . He picked a quarrel with
him at the village-council,—with that agent,—
things had got beyond endurance, you see. . .
A great matter, forsooth! So then he began
to peck at him,—at Antíp, I mean. Now he 'll
make an end of him. For he 's such a dirty dog,
a hound,—the Lord forgive my sin!—he knows
whom to oppress. The old men,—he does n't
touch those that are richer,—and with large
families, the bald-headed devil,—but now he 'll
let himself loose! You see, he gave Antíp's sons
for recruits out of their turn,—the cruel rascal,
the dirty dog,—may the Lord forgive my great
sin!"

We set off on our hunt.

Salzburg in Silesia, July, 1847.

XI

IT happened in the autumn. I had been roving about for several hours over the fields, with my gun; and, in all probability, would not have returned before the evening to the posting-station on the Kursk highway, where my tróïka was waiting for me, had not the extremely fine and cold, drizzling rain, which had been sticking to me ever since the morning, indefatigably and pitilessly, like an old maid, made me, at last, seek a temporary shelter, at least, somewhere in the vicinity. While I was deliberating in which direction to go, a low-roofed hut suddenly presented itself to my eyes, beside a field sown with peas. I went to the hut, cast a glance under the straw penthouse, and beheld an old man so decrepit, that he immediately reminded me of that dying goat which Robinson Crusoe found in one of the caves of his island. The old man was squatting on his heels, puckering up his purblind tiny eyes, and hurriedly but cautiously, like a hare (the poor fellow had not a single tooth), chewing a hard, dry pea, incessantly rolling it from side to side. He was so engrossed in his occupation, that he did not notice my approach.

"Grandpa! Hey there, grandpa!"—I said.

He ceased chewing, elevated his eyebrows and, with an effort, opened his eyes.

"What?"—he mumbled in a hoarse voice.

"Where is there a village near at hand?"—I asked.

The old man set to chewing again. He had not heard me. I repeated my question more loudly than before.

"A village? . . . . but what dost thou want?"

"Why, to shelter myself from this rain."

"What?"

"To shelter myself from the rain."

"Yes!" (He scratched his sunburned neck.) 'Well, thou must go, seest thou,"—he began suddenly, flourishing his hands loosely:—" yo . . . yonder, right past the little wood, thou must go, —yonder, as thou goest—there 'll be a road; do thou let it—the road, that is—alone, and keep on always to the right, keep right on, keep right on, keep right on. . . . . . Well, and then thou wilt come to Anányevo. Or thou canst go through to Sítovko."

It was with difficulty that I understood the old man. His moustache interfered with him, and his tongue obeyed him badly.

"But whence comest thou?"—I asked him.

"What?"

"Whence art thou?"

" From Anányevo."

" What art thou doing here? "

" What? "

" What art thou doing here? "

" I 'm the watchman."

" But what art thou guarding? "

" Why, the peas."

I could not help bursting into a laugh.

" Why, good gracious,—how old art thou? "

" God knows."

" Thy sight is bad, is n't it? "

" Yes. There are times when I hear nothing."

" Then, how canst thou act as watchman, pray? "

" My elders know."

" Thy elders," I thought, and surveyed the poor old man, not without compassion. He fumbled about his person, got a crust of stale bread from his bosom, and began to suck at it, like a child, drawing in with an effort his cheeks, which were sunken enough without that.

I walked off in the direction of the wood, turned to the right, kept on and on, as the old man had advised me, and at last reached a large village with a stone church in the new style, that is to say, with columns, and a spacious manor-house, also with columns. Already from afar, athwart the close network of the rain, I had observed a cottage with a board roof, and two chimneys taller than the others,—in all probability, the dwelling of the elder,—and thither I directed my steps, in the hope of finding in his house a samovár, tea, sugar, and cream which was not completely sour. Accompanied by my thoroughly benumbed dog, I ascended the porch, entered the anteroom, and opened the door; but, instead of the customary appliances of a cottage, I beheld several tables loaded down with papers, two red cupboards spattered with ink, a leaden sand-box weighing about a pud, very long pens, and so forth. At one of the tables sat a young fellow of twenty years, with a puffy and sickly face, tiny little eyes, a greasy forehead, and interminable curls on his temples. He was dressed, as was proper, in a grey nankeen kaftan shiny on the collar and the stomach.

"What do you want?"—he asked me, throwing his head upward, like a horse which has not been expecting to be seized by the muzzle.

"Does the manager live here . . . . . or . . . . ."

"This is the squire's principal counting-house,"—he interrupted me.—"I'm the clerk on duty. . . . Do you mean to say you didn't see the sign? That's what the sign is nailed up for."

"And where can I dry myself? Has any one in the village a samovár?"

"Why shouldn't there be a samovár?"—retorted the young fellow in the grey kaftan, pompously: "Go to Father Timoféi, or to the cot-

tage of the house-serfs, or to Nazár Tarásitch, o
to Agraféna the poultry-woman."

"Who's that thou art talking to, thou dolt
thou wilt not let one sleep, dolt!"—rang out
voice from the adjoining room.

"Why, here's some gentleman or other ha
come in, and is asking where he can dry himself.

"What gentleman is it?"

"I don't know. He has a dog and a gun."

A bed creaked in the adjoining room. Th
door opened, and there entered a man about fift
years of age, low of stature, squat, with a bull
neck, protruding eyes, remarkably round cheeks
and a polish all over his face.

"What do you want?"—he asked me.

"To dry myself."

"This is not the place for that."

"I did not know that this was a counting
house; moreover, I am ready to pay . . . . ."

"You might do it here,"—returned the fa
man:—"please to come this way." (He con
ducted me into another room, only not the on
from which he had emerged.)—"Shall you b
comfortable here?"

"Yes. . . . But cannot I get some tea wit
cream?"

"Certainly, directly. In the meantime, pleas
to undress yourself and rest, and the tea shall b
ready immediately."

"Whose estate is this?"

" The estate of Mme. Losnyakóff, Eléna Ni·oláevna."

He left the room. I looked about me: along he partition which separated my room from the ounting-house stood a huge, leather-covered livan; two chairs, also upholstered in leather, vith extremely high backs, reared themselves in he air, one on each side of the single window, vhich opened on the street. On the walls, hung vith dark-green paper with pink patterns, were hree enormous pictures, painted in oils. One epicted a setter hound with a blue collar and he inscription: " This is my delight; " at the log's feet flowed a river, and on the opposite hore of the river, beneath a pine-tree, sat a hare f extravagant size, with ears pricked up. In he other picture, two old men were eating watermelon: beyond the watermelon, in the distance, Greek portico was visible bearing the incription: " The Temple of Contentment." The hird picture presented a half-naked woman n a reclining attitude, *en raccourci,* with red nees and very thick heels. My dog, without he slightest delay, with superhuman effort, rawled under the divan, and apparently found great deal of dust there, for he began to sneeze 'rightfully. I walked to the window. Across he street, from the manor-house to the countinghouse of the estate, in a diagonal line, lay boards: very useful precaution, because everywhere around, thanks to our black soil, and to the prolonged rain, the mud was frightful. Round about the squire's residence, which stood with its back to the street, that was going on which usually does go on around the manors of the gentry: maids in faded cotton frocks were whisking to and fro; house-serfs were strolling through the mud, halting and meditatively scratching their spines, the rural policeman's horse, which was tied, was idly swishing its tail, and, with its muzzle tossed aloft, was nibbling the fence; hens were cackling; consumptive turkeys were incessantly calling to one another. On the porch of a dark and rotting building, probably the bathhouse, sat a sturdy young fellow with a guitar, singing, not without spirit, the familiar ballad:

> " E—I 'll to the desert hie myself away
> From these most lovely scenes "—

and so forth.[1]

The fat man entered my room.

" Here, they 're bringing your tea,"—he said to me, with a pleasant smile.

The young fellow in the grey kaftan, the clerk on duty, set out on an old l'ombre table the samovár, the tea-pot, a glass with a cracked saucer, a pot of cream, and a bundle of Bolkhóff ringrolls as hard as stone. The fat man withdrew.

---

[1] The man's atrocious pronunciation cannot be reproduced in English.—TRANSLATOR.

" Who is that,"—I asked the clerk on duty:—
" the manager? "

" Oh, no, sir; he used to be the head cashier,
but now he has been promoted to be the head
office-clerk."

" But have you no manager here? "

" No, sir, none. There 's a peasant overseer,
Mikhaílo Vikúloff, but there 's no manager."

" So there 's an agent? "

" Certainly, there is: a German, Lindamandol,
Kárlo Kárlitch;—only he does n't manage affairs."

" But who does the managing? "

" The mistress herself."

" You don't say so!—And have you a large
force in the office? "

The young fellow reflected.

" Six men."

" Who are they? "—I asked.

" Why, these:—first, there 's Vasíly Nikoláevitch, the head cashier; and next, Piótr
the clerk; Piótr's brother Iván, a clerk; another clerk, Iván; Koskenkín [1] Narkízoff, also a
clerk; and myself;—and you could n't reckon
up all."

" Your mistress has a great many menials, I
suppose? "

" No, not so very many. . . ."

" But how many? "

[1] Konstantín.—TRANSLATOR.

"They sum up to about a hundred and fifty persons, probably."

We both remained silent for a while.

"Well, and dost thou write well?"—I began again.

The young fellow grinned to the full capacity of his mouth, nodded his head, went into the office, and brought back a written sheet of paper.

"This is my writing,"—said he, without ceasing to grin.

I looked at it: on a quarter-sheet of greyish paper, the following was written in a large, handsome script:

"ORDINANCE"

"From the head home office of the Anányevo estate, to the Overseer Mikhaílo Vikúloff, No. 209."

"Thou art ordered, immediately on receipt of this, to institute an inquiry: who it was that, during the past night, in a state of intoxication and with improper songs, walked through the English park, and waked up and disturbed the French governess, Mme. Engenie? and what the watchman was about, and who was on guard in the park and permitted such disorder? Thou art ordered to report without delay to the office concerning the aforesaid, in full detail.

"Head clerk, NIKOLÁI KHVOSTÓFF."

A huge seal, bearing a coat of arms, was attached to the ordinance, with the inscription: " Seal of the head office of the Anányevo estate; " and below was the signature: " To be executed punctually: ELÉNA LOSNYAKÓFF."

" Did the mistress herself sign that, pray? "—I asked.

" Certainly, sir, she herself: she always signs herself. Otherwise, the order cannot take effect."

" Well, and shall you send this ordinance to the overseer? "

" No, sir. He will come himself and read it. That is to say, it will be read to him; for he can't read and write." (The clerk on duty lapsed into silence again.)

" Well, sir,"—he added, smilingly:—" it 's well written, is n't it, sir? "

" Yes."

" Of course, I did n't compose it. Koskenkín is a master-hand at that."

" What? . . . . . Dost thou mean to say that with you the orders are first composed? "

"How else, sir? They cannot be written out fairly straight off."

" And how much of a salary dost thou receive? "—I asked.

" Thirty-five rubles a year, and five rubles for boots."

" And art thou satisfied? "

" Certainly I am.—Not every one can get into

our counting-house. God himself ordered me there, to tell the truth: my uncle serves as butler."

" And art thou well off ? "

" Yes, sir. To tell the truth,"—he went on, with a sigh:—" the likes of us are better off with the merchants. Fellows like me are very well off with the merchants. Now, for instance, yesterday there came to us a merchant from Venyóvo,—so his workman told me. . . . They 're well off, there 's no denying it,—well off."

" But do the merchants give bigger wages? "

" God forbid! Why, a merchant would pitch you out of doors by the scruff of the neck if you were to ask wages from him. No, you must live in faith and in fear with a merchant. He gives you food, and drink, and clothing, and everything. If you please him,—he 'll give you even more. . . . What do you want with wages! you don't need any at all. . . . And the merchant lives simply in Russian fashion, in our own fashion: if you go on the road with him, he drinks tea, and you drink tea; what he eats, that you eat also. A merchant . . . . why, there 's no comparison: a merchant is not the same as a well-born master. A merchant is n't capricious; now, if he gets angry, he 'll thrash you, and that 's the end of it. He does n't nag and jeer. . . . But with the well-born master,—woe be to you! Nothing suits him: this is not right, and he is n't satisfied with the other. If you give him a glass of water or food,—' Akh, the water stinks! akh, the food stinks!' You carry it away, and stand outside the door a bit, and carry it in again:—' Well, now, that's good; well, now, that does n't stink.' And the lady mistresses, I can just tell you, the lady mistresses! . . . or, take the young ladies! . . . . ."

The clerk on duty briskly left the room. I finished my glass of tea, lay down on the divan, and fell asleep. I slept two hours.

On waking, I tried to rise, but indolence overpowered me; I closed my eyes, but did not get to sleep again. A low-voiced conversation was in progress in the office, on the other side of the partition. I involuntarily began to listen.

" Yis, sir, yis, sir, Nikolái Eremyéitch,"—said one voice:—" yis, sir. That cannot be taken into account, sir; it really can't. . . . H'm!" (The speaker coughed.)

" Pray believe me, Gavríla Antónitch,"—returned the fat man's voice:—" judge for yourself, whether I don't know the course of affairs here."

" Who else should know it, Nikolái Eremyéitch: you are the first person here, sir, one may say. Well, and how is it to be, sir; "—pursued the voice which was unfamiliar to me:—" what shall we decide on, Nikolái Eremyéitch?—permit me to inquire."

"What shall we decide on, Gavríla Antónitch? The matter depends on you, so to speak: you don't care about it, apparently."

"Good gracious, Nikolái Eremyéitch: what are you saying? I'm a merchant, a merchant; my business is to buy. That's what we merchants stand on, Nikolái Eremyéitch,—I may say."

"Eight rubles,"—said the fat man, pausing between his words.

A sigh was audible.

"Nikolái Eremyéitch, you are pleased to demand an awful lot."

"I can't do otherwise, Gavríla Antónitch,— 't is impossible,—I speak as in the presence of the Lord God."

A silence ensued.

I raised myself softly on my elbow, and peered through a crack in the partition. The fat man was sitting with his back toward me. Facing him, sat a merchant, about forty years old, gaunt and pale, as though smeared with fasting butter.[1] He kept incessantly running his fingers through his beard, blinking his eyes very rapidly, and twitching his lips.

"The crops are wonderfully fine this year, sir,"—he began again:—"all the time I have

[1] That is, with oil, butter being forbidden during the Great Fast (Lent), because it is an animal product. The wealthy replace it with costly nut-oils; the poor, with sunflower-seed and other strong, coarse oils.—TRANSLATOR.

been driving I have been admiring them. Beginning with Vorónezh, they are splendid, first-class, sir, I may say."

" The crops really are n't bad,"—replied the head of the counting-house: " but, surely, you know, Gavríla Antónitch, that the autumn gives good promise, but 't will be as the spring wills."

" That 's a fact, Nikolái Eremyéitch: everything is according to God's will; you have deigned to speak the exact truth. . . . . But I think your visitor has waked up, sir."

The fat man turned round . . . . and listened.

" No, he 's asleep. However, possibly you know . . . . ."

He stepped to the door.

" No, he 's asleep,"—he repeated, and returned to his place.

" Well, and how is it to be, Nikolái Eremyéitch? "—began the merchant again:—" we really must close the bargain. . . . Let it go at that then, Nikolái Eremyéitch, let it go at that,"—he went on, winking uninterruptedly: " two grey bank-notes and one white note for your grace, and yonder—" (he nodded his head in the direction of the manor-house) "—six rubles and a half. Shall we strike hands on it? "

" Four grey notes," [1]—replied the clerk.

---

[1] The (old-time) grey bank-note was for two rubles; the white, one ruble.—TRANSLATOR.

" Come, three."

" Four grey without the white."

" Three, Nikolái Eremyéitch."

" Three and a half, not a kopék less."

" Three, Nikolái Eremyéitch."

" Don't even mention such a thing, Gavríla Antónitch."

" What a pig-headed fellow! "—muttered the merchant.—" I think I 'd better settle the matter myself with the lady.'"

" As you like,"—replied the fat man:—" you ought to have done it long ago. Really, what 's the use of bothering yourself? . . 'T is much better so! "

" Come, enough! Stop that, Nikolái Eremyéitch. Why, he flies into a rage on the instant! I was only saying that, you know, to hear myself talk."

" No, really now . . . ."

" Have done, I tell you. . . . I was joking, I tell you. Come, take three and a half,—what can one do with you? "

" I ought to take four, but, like a fool, I have been too hasty,"—muttered the fat man.

" So, yonder, at the house, six and a half, sir, Nikolái Eremyéitch,—the grain is sold for six and a half? "

" Six and a half, yes, you 've already been told."

" Well, then, strike hands on the bargain, Nikolái Eremyéitch—" (the merchant smote the clerk's palm with his outspread fingers) "—and God bless us!" (The merchant rose.)—"So now I 'll be off to the lady mistress, dear little father, Nikolái Eremyéitch, and order them to announce me, and I 'll say: ' Nikolái Eremyéitch has settled on six and a half, ma'am.' "

" Say just that, Gavríla Antónitch."

" And now, please to accept."

The merchant handed over to the clerk a small bundle of paper-money, made his bow, shook his head, took up his hat with two fingers, twitched his shoulders, imparted to his figure an undulating motion, and left the room, his boots squeaking decorously. Nikolái Eremyéitch walked to the wall, and, so far as I could observe, began to sort over the money which the merchant had given him. A red head with thick side-whiskers thrust itself in at the door.

" Well, how are things? "—inquired the head: —" Is everything as it should be? "

" Yes."

" How much? "

The fat man waved his hand with vexation, and pointed toward my room.

" Ah, very good! " returned the head, and vanished.

The fat man went to the table, sat down, opened a book, got out his abacus,[1] and began to

[1] The merchants still use the counting-frame, rattling the colored balls on the wires to and fro with marvellous rapidity, and thus performing the most intricate calculations, instead of using paper and pencil.—TRANSLATOR.

deduct and add the bone balls, using for the purpose not his forefinger, but the third finger of his right hand, which is more decorous.

The clerk on duty entered.

" What dost thou want? "

" Sidór has arrived from Goloplyók."

" Ah! well, call him in. Stay, stay. . . . . Go first, and see whether that strange gentleman in there is still asleep, or whether he has waked up."

The clerk on duty cautiously entered my room. I laid my head on my game-bag, which served me in lieu of a pillow, and shut my eyes.

" He's asleep,"—whispered the office-boy, returning to the office.

The fat man emitted a growl between his teeth.

" Well, summon Sidór,"—he said at last.

Again I raised myself on my elbow. There entered a peasant of huge stature, about thirty years of age, healthy, rosy-cheeked, with light, chestnut hair, and a small, curly beard. He prayed before the holy pictures, bowed to the head clerk, took his cap in both hands, and straightened himself up.

" Good-day, Sidór,"—said the fat man, rattling his counting-frame.

" Good . . day, Nikolái Eremyéitch."

" Well, and how's the road? "

" Good, Nikolái Eremyéitch. A trifle muddy." (The peasant spoke neither fast nor loudly.)

" Is thy wife well? "

" What should ail her! She's all right."

The peasant heaved a sigh, and thrust out his leg. Nikolái Eremyéitch stuck his pen behind his ear, and blew his nose.

" Well, and why hast thou come? "—he went on with his questions, stuffing his checked hand-kerchief into his pocket.

" Why, we've heard, Nikolái Eremyéitch, that carpenters are required from us."

" Well, what of that—aren't there any among you, I'd like to know? "

" Of course there are, Nikolái Eremyéitch: ours is a forest hamlet,—you know well. But 't is our working season, Nikolái Eremyéitch."

" Your working season! That's precisely the point: you're fond enough of working for other folks, but you don't like to work for your own mistress. . . . It amounts to the same thing! "

" The work is the same, in fact, Nikolái Eremyéitch . . . . but . . . ."

" Well? "

" The pay is . . . you know . . . . awfully . . ."

" As if it wasn't enough for you! Just see, how spoiled you are! Get out with you! "

" Yes, and I want to say, Nikolái Eremyéitch, there's only work enough for a week, but we shall be detained a month. First the material

gives out, and then we'll be sent into the garden
to clean the paths.'"

"A pretty reason! The mistress herself has
deigned to command, and 't is not for me and
thee to make any argument."

Sidór said nothing for a while, and began to
shift from foot to foot.

Nikolái Eremyéitch twisted his head on one
side, and rattled the reckoning-beads vigorously.

"Our . . . . peasants . . . . Nikolái Eremyéitch . . . . ." began Sidór at last, stammering over every word:—"have ordered me to give
your grace . . . and here—there are . . . ."
(He thrust his huge hand into the breast of his
long coat, and began to draw thence a folded
towel with red patterns.)

"What dost thou mean, what dost thou mean,
fool? hast thou gone crazy, pray?"—the fat man
hastily interrupted him.—"Go, go to me in my
cottage,"—he continued, almost pushing out the
astounded peasant;—"ask there for my wife
. . . . she'll give thee some tea; I'll be there
directly. Go thy way! Pray, hast not thou been
told to go?"

Sidór left the room.

"What a . . . . . . bear!"—muttered the
head clerk after him, shook his head, and began
again on his reckoning-frame.

Suddenly shouts of: "Kupryá! Kupryá! you
can't upset Kupryá!"—resounded on the street

and on the porch, and a little later there entered the office a man of low stature, consumptive in appearance, with a remarkably long nose, large, impassive eyes, and a very haughty mien. He was clad in a tattered old great-coat, Adelaïda colour,—or, as it is called among us, ' oddeloida,' —with a velveteen collar and tiny buttons. He carried a fagot of firewood on his shoulders. Five house-serfs crowded around him, and all were shouting, " Kupryá! you can't upset Kupryá! Kupryá has been appointed to be stove-tender! " But the man in the great-coat with the velveteen collar paid not the slightest attention to the turbulence of his companions, and never changed countenance. With measured steps he walked to the stove, flung down his burden, rose, pulled a snuff-box from his rear pocket, opened his eyes wide, and began to stuff his nose with powdered melilot mixed with ashes.

When the noisy horde entered, the fat man was on the point of frowning, and half-rose from his seat; but on seeing what the matter was, he smiled, and merely ordered them not to shout: " There's a sportsman asleep in the next room," —said he.

" What sportsman? "—asked a couple of the men, with one accord.

" A landed proprietor."

" Ah! "

" Let them go on with their row,"—said the

man with the velveteen collar, flinging wide his arms:—"what do I care! if only they don't touch me. I have been appointed to be the stove-tender!"

"The stove-tender! the stove-tender!"—joyously chimed in the crowd.

"The mistress ordered it,"—he went on, shrugging his shoulders:—"but just you wait . . . . you'll be appointed swineherds yet. But that I have been a tailor, and a good tailor, and learned my business in the best workshops in Moscow, and sewed for 'Enerals,' is something that nobody can take away from me. But what are you putting on big airs about? . . . what? you are sluggards, drones, nothing more. If they were to set me free, I shouldn't die of hunger, I shouldn't go to destruction; give me a passport,—and I'll pay in a good quit-rent, and satisfy the masters. But how about you? You'd perish, perish like flies, and that's all about it!"

"Thou hast lied,"—interrupted a pockmarked young fellow with white eyebrows and lashes, a red neckerchief, and ragged elbows:—"thou hast had a passport, and the masters never saw a kopék of quit-rent from thee, and thou hast never earned a penny for thyself: thou hadst all thou could do to drag thy legs home, and ever since that time thou hast lived in one wretched kaftan."

"And what is one to do, Konstantín Narkízitch!"—retorted Kupriyán:—"if a man has fallen in love, and perished and gone to ruin? Do thou first go through my experience, Konstantín Narkízitch, and then thou mayest condemn me."

"And a pretty person thou didst choose to fall in love with! a regular monster!"

"No, don't say that, Konstantín Narkízitch."

"But to whom art thou making that assertion? Why, I 've seen her myself; last year, in Moscow, I saw her with my own eyes."

"Last year she really had gone off a bit in her looks,"—remarked Kupriyán.

"No, gentlemen, see here,"—interposed, in a scornful and negligent voice, a tall man, with a face sprinkled with pimples, and all curled and oiled,—probably the valet:—"here now, suppose we let Kupriyán Afanásitch sing his little song. Come on, begin, Kupriyán Afanásitch!"

"Yes, yes!"—chorused the others.—"Hey, there, Alexandra! thou hast caught Kupryá! there 's no denying it. . . . Sing away, Kupryá! —Gallant lad, Alexandra!" (House-serfs, by way of showing greater tenderness, frequently use the feminine terminations in speaking of a man.)—"Pipe up!"

"This is not the place to sing,"—retorted Kupryá, firmly:—"this is the gentry's counting-house."

"But what business is that of thine? I do believe thou art aiming at becoming head of the office thyself!"—replied Konstantín, with a coarse laugh.—" It must be so!"

" Everything is in the power of the mistress,"—remarked the poor fellow.

" See, see what he's aiming at! See there, what sort of a fellow he is! Phew! phew! ah!"

And all burst into violent laughter, and some even jumped. The one who laughed loudest of all was a wretched lad of fifteen, probably the son of an aristocrat among the house-serfs; he wore a waistcoat with bronze buttons, a neck-cloth of a lilac hue, and had already succeeded in acquiring a portly belly.

" Hearken now, Kupryá, confess,"—began Nikolái Eremyéitch, in a self-satisfied way, visibly in a sweat and affected:—" 't is a bad thing to be the stove-tender? Is n't it now? a trifling business, altogether, I fancy?"

" And what of that, Nikolái Eremyéitch,"—remarked Kupriyán:—" here you are now our head clerk, 't is true; there 's no disputing that, it 's a fact; but you were under the ban once, and lived in a peasant's hut yourself too."

" Just look out for thyself, don't forget thyself before me,"—the fat man interrupted snappishly:—" they 're jesting with thee, fool; thou should feel it, and be grateful, fool, that they bother themselves about thee, fool."

" It just slipped off my tongue, Nikolái Eremyéitch, pardon me. . . ."

" Just so, 't was a slip of the tongue."

The door flew wide open, and a page ran in.

" Nikolái Eremyéitch, the mistress summons you to her presence."

" Who is with the mistress? "—he asked the page.

" Aksínya Nikítishna and a merchant from Venyóvo."

" I 'll be there in a minute. And as for you, brothers,"—he went on, in a persuasive voice:— " you 'd better take yourself away from here, with the newly appointed stove-tender: nobody knows when the German may drop in, and he 'll complain on the spot."

The fat man smoothed his hair, coughed into his hand almost entirely covered by his coat-sleeve, hooked up his coat, and wended his way to the mistress, straddling his legs far apart as he walked. After waiting a while, the whole horde followed him, including Kupryá. My old acquaintance, the clerk on duty, was left alone. He started to clean a pen, but fell asleep where he sat. Several flies immediately took advantage of the fortunate opportunity, and stuck themselves around his mouth. A mosquito alighted on his forehead, planted its little legs in regular order, and slowly plunged its whole sting into his soft body. The former red-head with side-whiskers made its appearance again from behind the door, stared and stared, and entered the office with its decidedly ugly body.

" Fediúshka! Hey, Fediúshka! thou art eternally asleep! "—said the head cashier.

The clerk on duty opened his eyes, and rose from his chair.

" Has Nikolái Eremyéitch gone to the mistress? "

" He has, Vasíly Nikoláitch."

" Ah! ah! "—thought I:—" 't is he, the head cashier! "

The head cashier began to walk about the room. However, he stole about, rather than walked, and, altogether, bore a strong resemblance to a cat. From his shoulders depended an old, black dress-coat, with very narrow tails; he kept one hand on his breast, and with the other kept constantly clutching at his tall, tight stock of horsehair, and twisting his head in a strained way. He wore goatskin boots, and trod very softly.

" Squire Yagúshkin was asking for you to-day,"—added the clerk on duty.

" H'm,—was he? What did he say? "

" He said that he was going to Tiutiúrevo this evening, and would expect you. ' I must have a talk with Vasíly Nikoláitch about a certain matter,' says he,—but what the business was, he did n't mention: ' Vasíly Nikoláitch will know,' says he.

" H'm! "—returned the head cashier, and went to the window.

" Is Nikolái Eremyéitch in the office? "—rang out a loud voice in the anteroom, and a tall man, evidently in a rage, with an irregular, but bold and expressive face, and quite neatly dressed, strode over the threshold.

" Is n't he here? "—he asked, casting a swift glance around.

" Nikolái Eremyéitch is with the mistress,"—replied the cashier.—" Tell me what you want, Pável Andréitch: you can tell me. . . . What do you wish? "

" What do I want? You wish to know what I want? " (The cashier nodded his head in a sickly way.)—" I want to teach him a lesson, the fat-bellied wretch, the vile tale-bearing slanderer. . . I 'll teach him to tell tales! "

Pável flung himself on a chair.

" What do you mean, what do you mean, Pável Andréitch? Calm yourself. . . . . . Are n't you ashamed? Don't you forget of whom you are speaking, Pável Andréitch! "—stammered the cashier.

" Of whom I 'm speaking? And what do I care, that he has been appointed head clerk! A pretty one they have picked out for the appointment, I must say! They 've actually let the goat into the vegetable-garden, one may say! "

" That will do, that will do, Pável Andréitch, that will do! stop that . . . what nonsense! "

" Well, Lísa Patríkyevna,[1] go wag thy tail and fawn! . . . I 'll wait for him,"—said Pável, angrily, and banged his hand down on the table. —" Ah, yonder he comes,"—he added, glancing out of the window:—" talk of the devil. . . . You are welcome! " (He rose.)

Nikolái Eremyéitch entered the office. His face was beaming with satisfaction, but at the sight of Pável he grew somewhat embarrassed.

" Good day, Nikolái Eremyéitch,"—said Pável, significantly, as he moved slowly toward him:—" good day."

The head clerk made no reply. The merchant's face made its appearance in the doorway.

" Why don't you deign to answer me? "— went on Pável.—" But, no . . . . no,"—he added:—" that 's not the point; nothing is to be gained by shouting and abuse. No, you 'd better tell me amicably, Nikolái Eremyéitch, why do you persecute me? why do you want to ruin me? Come, speak, speak."

" This is not the place to give you an explanation,"—replied the head clerk, not without agitation:—" and this is not the proper time. Only, I must confess that one thing amazes me: whence have you derived the idea that I want to ruin you, or that I am persecuting you? And how, in short, can I persecute you? You are not in my office."

[1] The Russian equivalent of " Reynard the Fox."—TRANSLATOR.

"I should think not,"—replied Pável:—"that is the last straw! But why do you dissimulate, Nikolái Eremyéitch?—You understand me, you see."

"No, I don't understand you."

"Yes, you do."

"No,—by God, I don't!"

"And he swears into the bargain! Well, then, if it has come to that, tell me: come, you 're not afraid of God! Well, why can't you let the poor girl alone? What do you want of her?"

"Of whom are you speaking, Pável Andréitch?"—asked the fat man, with feigned amazement.

"Eka! you don't know, I suppose? I'm speaking of Tatyána. Have the fear of God before your eyes—what are you avenging yourself for? Shame on you: you are a married man, you have children as old as I am. But I mean nothing else than . . . . . I want to marry: I am acting honourably."

"How am I to blame in the matter, Pável Andréitch? Our mistress will not allow you to marry: 't is her ladyship's will! What have I to do with that?"

"What have you to do with it? and have n't you and that old witch, the housekeeper, entered into collusion, I 'd like to know? Are n't you a calumniator, I 'd like to know, hey! Tell me, are n't you accusing an innocent young girl of

all sorts of fictitious things? It is n't thanks to
your gracious offices, I suppose, that she has been
appointed dish-washer instead of laundress?
And they don't beat her, and keep her clad in
striped ticking, by your grace? . . . Shame on
you, shame on you, you old man! The first you
know, you 'll be smitten with paralysis. . . .
You will have to answer to God."

"Curse away, Pável Andréitch, curse away.
. . . . You won't have a chance to curse long! "

Pável flared up.

"What? Hast thou taken it into thy head
to threaten me? "—he began angrily.—" Dost
think that I fear thee? No, brother, thou hast
got hold of the wrong man! what have I to fear?
. . . . I can earn my bread anywhere. . But
thou—that 's another matter! Thou canst do
nothing but dwell here, and slander, and
steal. . . ."

" Just see how conceited he is! "—the clerk interrupted him, beginning to lose patience:—" a
medical man, a plain medical man, an ordinary
little peasant-surgeon; and just listen to him,—
whew, what an important personage! "

" Yes, I am a peasant-surgeon, and were it not
for that, your gracious person would now be rotting in the cemetery. . . . And 't was the Evil
One who prompted me to cure him,"—he added,
between his teeth.

" Thou didst cure me? . . . . No, thou didst

try to poison me; thou didst give me a potion of aloes,"—put in the clerk.

" And what if nothing but aloes would take effect on thee? "

" Aloes are prohibited by the medical authorities,"—went on Nikolái:—" I can enter a complaint about thee yet. . . . Thou didst try to murder me—that's what! But the Lord did not permit."

" That will do, that will do, gentlemen,"—the cashier tried to speak. . . .

" Stop that! "—shouted the clerk.—" He tried to poison me! Dost thou understand that? "

" Much I care! . . . . Hearken to me, Nikolái Eremyéitch,"—said Pável in desperation:— " For the last time I entreat thee . . . . thou hast forced me to it—my patience is exhausted. Leave us in peace, dost thou understand? otherwise, by God, 't will be the worse for some one of you, I tell thee."

The fat man flew into a rage.

" I 'm not afraid of thee,"—he yelled:—" dost hear me, booby! I mastered thy father, I broke his horns for him,—let that be a warning for thee, look out! "

" Don't remind me of my father, Nikolái Eremyéitch, don't remind me of him! "

" Get out! I don't take any orders from thee! "

" Don't remind me of him, I tell thee! "

"And I tell thee, don't forget thyself. . . . As the mistress does not need thee in thy line, if she had to choose between us two, thou wouldst not be the winner, my dear little dove! No one is permitted to mutiny, look out!" (Pável was quivering with rage.)—"And the girl Tatyána is getting what she deserves. . . . Just wait, and she 'll get something worse."

Pável darted forward with upraised arms, and the clerk rolled heavily to the floor.

"Handcuff him, handcuff him!"—moaned Nikolái Eremyéitch. . . .

I will not undertake to describe the end of this scene. I am afraid I have wounded the sensibilities of the reader as it is.

I returned home the same day. A week later, I learned that Mme. Losnyakóff had retained both Pável and Nikolái in her service, but had banished the girl Tatyána; evidently, she was not wanted.

XII

THE WOLF

I WAS driving from the chase one evening alone in a racing-drozhky.[1] I was eight versts from my house; my good mare was stepping briskly along the dusty road, snorting and twitching her ears from time to time; my weary dog never quitted the hind wheels, as though he had been tied there. A thunder-storm was coming on. In front of me a huge, purplish cloud was slowly rising from behind the forest; overhead, and advancing to meet me, floated long, grey clouds; the willows were rustling and whispering with apprehension. The stifling heat suddenly gave way to a damp chill; the shadows swiftly thickened. I slapped the reins on the horse's back, descended into a ravine, crossed a dry brook all overgrown with scrub-willows, ascended a hillock, and drove into the forest. The road in front of me wound along amid thick clumps of hazel-bushes, and was already inundated with gloom; I advanced with difficulty. My drozhky

[1] The racing-drozhky, which is also much used in the country, consists of a plank attached (without springs) to four small wheels. The driver sits astride of the plank, with his feet on the shafts.—TRANSLATOR.

jolted over the firm roots of the centenarian oaks and lindens, which incessantly intersected the long, deep ruts—the traces of cart-wheels; my horse began to stumble. A strong wind suddenly began to drone aloft, the trees grew turbulent, big drops of rain pattered sharply and splashed on the leaves, the lightning and thunder burst forth, the rain poured in torrents. I drove on at a foot-pace and was speedily compelled to halt; my horse had stuck fast. I could not see a single object. I sheltered myself, after a fashion, under a wide-spreading bush. Bent double, with my face wrapped up, I was patiently awaiting the end of the storm, when, suddenly, by the gleam of a lightning flash, it seemed to me that I descried a tall figure on the road. I began to gaze attentively in that direction—the same figure sprang out of the earth, as it were, by my side.

" Who is this? "—asked a sonorous voice.

" Who are you yourself? "

" I 'm the forester here."

I mentioned my name.

" Ah, I know; you are on your way home? "

" Yes; but you see what a storm . . . ."

" Yes, it is a thunder-storm,"—replied the voice. A white flash of lightning illuminated the forester from head to foot; a short, crashing peal of thunder resounded immediately afterward. The rain poured down with redoubled force.

THE WOLF

"It will not pass over very soon,"—continued the forester.

"What is to be done?"

"I 'll conduct you to my cottage, if you like,"—he said abruptly.

"Pray do."

"Please take your seat."

He stepped to the mare's head, took her by the bridle, and turned her from the spot. We set out. I clung to the cushion of the drozhky, which rocked like a skiff at sea, and called my dog. My poor mare splashed her hoofs heavily through the mire, slipping and stumbling: the forester swayed to right and left in front of the shafts, like a spectre. Thus we proceeded for quite a long time. At last my guide came to a halt.—"Here we are at home, master,"—he said, in a calm voice. A wicket-gate squeaked, several puppies began to bark in unison. I raised my head and by the glare of the lightning I descried a tiny hut, in the centre of a spacious yard, surrounded with a wattled hedge.[1] From one tiny window, a small light cast a dull gleam. The forester led the horse up to the porch, and knocked at the door. "Right away! Right away!"—resounded a shrill little voice, and a patter of bare feet became audible, the bolt

---

[1] In central and southern Russia, where timber is scarce, long boughs of trees are plaited into picturesque hedges, to replace board fences. Farm buildings frequently have their walls of the same wattled work.—TRANSLATOR.

screeched, and a little girl about twelve years of
age, clad in a miserable little smock, girt about
with a bit of list, and holding a lantern in her
hand, made her appearance on the threshold.

" Light the gentleman,"—he said to her:—
" and I will put his carriage under the shed."

The little lass glanced at me, and entered the
cottage. I followed her. The forester's cottage
consisted of a single room, smoke-begrimed, low-
ceiled, and bare, without any sleeping-shelf over
the oven, and without any partitions; a tattered
sheepskin coat hung against the wall. On the
wall-bench lay a single-barrelled gun; in one
corner trailed a heap of rags; two large pots
stood beside the oven. A pine-knot was burning
on the table, sputtering mournfully, and was on
the point of going out. Exactly in the middle
of the room hung a cradle, suspended from the
end of a long pole.[1] The little maid extinguished the lantern, seated herself on a tiny
bench, and began to rock the cradle with her left
hand, while with her right she put the pine-knot
in order. I looked about, and my heart grew sad:
it is not cheerful to enter a peasant's hut by

[1] A stout, long, supple sapling is fixed firmly against one wall.
The tip is in the middle of the room, and from it is suspended
the cradle, which depresses it, and acts as a natural spring. The
cradle may be (like Peter the Great's, which is in the museum
of the Kremlin in Moscow) of strong linen, distended by poles
at the ends, hammock-fashion; or even of a splint basket. It is
often rocked from a distance by means of a rope attached to one
of the angle-cords.—TRANSLATOR.

night. The baby in the cradle was breathing heavily and rapidly.

" Is it possible that thou art alone here? "—I asked the little girl.

" Yes,"—she articulated, almost inaudibly.

" Art thou the forester's daughter? "

" Yes,"—she whispered.

The door creaked, and the forester stepped across the threshold, bending his head as he did so. He picked up the lantern from the floor, went to the table, and ignited the wick.

" Probably you are not accustomed to a pine-knot,"—he said, tossing back his curls.

I looked at him. Rarely has it been my fortune to behold such a fine, dashing fellow. He was tall of stature, broad-shouldered, and splendidly built. From beneath his dripping shirt, which was open on the breast, his mighty muscles stood forth prominently. A curly black beard covered half of his surly and manly face; from beneath his broad eyebrows, which met over his nose, small brown eyes gazed gallantly forth. He set his hands lightly on his hips, and stood before me.

I thanked him, and asked his name.

" My name is Fomá " (Thomas), he replied —" but my nickname is ' The Wolf.' " [1]

" Ah, are you The Wolf? "

[1] In the Government of Orel, a solitary, surly man is called a wolf (biriúk).

I gazed at him with redoubled interest. .
From my Ermolái and from others I had often
heard about the forester—The Wolf, whom all
the peasants round about feared like fire.   According to their assertions, never before had
there existed in the world such a master of his
craft.   " He gives no one a chance to carry
off trusses of brushwood, no matter what the
hour may be; even at midnight he drops down
on you like snow on your head, and you need
not think of offering resistance—he 's as strong
and as crafty as the devil. . . . And it 's impossible to catch him by any means whatever;
neither with liquor, nor with money; he won't
yield to any allurement.   More than once good
men have made preparations to put him out of
the world; but no, he does n't give them a chance."

That was the way the neighbouring peasants
expressed themselves about The Wolf.

" So thou art The Wolf,"—I repeated.—
" I 've heard of thee, brother.   They say that
thou givest no quarter to any one."

He pulled his axe from his girdle, sat down
on the floor, and began to chop a pine-knot.

" Hast thou no housewife? "—I asked him.

" No,"—he replied, and brandished his axe
fiercely.

" She is dead, apparently."

" No—yes—she is dead,"—he added, and
turned away.

THE WOLF

I said nothing; he raised his eyes, and looked at me.

"She ran away with a petty burgher who came along,"—he remarked, with a harsh smile. The little girl dropped her eyes; the baby waked up, and began to cry; the girl went to the cradle. —"There, give him that,"—said The Wolf, thrusting into her hand a dirty horn.[1]—"And she abandoned him,"—he went on, in a low tone, pointing at the baby. He walked to the door, and turned round.

"Probably, master,"—he said,—"you cannot eat our bread; and I have nothing but bread."

"I am not hungry."

"Well, suit yourself. I would boil the samovár for you, only I have no tea. . . I'll go and see how your horse is getting along."

He went out and slammed the door. I surveyed my surroundings. The hut seemed to me more doleful than before. The bitter odour of chilled smoke oppressed my breathing. The little girl did not stir from her place, and did not raise her eyes; from time to time, she gave the cradle a gentle shove, or timidly hitched up on her shoulder her smock, which had slipped down; her bare legs hung motionless.

"What is thy name?"—I asked.

---

[1] The Russian peasants use a cow's horn, with a cow's teat tied over the tip, as a nursing-bottle. The dried teats are for sale in the common street-markets.—TRANSLATOR.

"Ulíta,"—she said, drooping her sad little face still lower than before. The forester entered, and seated himself on the wall-bench.

"The thunder-storm is passing over,"—he remarked, after a brief silence;—"if you command, I will guide you out of the forest."

I rose. The Wolf picked up his gun, and inspected the priming.

"What is that for?"—I inquired.

"They are stealing in the forest. They're felling a tree at the Hare's Ravine,"—he added, in reply to my glance of inquiry.

"Can it be heard from here?"

"It can from the yard."

We went out together. The rain had ceased. Heavy masses of cloud were piled up in the distance, long streaks of lightning flashed forth from time to time; but over our heads the dark-blue sky was visible; here and there, little stars twinkled through the thin, swiftly-flying clouds. The outlines of the trees, besprinkled with rain and fluttered by the wind, were beginning to stand forth from the gloom. We began to listen. The forester took off his cap, and dropped his eyes. "The—there," he said suddenly, and stretched out his arm;—"you see what a night they have chosen."

I heard nothing save the rustling of the leaves. The Wolf led my horse out from under the shed. —"But I shall probably let him slip, as matters stand,"—he added aloud.—" I 'll go with thee, may I? "—" All right,"—he replied, and backed the horse.—" We 'll catch him in a trice, and then I 'll guide you out. Come on! "

We set off, The Wolf in advance, I behind him. God knows how he found the road, but he rarely halted, and then only to listen to the sound of the axe.—" You see,"—he muttered between his teeth.—" You hear? do you hear? "—" But where? "—The Wolf shrugged his shoulders. We descended into a ravine, the wind died down for an instant, measured blows distinctly reached my ear. The Wolf glanced at me, and shook his head. On we went, over the wet ferns and nettles. A dull, prolonged roar rang out. . . . . . .

" He has felled it,"—muttered The Wolf.

In the meantime the sky had continued to clear; it was almost light in the forest. We made our way out of the ravine at last.—" Wait here,"—whispered the forester to me, crouched down, and raising his gun aloft, vanished among the bushes. I began to listen with strained intentness. Athwart the constant noise of the wind, I thought I discerned faint sounds not far away: an axe was cautiously hewing branches, a horse was neighing.

" Where art thou going? Halt! "—the iron voice of The Wolf suddenly thundered out. Another voice shrieked plaintively, after the fashion of a hare. . . . . . A struggle began.—" Thou

li-iest, thou li-iest,"—The Wolf kept repeating,
panting the while; "thou shalt not escape."—I
dashed forward in the direction of the noise, and
ran to the scene of battle, stumbling at every
step. Beside the felled tree on the ground, the
forester was tumbling about: he held the thief
beneath him, and was engaged in binding the
man's hands behind his back with his girdle. I
stepped up. The Wolf rose, and set him on his
feet. I beheld a peasant, soaked through, in
rags, with a long, dishevelled beard. A miserable little nag, half-covered with a small, stiff
mat, stood hard by, with the running-gear of a
peasant-cart. The forester uttered not a word;
the peasant, also, maintained silence, and merely
shook his head.

"Let him go,"—I whispered in The Wolf's
ear.—"I will pay for the tree."

The Wolf, without replying, grasped the
horse's foretop with his left hand; with his right
he held the thief by the girdle.—"Come, move
on, booby!"—he ejaculated surlily.

"Take my axe yonder,"—muttered the peasant.—"Why should it be wasted?"—said the
forester, and picked up the axe. We started. I
walked in the rear. . . . . . . The rain began to
descend again in a drizzle, and soon was pouring
in torrents. With difficulty we made our way
to the cottage. The Wolf turned the captured
nag loose in the yard, led the peasant into the

house, loosened the knot of the girdle, and seated him in one corner. The little girl, who had almost fallen asleep by the oven, sprang up, and began to stare at us in dumb affright. I seated myself on the wall-bench.

"Ekh, what a downpour!"—remarked the forester.—"We must wait until it stops. Would n't you like to lie down?"

"Thanks."

"I would lock him up in the lumber-room, on account of your grace,"—he went on, pointing at the peasant,—"but, you see, the bolt . . . . ."

"Leave him there,—don't touch him,"—I interrupted The Wolf.

The peasant darted a sidelong glance at me. I inwardly registered a vow that I would save the poor fellow at any cost. He sat motionless on the wall-bench. By the light of the lantern I was able to scrutinise his dissipated, wrinkled face, his pendent, yellow eyebrows, his thin limbs. . . . The little girl lay down on the floor, at his very feet, and fell asleep again. The Wolf sat by the table, with his head propped on his hand. A grasshopper was chirping in one corner. . . . The rain beat down upon the roof, and dripped down the windows; we all maintained silence.

"Fomá Kúzmitch,"—began the peasant, suddenly, in a dull, cracked voice:—"hey, there, Fomá Kúzmitch!"

MEMOIRS OF A SPORTSMAN

"What dost thou want?"

"Let me go."

The Wolf made no reply.

"Let me go. . . . . Hunger drove me to it. . . . . Let me go."

"I know you,"—retorted the forester, grimly. "You're all alike in your village,—a pack of thieves."

"Let me go,"—repeated the peasant.—"The manager . . . . we're ruined, that's what it is . . . . . . let me go!"

"Ruined! . . . . No one ought to steal!"

"Let me go, Fomá Kúzmitch . . . . . don't destroy me. Thy master, as thou knowest, will devour me, so he will."

The Wolf turned away. The peasant was twitching all over, as though racked with fever. He kept shaking his head, and his breath came irregularly.

"Let me go,"—he repeated, with mournful desperation.—"Let me go, for God's sake, let me go! I'll pay, that I will, God is my witness. As God is my witness, hunger drove me to it . . . . . the children were squalling, thou knowest how it is thyself. 'T is hard on a man, that it is."

"All the same, don't go a-thieving."

"My horse,"—went on the peasant,— "there's my horse, take it if thou wilt . . . . 't is my only beast . . . . . let me go!"

" Impossible, I tell thee. I, also, am a sub-ordinate; I shall be held responsible. And it is n't right, either, to connive at thy deed."

" Let me go! Poverty, Fomá Kúzmitch, pov-erty, that 's what 's the trouble . . . . . let me go! "

" I know thee! "

" But do let me go! "

" Eh, what 's the use of arguing with thee; sit still, or I 'll give it to thee, understand? Dost thou not see the gentleman? "

The poor fellow dropped his eyes. . . . . The Wolf yawned, and laid his head on the table. The rain had not stopped. I waited to see what would happen.

The peasant suddenly straightened himself up. His eyes began to blaze, and the colour flew to his face.—" Well, go ahead, devour! Go ahead, oppress! Go ahead! "—he began, screw-ing up his eyes, and dropping the corners of his lips:—" Go ahead, damned murderer of the soul, drink Christian blood, drink! "

The forester turned round.

" I 'm talking to thee,—to thee, Asiatic, blood-drinker,—to thee! "

" Art drunk, that thou hast taken it into thy head to curse! "—said the forester in amaze-ment.—" Hast thou gone crazy? "

" Drunk! . . . . It was n't on thy money, thou damned soul-murderer, thou wild beast, beast, beast! "

" Akh, thou . . . . I 'll give it to thee ! "

" What do I care? 'T is all one to me—I shall perish anyway; what can I do without a horse? Kill me—it comes to the same thing; whether with hunger, or thus, it makes no difference. Let everything go to destruction: wife, children, —let them all perish. . . . But just wait, thou shalt hear from us ! "

The Wolf half-rose to his feet.

" Kill, kill,"—the peasant began again, in a savage voice: " Kill, go ahead, kill. . . . ." (The little girl sprang hastily from the floor, and riveted her eyes on him.)—" Kill, kill ! "

" Hold thy tongue ! "—thundered the forester, and advanced a couple of strides.

" Enough, that will do, Fomá Kúzmitch,"—I shouted:—" let him alone. . . . Don't bother with him. . . ."

" I won't hold my tongue,"—went on the unfortunate man.—" It makes no difference how he murders me. Thou soul-murderer, thou wild beast, hanging is too good for thee. . . . . . But just wait a bit. . . Thou hast not long to vaunt thyself! They 'll strangle thy throat for thee. Just wait a bit ! "

The Wolf seized him by the shoulder. . . I rushed to the rescue of the peasant.

" Don't touch us, master ! "—the forester yelled at me.

I did not fear his threats, and was on the point

of stretching forth my arm when, to my extreme amazement, with one twist of the hand, he tore the girdle from the peasant's elbows, grasped him by the collar, banged his cap down over his eyes, flung open the door, and thrust him out.

" Take thyself and thy horse off to the devil! " —he shouted after him:—" and look out, another time I 'll . . . ."

He came back into the cottage, and began to poke about in the corner.

" Well, Wolf,"—I said at last;—" thou hast astonished me. I see that thou art a splendid young fellow."

" Ekh, stop that, master,"—he interrupted me, with vexation.—" Only, please don't tell about it. Now I 'd better show you your way," —he added;—" because you can't wait for the rain to stop."

The wheels of the peasant's cart rumbled through the yard.

" You see, he has dragged himself off,"—he muttered;—" but I 'll give it to him! "

Half an hour later he bade me farewell on the edge of the forest.

XIII

I HAVE already had the honour of introducing
to you, my indulgent readers, several of my gentlemen neighbours; permit me now, therefore, by
the way (for us writers everything is " by the
way "), to make you acquainted with two more
landed proprietors, on whose property I have
often hunted, extremely worthy, well-intentioned individuals, who enjoy the universal respect of several counties.

I will first describe to you retired Major-General Vyátcheslaff Ilariónovitch Khvalýnsky.
Picture to yourselves a tall man, finely propor-
tioned in days gone by, but now somewhat pot-
bellied, though not in the least decrepit, not even
aged, a man of mature years, in the very prime
of life, as the expression is. His once regular
and still agreeable features have changed somewhat, 't is true; his cheeks have grown pendent
in jowls, numerous radiating wrinkles have clus-
tered round his eyes, some teeth are already miss-
ing, as Saadi said, according to Púshkin's statement; his light-chestnut hair—all that is left
of it, at least—has turned lilac, thanks to a
preparation bought at the Romný horse-fair

TWO LANDED PROPRIETORS

from a Jew who gave himself out as being an Armenian; but Vyátcheslaff Ilariónovitch steps out alertly, has a ringing laugh, clanks his spurs, twirls his moustache, calls himself, in short, an old cavalryman, while it is a well-known fact that real old men never call themselves old men. He generally wears a surtout buttoned up to the throat, a tall stock with a starched collar, and trousers of a speckled grey, of military cut; and he wears his hat straight on his forehead, leaving the whole back of his head outside. He is a very kind-hearted man, but with decidedly peculiar ideas and habits. For example: he is utterly unable to treat noblemen who are not wealthy nor of official rank as his equals. In talking with them, he generally gazes at them askance, with his cheek leaning heavily on his firm, white collar, or he will suddenly take and illumine them with a clear, impassive stare, maintain silence, and wriggle the whole of his skin on his head under his hair; he even pronounces his words in a different way, and does not say, for instance: "Thanks, Pável Vasílitch," or: "Please come hither, Mikhaílo Ivánitch," but: "T'anks, Páll 'Asílich," or: "Pe-ease come hither, Mikhal' 'Vánitch." And he behaves in a still stranger manner to people who stand on the lower rungs of the society ladder: he does not look at them at all, and before announcing his wishes to them, or giving them an order, he repeats several times in succession, with a preoccupied and dreamy aspect: " *What* 's thy name? . . . *What* 's thy name? "— generally with a remarkably sharp emphasis on the first word, " what," and uttering the rest very rapidly, which imparts to his whole mode of speech a pretty close likeness to the cry of the male quail. He is a frightfully fussy man, and a skinflint, and a bad farmer: he has taken to himself as manager a retired quartermaster, a Little Russian, a remarkably stupid man. However, in the matter of estate management, no one in our parts has, so far, outdone a certain important Petersburg official, who, on perceiving from his overseer's report that grain-kilns on his estate were subject to frequent conflagrations, which caused the loss of much grain, issued stringent orders that, henceforth, no sheaves were to be placed in the kiln until the fire was completely extinguished. This same dignitary once took it into his head to sow all his fields with poppies, in consequence of what was, apparently, an extremely simple calculation. " Poppies are more expensive than rye," said he: " therefore, it will be more profitable to plant poppies." And he also commanded his peasant women to wear kokóshniki [1] made after a pattern

---

[1] The *kokóshnik* is the round, coronet-shaped head-dress of the peasant women. It varies in shape and appellation in different districts, *kokóshnik* being the generic name. The *kíka* is tall and pointed in front, like the mitre of a Roman or an Anglican bishop. —Translator.

sent from Petersburg; and, as a matter of fact, to this day the peasant women on his estates wear the round-coronet head-dress . . . . . only, it runs up to a sharp point at the front, like a kíka. . . . . But let us return to Vyátcheslaff Ilariónovitch. Vyátcheslaff Ilariónovitch is terribly fond of the fair sex, and, just as soon as he catches sight of a pretty person on the boulevard of his county town, he instantly sets out in pursuit of her, but also immediately takes to limping —which is a noteworthy circumstance. He is fond of playing cards, but only with persons of a lower class; they say to him, " Your Excellency," and he can chide them and scold them to his heart's content. But when he chances to play with the Governor, or with some official personage, a wonderful change takes place in him: he smiles, and nods his head, and stares with all his eyes,—he is fairly redolent of honey. . . . . He even loses without complaint. Vyátcheslaff Ilariónovitch reads little, and while he is reading he keeps his moustache and his brows in incessant motion, as though a wave were flowing over his face, from below upward. Especially noteworthy is this undulating movement on Vyátcheslaff Ilariónovitch's face, when he happens (in the presence of visitors, of course) to run through the columns of the *Journal des Débats*. He plays quite an important part at the elections, but declines the honourable post of Marshal of the Nobility out of parsimony.—" Gentlemen," —he generally says to the nobles who approach him, and he says it in a voice filled with patronage and independence:—" I am greatly obliged for the honour; but I have decided to devote my leisure to solitude."—And, having uttered these words, he turns his head several times to right and left, and then, with dignity, drops his chin and his cheeks on his neckerchief. In his youth, he served as adjutant to some distinguished person, whom he never mentions otherwise than by his baptismal name and patronymic; 't is said, that he took upon himself not alone the duties of an adjutant,—that, for instance, donning his full parade-uniform, and even fastening the hooks, he steamed his superior in the bath—but one cannot believe every rumour. Moreover, General Khvalýnsky is not fond of referring to his career in the service, which is, on the whole, rather odd; it appears, also, that he has not been to war. General Khvalýnsky lives in a small house, alone; he has never experienced conjugal bliss in his life, and therefore, to this day, he is regarded as a marriageable man, and even a good catch. On the other hand, his housekeeper, a woman of three-and-thirty years, black-eyed, blackbrowed, plump, fresh, and with a moustache, wears starched gowns on week-days, and puts on muslin sleeves of a Sunday.[1] Vyátcheslaff

---

[1] " Sleeves," in central and southern Russia, means the chemise, of which the *full sleeves* and the guimpe-like neck portion are

TWO LANDED PROPRIETORS

Ilariónovitch is happy at great, formal dinners, given by landed proprietors in honour of governors and other powers that be: then he is, so to speak, thoroughly in his element. On such occasions he sits, if not at the right hand of the Governor, at least not very far from him; at the beginning of the banquet, he is generally engaged in maintaining the sense of his own dignity, and throwing himself back in his chair, but not turning his head, he drops a sidelong look upon the round napes and standing collars of the guests; on the other hand, toward the end of the dinner, he cheers up, begins to smile on all sides (he has been smiling in the direction of the Governor from the very beginning of the feast), and sometimes even proposes a toast in honour of the fair sex, " the ornament of our planet," as he phrases it. General Khvalýnsky also makes a far from bad appearance at all solemn and public sessions, examinations, assemblies, and exhibitions; and he is, moreover, a master-hand at approaching an ecclesiastical dignitary and receiving his blessing.[1] Vyátcheslaff Ilariónovitch's people do not shout and create an uproar when they meet another carriage at the cross-roads or ferries, and in other similar circumstances; on visible above the *sarafán*, or full frock. The *sarafán* itself has no sleeves, and its upper edge passes under the arms, from which narrow straps pass over the shoulders.—TRANSLATOR.

[1] Considerable art and practice are required to receive a bishop's hand properly and gracefully, on the upturned palms, held in boat-shape, raise it reverently to the lips, and kiss it, in return for the cross of blessing bestowed.—TRANSLATOR.

the contrary, when pushing people aside, or calling the carriage, they say, in an agreeable gut-
tural baritone voice: " Pray, pray, allow General
Khvalýnsky to pass through," or: " General
Khvalýnsky's equipage." . . . . Khvalýnsky's
equipage is, truth to tell, of rather ancient fashion; his lackeys' liveries are decidedly threadbare
(that they are grey, with trimmings of red braid,
it is hardly necessary to mention);[1] the horses,
also, are somewhat aged, and have seen hard service; but Vyátcheslaff Ilariónovitch makes no
pretensions to foppishness, and does not even
consider it becoming to his rank to throw dust in
the eyes of the public. Khvalýnsky is not endowed with any special gift of language, or, perhaps, he has no opportunity to display his eloquence, because he not only will not tolerate dis-
cussion, but even rejoinder in general, and sedu-
lously avoids all long conversations, particularly
with young persons. 'T is safer, in fact; otherwise, with the present generation of men, a calamity might befall: they might immediately become insubordinate and lose their reverence.
In the presence of persons of superior rank,
Khvalýnsky maintains silence, in the majority
of cases, but to persons of a lower rank, whom,
evidently, he despises, but with whom alone
he consorts, he makes abrupt and harsh speeches,

---

[1] The regular prerogative of a general: the cape-coats are trimmed
with rows of scarlet braid.—TRANSLATOR.

incessantly employing expressions such as the
following: " But what you are saying is nonsense;" or: "I find myself compelled, in
short, m' dea' si', to call to your attention," or:
" But, after all, you ought to know with whom
you are dealing," and so forth. He is especially dreaded by postmasters, permanent jus-
tices of the peace, and station superintendents.
He never invites any one to his own house,
and lives, so says rumour, after the fashion of
a miser. Notwithstanding all which, he is a very
fine landed proprietor,—" an ex-soldier, a disinterested man, with principles, *vieux grognard,*"
his neighbours say of him. One governmental
procurator permits himself to smile when General Khvalýnsky's excellent and solid qualities
are referred to in his presence,—but what will
not envy do! . . . . . .

However, let us pass on to the other landed
proprietor.

Mardáry Apollónitch Stegunóff does not resemble Khvalýnsky in any respect. 'T is not
likely that he was ever in the service anywhere,
and he never has regarded himself as a beauty.
Mardáry Apollónitch is a short, plump, bald old
gentleman, with a double chin and a good-sized
paunch. He is very hospitable and fond of jesting; he lives, as the saying is, at his ease; winter
and summer he goes about in a wadded striped
dressing-gown. In one point only does he agree

with General Khvalýnsky: he, also, is a bachelor. He has five hundred souls.[1] Mardáry Apollónitch busies himself with his estate in a pretty superficial manner; ten years ago he purchased from Butenop, in Moscow,—in order not to be behind his age,—a threshing-machine, locked it up in a barn, and relapsed into contentment. Occasionally, on a fine summer's day, he will order his racing-drozhky to be harnessed up, and will drive to the fields to take a look at the grain and to pluck corn-flowers. Mardáry Apollónitch lives thoroughly in the ancient fashion. And his house, also, is of ancient construction: the anteroom, as is fitting, reeks of kvas, tallow candles, and leather; there, also, on the right, is a buffet, with smoke-pipes[2] and towels; in the dining-room are family portraits, flies, a huge pot of geranium, and a jingling piano; in the drawing-room are three couches, three tables, two mirrors, and a hoarse clock with carved hands of blackened enamel and bronze; in the study are a table with papers, a screen of bluish hue with small pictures pasted on it which have been cut from various publications of the last century, a cupboard filled with stinking books, spiders, and black dust, a fat arm-chair, an Italian window, a nailed-up door leading to the garden. . . . .

[1] That is, male serfs. The women were not included in the Revision Lists.—TRANSLATOR.

[2] For preparing the samovár: the pipes, leading to the outer air, being attached to the samovár at need.—TRANSLATOR.

TWO LANDED PROPRIETORS

In a word, everything is as it should be. Mardáry
Apollónitch has a multitude of domestics, and all
are garbed in ancient fashion: in long, blue
kaftans, with tall collars, trousers of a muddy
colour, and short, yellowish waistcoats. They
address visitors as: "Dear little father." His
farming operations are presided over by a peasant bailiff, who has a beard that spreads all over
his sheepskin coat; his house, by a wrinkled and
stingy old woman, with her head enveloped in
a light-brown kerchief. In Mardáry Apollónitch's stables stand thirty horses, of varied quality; he drives out in a home-made calash,
weighing one hundred and fifty puds.[1] He receives visitors very cordially, and entertains
them gloriously,—that is to say, thanks to the stu-
pefying properties of Russian cookery, he de-
prives them of all possibility of occupying themselves with anything but preference until close
on nightfall. But he himself never occupies
himself with anything whatsoever, and has even
ceased to peruse the "Dream-book." But there
are still a good many landed proprietors of that
sort, among us in Russia—the question is: To
what end have I begun to speak about him,
and why? . . . . So now, permit me, in lieu of
a reply, to tell you the story of one of my visits
to Mardáry Apollónitch.

I arrived at his house in summer, about seven

[1] A pud is a little over thirty-six pounds.—TRANSLATOR.

o'clock in the evening. The Vigil service had just ended,[1] and the priest, evidently a very timid young man, who had not been long out of the theological seminary, was sitting in the drawing-room, near the door, on the very edge of a chair. Mardáry Apollónitch received me very affectionately, according to his wont: he sincerely rejoiced over every guest, and, in general, he was a very kind-hearted man. The priest rose, and picked up his hat.

" Wait, wait, bátiushka," [2] said Mardáry Apollónitch, without releasing my hand.— " Don't go. . I have ordered them to bring thee some vódka."

" I don't drink, sir,"—murmured the priest in confusion, and flushed scarlet to his very ears.

" What nonsense! "—replied Mardáry Apollónitch:—" Míshka! Yúshka! vódka for the bátiushka! "

Yúshka, a tall, thin old man of eighty years, entered with a wine-glass of vódka on a dark-painted tray variegated with spots of flesh-colour.

The priest began to refuse.

[1] The All-Night Vigil, consisting of Vespers (or Compline) and Matins, which is obligatory before the celebration of the morning Liturgy, may be read in an unconsecrated building, even by a layman, and is not infrequently requested by the devout.—Translator.

[2] "Dear little father": the form of address for ecclesiastics, in particular.—Translator.

TWO LANDED PROPRIETORS

"Drink, bátiushka, don't put on airs, it isn't nice,"—remarked the squire, reprovingly.

The poor young man obeyed.

"Well, now thou mayest go, bátiushka."

The priest began to bow his farewell.

"Come, very good, very good, go along. . . . A very fine man,"—went on Mardáry Apolló-nitch, glancing after him:—"I'm very well satisfied with him, only—he's young yet. But how about you, my dear fellow? [1] . . . . How are you? what have you been doing with yourself? Let's go out on the balcony—just see what a magnificent evening it is."

We went out on the balcony, sat down, and began to chat. Mardáry Apollónitch glanced down, and suddenly became frightfully agitated.

"Whose hens are those? whose hens are those?"—he began to shout:—"whose hens are those running in the garden? . . . . Yúshka! Yúshka! go, find out instantly whose hens those are running in the garden!—Whose hens are those? How many times have I forbidden it— how many times have I spoken about that?"

Off rushed Yúshka.

"What disorder!" Mardáry Apollónitch kept reiterating:—"'t is frightful!"

The unlucky hens, as I now recall the circumstances, two speckled and one white with a crest,

[1] *Bátiushka,* in addressing social equals, has this sense.—TRANSLATOR.

303

continued to stalk about very quietly under the apple-trees, now and then giving vent to their feelings by a prolonged cackling, when suddenly Yúshka, hatless and stick in hand, and three other adult house-serfs, all fell upon them energetically and in unison. The fun began. The hens shrieked, flapped their wings, cackled deafeningly; the house-serfs rushed about, stumbled, and fell; the master, from the balcony, yelled like a fanatic: " Catch, catch, catch, catch them! catch, catch, catch them! . . . Whose hens are those—whose hens are those?"

At last, one of the men succeeded in seizing the crested hen and squeezing her throat to the ground, and, at the same moment, over the hedge of the garden leaped a little girl of eleven years, all dishevelled and with a switch in her hand.

" Hey, so that's the owner of the hens!" exclaimed the squire, triumphantly:—" Ermíl the coachman's hens! There, he has sent his Natálka to drive them home—I wonder why he did n't send Parásha,"—added the squire in an undertone, and grinned significantly.—" Hey, Yúshka! drop those hens: catch Natálka for me."

But before the panting Yúshka could overtake the frightened little maid, the housekeeper made her appearance from somewhere or other, grasped her by the arm, and slapped her several times on the back.

TWO LANDED PROPRIETORS

" That 's right, that 's right,"—chimed in the squire,—" te, te, te! te, te, te!—But take the hens away from her, Avdótya,"—he added in a loud voice, and, turning to me with a radiant countenance:—" What a hunt, was n't it, my dear fellow, hey?—Just look, I 'm all in a perspiration."

And Mardáry Apollónitch burst out laughing.

We remained on the balcony. The evening really was extremely fine.

Tea was served.

" Pray tell me,"—I began,—" Mardáry Apollónitch: are those your homesteads transplanted over yonder, on the highway, beyond the ravine? "

" Yes—why? "

" How could you do such a thing, Mardáry Apollónitch? Why, that 's a sin. The peasants have been assigned to wretched, cramped little huts; there is n't a single tree to be seen all around; there 's not even a pond; there is only one well, and that is good for nothing. Is it possible that you could find no other spot?—And 't is said that you have even deprived them of their old hemp-patches? "

" But what is one to do with the boundary-survey? " replied Mardáry Apollónitch. " This is where the survey sits with me." (He pointed to the nape of his neck.) " And I foresee no profit whatever from that survey. And as for

my having deprived them of their hemp-patches
and ponds, or not having dug any there,—why
my dear fellow, I know my own business. I 'm
a simple man,—I proceed in the good old way
In my opinion, if one is a gentleman—why, let
him be a gentleman; if he 's a peasant—then let
him be a peasant.—So there you have it."

Of course, it was impossible to make any an
swer to such a clear and convincing evasion.

" And besides,"—he went on:—" they are
bad, disgraced peasants. There are two families
there, in particular: my late father, even,—God
grant him the kingdom of heaven!—did not fa
vour them, was very far from favouring them
And I take this as a sign, I must tell you: if the
father is a thief, the son is a thief also; you may
say what you like—oh, blood, blood is a great
thing!"

In the meantime the air had become perfectly
quiet. Only now and then did the breeze blow
in gusts, and, as it died down, for the last time
around the house, it wafted to our ears measured
blows which followed one another quickly, re
sounding from the direction of the stables. Mar
dáry Apollónitch had only just raised his saucer
of tea to his lips, and was already inflating his
nostrils, without which, as every one knows, not
a single genuine primitive Russian imbibes tea
—but he paused, listened, nodded his head, took
a sip, and setting the saucer on the table, he an

ticulated, with the most good-natured of smiles, and as though involuntarily keeping time to the blows: " Tchiúki-tchiúki-tchiúk! tchiúki-tchiúk! tchiúki-tchiúk!"

"What's that?"—I asked in amazement.

"Why, by my orders, that mischievous monkey is being whipped yonder.—Do you know Vásya the butler?"

"What Vásya?"

"Why, the one who waited on us at dinner a little while ago. The one who wears such huge side-whiskers."

The fiercest wrath could not have withstood the clear and gentle gaze of Mardáry Apollónitch.

"What do you mean, young man, what do you mean?"—he said, shaking his head. "Am I a malefactor, I'd like to know, that you stare at me like that? Whom he loveth, he chasteneth: you know that yourself."

A quarter of an hour later I bade Mardáry Apollónitch farewell. As I drove through the village, I caught sight of Vásya the butler. He was walking along the street, nibbling nuts. I ordered my coachman to stop the horses, and called him to me.

"Well, brother, so they have been flogging thee to-day?"—I asked him.

"And how do you know?"—answered Vásya.

"Thy master told me."

" The master himself? "

" What did he order thee to be whipped for? "

" I deserved it, dear little father, I deserved it. We are not whipped for trifles; that's not the custom with us—naw, naw. Our master is not that sort of a man; our master—why, you could n't find such another master in the whole government."

" Drive on! "—I said to my coachman. " Here's ancient Russia for you! "—I said to myself, on my homeward journey.

MEMOIRS OF A SPORTSMAN

CONTENTS

II

MEMOIRS OF A SPORTSMAN

I

LEBEDYÁN [1]

ONE of the chief advantages of hunting, my dear readers, consists in this—that it forces you to go about constantly from place to place, which is extremely agreeable for an unoccupied man. In sooth, it is not always a very cheerful matter, especially in rainy weather, to roam about on the country roads, to go " cross-country," to stop any peasant you may meet with the question: " Hey there, my good fellow! how can we get to Mordóvka? " and in Mordóvka inquire of a dull-witted peasant wife (for the labourers are all in the fields) whether it is far to the posting-stations on the highway, and how one is to reach them,—and, after having traversed ten versts, instead of a posting-house, to find one's self in the extremely dilapidated little manorial hamlet of Khudobúbnovo, to the intense surprise of a whole herd of swine, buried to their ears in the dark-

---

[1] Lebedyán is the capital of the Government of Tambóff, and is celebrated for its horse-fair, to which cavalry remount-officers resort to purchase horses.—TRANSLATOR.

brown mud in the very middle of the street, and
not at all expecting to be disturbed. Neither is it
exhilarating to cross quaking little bridges, descend into ravines, and ford swampy brooks; it is
not exhilarating to drive—for whole days to drive
along the greenish sea of the highways, or, which
God forbid, to get bemired for several hours in
front of a striped mile-post with the figures " 22 "
on one side and " 23 " on the other; it is not exhilarating to subsist for weeks on eggs, milk, and
the vaunted sour rye bread. . . . But all these
discomforts and misadventures are redeemed by
another sort of benefits and pleasures. However
let us begin the story.

After all that has been said above, there is no
necessity for my explaining to the reader, how I
happened to come upon Lebedyán, five years
ago, at the very height of the annual fair.[1] We
sportsmen may drive forth, some fine morning
from our more or less hereditary estates, with the
intention of returning by the evening of the following day, and, little by little, without ceasing
to shoot woodcock, finally arrive on the blessed
shores of the Petchóra River. Moreover, every
one who is fond of dog and gun is a passionate
respecter of the most noble animal in the world
—the horse. Thus, I arrived at Lebedyán, put
up at the inn, changed my clothes, and set out

[1] There are innumerable annual fairs in Russia, in the governments and districts.—TRANSLATOR.

4

for the fair. (The waiter, a long and gaunt
young fellow, of twenty years, with a sweet,
nasal tenor voice, had already contrived to impart to me, that Their [1] Illustrious Highness,
Prince N., remount-officer of the * * * regiment,
was stopping at our inn; that many other gentlemen had arrived; that the gipsies sang in the
evenings, and that "Pan Tvardovsky" [2] was
being played in the theatre; that horses, 't was
said, were selling for high prices,—and good
horses had been brought to the fair.)

On the fair-ground, in interminable rows,
stretched peasant carts, and behind the carts
were horses of all possible sorts: trotters, stud-
farm horses, *bitiúki* [3] draught-horses, posting-
horses, and plain peasant-horses. Some, well-
fed and smooth, assorted according to colour,
covered with horse-cloths of varied hues, hitched
short to a high rack, were apprehensively rolling
their eyes backward at the too familiar whips of
their owners, the horse-dealers; the horses of
landed proprietors, sent by noblemen of the
steppes one or two hundred versts away, under
the supervision of some decrepit coachman and
two or three hard-headed grooms, were flourishing their long necks, stamping their hoofs, and
gnawing the posts out of boredom; roan Vyátka

[1] The respectful form for *His*.—TRANSLATOR.
[2] The dramatisation of a novel of that title, published (1859)
by Jospeh Ignatius Krasçewsky (1812–1887).—TRANSLATOR.
[3] See note on p. 101, Vol. I.

horses pressed close to one another; in majestic immobility, like lions, stood the broad-haunched trotters with waving tails and shaggy pasterns, dapple-grey, black, and brown. Experts paused respectfully in front of them. In the streets formed by the carts, people of all sorts of classes, stature, and aspect thronged: the horse-dealers, in blue kaftans and tall caps, craftily watched and waited for purchasers; goggle-eyed, curly-haired gipsies darted to and fro like madmen, inspected the horses' teeth, lifted their feet and tails, shouted, wrangled, served as go-betweens, cast lots, or fawned upon some remount-officer in military cap and cloak with beaver collar. A stalwart kazák towered up astride of a lank gelding with a deer-neck and sold it, " in one lot," that is to say, with saddle and bridle. Peasants, in sheepskin coats tattered under the armpits, descended by tens on a cart, drawn by a horse which must be " tried," or, somewhere apart, with the aid of a cunning gipsy, they bargained until they were worn out, struck hands on the deal a hundred times in succession, each insisting on his own price, while the object of their dispute, a wretched little nag covered with a shrunken rug, merely blinked its eyes, as though the matter did not concern it. . . . And, in fact, was it not all the same to it who would beat it! Broad-browed landed proprietors with dyed moustaches, and an expression of dignity

on their faces, in braided jackets and camelot
peasant-coats, worn with an arm in one sleeve,
condescendingly conversed with pot-bellied merchants in beaver hats and green gloves. Officers
of various regiments were discussing matters
there also; a remarkably tall cuirassier, of German extraction, was coolly asking a horse-dealer
how much he expected to get for that sorrel
horse. A fair-haired young hussar, nineteen
years of age, was picking out a trace horse to go
with an emaciated pacer; a postilion, in a low-
crowned hat, surrounded with peacock feathers,
in a brown long-coat, and with leather mittens
thrust into his narrow, greenish belt, was looking
for a shaft-horse for a tróïka. The coachmen
plaited their horses' tails, dampened their manes,
and gave deferential advice to their masters. On
concluding the trade, they hastened to the eating-
tavern or the dram-shop, according to their
means. . . . And all this uproar, shouting,
bustle, wrangling, reconciliations, cursing, and
laughter was going on in mud knee-deep. I
wanted to buy a tróïka of fairly good horses, for
my britchka: mine were beginning to shirk their
work. I found two, but could not manage to
match them with a third. After dinner, which
I will not undertake to describe (even Æneas
knew how unpleasant it is to recall bygone woe),
I set out for the so-called coffee-house, where
every evening the remount-officers, stud-farm

men, and other visitors were wont to assemble. In the billiard-room, drowned in floods of leaden-hued tobacco-smoke, were about a score of men. There were free-and-easy young landed proprietors in braided hussar-jackets and grey trousers, with long mutton-chop whiskers and pomaded moustaches, gazing loftily and boldly about; other nobles in kazák coats, with remarkably short necks and little eyes swimming in fat, were painfully snoring away there also; the merchants sat apart, " pricking up their ears," as the saying is; the officers chatted freely among themselves. Prince N., a young man of five and twenty, with a merry and somewhat scornful face, clad in a coat thrown open on the breast, a red silk shirt, and full velvet trousers, was playing billiards; he was playing with Viktór Khlopakóff, a retired lieutenant.

Ex-Lieutenant Viktór Khlopakóff, a thin and swarthy little man of thirty years, with thin, black hair, brown eyes, and a short, tip-tilted snub-nose, is a diligent attendant upon elections and fairs. He skips as he walks, sets his arms akimbo swaggeringly, wears his cap on one ear, and turns up the sleeves of his military coat, lined with bluish calico. Mr. Khlopakóff understands how to curry favour with the wealthy Petersburg rakes, smokes, drinks, and plays cards with them, and addresses them as " thou." Why they favour him is a good deal of a puzzle.

LEBEDYÁN

He is not clever, he is not even amusing; neither is he useful as a buffoon. To tell the truth, they treat him in an amicably-careless way, like a good-natured but empty-pated fellow; they haunt his society for the space of two or three weeks, and then suddenly cease even to bow to him, and he, also, no longer bows to them. A peculiarity of Lieutenant Khlopakóff consists in this: that he uses one and the same expression constantly for the period of a year, sometimes two years, appropriately and inappropriately, an expression not in the least amusing, but which, God knows why, sets every one to laughing. Eight years ago, he used to say, at every step, "My respects to you, I thank you most humbly," and his patrons of that epoch fairly expired with laughter every time and made him repeat, "My respects"; then he began to use a rather complicated expression, "No, now you know, keskese—that proves proved," and with the same dazzling success; two years later, he invented a new quaint saying, "*Ne vous goryatchez*[1] *pas,* you man of God, sewn up in a sheepskin," and so forth. And lo! as you see, his far from ingenious little remarks supply him with food, drink, and apparel. (He has long ago squandered his property, and lives exclusively at the expense of his friends.) Observe, that he possesses positively no other amiable

[1] *Goryatchitsya,* to get heated, angry.—TRANSLATOR.

9

characteristics: 't is true, that he will smoke a hundred pipes of Zhúkoff [1] tobacco a day, and, when playing billiards, he raises his right foot higher than his head, and as he takes aim, wriggles his cue violently in his hand;—well, but not every one is an admirer of such merits. He is a good drinker, also . . . . but it is difficult to distinguish one's self in Russia by that means. . . . In a word, his success is a complete mystery to me. . . . There may be one reason for it, perhaps: he is cautious, never tells tales out of school, never utters a bad word about anybody.

" Come,"—I thought, at sight of Khlopakóff: —" what 's his catchword at present? "

The Prince pocketed the white.

" Thirty and nothing," roared the consumptive marker.

The Prince drove the yellow ball into the furthest pocket with a crash.

" Ekh! " approvingly grunted, with his whole body, a fat merchant, who sat in one corner at a tottering little table on a single leg,—grunted and quailed. But, luckily, no one noticed him. He sighed and stroked his beard.

" Thirty-six and very little! " [2] shouted the marker through his nose.

[1] Equivalent to " navy-plug "—the coarsest sort of tobacco.— TRANSLATOR.

[2] The game alluded to is a game with five balls. It is a fashionable fad for the marker to say, instead of " thirty and nothing," " thirty and very little," even substituting " nobody " for " nothing."—TRANSLATOR.

LEBEDYÁN

" Well, what do you think of that, brother? "
the Prince asked Khlopakóff.

" Why, of course, rrrrakaliooon, a regular
rrrrakaliooon! " [1]

The Prince burst out laughing.

" What, what 's that? say it again! "

" Rrrrakalioon! " repeated the ex-lieutenant,
conceitedly.

" That 's the word! " I thought.

The Prince pocketed the red.

" Ekh! that 's wrong, Prince, that 's wrong,"
—suddenly stammered the fair-haired young
officer with the reddened eyes, the tiny nose, and
the childishly sleepy face. . . . " You don't play
right . . . . you ought to have . . . . that 's
wrong! "

" How so? " asked the Prince over his
shoulder.

" You ought to have . . . . you know . . . .
with a triplet. . . ."

" Really? " muttered the Prince through his
teeth.

" Well, Prince, shall we go to the gipsies to-
day? " put in the embarrassed young man.
" Styóshka is going to sing. . . . Iliúshka . . . ."

The Prince did not answer him.

" Rrrrakaliooon, my good fellow," said Khlopakóff, cunningly screwing up his left eye.

[1] *Rakalíya* means a scamp or good-for-nothing. But it has no
apparent connection with this nonsense.—TRANSLATOR.

And the Prince burst into a roar of laughter.

"Thirty-nine and nothing," proclaimed the marker.

"All . . . . just look now, what I 'm going to do with that yellow . . . ." Khlopakóff wriggled the cue in his hand, took aim, and missed.

"Eh, rrakalioon," he shouted wrathfully.

Again the Prince laughed.

"What, what, what?"

But Khlopakóff did not wish to repeat his word: one must coquet a bit.

"You have made a miscue,"—remarked the scorer.—"Please to chalk . . . . Forty and very little!"

"Yes, gentlemen," said the Prince, turning to the whole assembly, but not looking at any one in particular:—"you know, we must call out Verzhembítzkaya."

"Of course, of course, without fail," several visitors vied with each other in exclaiming, being wonderfully flattered by the possibility of replying to the remark of a Prince:—"Verzhembítzkaya. . . ."

"Verzhembítzkaya is a capital actress,—far better than Sopnyakóva," squeaked a rascally-looking man, with moustache and spectacles, from one corner. Unhappy man! in secret he was sighing violently for Mme. Sopnyakóff, but the Prince did not deign even to look at him.

LEBEDYÁN

"Wai-er, hey, a pipe," said a tall man in a stock, with a regular face, and the most noble of miens,—but yet by all the signs, a card-sharper.

The waiter ran for a pipe, and on his return announced to His Illustrious Highness: " Positilion Baklága is asking for you, sir."

" Ah! well, order him to wait, and give him some vódka."

" Very good, sir."

Baklága (The Flask), as I was afterward told, was the nickname of a young, handsome, and extremely petted postilion; the Prince was fond of him, gave him horses, drove races with him, spent whole nights with him. . . . You would not recognise that Prince—formerly a scapegrace and a spendthrift—now. . . . How puffed up, tight-laced, and perfumed he is! How engrossed in the service,—and, chief of all, how sober-minded!

But the tobacco-smoke began to irritate my eyes. After listening to Khlopakóff's exclamation and the Prince's shout of laughter, for the last time, I betook myself to my chamber, where, on a narrow divan, with broken springs, covered with horse-hair, and with a tall, curved back, my man had already made up my bed.

On the following day I inspected the horses in the yards, and began with the well-known horse-dealer Sítnikoff. Through a wicket I entered a courtyard sprinkled with sand. In front

13

of the wide-open door of the stable stood the
proprietor himself, a man no longer young, tall
and stout, in a short-coat of peasant shape,
lined with hareskin, and with a standing collar
turned down. On perceiving me, he slowly
moved to meet me, held his cap above his
head with both hands, and said, in a singsong
tone:

" Ah, our respects to you. I suppose you
want to look at horses?"

" Yes, I came to look at horses."

" And what sort, exactly, may I venture to
inquire?"

" Show me what you have."

" With pleasure."

We entered the stable. Several white curs
rose from the hay, and ran to us, wagging their
tails; a long-bearded goat stalked off to one side,
in displeasure; three grooms, in strong but dirty
sheepskin coats, bowed to us in silence. On the
right and the left, in cleverly raised stalls, stood
about thirty horses, splendidly groomed and
cleaned. Pigeons were hopping along the cross-
beams and cooing.

" For what, that is to say, do you require the
horse: for driving or the stud-farm? "—Sítnikoff
asked me.

" Both for driving and for the stud."

" I understand, sir, I understand, sir, I understand, sir," articulated the horse-dealer, pausing between his words.—" Pétya, show the gentleman Ermine."

We went out into the yard.

" Would n't you like to have a bench brought out from the house? . . . . You don't want it? . . . . As you please."

Hoofs thundered over planks, a whip cracked, and Pétya, a man of forty years, pockmarked and swarthy, sprang forth from the stable, in company with a grey and fairly well-made stallion, allowed him to rear up, ran with him a couple of times round the yard, and cleverly pulled him up at the show spot. Ermine stretched himself out, snorted with a whistling sound, flirted his tail, twitched his muzzle, and gazed askance at us.

" A well-trained bird! " thought I.

" Give him his head, give him his head," said Sítnikoff and fixed his eyes on me.

" What do you think of him, sir? "—he asked, at last.

" He is n't a bad horse—his fore legs are not sound."

" His legs are splendid! "—returned Sítnikoff, with conviction.—" And his loins . . . . be so good as to look . . . . a regular oven; you might even sleep your fill on them."

" His cannon-bones are long."

"What do you call long—good gracious! Run, Pétya, run, and at a trot, trot, trot . . . . don't let him gallop."

Again Pétya ran round the yard with Ermine. We all maintained silence.

"Well, put him back in his place," said Sítnikoff:—"and bring out Falcon."

Falcon, a stallion black as a beetle, of Dutch pedigree, with a sloping back, and lean, proved to be little better than Ermine. He belonged to the category of horses of which sportsmen say that "they hack and cut and take prisoner,"— that is to say, in action they turn out and fling out their fore legs to the right and left, but make little headway.[1] Middle-aged merchants admire that sort of horses: their gait is suggestive of the dashing pace of an alert waiter; they are good in single harness, for a drive after dinner; stepping out cock-a-hoop, curving their necks, they zealously drag the clumsy drozhky, laden with a coachman who has eaten himself into a state of numbness, and a squeezed merchant[2] suffering from heart-burn, and a lymphatic merchant's wife, in a sky-blue silk sleeved coat, and

[1] Dishing, in English.—TRANSLATOR.
[2] The smaller the drozhky, the more popular and stylish it is. If the passengers bulge over, and the coachman, through his own admired fat and the tightness of the drozhky, has to straddle the dashboard with his knees, and keep his feet on iron supports outside, the height of fashion and happiness is assured. If not fat enough naturally, cushions are added to secure the "broad seat" which Russians consider stylish and safe.—TRANSLATOR.

16

with a lilac kerchief on her head.[1] I declined
Falcon. Sítnikoff showed me several other
horses. . . . At last one, a dappled-grey stallion,
of Voiéikoff breed, pleased me. I could not refrain from patting him on the forelock with
pleasure. Sítnikoff immediately feigned indifference.

"Does he drive well?"—I inquired.   (The
word "go" is not used of trotters.)

"Yes,"—replied the horse-dealer, calmly.

"Cannot I see him?" . . . .

"Why not?—certainly, sir. Hey, there,
Kúzya, put Overtaker in a drozhky."

Kúzya, the jockey, a master of his business,
drove past us three times along the street. The
horse went well, did not break, did not sway, his
action was free, he held his tail up and stepped
out firmly, with a long, regular stride.

"And what do you ask for him?"

Sítnikoff mentioned a preposterous price.
We had begun to chaffer there, in the street,
when, suddenly, from round the corner thundered swiftly a splendidly matched posting-
tróïka, and drew up in dashing fashion in front
of the gate to Sítnikoff's house. In the dandified sporting-cart sat Prince N.; beside him
towered Khlopakóff. The Flask was driving,—

---

[1] Old-fashioned women of the merchant class, no matter how
wealthy they may be, still wear no bonnets, but merely a silk kerchief on the head.—TRANSLATOR.

and how he drove! he could have got through an earring, the rascal! The brown side-horses, small, vivacious, black-eyed, black-legged, were fairly on fire, fairly gathered themselves together with nervous tension; if one had whistled, they would have vanished like a shot. The dark-bay shaft-horse stood firmly, with his neck curved like a swan's, his chest thrown forward, his legs like arrows; he shook his head and proudly screwed up his eyes.—Good! 'T was like some one taking a drive on the bright festival (Easter).

"Your Illustrious Highness! Deign to favour us!" cried Sítnikoff.

The Prince sprang from his cart. Khlopakóff slowly alighted on the other side.

"Good morning, brother. . . . Have you any horses?"

"Of course I have for Your Illustrious Highness. Be pleased to enter.—Pétya, bring out Peacock,—and let Meritorious be made ready. And you and I, dear little father,"—he continued, addressing me:—"will settle our business another time. . . . Fómka, a bench for His Illustrious Highness."

Peacock was led out from a special stable, which I had not noticed before. The powerful dark-brown horse fairly reared with all four feet in the air. Sítnikoff even turned his head away and narrowed his eyes.

"Ugh, rrakalion!"—proclaimed Khlopakóff. —"Zhemsà" (J'aime ça).

The Prince laughed.

Peacock was halted with difficulty: he fairly dragged the stablemen round the yard; at last they pressed him against the wall. He snorted, quivered, and gathered himself together, but Sítnikoff still teased him, flourishing a whip at him.

" Where art thou staring? I 'll give it to thee! ugh! " said the horse-dealer, with affectionate menace, himself involuntarily admiring his horse.

" How much? "—asked the Prince.

" For Your Illustrious Highness, five thousand."

" Three."

" Can't be done, Your Illustrious Highness, upon my word—"

" You 've been told three, rrakalion," put in Khlopakóff.

I did not wait to see the end of the bargain, and went away. At the extreme end of the street I noticed at the gate of a greyish little house a large sheet of paper pasted up. At the top was a pen-and-ink sketch of a horse, with a tail in the shape of a trumpet and an endless neck, and under the horse's hoofs stood the following words, written in old-fashioned script:

" For sale here, horses of various colours, brought to the Lebedyán fair from the well-known stud-farm on the steppe of Anastásey Ivánitch Tchernobáy, landed proprietor of Tambóff. These horses are of excellent form, perfectly trained, and of gentle disposition. Messrs. Buyers will be so good as to ask for Anastásey Ivánitch himself: should Anastásey Ivánitch be absent, then ask for his coachman, Nazár Kubýshkin. We beg the Messrs. Buyers to honour an old man."

I halted. " Come," I thought, " I 'll take a look at the horses of the well-known horse-breeder, Mr. Tchernobáy."

I tried to enter the wicket-gate, but, contrary to custom, I found it locked. I knocked.

" Who 's there? . . . . A buyer? "—piped a feminine voice.

" Yes."

" Directly, dear little father, directly."

The wicket opened. I beheld a peasant woman about fifty years of age, her hair uncovered, in boots and a sheepskin coat open on the breast.

" Please to enter, benefactor, and I 'll go at once and announce you to Anastásey Ivánitch. . . . Nazár, hey, Nazár! "

" What 's wanted? " mumbled the voice of an old man of seventy from the stable.

" Get the horses ready; a buyer has come."

The old woman ran into the house.

" A buyer, a buyer," Nazár growled after her in reply.—" I have n't got all their tails washed yet."

" Oh, Arkadia! " I thought.

" Good morning, dear little father, I beg your favour,"—a succulent and agreeable voice resounded behind my back. I glanced round: in front of me, in a long-skirted, blue cloak, stood an old man of medium height, with white hair, an amiable smile, and very handsome blue eyes.

" Didst thou want a horse? Certainly, dear little father, certainly. . . . But wilt not thou first come in and drink a cup of tea with me? "

I declined, with thanks.

" Well, as thou wilt. Thou must excuse me, dear little father: I hold to the old-fashioned ways, seest thou? " (Mr. Tchernobáy spoke without haste, with a rotund pronunciation of the o.[1])—" Everything about me is very simple, thou knowest. . . . Nazár, hey, Nazár,"—he added in a drawl, and without raising his voice.

Nazár, a wrinkled little old man with a hawk-like nose and a wedge-shaped little beard, made his appearance on the threshold of the stable.

" What sort of horses dost thou require, dear little father? " went on Mr. Tchernobáy.

" Some that are not too dear, well broken to harness, for my kibítka."

" Very well—I have such . . . . certainly.

---

[1] Unless the accent—which is variable—happens to fall on the o, it is pronounced slightingly, somewhat like a. This is the new-fangled, fashionable method. The other form indicates either rusticity, clinging to old fashions, or that the speaker belongs to the ecclesiastical class, the o being very rotund in the Old Slavonic, which is always used in the services of the Church.—TRANSLATOR.

. . . Nazár, Nazár, show the gentleman the grey gelding, the one which stands at the end, thou knowest, and the bay with the star,—or no, not that one . . . . the other bay, the one of Beauty's get, knowest thou? "

Nazár went back into the stable.

" And do thou lead them out by their halters," shouted Mr. Tchernobáy after him.

" I don't do, dear little father," he went on, looking me frankly and gently in the face, " as horse-dealers do—confound them! they use ginger in various shapes, and salt and malt;[1] I wash my hands of them completely!—But I have everything aboveboard, without trickery, please to observe."

The horses were led out. I did not like them.

" Well, put them in their places, with God's blessing," said Anastásey Ivánitch. " Show us some others."

They showed some others. At last I selected one as cheap as possible. We began to haggle. Mr. Tchernobáy did not get heated, he talked so sensibly, with so much pompousness, that I could not help " honouring the old man "; I made a deposit.

" Well, now," said Anastásey Ivánitch:— " permit me, in accordance with ancient custom, to transfer the horse to thee from coat-skirt to

[1] Salt and malt fatten a horse very quickly.

22

coat-skirt. . . . . Thou wilt thank me for it . . . .
't is a fresh beast, sound as a nut . . . . without
a flaw . . . . a gen-u-ine horse of the steppe!
It will go in any harness."

He crossed himself, laid the skirt of his great
cloak on his hand, took the halter and transferred
the horse to me.

" Possess it, with God's blessing, now. . . . .
And thou still dost not wish any tea? "

" No, I 'm greatly obliged to you: it is time I
was going home."

" As thou wilt. . . . And shall my coachman
lead the horse after thee now? "

" Yes, now, if you will permit."

" Certainly, my dear man, certainly. . . .
Vasíly, hey, Vasíly, go with the gentleman; lead
the horse, and receive the money. Well, good-
bye, dear little father, God bless thee."

" Good-bye, Anastásey Ivánitch."

My horse was led home. On the following
day, it turned out to be foundered and lame. I
undertook to harness it: my horse backed, and it
was struck with the whip; it began to balk, kick,
and lie down. I betook myself at once to Mr.
Tchernobáy. I asked:

" Is he at home? "

" He is."

" What do you mean by it? " said I:—" you
have sold me a foundered horse."

" Foundered?—God forbid! "

"And it's lame to boot, and balks into the bargain."

"Lame? I know nothing about that; evidently thy coachman has ruined it somehow,—but, I, as in the sight of God—"

"By rights, Anastásey Ivánitch, you ought to take it back."

"No, dear little father, don't be angry: once the horse has left the yard—there's an end of it. Thou shouldst have looked at it before."

I understood how the land lay, submitted to my fate, laughed, and departed. Fortunately, I had not paid so very dear for my lesson.

Two days later I drove away, and after the lapse of a week I passed through Lebedyán on my way home. In the coffee-house I found nearly the same persons as before, and Prince N. at the billiard-table. But the customary change in Mr. Khlopakóff's fate had already had time to take place. The fair-haired young officer had replaced him in the Prince's favour. The poor ex-lieutenant made an effort to set off his little word once more in my presence,—perchance, thought he, it will please as heretofore,—but the Prince not only did not smile, he even frowned and shrugged his shoulders. Mr. Khlopakóff dropped his eyes, shrunk together, stole into a corner, and began softly to stuff his pipe full. . . . .

II

TATYÁNA BORÍSOVNA AND HER NEPHEW

GIVE me your hand, my amiable reader, and
come with me. The weather is magnificent; the
May sky is of a soft azure hue; the smooth,
young leaves of the willows glisten as though
they had been washed; the broad, level road is
all covered with that fine, reddish-bladed grass
which the sheep are so fond of nibbling; to right
and left, on the long declivities of the sloping
hills, the green rye is waving gently; the shadows
of small cloudlets slip across it in thin splotches.
In the distance forests darkle, ponds glimmer,
villages gleam yellow; larks soar upward by hundreds, warble, fall headlong downward, and perch
upon small clods with outstretched necks; daws
halt on the highway, stare at you, and cower
down to the ground; they allow you to pass, and,
giving a couple of hops, fly off to one side; on
the height, beyond the ravine, a peasant is
ploughing; a piebald colt, with a stubby tail and
dishevelled mane, is running on unsteady legs
after its mother; its shrill neighing is audible.
We drive into a birch coppice; the strong, fresh
odour agreeably oppresses our breath. Here is

25

the boundary-fence; the coachman descends from his seat, the horses snort, the side-horses glance around, the shaft-horse flirts his tail, and leans his head against the arch[1] . . . . . . the rude bars open with a squeak. The coachman resumes his seat. . . . Drive on! ahead of us is a village. After passing five homesteads, we turn to the right, descend into a hollow, and drive on the dam. Beyond the small pond, from behind the rounded heads of apple-trees and lilac-bushes, a board roof which has once been red, with two chimneys, is visible. The coachman directs his course along the fence to the left; accompanied by the hoarse and yelping barks of very aged curs, he drives through the wide-open gate, dashes adroitly round the spacious yard, past the stables and carriage-houses, bestows a swaggering bow upon the old housekeeper, who is stepping sideways over the lofty threshold into the open door of the storehouse, and draws up, at last, in front of the small porch of a tiny, dark house, with bright windows. . . . . We are at Tatyána Borísovna's. And yonder is she herself, opening the hinged pane, and nodding to us. . . . . Good morning, mátushka![2]

Tatyána Borísovna is a woman about fifty years of age, with large, grey, prominent eyes, a rather blunt nose, red cheeks, and a double chin.

---

[1] The arch connecting the shafts.—TRANSLATOR.

[2] Literally, "Dear little mother"; an affectionately respectful mode of address for any woman, of any class.—TRANSLATOR.

TATYÁNA BORÍSOVNA

Her face breathes forth welcome and cordiality. She was married once, but soon was left a widow. Tatyána Borísovna is an extremely remarkable woman. She resides on her tiny estate, never leaves it, has very little intercourse with her neighbours, and receives and likes only young people. She was the daughter of very poor gentry, and received no education whatever,—that is to say, she does not speak French; she has never even been in Moscow,—and, despite all these defects, she bears herself so simply and finely, she feels and thinks so freely, she is so little infected with the ordinary infirmities of the petty landed proprietress, that, in truth, it is impossible not to feel amazed. . . . And, in fact, think of a woman who lives the year round in the country, in the wilds—and does not gossip, does not squeal, does not courtesy, does not get excited, does not choke, does not quiver with curiosity. . . . . She's a marvel! She generally wears a grey taffeta gown and a white cap with pendent lilac ribbons; she is fond of good eating, but not to excess; she leaves the preparation of preserves and dried and salted provisions to the housekeeper. " What does she do all day long? " you ask. . . . . " Does she read? "—No, she does not read; and, to tell the truth, books are not printed for her benefit. . . . If she has no visitors, my Tatyána Borísovna sits at the window and knits stockings in winter; in summer she strolls in the garden, plants and waters her flowers, plays with the kittens for hours together, feeds the pigeons. . . . . She occupies herself very little with the housekeeping. But if a guest comes, some young neighbour whom she likes, then Tatyána Borísovna brightens up all over; she gives him a seat, treats him to tea, listens to his stories, laughs, pats him on the cheek from time to time, but she herself says little: in calamity, in grief, she will comfort, will give good advice. How many people have confided to her their domestic, their intimate secrets, and have wept in her arms! She will seat herself opposite a guest, lean softly on her elbows, and gaze into his eyes with so much sympathy, will smile in so friendly a manner, that the thought will, inevitably, occur to the visitor: "What a splendid woman thou art, Tatyána Borísovna! Come now, I 'll tell thee what I have on my heart." A man feels at ease and warm in her small, cosy rooms; the weather is always fine in her house, if one may so express one's self. A wonderful woman is Tatyána Borísovna, but no one is surprised at her: her sound sense, firmness, and freedom, her ardent sympathy with the woes and joys of other people, in a word, all her fine qualities seem to have been born with her, to have cost her no labour or anxiety. . . . It is impossible to imagine her otherwise; consequently, there is nothing to thank her for. She is particu-

larly fond of watching the games and pranks of
young people; she will fold her hands on her lap,
lay her head on one side, screw up her eyes, and
sit smiling; then, all of a sudden, she will sigh and
say: " Akh, you, my children, children! " . . . . .
So that you feel like going to her, and taking her
hand, and saying to her: " Listen, Tatyána Borísovna, you don't know your own value, for, with
all your simplicity and lack of education, you are
a remarkable being! " Her very name has a sort
of familiar, cordial ring, one utters it with pleasure, it evokes a friendly smile. How many times
has it happened to me, for instance, to ask a peasant whom I chanced to meet: " How am I to get
to Gratchyóvko," let us say, " brother? "—"Well,
dear little father, do you go first to Vyazovóe,
and thence to Tatyána Borísovna's, and from
Tatyána Borísovna's any one will point out the
way to you." And at the name of Tatyána Borísovna the peasant will shake his head in quite a
peculiar manner. She keeps only a small staff
of servants, in consonance with her means. In
the house, the laundry, storeroom, and kitchen
are under the charge of the housekeeper, Agáfya, formerly her nurse, an extremely good-
hearted, tearful, and toothless creature; two
buxom maids, with strong, purplish-red cheeks,
after the pattern of Antónoff (winter) apples,
are under her orders. The duties of valet, butler,
and pantry-man are discharged by Polikárp, ♪

MEMOIRS OF A SPORTSMAN

servant of seventy years, a remarkably eccentric
person, a well-read man, a former violinist and
worshipper of Viotti, a personal foe of Napoleon, or, as he says, of " Bonapartíshka," [1] and a
passionate adorer of nightingales. He always
keeps five or six of them in his room; early in the
spring, he sits beside their cages for whole days
at a time, awaiting their first " warble "; and
when it comes he covers his face with his hands
and moans: " Okh, 't is pitiful, pitiful! "—and
begins to weep as though his heart would break.
Polikárp's grandson, Vásya, a lad of twelve
years, curly-haired and keen-eyed, is appointed
to assist him; Polikárp loves him unboundedly,
and grumbles at him from morning until night.
But he busies himself with his education.—
" Vásya,"—he says, " tell me: is Bonapartíshka
a brigand? "—" What wilt thou give, daddy? "
—" What will I give? . . . I won't give thee
anything . . Who art thou, I 'd like to know?
Art thou a Russian? "—" I 'm an Amtchanín,
daddy; I was born in Amtchénsk." [2]   " Oh,
stupid head! and where 's Amtchénsk? "—
" How should I know! "—" Is Amtchénsk in
Russia, stupid? "—" Well, and if it is in Russia,
what then? "—" What dost thou mean by ' what

[1] The diminutive of scorn and utter worthlessness ends thus in
ishka.—TRANSLATOR.
[2] In popular speech, the town of Mtzensk is called Amtchénsk,
and its citizens Amtcháni. The Amtcháni men are daring; not
without reason is an enemy with us promised " an amtchanín."

30

then'? His Ill
Mikhaílo Ilari
zoff-Smolénsky
pleased to exp
fines of Russia.
lad was compos
dancing, he ha
understand? H
what care I for
thou stupid! W
Mikhaílo Ilarió
partíshka, some
whacking thee

MEMOIRS OF

we'd say to him: '
damned Frenchm
. . Come, no
gand!'"—"
—"Wha
Tat
the

thou? He would come up to thee and say:
'Coman vu porte vu?'—and whack, whack!"—
"Then I'd hit him in the belly with my fist."—
"And he'd say to thee: 'Bonzhur, vene isi,'—and
he'd grab thee by the hair, by the hair!"—"And
I'd stamp on his feet, his feet, his knobby feet."
—"That's so, they do have knobby feet. . . . .
Well, and when he began to bind thy arms, what
wouldst thou do then?"—"I wouldn't let him:
I'd call Mikhéi the coachman to my assis-
tance."—"And dost thou think, Vásya, that the
Frenchman could not overpower Mikhéi?"—
"Overpower him, indeed! just see how robust
Mikhéi is!"—"Well, and what would you two
do to him?"—"We'd beat him on his back,—yes,
on his back."—"And he'd begin to shriek:
'Pardon! pardon, pardon, sivuplay!'"—"And

No sivuplay for thee, thou
an! . . .' " " Brave lad, Vásya!
, shout: ' Bonapartíshka is a bri-
Then do thou give me some sugar! "
a boy! " . . . .

ána Borísovna consorts very little with
landed proprietors: they go to her reluc-
antly, and she does not know how to entertain
them; she falls into a doze at the noise of their
remarks, gives a start, makes an effort to open
her eyes, and again relapses into slumber. In
general, Tatyána Borísovna is not fond of women. One of her friends, a fine, peaceable young
man, had a sister, an old maid of eight and thirty
years and a half, the kindest of beings, but unnatural, affected, and given to enthusiasms. Her
brother frequently narrated to her anecdotes of
their neighbour. One fine morning, my old
maid, without saying a word to any one, ordered
her horse to be saddled, and set out to see Tatyána Borísovna. In her long habit, with her hat
on her head and a green veil and curls floating,
she entered the anteroom, and dodging the panic-
stricken Vásya, who took her for a water-nymph,
she ran into the drawing-room. Tatyána Borísovna was frightened, and tried to rise, but her
limbs gave way beneath her.—" Tatyána Borísovna,"—began the visitor, in a tone of entreaty,
" excuse my boldness; I am the sister of your
friend, Alexyéi Nikoláevitch K * * *, and I

have heard so much about you from him, that I made up my mind to become acquainted with you."—" I feel greatly honoured," murmured the astounded hostess. The visitor threw off her hat, shook back her curls, seated herself beside Tatyána Borísovna, and took her hand. . . . " So, this is she,"—she began in a pensive, touched voice:—" this is that good, serene, noble, holy being! This is she! this simple and, at the same time, profound woman! How glad I am, how glad I am! How we shall love each other! I shall rest, at last. . . . She is exactly as I have pictured her to myself,"—she added, in a whisper, boring her eyes into the eyes of Tatyána Borísovna. " You will not be angry with me, will you, my kind, my good one! "—" Really, I am very glad. . . . . . Would not you like some tea? "—The visitor smiled condescendingly.

" *Wie wahr, wie unreflechirt,*"—she whispered, as though to herself. " Permit me to embrace you, my dear."

The old maid sat for three hours with Tatyána Borísovna, and never held her peace for a moment. She tried to expound to her new acquaintance her own significance. . . . Immediately after the departure of the unexpected visitor, the poor gentlewoman betook herself to the bath, drank a dose of linden-flower tea, and went to bed. But on the following day, the old maid returned, sat four hours, and withdrew promising to visit

Tatyána Borísovna every day. You will please
to observe, that she had taken it into her head to
develop, to put the finishing touches to the education of such a rich nature, as she expressed
herself; and, probably, she would have completely exhausted it in the end, had it not been
for the fact that, in the first place, she got
" utterly " disenchanted as to her brother's friend
in the course of a fortnight; and, in the second
place, if she had not fallen in love with a passing
student, with whom she instantly entered into an
active and ardent correspondence; in her epistles,
as was fitting, she blessed him for a holy and most
beautiful life, offered " the whole of herself " as
a sacrifice, demanded only the name of sister,
plunged into descriptions of nature, alluded to
Goethe, Schiller, Bettina, and German philosophy,—and, at last, drove the poor young man to
grim despair. But youth asserted its rights: one
fine morning, he awoke with such exasperated
hatred for his " sister and best friend," that he
came near knocking his valet down, in the heat of
passion, and, for a long time, all but bit at the
slightest hint about exalted and disinterested
love. . . . But, from that time forth Tatyána
Borísovna began more than ever to avoid inti-
macy with her neighbours.

Alas! nothing is stable upon earth. Everything which I have related concerning my kind
gentlewoman's mode of life is a thing of the

past; the tranquillity which reigned in her house has been destroyed forever. For more than a year now, her nephew, an artist from Petersburg, has been living with her. This is the way it came about.

Eight years ago, there lived with Tatyána Borísovna a boy of twelve, orphaned of father and mother, Andriúsha, the son of her deceased brother. Andriúsha had large, bright, humid eyes, a tiny mouth, a regular nose, and a very handsome, lofty brow. He spoke in a soft, sweet voice, kept himself tidy and decorous, was cordial and attentive to visitors, and kissed his aunt's hand with an orphan's sensibility. No sooner would you make your appearance than, lo and behold, he was already bringing you an armchair. He never played any pranks at all; he never made any noise; he would sit by himself in a corner, over his book, so modestly and submissively, and not even lean against the back of the chair. A visitor would enter,—my Andriúsha would rise, smile courteously, and flush; the visitor would leave the room;—he would seat himself again, pull a little brush and mirror from his pocket, and arrange his hair. He had felt an inclination for drawing from his earliest years. If a scrap of paper fell into his hands, he would immediately ask Agáfya the housekeeper for her scissors, carefully cut from the paper a regular square, draw a narrow frame around it, and set to work; he would draw an eye with a huge pupil, or a Grecian nose, or a house with a chimney and smoke in the form of a screw, a dog " en face," resembling a bench, a tree with two doves, and sign it: " Drawn by Andréi Byelovzóroff, on such a date, of such a year, village of Máliya Brýki." He toiled with particular zeal, for a couple of weeks before Tatyána Borísovna's name-day,[1] was the first to present himself to congratulate her, and offered a roll tied up with a pink ribbon. . Tatyána Borísovna kissed her nephew on the brow, and untied the knot; the roll spread out, and disclosed to the curious view of the spectator a round temple with an altar in the middle, boldly washed in in India ink; on the altar lay a flaming heart and a wreath, and above, on an undulating scroll, in plain letters, stood written: " To my aunt and benefactress Tatyána Borísovna Bogdánoff, from her respectful and loving nephew, in token of the most profound devotion." Tatyána Borísovna kissed him again and gave him a ruble. But she felt no great affection for him: Andriúsha's obsequiousness did not altogether please her. In the meantime, Andriúsha was growing up; Tatyána Borísovna was beginning to grow anxious as to his future. An unexpected event rescued her from her dilemma. . . .

---

[1] The name-day—the day of the Saint after whom a person is named—is celebrated instead of the birthday.—TRANSLATOR.

TATYANA BORISOVNA

To wit: one day, eight years ago, a certain Mr. Benevolénsky, a collegiate assessor [1] and cavalier of an order, dropped in to call. Mr. Benevolénsky had formerly been in the service in the neighbouring county town, and had been an assiduous visitor at Tatyána Borísovna's; he had removed to Petersburg, had entered a ministry, had attained to a fairly important post, and during one of his frequent trips on government business he had recalled his old friend, and dropped in to see her, with the intention of resting for a couple of days from the cares of the service, "in the lap of rustic tranquillity." Tatyána Borísovna received him with her habitual cordiality, and Mr. Benevolénsky . . . . But before we go on with our story, permit us, dear reader, to make you acquainted with this new person.

Mr. Benevolénsky was a rather fat man, of medium height, soft in aspect, with small, short feet, and plump little hands; he wore a capacious and extremely neat swallow-tailed coat, a tall and broad neckerchief, snow-white linen, a gold chain on his silk waistcoat, a ring with a stone on his forefinger, and a blond wig; he talked persuasively and gently, walked noiselessly, smiled pleasantly, rolled his eyes about pleas-

[1] Grade No. 8, corresponding to the (former) title of Major, in Peter the Great's famous Table of Ranks. There are fourteen grades in all.—TRANSLATOR.

antly, plunged his chin into his neckerchief pleasantly: altogether, he was a pleasant man. The Lord had also endowed him with the kindest of hearts: he wept and went into raptures easily; above all, he burned with disinterested ardour for art, and this ardour was genuinely disinterested, for, if the truth must be told, it was precisely in the matter of art that Mr. Benevolénsky had positively no understanding whatsoever. One even marvelled whence, by virtue of what mysterious and incomprehensible laws, he had become infected with that passion. Apparently, he was a sedate, even a commonplace man . . . . . however, there are quite a good many such people among us in Russia.

Love for art and artists imparts to these people an inexplicable mawkishness; it is torture to know them, to converse with them: they are regular blockheads smeared with honey. For example, they never call Raphael Raphael, or Correggio Correggio: they say, " the divine Sanzio, the incomparable de Allegris," and invariably they pronounce their *o's* broadly. They laud every homespun, conceited, over-elaborated and mediocre talent as a genius, or, to be more accurate, " janius "; the blue sky of Italy, the southern lemon, the perfumed gales of the shores of the Brenta, are eternally on their lips. " Ekh, Ványa, Ványa," or " Ekh, Sásha, Sásha," they say to each other with ecstasy, " we ought to go

to the south, to the southland . . . for you and I
are Greeks in spirit, ancient Greeks!" They
may be observed at exhibitions, in front of the
productions of certain Russian painters. (We
must remark, that the majority of these gentlemen are frightfully patriotic.) First they
retreat a pace, and loll their heads on one side,
then they approach the picture again; their little
eyes become suffused with an oily moisture. .
" Phew, O my God,"—they say, at last, in a voice
broken with emotion,—" what soul, what soul!
What heart, what heart! how much soul he has
put into it! a vast amount of soul! . . . . And
how it is conceived! conceived in a masterly manner! "—And what pictures they have in their
own drawing-rooms! What artists frequent
them of an evening, drink their tea, listen to their
conversation! What perspective views of their
own rooms they offer them, with a brush in the
right foreground, a pile of dirt on the polished
floor, a yellow samovár on a table by the window,
and the master of the house himself, in dressing-
gown and skull-cap, with a brilliant spot of light
on his cheek! What long-haired nurslings of
the Muses, with feverishly-scornful smile, visit
them! What pale-green young ladies squeal at
their pianos! For that is the established order of
things with us in Russia: a man cannot devote
himself to one art alone—give him all! Hence.
it is not in the least surprising, that these gentle-

men-amateurs also display great patronage to
Russian literature, especially to dramatic literature. . . . The " Jacob Sanpasaros " are written
for them; the conflict of unrecognised talent with
people, with the whole world, which has been depicted a thousand times, shakes them to the very
bottom of the soul. . . .

On the day following the arrival of Mr.
Benevolénsky, Tatyána Borísovna, at tea, commanded her nephew to show the visitor his
drawings. " And does your relative draw? "
ejaculated Mr. Benevolénsky, not without surprise, and turned sympathetically to Andriúsha.
" Certainly he does! "—said Tatyána Borísovna:
—" he 's so fond of it! and he does it all alone,
without any teacher, you know."—" Akh, show
me, show me,"—interposed Mr. Benevolénsky.
Andriúsha, blushing and smiling, brought his
sketch-book to the visitor. Mr. Benevolénsky
began, with the air of a connoisseur, to turn over
the leaves. " Good, young man,"—he said at
last:—" Good, very good." And he stroked
Andriúsha's head. Andriúsha kissed his hand on
the fly.—" Just see, what talent! . . . . . I congratulate you, Tatyána Borísovna, I congratulate you! "—" But what is to be done, Piótr
Mikhaílitch? I cannot find any teacher for him
here. It costs too much to have one come from
town; there is an artist at my neighbours', the
Artamónoffs, and a capital one he is, they say,

40

but the lady forbids him to give lessons to outsiders. She says he will spoil his taste."— "H'm,"—ejaculated Mr. Benevolénsky, as he fell to meditating, and cast sidelong glances at Andriúsha. "Well, we will talk the matter over,"—he suddenly added, rubbing his hands. That same day he requested permission of Tatyána Borísovna to have a private conversation with her. They locked themselves up. Half an hour later, they called Andriúsha. Andriúsha entered. Mr. Benevolénsky was standing at the window, with his face slightly flushed and his eyes beaming. Tatyána Borísovna was sitting in one corner, and wiping away her tears.—" Well, Andriúsha,"—she began at last:—" thank Piótr Mikhaílitch: he is going to take thee under his charge, and carry thee off to Petersburg." Andriúsha was fairly petrified where he stood.— "Tell me frankly,"—began Mr. Benevolénsky, in a voice permeated with dignity and condescension:—" Do you wish to become an artist, young man, do you feel a sacred vocation for art? "— " I do want to be an artist, Piótr Mikhaílitch,"— affirmed Andriúsha, tremulously.—" In that case, I am very glad. Of course,"—pursued Mr. Benevolénsky,—" you will find it hard to part from your respected aunt; you must feel the liveliest gratitude to her."—" I adore my aunty,"— Andriúsha interrupted him, blinking his eyes.— " Of course, of course, that is very natural and

does you much honour; but, on the other hand,
just imagine, what joy, in course of time . . . .
your successes. . ."—" Embrace me, Andriúsha,"—murmured the kind lady. Andriúsha
flung himself on her neck.—" Well, and now
thank thy benefactor. . . ." Andriúsha embraced Mr. Benevolénsky's paunch, raised himself on tiptoe, and so managed to grasp his hand,
which the benefactor, truth to tell, accepted, yet
made no great haste to accept. . . . The child
must be soothed, satisfied,—well, and one may
indulge one's self also. Two days later Mr. Benevolénsky departed, and carried with him his
new protégé.

During the first three years of his absence,
Andriúsha wrote with tolerable frequency, sometimes enclosing drawings in his letters. Mr.
Benevolénsky occasionally added also a few
words from himself, chiefly of approval; then
the letters became more and more infrequent,
and, at last, ceased altogether. Tatyána Borísovna's nephew maintained silence for a whole
year: she had already begun to worry, when,
suddenly, she received a note whose contents
were as follows:

" DEAR AUNTY!

" Two days ago, Piótr Mikhaílovitch, my benefactor,
died. A severe shock of paralysis has deprived me of
my last support. Of course, I am already twenty years

of age; in the course of seven years I have made notable progress; I have strong hopes of my talent and can earn my living by means of it; I am not downcast, but, nevertheless, if you can, send me, for present expenses, two hundred and fifty rubles. I kiss your hands, and remain,"—and so forth.

Tatyána Borísovna sent her nephew the two hundred and fifty rubles. Two months later, he demanded some more; she gathered together her last resources, and sent again. Six weeks had not elapsed after the last despatch, when he asked for the third time, nominally for the purpose of purchasing paints for a portrait which a Princess Terteréshneff had ordered from him. Tatyána Borísovna refused. "In that case," he wrote to her, "I intend to come to you, in the country, to recuperate my health." And, in fact, in the month of May of that same year, Andriúsha returned to Máliya Brýki.

At first, Tatyána Borísovna did not recognise him. From his letters, she had expected a thin and sickly man, but she beheld a broad-shouldered, stout young fellow, with a broad, red face and curly, greasy hair. The pale, slender Andriúsha had been converted into sturdy Andréi Ivánoff Byelovzóroff. His external appearance was not the only thing in him which had undergone a change. The sensitive shyness, the caution and neatness of former years, had been replaced by a careless swagger, by intolerable slovenliness; he swayed to right and left as he walked, flung himself into arm-chairs, sprawled over the table, lolled, yawned to the full extent of his jaws, and behaved impudently to his aunt and the servants,—as much as to say: " I 'm an artist, a free kazák! I 'll show you what stuff I 'm made of!" For whole days together, he would not take a brush in his hand; when the so-called inspiration came upon him, he would behave as wildly as though he were intoxicated, painfully, awkwardly, noisily; his cheeks would burn with a coarse flush, his eyes would grow inebriated; he would set to prating about his talent, his successes, of how he was developing and advancing. . . . But, as a matter of fact, it turned out that his gift barely sufficed for tolerably fair petty portraits. He was an utter ignoramus, he had read nothing; and why should an artist read? Nature, freedom, poetry,—those are his elements. So, shake thy curls, and chatter away volubly, and inhale Zhukóff [1] with frenzy! Russian swagger is a good thing, but it is not becoming to many; and talentless second-rate Polezháeffs are intolerable. Our Andréi Ivánitch continued to live at his aunt's: evidently, gratuitous food was to his taste. He inspired visitors with deadly ennui. He would seat himself at the piano (Tatyána Borísovna had set up a piano also) and begin to pick out with one

[1] The coarsest sort of tobacco.—TRANSLATOR.

finger "The dashing Tróïka"; he would strike chords, and thump the keys; for hours at a stretch he would howl Varlámoff's romances "The solitary Pine," or "No, Doctor, no, do not come," and the fat would close over his eyes, and his cheeks would shine like a drum. . . . . And then, suddenly, he would thunder: "Begone, ye tumults of passion!" . . . . And Tatyána Borísovna would fairly jump in dismay.

"'T is extraordinary,"—she remarked to me one day,—"what songs are composed nowadays, —they are all so despairing, somehow; in my day, they used to compose a different sort: there were sad ones then too, but it was always agreeable to listen to them. . . . . For example:

> "Come, come to me in the meadow,
>   Where I wait for thee in vain;
>   Come, come to me in the meadow,
>   Where my tears flow hour after hour . . . .
>   Alas, thou wilt come to me in the meadow,
>   But then 't will be too late, dear friend!"

Tatyána Borísovna smiled guilefully.

"'I shall suf-fer, I shall suf-fer,'" howled her nephew in the adjoining room.

"Stop that, Andriúsha!"

"'My soul is lan-guishing in part-ing,'" continued the irrepressible singer.

Tatyána Borísovna shook her head.

" Okh, those artists! " . . . .

A year has passed since then. Byelovzóroff is still living with his aunt, and still preparing to go to Petersburg. He has become broader than he is long in the country. His aunt—who would have thought it?—is perfectly devoted to him, and the young girls of the neighbourhood fall in love with him. . . .

Many of Tatyána Borísovna's former acquaintances have ceased to visit her.

III

I HAVE a neighbour, a young agriculturist and young sportsman. One fine morning I dropped in on him for a call, on horseback, with the suggestion that we should set out together in quest of woodcock. He consented. "Only," said he, "let us go through my tract of second growth of trees to the Zúsha; I 'll take a look at Tchaplý- gino by the way. Do you know my oak forest? It is being felled."—"Come on."—He ordered his horse to be saddled, donned a green surtout with bronze buttons representing boars' heads, a game- bag embroidered in worsted, and a silver flask, threw over his shoulder a rather new French gun, turned himself about, not without pleasure, in front of the mirror, and called his dog Espérance, which had been presented him by his cousin, an old maid with an excellent heart, but without any hair. We set out. My neighbour took with him the village policeman Arkhíp, a fat and ex- tremely short peasant with a square face and cheek-bones of antediluvian development, and a recently-engaged superintendent from the Baltic

47

provinces, a young fellow of nineteen years, thin, fair-haired, mole-eyed, with sloping shoulders, and a long neck, Mr. Gottlieb von der Koch. My neighbour himself had entered into possession of his estate not long before. It had come to him by inheritance from his aunt, the wife of Councillor of State [1] Kardón-Katáeff, a remarkably fat woman, who, even when she was lying in bed, groaned in a prolonged and plaintive manner. We rode into the tract of second growth trees. " Wait for me here, in the glade," said Ardalión Mikhaílitch (my neighbour), turning to his satellites. The German bowed, slipped off his horse, pulled a small book from his pocket, apparently a romance by Johann Schopenhauer, and sat down under a bush; Arkhíp remained in the sun, and never moved for the space of an hour. We made a circuit through the bushes, and found not a single covey. Ardalión Mikhaílitch announced that he intended to betake himself to the forest. For some reason or other, I myself had no faith in the success of our hunt on that day: I wended my way after him. The German noted his page, rose, put the book in his pocket, and mounted, not without difficulty, his bob-tailed, imperfect mare, which squealed and kicked out at the slightest touch; Arkhíp gave a start, jerked both reins simultaneously, flung his feet about, and, at last,

---

[1] The fifth grade from the top, in Peter the Great's Table of Ranks.—TRANSLATOR.

got his stupefied and spiritless little nag to move from the spot. We rode off.

Ardalión Mikhaílitch's forest had been familiar to me from my childhood. In company with my French tutor, M—r. Désire Fleury, the kindest of men (who, nevertheless, came near ruining my health for life, by making me drink De Roy's potion of an evening), I frequently walked to Tchaplýgino. The entire forest consisted of about two or three hundred enormous oak-trees and maples. Their stately, mighty boles darkled magnificently against the translucent golden-green of the hickories and mountain-ashes; they rose higher, outlined themselves gracefully against the clear azure, and there, at last, flung wide the canopy of their broad, gnarled boughs; hawks, honey-buzzards, kestrels soared whistling over the motionless crests, spotted woodpeckers tapped vigorously on the thick bark; the resonant song of the black thrush suddenly rang forth in the dense foliage, following the variable cry of the oriole; down below, in the bushes, hedge-sparrows, finches, and pewits twittered and warbled; chaffinches hopped briskly along the paths; a white hare stole along the edge of the woods, cautiously "limping"; a reddish-brown squirrel leaped in an offhand way from tree to tree, and suddenly sat down, with tail aloft, over our heads. In the grass, near the tall ant-hills, beneath the light shadow of the deeply dented beautiful fronds of the ferns, violets and lilies of the valley bloomed, and mushrooms of various sorts, and crimson fly-agaric grew; in the little glades, amid the bushes, strawberries gleamed red. . . And what shade there was in the forest! In the very height of the heat, at noonday, it was perfect night: silence, perfume, coolness. . . . Cheerfully had I passed the time in Tchaplýgino, and therefore, I confess, it was not without a feeling of sadness that I now rode into the forest which was but too familiar to me. The pernicious, snowless winter of 1840 had not spared my old friends, the oaks and maples; withered, stripped bare, here and there covered with consumptive foliage, they drooped mournfully over the young coppice which had " taken their place but not replaced them." [1] Some, still clothed with leaves below, reared their lifeless, broken boughs aloft as though with reproach and despair; in the case of others, from the foliage, still tolerably dense, though not abundant, not copious as of yore, thick, dry, dead branches protruded; the bark of others had fallen at a dis-

---

[1] In the year 1840, although there was a most rigorous frost, no snow fell until the very end of December; all the crops were frozen, and many fine oak forests were ruined by that ruthless winter. It is difficult to replace them: the productive power of the soil is evidently lessening; on " forbidden " winter-killed lands (around which there had been a procession with holy pictures), in place of the former noble trees, birches and aspens are springing up of themselves; and with us no one knows how to propagate woods otherwise.

DEATH

'tance; others still had fallen altogether, and were rotting, like corpses, on the ground. Who could have foreseen it—that it would be impossible to find shade—shade in Tchaplýgino—anywhere! Well, I thought, as I gazed at the moribund trees: I think you must feel ashamed and bitter. . . . . Koltzóff's [1] verse recurred to my mind:

> " What has become
>   Of the lofty speech,
>   The haughty power,
>   Th' imperial valour?
>   Where now is thy
>   Green might . . . . "

" Why is this, Ardalión Mikhaílitch,"—I began:—" Why did n't you fell these trees last year? You will not get a tenth part as much for them now, you see, as you would have got then."

He merely shrugged his shoulders.

" You 'd better have asked my aunt;—but the merchants came, brought their money, and importuned her."

" Mein Gott! "—von der Koch exclaimed at every step.—" Vat a prank! vat a prank! "

" What prank do you mean? "—remarked my neighbour, with a smile.

" Dat is, vat a peety, I meanttt to zay." (It is a well-known fact, that all Germans, when they

---

[1] Alexyéi Vasílievitch Koltzóff (1809–1842), a writer of extremely original national ballads.—TRANSLATOR.

have at last mastered our letter *l,* with hard pronunciation, throw remarkable stress upon it.[1])

His regret was particularly aroused by the
oaks which lay on the ground,—and, as a matter of fact, any miller would have paid a high
price for them.   On the other hand, Arkhíp,
the village policeman, maintained imperturbable
composure, and did not grieve in the least; on the
contrary, he leaped over them not without satisfaction, and lashed them with his whip.

We were making our way to the spot where the
felling was in progress, when suddenly, following the noise of a falling tree, a shout and talking
rang out, and a few moments later a young peasant, pale and dishevelled, sprang out of the
thicket toward us.

" What 's the matter?—Whither art thou running? "—Ardalión Mikhaílitch asked him.

He immediately came to a halt.

" Akh, dear little father, Ardalión Mikhaílitch, 't is a catastrophe! "

" What has happened? "

" Maxím, dear little father, has been hurt by a
tree."

" How did that happen? . . . Maxím the
contractor? "

" Yes, the contractor, dear little father.   We

---

[1] The hard *l* is so difficult of pronunciation that some Russians
renounce the attempt, and substitute *oo:* e. g., *ooá*shad (horse) for
lóshad. The word here is *khotyélll,* and I have trebled the *t* to represent the author's trebled *l.*—TRANSLATOR.

began to fell a maple, and he stood and watched.
. . . He stood and stood, then went off to the
well for water: he wanted a drink, you see; when,
all at once, the maple began to crack and fell
straight toward him. We shouted at him, ' Run,
run, run!' . . . He ought to have leaped to one
side, but he took and ran straight toward it . . . .
he must have got frightened. And the maple
covered him with its upper boughs. And why it
fell so suddenly,—the Lord knows. . . . The
heart must have been rotten."

" Well, and did it injure Maxím? "

" It did, dear little father."

" Mortally? "

" No, dear little father, he is still alive,—but
what of that? it has broken his arms and legs. So
I'm running for Selivéstritch,—for the doctor."

Ardalión Mikhaílitch ordered the policeman to
gallop to the village for Selivéstritch, and he
himself rode forward at a swift trot to the clearing. . . . I followed him.

We found poor Maxím on the ground. Half
a score of peasants were standing around him.
We alighted. He was hardly groaning; from
time to time he opened and dilated his eyes, gazed
around him, as though in surprise, and bit his lips,
which were turning blue. . . . His chin quivered, his hair adhered to his brow, his chest
heaved unevenly: he was dying. The light shade
of a young linden flitted across his face.

We bent over him. He recognised Ardalión Mikhaílitch.

"Dear little father,"—he began, in a barely audible tone:—"order . . . . the priest . . . . . to be sent for. . . . . The Lord . . . . has punished me . . . . my legs and arms are all smashed. . . . To-day . . . . is Sunday . . . . and I . . . . and I . . . . you see . . . did not let the lads go."

He ceased speaking. His breath failed him.

"And give . . . . . my money . . . . to my wife . . . . to my wife . . . . after deducting . . . . for my debts. . . Onísim here knows . . . . . to whom I . . . . . am in debt."

"We have sent for the doctor, Maxím,"—said my neighbour:—"perhaps thou wilt not die yet."

He tried to open his eyes, and raised his lids and his eyebrows with the effort.

"Yes, I shall die. Yonder . . . . yonder it is tapping, yonder it is, yonder . . . . For-give me, my lads, if in anything . . . . ."

"God pardons thee, Maxím Andréitch,"—said the peasants dully with one voice, and took off their caps:—"do thou forgive us."

He suddenly shook his head in a desperate way, painfully heaved his chest, and lowered it again.

"But he cannot be left to die here,"—exclaimed Ardalión Mikhaílitch:—"fetch hither a mat from the cart yonder, my lads,—let's carry him to the hospital."

A couple of men rushed to the cart.

DEATH

" I bought a horse . . . yesterday,"—stammered the dying man,—" from Efrím . . . . Sytchóvsky . . . . I gave him . . . . a deposit . . . . . so the horse is mine . . . . give it . . . . to my wife . . . . also . . . . ."

They began to lay him on the mat . . . . . he quivered all over like a bird which has been shot, and straightened himself. . . . .

" He is dead,"—muttered the peasants.

We mounted our horses in silence, and rode away.

The death of poor Maxím caused me to reflect. 'T is wonderful how the Russian man dies! It is impossible to call his condition before the end indifference or stupidity; he dies, as though he were performing a rite, coldly and simply.

Several years ago, in the village of another of my neighbours, a peasant was fatally burned in the grain-kiln. (He would have remained in the kiln, but a petty burgher who was passing by dragged him out,—he threw himself into a vat of water, and with the force of his flight he burst open the door beneath the flaming shed.) I went to see him in his cottage. It was dark, stifling, smoky in the cottage. I inquired where the sick man was.—" Why, yonder, dear little father, on the oven-bench,"—answered the grieving peasant-wife in a sing-song tone. I stepped up to him—the man was lying there, covered with his sheepskin coat, breathing heavily.—" Well, how dost thou feel? "—The sick man fidgeted about on the oven, and tried to raise himself, but was covered with wounds and on the verge of death. " Lie still, lie still, lie still. . . . Well, how goes it? how art thou? "—" Bad, of course," said he.— " Art thou in pain? "—No answer.—" Dost thou want anything? "—No answer.—" Shall not I send thee some tea? "—" It is n't necessary."— I left him, and seated myself on the bench. I sat there for a quarter of an hour. I sat for half an hour,—the silence of the grave reigned in the cottage. In the corner, at the table beneath the holy pictures,[1] a little maiden of five years was hiding, and eating bread. The mother shook her finger at her now and then. People were walking about, pounding and chattering in the anteroom. The brother's wife was chopping up cabbage.—"Hey, Aksínya!"—said the sick man at last.—" What is it? "—" Give me some kvas."—Aksínya gave him the kvas. Again silence reigned. I asked in a whisper: " Has he received the communion? "— " Yes."—Well, then everything was in due order: he was waiting for death, that was all. I could not endure it, and left the house. . . .

I remember, too, that I once dropped in at the hospital in the village of Krasnogórye, to see my acquaintance, Peasant-Surgeon Kapitón, an ardent sportsman.[2]

[1] That is, in the right-hand corner, facing the door.—TRANSLATOR.

[2] The German *feldsherr,* a doctor's assistant; or (in cases like the one here referred to) an independent doctor, for the peasants, with minor diploma.—TRANSLATOR.

DEATH

This hospital consisted of a former wing of the seigniorial manor-house; the lady-owner of the estate herself had arranged it,—that is to say, she had given orders that over the door should be nailed up a blue board, with the inscription in white letters, " The Krasnogórye Hospital," and she had personally handed to Kapitón a handsome album wherein to jot down the names of the patients. On the first page of this album one of the philanthropic benefactress's dish-lickers and servile fawners had traced the following lines:

> " Dans ces beaux lieux, où règne l'allégresse,
> Ce temple fut ouvert par la Beauté;
> De vos seigneurs admirez la tendresse,
> Bons habitants de Krasnogorié! "

And another gentleman had added below:

> " Et moi aussi j'aime la nature!
>   "Jean Kobyliátnikoff."

The doctor had purchased six beds with his own money, and had started out, invoking a blessing on himself with the sign of the cross, to heal God's people. There were, in addition to himself, two persons attached to the hospital: Pável the carver, who was subject to fits of insanity, and a peasant woman with a withered hand, Melikitrísa, who discharged the functions of cook. Both of them prepared the medicines, and dried and infused the herbs; they also restrained the fever patients. The crazy carver was gloomy of aspect, and parsimonious as to words: at night he was wont to sing a song about "Venus most fair," and to appeal to every passer-by for permission to wed a certain maiden, Malánya by name, who had long been dead. The cripple-handed peasant-wife beat him, and forced him to tend her turkeys. Well, then, I was sitting one day with Doctor Kapitón. We had begun to chat about our last hunt, when, suddenly, there drove into the yard a peasant-cart drawn by a remarkably fat grey horse, such as millers use. In the cart sat a robust peasant, in a new long-coat, and with a streaky beard.—"Hey there, Vasíly Dmítritch,"—shouted Kapitón from the window:— "pray come in . . . . 'T is the miller from Lybóff"—he whispered to me. The peasant descended, grunting, from his cart, entered the doctor's room, sought the holy pictures with his eyes, and crossed himself.—"Well, what now, Vasíly Dmítritch, what 's the news . . . . But you must be ill: your face does n't look right."—"Yes, Kapitón Timoféeitch, something 's wrong."— "What 's the matter with you?"—"Why, this, Kapitón Timoféeitch. Not long ago, I bought a mill-stone in town: well, I brought it home, and when I began to unload it from the cart, I strained myself, probably, or something of the sort, and there was a ripping in my belly, as though something had broken . . . and ever since then I have been ailing all the time. To-day I even feel very bad."—" H'm,"—said Kapitón, and took a pinch of snuff: " that means, you 've ruptured yourself. And did this happen to you long since? "—" Why, ten days ago."— "Ten days?" (The doctor inhaled the air through his teeth, and shook his head.) " Allow me to feel of you. . . . Well, Vasíly Dmítritch," he said at last: " I 'm sorry for thee, my dear fellow, but thou 'rt in a bad way, thou 'rt seriously ill; remain here with me; I will use every effort, but I will guarantee nothing."—" Is it as bad as that? "—muttered the astonished miller.—" Yes, Vasíly Dmítritch, it is very bad; you ought to have come to me a couple of days earlier, and it would n't have amounted to anything; I could have relieved you easily; but now there is inflammation, that 's what 's the matter: the first you know, gangrene will set in."—" But it cannot be, Kapitón Timo-féeitch."—" But I tell you it is so."—" But why? "—(The doctor shrugged his shoulders.) —" And must I die from that trifle? "—" I don't say that . . . . but do stay here." The peasant meditated, meditated, stared at the floor, then at us, scratched his head, then caught up his cap. " Whither art thou going, Vasíly Dmítritch? "— " Whither? home, of course, if matters are as bad as that. I must make my arrangements, if that is so."—" But, good heavens! you will do yourself an injury, Vasíly Dmítritch; I 'm amazed that

you managed to get here, as it is. Do stay."—
" No, brother, Kapitón Timoféeitch, if I must
die, then I'll die at home; for if I were to die
here, the Lord only knows what would happen at
my house."—" We don't know, as yet, Vasíly
Dmítritch, how the affair will turn out. . . . . .
There is danger, of course, very great danger,
there's no disputing that . . . . . but that is
precisely the reason why you ought to remain."
(The peasant shook his head.)—" No, Kapitón
Timoféeitch, I will not stay . . . . . but won't
you prescribe some medicine?"—" Medicine
alone will not help."—" I won't stay, I tell you."
—" Well, do as you please . . . . only, look out,
that you don't blame me afterward!"

The doctor tore a leaf out of the album, and,
having written a prescription, he advised him
what to do in addition. The peasant took the
paper, gave Kapitón half a ruble, left the room,
and climbed into his cart.—" Well, good-bye,
Kapitón Timoféeitch; don't bear me ill-will, and
don't forget my orphans, if anything . . . . ."
" Hey, stay here, Vasíly!"—The peasant merely
shook his head, slapped his horse with the reins,
and drove out of the yard. I went out into the
street and gazed after him. The road was muddy
and full of holes; the miller drove cautiously,
without haste, guiding the horse skilfully, and
nodding to the persons whom he met. . . . . On
the fourth day he died.

DEATH

On the whole, it is wonderful how Russians die. Many dead now recur to my mind. I recall thee, my old friend, Avenír Sorokoúmoff, my fellow-student, who did not finish his course, a fine, noble man! Again I behold thy consumptive, greenish face, thy thin, reddish hair, thy gentle smile, thy ecstatic glance, thy long limbs; I hear thy weak, caressing voice. Thou livedst with the Great Russian landed proprietor, Gur Kupryánikoff; thou didst teach his children, Fófa and Zyózo, to read and write Russian, together with geography and history; thou didst patiently endure the heavy jokes of Gur himself, the coarse amiability of the butler, the stale pranks of the malicious little boys; not without a bitter smile, but also without complaint, didst thou comply with the capricious demands of the bored lady of the manor; on the other hand, when thou wert resting, how blissfully happy wert thou in the evening, after supper, when, having rid thyself, at last, of all obligations and occupations, thou wert wont to seat thyself at the window, and pensively smoke thy pipe, or eagerly turn over the leaves of a mutilated and soiled number of the thick journal brought from town by the surveyor, the same sort of homeless wight as thyself! How pleased wert thou then by all poems and novels, how easily did the tears well up to thine eyes, with what pleasure didst thou laugh, with what genuine love for mankind, with what noble sympathy for everything that was good and beautiful was thy soul—pure as that of a child— permeated! I must say, to tell the truth, thou wert not distinguished for extraordinary wit; nature had not gifted thee with either memory or studiousness; in the university thou wert reckoned one of the worst students; at the lectures thou wert wont to sleep,—at the examinations, to maintain a solemn silence; but whose eyes beamed with joy, whose breath came short over the success, over the good fortune of a comrade? —Avenír's. . . . Who believed blindly in the lofty mission of his friends, who extolled them with pride, who defended them with obduracy? Who was it that knew neither envy nor self-love, who was it that disinterestedly sacrificed himself, who was it that willingly yielded submission to people who were not worth the soles of his shoes? . . . . . Always thou, always thou, our kind Avenír! I remember, that thou badest thy comrades farewell with broken heart, when thou wert setting off to become a tutor; evil premonitions tormented thee. . . . And, in fact, thou didst fare but ill in the country; in the country there was no one for thee to listen to adoringly, no one to admire, no one to love. . . . . And those steppe-dwellers and cultivated gentry treated thee like a teacher: some roughly, others carelessly. And moreover, thou didst not predispose in thy favour by thine appearance; thou wert shy, thou didst blush, cast down thine eyes, stammer. . . . The country air did not even restore thy health: thou didst melt away like a candle, poor fellow! Truth to tell, thy chamber looked on the garden; bird-cherry trees, apple-trees, linden-trees shed their light blossoms on thy table, on thy ink-bottle, on thy books; on the wall hung a little blue silk cushion for thy watch, given to thee at the hour of parting by a kind, sentimental little German governess with blonde curls and small blue eyes; sometimes an old friend from Moscow dropped in to see thee, and wrought thee to ecstasy by other people's verses, or even by his own; but solitude, the intolerable slavery of the teacher's calling, the impossibility of winning freedom, the endless autumns and winters, importunate illness. . . . Poor, poor Avenír!

I visited Sorokoúmoff not long before his death. He was hardly able to walk. Squire Gur Kupryánikoff did not eject him from his house, but he ceased to pay him any salary, and hired another tutor for Zyózo. . . . Fófa had been sent off to the cadet school. Avenír was sitting by his window, in an old Voltaire chair. The weather was magnificent. The bright autumnal sky gleamed blue above the dark-brown row of naked lindens; here and there the last bright-yellow leaves on them were rustling and whispering. The earth, penetrated with frost, was sweating and thawing in the sun; its slanting crimson rays beat obliquely on the pale grass; one felt conscious of a slight crackling in the air; the voices of the labourers resounded clearly and intelligibly in the garden. Avenír wore an old Bukhará dressing-gown; a green neckerchief cast a deathly hue upon his dreadfully emaciated face. He was extremely delighted to see me, stretched out his hand, and began to speak, and to cough. I allowed him to quiet down, and seated myself beside him. . . . On Avenír's lap lay a notebook filled with poems of Koltzóff, carefully copied; he tapped it with the other hand. " There was a poet," he faltered, with an effort repressing his cough, and tried to declaim, in a barely audible voice:

> " Or hath the falcon
> Fettered wings?
> Or are his paths
> All ordered? "

I stopped him: the doctor had forbidden him to talk. I knew what would please him. Sorokoúmoff had never, as the saying is, " kept in touch " with science, but he was curious to know what the great minds had done, and how far they had got now. He would, sometimes, take a comrade off in one corner, and begin to interrogate him: he would listen, and marvel, and believe him implicitly, and then repeat it all after him. German philosophy in particular possessed a strong interest for him.—I began to talk to him about Hegel (this happened long ago, as you see). Avenír nodded his head affirmatively, elevated his eyebrows, smiled, whispered: " I understand, I understand . . . . ah! good, good! . . . ." The childlike curiosity of the poor, dying, homeless, and discarded fellow touched me to tears, I admit. I must remark, that Avenír, contrary to the habit of most consumptives, did not deceive himself in the least as to his malady . . . . and what then? He did not sigh, he did not grieve, he did not even once refer to his condition. . . .

Collecting his forces, he talked of Moscow, of his comrades, of Púshkin, of the theatre, and of Russian literature; he recalled our merry-makings, the heated discussions of our circle, with regret he mentioned the names of two or three friends who had died. . . . .

" Dost thou remember Dásha? "—he added at last:—" that was a soul of gold! that was a heart! and how she loved me! . . . . What has become of her now?—I think she must have withered away, gone into a decline, has n't she, poor girl? "

I did not dare to undeceive the sick man,— and, in fact, why should he know that his Dásha was now twice as broad as she was long, and consorted with merchants—with the brothers Kondatchkóff, powdered and painted herself, squealed and wrangled?

" But," I said to myself, as I gazed at his ex-

hausted face, " cannot he be got away from here?
Perhaps there is still a possibility of curing
him . . . ." But Avenír did not permit me to
finish my proposal.

" No, brother, thanks,"—he said:—" it makes
no difference where I die. I certainly shall not
survive until the winter. . . . Why disturb people unnecessarily? I have become accustomed to
this house. To tell the truth, the master and mistress here are . . . ."

" Are unkind, thou meanest? " I interpolated.

" No, not unkind! they are wooden creatures,
somehow. However, I cannot complain of them.
There are neighbours: Landed Proprietor Kasát-
kin has a daughter, a cultivated, amiable, extremely kind young girl . . . . not proud . . . ."

Again Sorokoúmoff had a fit of coughing.

" Nothing would matter,"—he went on, after
resting:—" if I were only permitted to smoke
my pipe. . . . But I 'm not going to die like
this. I will smoke my pipe! "—he added, with a
sly wink.—" Thank God, I 've lived enough,
enough. I 've known good people. . . ."

" But thou shouldst write to thy relatives,"—
I interrupted him.

" What 's the good of writing to my relatives?
So far as helping is concerned,—they won't help
me; when I die, they will hear of it. But what 's
the use of talking about this. . . . Tell me,
rather, what hast thou seen abroad? "

DEATH

I began to narrate. He fairly bored his eyes into me. Toward evening I went away, and ten days later I received the following letter from Mr. Kupryánikoff:

" I have the honour to inform you herewith, my dear sir, that your friend, the student Mr. Avenír Sorokoú-moff, who resided in my house, died three days ago, at two o'clock in the afternoon, and was buried to-day in my parish church at my expense. He requested me to send you the accompanying seven books and note-books. It turned out that he had twenty-two rubles and a half, which, together with his remaining things, become the property of his relatives. Your friend died perfectly conscious, and, I may say, with equal lack of feeling, without having displayed any signs whatsoever of regret, even when our entire family bade him farewell. My consort, Kleopátra Alexándrovna, sends you her compliments. The death of your friend could not fail to have an effect upon her nerves; so far as I am concerned, I am well, thank God, and have the honour to be—

Your most humble servant
G. Kupryánikoff."

Many other instances occur to my mind,—but it would be impossible to recount them all. I will confine myself to one.

An aged landed proprietress died in my presence. The priest began to read over her the prayers for a departing soul, but suddenly observed that she was actually dying, and with all haste gave her the cross to kiss. The lady thrust it aside impatiently. "Why art thou in such a hurry, bátiushka?"—she said with her sluggish tongue:— "thou wilt have plenty of time." . . . She kissed the cross, tried to thrust her hand under the pillow, and drew her last breath. Under the pillow lay a silver ruble: she wanted to pay the priest for her own prayer-service. . . .

Yes, wonderful is the way in which Russians die!

IV

THE small village of Kolotóvka, which formerly
belonged to a landed proprietress who was known
throughout the neighbourhood as the Planer
on account of her energetic and evil disposition
(her real name remained unknown), but now the
property of some Petersburg Germans or other,
lies on the slope of a bare hill, intersected from
top to bottom by a frightful ravine, which, yawning like a bottomless pit, winds its way, cleft and
excavated by torrents, through the very middle
of the street, and separates the two sides of the
poor little hamlet worse than a river,—for across
a river a bridge may, at least, be built. A few
spindling willows timidly descend its sandy
slopes; at the very bottom, dry and yellow as
brass, lie huge slabs of clayey stone. The aspect
is cheerless, there's no denying that,—and yet,
all the inhabitants of the neighbourhood are well
acquainted with the road to Kolotóvka: they resort thither often and gladly.

At the very apex of the ravine, a few paces

from the point where it has its beginning as a narrow cleft, stands a tiny four-square cottage,— alone, apart from the rest. It is roofed with straw thatch, and has a chimney; one window is turned to the ravine, like a vigilant eye, and on winter evenings, illuminated from within, it is visible from afar, athwart the dim mist of the frost, and twinkles forth as a guiding star to many a wayfaring peasant. Over the door of the cottage a blue board is nailed up: this cot is a dram-shop, called " The Prítynny." [1] Probably the liquor in this dram-shop is not sold for any less than the current price, but it is much more diligently frequented than all the other establishments of the same character in the vicinity. Nikolái Ivánitch, the tapster, is the cause.

Nikolái Ivánitch, once upon a time a slender, curly-haired, rosy-cheeked young fellow, but now a remarkably obese man, already turning grey, with a face swimming in fat, cunning but good-natured little eyes, and a fleshy brow, intersected by thread-like wrinkles, has been living in Kolotóvka for more than twenty years. Nikolái Ivánitch is a smart, shrewd man, like the majority of dram-shop keepers. Without being distinguished by any special amiability or loquacity, he possesses the gift of attracting and retaining his patrons, who, for some reason, find it particu-

---

[1] Any place where people are fond of assembling, any agreeable (priyátny) place, is called " prítynny."

larly jolly to sit in front of his counter, beneath the calm and cordial, though keen gaze of the phlegmatic host. He has a great deal of common sense; he is well acquainted with the ways of the gentry and of the peasantry and of the burghers; in difficulties, he might give advice which was far from stupid, but, as a cautious man and an egoist, he prefers not to interfere, and, at most, merely by distant hints uttered as though wholly devoid of intention, will he guide his patrons—and even then only his favourite patrons —into the way of truth. He is a good judge of everything which is important or interesting to the Russian man: of horses and cattle, of forests and of bricks, of crockery and dry-goods and leather wares, of songs and dances. When he has no guests, he generally sits, like a sack, on the ground in front of his cottage, with his thin legs tucked up under him, and exchanges affable remarks with all the passers-by. He has seen a great deal in his day, he has outlived scores of petty gentry who have come to him for " alcohol," he knows everything that is going on for a hundred versts round about, and never blurts it out, never even has the appearance of knowing that which not even the most penetrating commissioner of rural police so much as suspects. He minds his own business, holds his tongue, smiles to himself, and shifts his drinking-glasses about. The neighbours respect him. The ci-

vilian General [1] Shshtcherspeténko, the leading
squire of the district as to rank, always nods condescendingly to him whenever he passes his little
house. Nikolái Ivánitch is a man of influence: he
forced a well-known horse-thief to restore a horse
which he had abstracted from the yard of one of
his acquaintances, he brought to their senses the
peasants of a neighbouring village who were un-
willing to accept a new manager, and so forth.
But it must not be supposed that he did this out
of love for justice, out of zeal for his neighbours
—no! he simply endeavours to prevent anything
which may in any way disturb his tranquillity.
Nikolái Ivánitch is married, and has children.
His wife, an alert, sharp-nosed, and quick-eyed
woman of the burgher class, has also grown
rather heavy in body of late, like her husband.
He relies upon her thoroughly, and she keeps
their money under lock and key. Boisterous
drunkards fear her; she is not fond of them: there
is little profit from them, but much uproar; the
silent, surly sort are more to her taste. Nikolái
Ivánitch's children are still small; all the first-
born have died, but the rest resemble their parents: it is a pleasure to look at the clever faces
of these robust youngsters.

[1] According to Peter the Great's famous Table of Ranks, civilians hold military titles (though they are rarely used, except in
the case of " general ") which correspond with the grade they
have attained. In order of precedence, the " generals " run as
follows: Actual Privy Councillor corresponds to General of Cavalry, Infantry, or Artillery; Privy Councillor, to Lieutenant-General; Actual Councillor of State, to Major-General.—TRANSLATOR.

THE SINGERS

It was an intolerably hot July day, when, slowly putting one foot before the other, and accompanied by my dog, I made my way upward along the Kolotóvka ravine in the direction of the Prítynny dram-shop. The sun was blazing in the sky, as though in a furious rage; it stewed and baked one unremittingly; the air was impregnated with stifling dust. The daws and crows, covered with gloss, with gaping bills stared at the passers-by, as though entreating their sympathy; the sparrows were the only ones who did not grieve, and puffing out their feathers, they twittered more violently than ever, and fought in the hedges, flew amicably from the dusty road, and soared in grey clouds above the green patches of hemp. I was suffering tortures from thirst. There was no water near; in Kolotóvka, as in many other villages of the steppes, the peasants drink a sort of liquid mud from the pond, in default of springs or wells. . . . But who would call that repulsive beverage water? I wanted to ask Nikolái Ivánitch for a glass of beer or kvas.

I must admit that Kolotóvka does not present a very cheerful spectacle at any season of the year; but it arouses a particularly sad feeling when the glittering July sun with its pitiless rays is heating the dark-brown, half-dispersed thatches of the houses, and that deep ravine, and the burnt-up, dusty pasture, across which hopelessly wander gaunt, long-legged hens, and the grey, aspen framework with holes in lieu of windows, the remnant of the former manor-house, completely overgrown with nettles, steppe-grass, and wormwood, and covered with goose-down, the black pond, red-hot as it were, with a fringe of half-dried mud, and a dam, twisted awry, by whose side, on the ash-like soil, trodden fine, sheep, barely breathing and sneezing with the dust, sadly huddle close to one another, and with dejected patience bow their heads as though waiting for that intolerable heat to pass off at last. With weary steps I approached the abode of Nikolái Ivánitch, evoking in the small brats, as was proper, a surprise which rose to the pitch of strainedly-irrational stares, and in the dogs wrath which was expressed by barking so hoarse and vicious, that it seemed as though all their entrails were being torn out of them, and they themselves coughed and panted after it,—when, all of a sudden, on the threshold of the dram-shop there made his appearance a peasant of lofty stature, capless, in a frieze cloak, girt low with a sky-blue girdle. From his appearance, he seemed to be a house-servant; his thick grey hair rose in disorder above his lean, wrinkled face. He called some one, hurriedly gesticulating with his arms, which, evidently, made more sweeping flourishes than he himself intended. It was obvious that he had already succeeded in getting intoxicated.

" Come along, come along, I say! "—he stammered, elevating his thick eyebrows with an effort:—" come along, Blinker, come along! deuce take thee, my good fellow, thou fairly crawlest, upon my word. 'T is not well, my good fellow. They are waiting for thee, and here thou art crawling. . . . Come along."

" Well, I 'm coming, I 'm coming,"—resounded a quavering voice, and from behind the cottage, on the right, a short, fat, lame man made his appearance. He wore a fairly clean woollen overcoat, with his arm in one sleeve only; a tall, conical cap, pulled straight down to his brows, imparted to his round, plump face a sly and jeering expression. His small, yellow eyes fairly darted about, a repressed, constrained smile never left his lips, and his long, sharp nose projected audaciously in front like a rudder.— " I 'm coming, my dear fellow,"—he went on, hobbling in the direction of the dram-shop:— " why dost thou call me? . . . Who is waiting for me? "

" Why do I call thee? "—said the man in the frieze coat, reproachfully.—" Thou 'rt a queer fellow, Blinker: thou art called to the dram-shop, and thou askest: ' Why? ' Good men are waiting for thee: Turk-Yáshka, and Wild Gentleman, and the contractor from Zhísdra. Yáshka and the contractor have made a bet: they have wagered a gallon of beer as to which one of them will outdo the other,—that is to say, which will sing the best. . . . . Dost understand? "

" Is Yáshka going to sing? "—said the man called Blinker, with vivacity,—"And art not thou lying, Ninny? "

" I 'm not lying,"—replied The Ninny, with dignity:—" but thou art talking crazy nonsense. Of course he 's going to sing, if he has made a bet, thou lady-bug, thou rogue, Blinker! "

" Well, come on then, silly," retorted Blinker.

" Come, kiss me at least, my darling,"—stammered The Ninny, opening his arms widely.

" Pshaw, what a tender Æsop,"—replied Blinker, scornfully, repulsing him with his elbow, and both, bending down, entered the low-browed door.

The conversation I had overheard powerfully excited my curiosity. More than once rumours had reached me about Turk-Yáshka as the best singer in the vicinity, and an opportunity had now presented itself to me to hear him in competition with another master of the art. I redoubled my pace, and entered the establishment. In all probability, not many of my readers have had a chance to take a peep at country dram-shops; but into what places do not we sportsmen enter! Their arrangement is extremely simple. They usually consist of a dark anteroom and a light cottage, separated into two divisions by a partition, behind which no visitor has the right to go. In this partition, above the broad, oaken table, a large, oblong opening is made. On the table or counter the liquor is sold. Sealed square bottles of various sizes stand in rows on shelves, directly opposite the aperture. In the central part of the cottage, designed for patrons, are benches, two or three empty casks, and a corner table. The majority of country dram-shops are rather dark, and almost never will you see on their board walls any of the brilliantly coloured cheap pictures which are lacking in very few cottages.

When I entered the Prítynny dram-shop, a fairly numerous company was already assembled there.

Behind the counter, as was proper, almost to the full extent of the aperture, Nikolái Ivánitch was standing in a gay-coloured cotton shirt and with a languid smile on his plump cheeks, and pouring out with his fat, white hands two glasses of liquor for the friends who had just entered, Blinker and The Ninny; and behind him, in the corner, near the window, his brisk-eyed wife was to be seen. In the middle of the room stood Yáshka-the-Turk, a spare and well-built man of three-and-twenty years, clad in a long-tailed nankeen kaftan, blue in colour. He looked like a dashing factory-hand, and, apparently, could not boast of very robust health. His sunken cheeks, his large, uneasy grey eyes, his straight nose with thin, mobile nostrils, his white receding brow, with light chestnut curls tossed back, his large but handsome and expressive lips—his whole countenance denoted an impressionable and passionate man. He was in a state of great excitement: his eyes were winking hard, he was breathing irregularly, his hands were trembling as though with fever,—and he really had a fever, that palpitating, sudden fever which is so familiar to all people who speak or sing before an audience. Beside him stood a man about forty years of age, broad-shouldered, with broad cheek-bones, and a low brow, narrow Tatár eyes, a short, thick nose, a square chin, and shining black hair as stiff as bristles. The expression of his swarthy and leaden-hued face, especially of his pallid lips, might have been designated as almost fierce, had it not been so composedly-meditative. He hardly stirred, and only slowly glanced around him, like an ox from beneath his yoke. He was dressed in some sort of a threadbare coat with smooth, brass buttons; an old, black silk kerchief encircled his huge neck. He was called the Wild Gentleman. Directly opposite him, on the bench, beneath the holy pictures, sat Yáshka's competitor,— the contractor from Zhísdra: he was a thick-set peasant, low of stature, aged thirty, pockmarked and curly-haired, with a stubby, snub nose, small, lively brown eyes, and a small, thin beard. He cast bold glances about him, with his hands tucked under him, chattered incessantly, and kept tapping with his feet, which were shod in dandified boots with a border.

THE SINGERS

He wore a new, thin armyák [1] of grey cloth, with a velveteen collar, against which the edge of a scarlet shirt, closely buttoned around the throat, stood out sharply. In the opposite corner, to the right of the door, at the table, an insignificant little peasant was sitting, clad in a scant, threadbare smock-frock with a huge hole in the shoulder. The sunlight streamed in a thin, yellowish flood through the dusty panes of two tiny windows, and, apparently, could not conquer the habitual gloom of the room: all the objects were scantily illuminated,—in spots, as it were. On the other hand, it was almost cool there, and the sensation of suffocation and sultry heat slipped from my shoulders, like a burden, as soon as I had stepped across the threshold.

My arrival—I could see it—somewhat disconcerted Nikolái Ivánitch's guests at first; but, perceiving that he bowed to me, as to an acquaintance, they recovered their composure, and paid no further attention to me. I ordered some beer, and seated myself in the corner, beside the peasant in the torn smock.

" Well, what now! "—suddenly roared The Ninny, tossing off a glass of beer at one gulp, and accompanying his exclamation with the same strange flourishing of the hands, without which,

[1] A coat which is fitted as far as the waist-line, folds diagonally across the front, and has considerable fullness imparted to the tails by plaits inserted at the waist where the curving seams from the shoulders join the skirt.—TRANSLATOR.

evidently, he never uttered a single word.—
" What are we waiting for? If you 're going to
begin, why begin. Hey? Yáshka? . . ."

" Begin, begin,"—chimed in Nikolái Ivánitch,
approvingly.

" We will begin, if you like,"—said the contractor, coolly, and with a self-satisfied smile:—
" I 'm ready."

" And I 'm ready,"—enunciated Yákoff, with
agitation.

" Well, begin, my lads, begin," piped Blinker.

But, despite the unanimously expressed desire,
no one did begin; the contractor did not even rise
from his bench,—all seemed to be waiting for
something.

" Begin!"—said the Wild Gentleman, sharply
and morosely.

Yákoff gave a start. The contractor rose,
pulled down his girdle, and cleared his throat.

" But who 's to begin?"—he asked, in a
slightly altered voice of the Wild Gentleman,
who still continued to stand motionless in the
middle of the room, with his thick legs straddled far apart, and his mighty arms thrust into
the pockets of his full trousers almost to the
elbow.

" Thou, thou, contractor,"—lisped The Ninny,
—" thou, my good fellow."

The Wild Gentleman darted a sidelong glance
at him. The Ninny gave a faint squeak, grew

confused, stared at some point on the ceiling, twitched his shoulders, and relapsed into silence.

" Cast lots,"—said the Wild Gentleman with a pause between his words:—" and let the measure of beer be placed on the counter."

Nikolái Ivánitch bent down, picked up the measure from the floor, with a grunt, and set it on the table.

The Wild Gentleman glanced at Yákoff, and said: " Go ahead!"

Yákoff fumbled in his pockets, drew forth a two-kopék piece, and bit a mark in it. The contractor pulled from beneath the tails of his kaftan a new leathern purse, deliberately untied the cords, and pouring out a quantity of small change into his hand, selected a new two-kopék bit. The Ninny held out his well-worn cap, with its broken and ripped visor; Yákoff tossed his coin into it, and the contractor tossed in his.

" 'T is for thee to draw,"—said the Wild Gentleman, turning to Blinker.

Blinker laughed in a self-satisfied way, took the cap in both hands, and began to shake it.

Instantaneously a profound silence reigned: the coins, faintly jingling, clinked against each other. I cast an attentive glance around: all faces expressed strained expectation; the Wild Gentleman himself screwed up his eyes; my neighbour, the wretched little peasant in the torn smock, even craned out his neck with curiosity.

Blinker thrust his hand into the cap and drew out the contractor's coin; all heaved a sigh. Yákoff flushed scarlet, and the contractor passed his hand over his hair.

" There, did n't I say that thou shouldst begin,"—exclaimed The Ninny. " I told you so! "

" Well, well, don't squawk," [1]—remarked the Wild Gentleman, disdainfully. " Begin,"—he added, nodding his head at the contractor.

"What song shall I sing? "—inquired the contractor, becoming flustered.

" Whatever one thou wilt,"—replied Blinker. —" Whatever song comes into thy head, sing that."

" Whatever one thou pleasest, of course,"—added Nikolái Ivánitch, slowly folding his arms on his chest.—" There 's no decree for thee on that matter. Sing what thou wilt; only, sing well; and afterward, we will decide according to our consciences."

" According to our consciences, of course,"—put in The Ninny, and licked the rim of his empty glass.

" Let me clear my throat a bit, my good fellows,"—began the contractor, drawing his fingers along the collar of his kaftan.

" Come, come, don't dawdle—begin! "—said the Wild Gentleman, with decision, and dropped his eyes.

[1] Hawks squawk when they are frightened by anything.

THE SINGERS

The contractor reflected a while, shook his head, and advanced a pace. Yákoff riveted his eyes upon him. . . .

But before I enter upon a description of the contest itself, I consider it not superfluous to say a few words about each of the acting personages of my tale. The life of several of them was already known to me, when I encountered them in the Prítynny dram-shop; I collected information concerning the others later on.

Let us begin with The Ninny. This man's real name was Evgráf Ivánoff; but no one in all the country round about called him anything but The Ninny, and he alluded to himself by this nickname also: so well did it fit him. And, as a matter of fact, nothing could have been better suited to his insignificant, eternally alarmed features. He was an idle, unmarried house-serf, who had very long since been discarded by his owners, and who, although he had no duties and received not a penny of wages, found the means, nevertheless, to indulge in daily sprees at other people's expense. He had a multitude of acquaintances, who treated him to liquor and to tea, without themselves knowing why they did so, because he not only was not entertaining in company, but even, on the contrary, bored every one with his senseless chatter, his unbearable insolence, his feverish movements and incessant, unnatural laughter. He could neither sing nor dance; in all his life he had not uttered a witty nor even a sensible word: he did nothing but " tipple " and lie at random—a regular ninny! And yet, not a single drinking-bout took place within a circuit of forty versts without his long-limbed figure turning up among the guests,—so wonted had they become to him, and so tolerant of his presence as an inevitable evil. He was treated scornfully, it is true, but no one except the Wild Gentleman knew how to put a stop to his inopportune outbursts.

Blinker did not in the least resemble The Ninny. The name Blinker suited him also, although he did not blink his eyes more than other people: 't is a well-known fact that the Russian populace are master-hands at bestowing nicknames. Despite my efforts to investigate more circumstantially the past of this man, there yet remained for me— and, probably, for others also—dark spots in his life, places, as the men learned in book-lore express it, veiled in the profound gloom of obscurity. All I found out was, that he had formerly been the coachman of an old, childless landed proprietress, had absconded with the team of three horses entrusted to him, had disappeared for a whole year, and having become convinced by experience, it is to be presumed, of the disadvantages and miseries of a vagabond existence, had returned of his own accord, but lame, had flung himself at the feet of his mistress, and,

having for the space of several years atoned
for his crime by exemplary conduct, had gradually got into her good graces, had at last won
her complete confidence, had been made overseer, and after the death of his mistress now
turned cut to have been emancipated, no one
knew how, had inscribed himself in the burgher
class, had begun to hire ground for raising mel-
ons and cucumbers from the neighbours, had
grown rich, and now lived in clover. He was a
man of experience, opinionated, neither good-
natured nor malicious, but calculating, rather;
he was a cunning rogue, acquainted with men's
ways, and knew how to take advantage of
them. He was cautious and, at the same time,
enterprising, like a fox; loquacious as an old woman, yet never made a slip of the tongue, while
he made every one else betray himself in speech;
moreover, he did not pretend to be a simpleton, as
some crafty persons of the same stamp do; and,
indeed, it would have been difficult for him to dissimulate: I have never seen more piercing and
clever eyes than his tiny, crafty " peepers." [1]
They never simply looked—they were always
watching or spying out. Blinker would sometimes consider for weeks at a stretch some apparently simple undertaking, and then suddenly decide upon some desperately-bold operation, in

[1] The people of the Orel (Aryól) Government call eyes " peepers,"
as they call the mouth "the eater."

which, to all appearances, he was sure to break his neck . . . . . And the first you knew,—everything had turned out a success, everything was running as though on oiled wheels. He was lucky, and believed in his luck, and believed in omens. Altogether, he was very superstitious. He was not beloved, because he cared nothing for any one, but he was respected. His entire family consisted of one small son, whom he fairly adored, and who, reared by such a father, would in all probability go far. " Little Blinker " (Morgatchónok) " takes after his father," the old people already said of him, with bated breath, as they sat on the earthen banks around the cottages and chatted among themselves on summer evenings; and everybody understood what that meant, and added not a word more.

There is no necessity for occupying ourselves long with Yákoff-the-Turk and the contractor. Yákoff, nicknamed the Turk, because he really was descended from a Turkish woman captive, was in soul an artist in every sense of the word, and by profession a moulder in the paper-mill of a merchant; as for the contractor, he seemed to me to be a resourceful and dashing town-dweller of the burgher class. But it is worth while to speak in more detail concerning the Wild Gentleman.

The first impression which the aspect of this man made upon you was a sensation of some coarse, heavy but irresistible force. He was awkwardly built, "flung together," as our expression runs, but he exhaled an atmosphere of invincible health, and, strange to say, his ursine figure was not devoid of a certain peculiar grace, emanating, possibly, from perfectly composed confidence in his own might. It was difficult to decide, off-hand, to what social class this Hercules belonged; he resembled neither a house-serf nor a burgher, nor an impoverished pettifogger out of a job, nor a ruined nobleman of small estate—a keeper of dogs and bully: in truth, he was a unique specimen. No one knew whence he had descended upon our district; it was said that his ancestors had been peasant-freeholders,[1] and it was supposed that he had formerly been in the government service somewhere, but no one knew anything definite in regard to that; and from whom were they to find out—certainly not from the man himself: there never was a more taciturn and surly person. Moreover, no one could say with authority what were his means of subsistence; he occupied himself with no handicraft, he visited no one, he knew hardly any one, yet he was supplied with money,—not much, to tell the truth, but enough. His demeanour was not precisely unassuming,—on the whole, there was nothing unassuming about him,—but quiet: he lived as though he did not notice any one around him,

[1] See the sketch in Vol. I, "Freeholder Ovsyánikoff," p. 98.

and decidedly stood in no need of any one. The
Wild Gentleman (such was the nickname which
had been conferred upon him; but his real name
was Perevlyésoff) enjoyed immense influence
throughout the whole countryside; people yielded
him instantaneous and willing obedience, although he not only had no shadow of right to
issue orders to any one whomsoever, but did not
even manifest the slightest pretensions to the obedience of the people with whom he came into contact. He spoke,—he was obeyed; power always
asserts its rights. He drank hardly any liquor,
did not consort with women, and was passionately
fond of singing. There was a great deal that was
mysterious about this man; it seemed as though
some vast forces or other were morosely reposing
within him, as though aware that, having once
risen up, having once broken loose, they were
bound to destroy both themselves and everything
with which they should come into contact; and I
am greatly mistaken, if such an outburst had not
already taken place in that man's life, if he,
taught by experience and barely rescued from
perdition, were not now holding a very tight rein
over himself. What especially struck me in him
was the mixture of a certain innate, natural
fierceness and an equally innate nobility,—a mixture which I have never encountered in any one
else.

So then, the contractor stepped forward, half-closed his eyes, and began to sing in a high falsetto. His voice was tolerably agreeable and sweet, although somewhat husky; he played with his voice and flung it about like a whirligig, incessantly trilling and executing roulades in a descending scale, and incessantly returning to his upper notes, which he held and drew out with peculiar pains, then paused, and again suddenly took up his former refrain with a certain daring, spirited dash. His transitions were sometimes quite bold, sometimes quite amusing: they would have afforded connoisseurs great satisfaction; a German would have been enraged by them. He was a Russian *tenore di grazia, tenor léger.* He sang a merry dance-tune, the words of which, so far as I could make them out amid the interminable ornamentation, the supplementary consonants and exclamations, were as follows:

> " I 'll plough, will I, the stripling young,
>   A little patch of ground:
>   I 'll sow, will I, the stripling young,
>   A little flower of scarlet hue."

He sang; all listened to him with great attention. He evidently felt that he had to deal with people who were good judges, and therefore, as the saying is, he fairly " crawled out of his skin " in his efforts. As a matter of fact, people in our parts are good judges of singing, and not with-

out cause is the village of Sérgievskoe, on the
great Orel highway, renowned throughout the
whole of Russia for its peculiarly agreeable and
harmonious melody. For a long time the contractor continued to sing, without evoking any
special sympathy in his hearers.

He lacked the support of a chorus; at last, at
one particularly successful passage, which made
even the Wild Gentleman smile, The Ninny could
contain himself no longer, and shouted aloud with
delight. Every one gave a start. The Ninny
and Blinker began to hum in an undertone, to
accompany him, and to shout: " That 's a dandy!
. . . . . . Go ahead, thou rascal! . . . Go
ahead, keep on, thou brigand! Lash out again!
Split thy throat again, thou dog, thou hound!
. . . Let Herod slay thy soul!" . . . and so
forth. Nikolái Ivánitch, behind his counter,
nodded his head to right and left in approbation.
At last, The Ninny began to stamp his feet, to
shift from foot to foot, and to twitch his shoulders,—and Yákoff's eyes fairly blazed up like
coals of fire, and he quivered all over like a leaf,
and smiled flabbily. The Wild Gentleman alone
did not change countenance, and, as before, did
not stir from his seat; but his gaze, riveted upon
the contractor, became somewhat softer, although
the expression of his lips remained scornful. Encouraged by these tokens of universal approval,
the contractor became a perfect whirlwind, and

began to emit such *fioriture*, clicked and drummed
so with his tongue, made his throat perform such
frantic feats, that when, at last, exhausted, pale,
and drenched in boiling perspiration, he threw
his whole body backward and gave vent to a final
expiring outcry, a general unanimous shout responded to him in a vehement outburst. The
Ninny flung himself upon his neck, and began to
choke him with his long, bony arms; on Nikolái
Ivánitch's fat face a flush broke forth, and he
seemed to have grown young again; Yákoff
shouted like a madman: "Well done! well
done!"[1]—even my neighbour, the peasant in the
torn smock, could not contain himself, and smiting the table with his fist, he shouted: "A-ha!
good, devil take it—'t is good!"—and spat decisively to one side.

"Well, brother, thou hast diverted us!"—cried
The Ninny, without releasing the exhausted contractor from his embrace,—"thou hast diverted
us, there's no denying that! Thou hast won,
brother, thou hast won! I congratulate thee,—the
measure of beer is thine! Yáshka is far behind
thee. . . . Just mark what I am saying to thee:
thou 'rt far ahead of him. . . . Believe me!"
(And again he clasped the contractor to his
breast.)

"Come, let him go, let him go, thou nui-

---

[1] Literally: "Fine, dashing young fellow." Possibly, "Bully for
you!" would be the more accurate translation.—TRANSLATOR.

sance . . ." said Blinker, with vexation:—" let him sit down on the bench; dost not thou see he 's tired! . . . What a ninny thou art, my good fellow,—really, a ninny! Why dost thou stick to him like a bath-leaf?" [1]

" Well, all right, let him sit down, and I 'll drink to his health,"—said The Ninny, stepping up to the counter.—" At thy expense, brother,"—he added, addressing the contractor.

The latter nodded in assent, seated himself on the bench, pulled a towel out of his cap, and began to mop his face; but The Ninny, with greedy haste, drained his glass, and, according to the custom of confirmed drunkards, he assumed a grieved and careworn aspect.

" Thou singest well, brother, well,"—remarked Nikolái Ivánitch, caressingly.—" And now 't is thy turn, Yáshka: look out, don't be timid. Let 's see who 's who; let 's see. . . But the contractor sings well,—by heaven, he does!"

" Very well, indeed,"—remarked Nikolái Ivánitch's wife, glancing at Yákoff with a smile.

" Very well indee-ed!" repeated my neighbour, in an undertone.

" Hey, Savage-Polyékha!" [2] suddenly roared

---

[1] The usual bath-besom, for agreeable massage after the steam-bath, is a fan-like bunch of birch-branches, with the leaves left on, and dipped in hot water to prevent their falling off. Sometimes the peasants use bunches of nettles.—TRANSLATOR.

[2] The inhabitants of southern Polyésye are called Polyékhi. The Polyésye is a long forest tract which begins at the boundary of the Bolkhóff and Zhízdra districts. Its inhabitants are distin-

The Ninny, and stalking up to the peasant with the hole on his shoulder, he pointed his finger at him, began to skip about, and burst into a peal of laughter. — " A Polyékha! a Polyékha! Ha, *bádye,*[1] drive on, Savage? Why hast thou favoured us with thy company? " he shouted, through his laughter. The poor peasant was disconcerted, and was making ready to rise and depart as speedily as possible, when suddenly the Wild Gentleman's brazen voice rang out:

" Why, what intolerable animal is this? "—he ejaculated, gnashing his teeth.

" I did n't do anything," — mumbled The Ninny:—" I did n't do anything. . . . I only just . . . . "

" Well, very good, hold thy tongue! "—retorted the Wild Gentleman.—" Yákoff, begin! "

Yákoff clutched his throat with his hand.

" Well, brother, you know . . . somehow . . . H'm . . . . I don't know, really, somehow, you know . . . . "

" Come, have done with that, don't get frightened. Art ashamed? . . . Why dost thou wriggle? Sing as God prompts thee."

And the Wild Gentleman lowered his eyes in anticipation.

guished by many peculiarities in their manner of life, customs, and dialect. They are called savages because of their suspicious and dull disposition.

[1] The Polyékhi add the exclamation " ha! " to nearly every word, also " bádye." The Ninny says " panyái " instead of " pogonyái " (" drive on "), also in mimicry.

Yákoff held his peace for a little, cast a glance round him, and covered his face with his hand. Every one fairly bored into him with his eyes, especially the contractor, upon whose countenance, athwart his wonted self-assurance, and the triumph of success, there broke forth a faint, involuntary uneasiness. He leaned back against the wall and again tucked both his hands under him, but he no longer swung his feet to and fro. When, at last, Yákoff uncovered his face, it was pale as that of a corpse, and his eyes barely gleamed through his lowered lashes. He heaved a deep sigh, and began to sing. . . . The first sound of his voice was weak and uneven, and, apparently, did not emanate from his chest, but was wafted from some distant place, as though it had flown accidentally into the room. This tremulous, ringing sound had a strange effect on all of us; we glanced at one another, and Nikolái Ivánitch's wife actually straightened herself up. This first sound was followed by another, more firm and prolonged, but still obviously tremulous, like a chord when, suddenly resounding beneath a strong finger, it quivers with a final, expiring tremor; the second note was followed by a third, and, gradually, warming up and broadening, a melancholy song poured forth.

" Not one path alone in the field is trodden,"

he sang, and we all felt sweetness and sadness in
our hearts. I am bound to confess, that rarely
have I heard such a voice: it was slightly broken,
and had a cracked ring; at first it even had a sort
of sickly sound; but it contained both genuine
and profound passion, and youth, and power, and
sweetness, and a certain captivatingly-care-free,
despondent pain. An upright, burning, Russian
soul resounded and breathed in it, and fairly
gripped our hearts, laid hold directly upon their
Russian chords. The song swelled and broad-
ened. Yákoff, evidently, had been seized with a
fit of rapture; he was no longer timid, he surrendered himself wholly to his bliss; his voice no
longer trembled,—it quivered, but with that
barely perceptible inward quiver of passion,
which pierces the soul of the hearer like an arrow,
and grew constantly stronger, firmer, more volu-
minous. I remember having seen, once upon a
time, of an evening, at ebb-tide, on the flat, sandy
shore of the sea, which was roaring menacingly
and heavily in the distance, a large white sea-gull;
it was sitting motionless, with its silky breast
exposed to the crimson glow of the sunset, and
only now and then did it slowly spread its long
wings in the direction of its familiar ocean,
toward the purpling sun: I recalled that sea-gull
as I listened to Yákoff. He sang on, utterly
oblivious of his rival, and of us all, but evidently
upborne, like a vigorous swimmer by the waves,

by our silent, passionate interest. He sang, and
every sound of his voice breathed forth something
which was akin to us, and boundlessly vast, as
though the familiar steppes were unrolling themselves before us, stretching out into the illimitable
distance. I felt that tears were gathering in my
heart, and welling up into my eyes; dull, sup-
pressed sobs suddenly startled me. I
glanced around—the publican's wife was weeping, bent forward, with her bosom against the
window. Yákoff shot a swift glance at her, and
began to warble even more sweetly than before. Nikolái Ivánitch dropped his eyes; Blinker
turned away; The Ninny, completely melted,
stood with his mouth stupidly agape; the grey
little peasant was sobbing softly in his corner,
shaking his head with a bitter whisper; and across
the iron face of the Wild Gentleman, from beneath his brows, which were completely contracted
in a frown, a heavy tear was trickling slowly;
the contractor raised his clenched fist to his brow,
and did not stir. . . . I know not in what the universal anguish would have culminated, had not
Yákoff suddenly wound up on a high, remarkably thin note—as though his voice had broken off
short. No one cried out, no one even stirred; all
seemed to be waiting to see whether he would not
sing some more; but he opened his eyes, as though
surprised at our silence, surveyed us all with an
inquiring glance, and saw that the victory was
his. . . .

THE SINGERS

" Yáshka,"—said the Wild Gentleman, laying his hand on his shoulder, and—said no more.

We all stood as though stunned. The contractor rose softly, and stepped up to Yákoff.— " Thou . . . . thy . . . . thou hast won,"—he enunciated at last with difficulty, and rushed headlong from the room.

His swift, decisive movement seemed to break the spell: all suddenly began to talk noisily, joyously. The Ninny gave an upward leap, stammered, fluttered his arms like the wings of a windmill; Blinker hobbled up to Yákoff and began to kiss him; Nikolái Ivánitch half rose, and solemnly announced that he would add an extra measure of beer on his account. The Wild Gentleman laughed with a good-natured sort of laugh, which I had never expected to encounter on his face; the wretched little peasant kept reiterating in his corner, as he wiped his eyes, cheeks, nose, and beard with both his sleeves: " But 't is good,—by heaven, 't is good! Well, now, I 'll renounce my parents and become a dog if it is n't good! " while Nikolái Ivánitch's wife, all flushed, rose hastily and withdrew. Yákoff enjoyed his victory like a child; his whole face was transfigured; his eyes, in particular, fairly beamed with happiness. He was dragged to the counter; he called to him the tear-sodden peasant, despatched the tapster's little son for the contractor, whom the boy did not find, however, and the carouse began,—" Thou wilt sing for us again,

thou wilt sing for us until the evening," The
Ninny kept repeating, raising his hands on
high.

I cast one more glance at Yákoff, and departed. I did not wish to remain,—I was afraid
of spoiling my impression. But the sultry heat
was as unbearable as ever. It seemed to be hanging close to the very earth, in a dense, heavy
stratum; in the dark-blue sky, certain tiny, bright
flames seemed to be whirling about, athwart the
very fine, almost black dust. All was silent; there
was something hopeless, oppressive in that profound silence of debilitated nature. I wended
my way to the hay-loft and lay down on the
freshly-mown but already almost dry grass. For
a long time I did not fall asleep; for a long time,
Yákoff's irresistible voice rang in my ears. . . . . .
At last the heat and my fatigue asserted their
rights, however, and I sank into a death-like
slumber. When I awoke, all was dark; the grass
scattered round about emitted a strong fragrance, and had grown somewhat damp; through
the thin boards of the half-open roof pale little
stars were twinkling. I went outside. The sunset glow had long since died out, and its last traces
were barely visible, like a white streak on the
horizon; but in the air, recently red-hot, warmth
was still perceptible athwart the nocturnal coolness, and the lungs still thirsted for a cold blast.
There was no breeze, there was not even a cloud;

round about, the sky was perfectly clear and transparently-dark, softly scintillating with innumerable but barely visible stars. Lights gleamed in the village; from the brilliantly-lighted dram-shop hard by was wafted a confused, discordant uproar, amid which it seemed to me that I recognised Yákoff's voice. Shrill laughter arose thence in gusts, from time to time. I stepped up to the tiny window, and pressed my face to the pane. I beheld a cheerless, though motley and lively picture: everybody was drunk —everybody, beginning with Yákoff. He was sitting, with bared breast, on the wall-bench, and singing in a hoarse voice some dancing-tune of the street, as he lazily ran his fingers over and twanged the strings of a guitar. His damp hair hung in elf-locks over his horribly pale face. In the middle of the dram-shop, The Ninny, completely " unscrewed " and minus his kaftan, was dancing with leaps and squattings in front of the peasant in the greyish armyák; the miserable little peasant, in his turn, was stamping and shuffling his enfeebled feet with difficulty, and smiling foolishly through his dishevelled beard, and flourished one hand from time to time, as much as to say: "I don't care a rap for anybody!" Nothing could be more ridiculous than his face: no matter how much he twitched his brows upward, his fatigue-laden lids would not rise, and continued to lie upon the barely perceptible, intoxicated, but still very sweet little eyes. He was in the engaging condition of a man who has got thoroughly tipsy, when every passer-by, on glancing at his face, will infallibly say: " 'T is good, brother, 't is good!" Blinker, all scarlet as a crayfish, and with his nostrils widely inflated, was jeering spitefully from a corner; Nikolái Ivánitch alone, as is befitting a genuine publican, preserved his invariable coolness. A number of new individuals had assembled in the room; but I did not see the Wild Gentleman among them.

I turned away, and with swift steps began to descend the hill on which Kolotóvka lies. At the foot of this hill, the broad ravine spreads out; submerged in the misty billows of the evening fog, it appeared more limitless than ever, and seemed to merge into the darkened sky. I was proceeding with great strides on the road which runs along the precipice, when suddenly, far away in the ravine, there rang out the resonant voice of a boy.—" Antrópka! Antrópka-a-a!"—it shouted in persistent and tearful desperation, prolonging the last syllable for a very, very long time.

He stopped for a few moments, and again began to shout. His voice rang out sonorously on the motionless, lightly-slumbering air. Thirty times, at least, had he shouted the name of Antrópka, when suddenly from the opposite end of the field, as though from another world, the barely audible reply was wafted:

" Wha-a-a-aat? "

The boy's voice instantly shouted with joyous wrath:

" Come hither, thou devil, thou forest-fi-i-i-iend! "

" Why-y-y-y? "—replied the second voice, after a long pause.

" Why, because thy daddy wants to spa-a-a-ank thee,"—hastily shouted the first voice.

The second voice did not respond again, and again the boy began to call Antrópka. His shouts, which grew ever weaker and more infrequent, still continued to reach my ear, when it had already grown completely dark, and I was doubling the edge of the forest which surrounded my hamlet and was situated four versts from Kolotóvka. . . . .

" Antrópka-a-a! " seemed to be still audible in the air, filled with the shades of night.

V

FIVE years ago, in autumn, I was compelled to sit
for almost an entire day in a posting-house on the
highway from Moscow to Túla, for lack of
horses. I was returning from a hunting-expedition, and had been so incautious as to send my
tróïka on ahead. The superintendent, a surly
fellow, already aged, with hair which hung over
his nose, and tiny, sleepy eyes, replied to all my
complaints and requests by a growl, slammed the
door wrathfully, as though cursing his own office,
and emerging upon the porch, set to berating the
postilions, who were slowly tramping through
the mud with arches weighing about forty
pounds apiece in their arms, or were sitting on
the bench, yawning and scratching their heads,
and paid no particular attention to the angry exclamations of their superior. I had already set
to work three times to drink tea, I had several
times vainly endeavoured to get to sleep, I had
perused all the inscriptions on the windows and
on the walls; I was oppressed by frightful tedium. I was staring with chill and hopeless despair at the upturned shafts of my tarantás, when

102

suddenly a small bell resounded, and a little cart, drawn by three weary horses, drew up before the porch. The newcomer sprang from his cart, and with the shout: " Horses, and be quick about it! " entered the room. While he listened, with the customary strange surprise, to the superintendent's reply, that there were no horses, I succeeded, with the eager curiosity of a bored man, in scanning my new companion from head to foot with a glance. Apparently, he was about thirty years of age. The smallpox had left ineffaceable traces on his face, which was harsh and yellow, with an unpleasant brazen tint; his long, bluish-black hair fell in rings upon his collar behind, in front it curled in dashing ringlets on the temples; his small, swollen eyes had sight, and that was all; on his upper lip, several small hairs stuck out. He was dressed like a dissolute landed proprietor, a frequenter of horse-fairs, in a flowered Caucasian overcoat, considerably soiled, a faded silk neckerchief of lilac hue, a waistcoat with brass buttons, and grey trousers with huge bell-bottoms, from beneath which the tips of his uncleaned boots were barely visible. He reeked strongly of tobacco and vódka; on his fat, red fingers, which were almost covered by the sleeves of the overcoat, silver and Túla rings of gold and black steel were discernible. Such figures are to be encountered in Russia not by the dozen but by the hundred; acquaintance with them, truth to tell, does not afford any pleasure whatever, but, in spite of the prejudice wherewith I surveyed the newcomer, I could not but notice the unconcernedly good-natured and passionate expression of his face.

" They [1] have been waiting here for more than an hour, sir,"—said the superintendent, pointing at me.

More than an hour!—The malefactor was making fun of me.

" But perhaps he does not need them so badly," —replied the newcomer.

" We can't tell about that, sir,"—said the superintendent, surlily.

" And isn't it possible to manage it in some way? Are there positively no horses? "

" Can't be done, sir. There isn't a single horse."

" Well, then, order the samovár to be brought for me. I'll wait, there's nothing else to be done."

The newcomer seated himself on the wall-bench, flung his cap on the table, and passed his hand over his hair.

" And have you already drunk tea? "—he asked me.

" Yes."

" Won't you drink again, to keep me company? "

[1] Respectful form for " he."—TRANSLATOR.

PIÓTR PETRÓVITCH KARATÁEFF

I consented. The fat, reddish samovár made its appearance on the table for the fourth time. I produced a bottle of rum. I had made no mistake in taking my interlocutor for a noble of small estate. His name was Piótr Petróvitch Karatáeff.

We entered into conversation. Half an hour had not elapsed since his arrival before he, with the most good-humoured frankness, had related to me the story of his life.

" Now I 'm going to Moscow,"—he said to me, as he drained his fourth cup:—" there 's nothing more for me to do in the country now."

" Why not? "

" Just because there is n't . . . not a thing. My farming operations are thoroughly disorganised, I have ruined the peasants, I must confess; we have had bad years; poor harvests, various calamities, you know. . . . And besides,"—he added, with a dejected glance aside:—" I 'm no sort of a landlord! "

" How so? "

" Because I 'm not," — he interrupted me. " There are good landlords of a very different sort from me. See here, now,"—he went on, twisting his head on one side, and sucking diligently at his pipe:—" Perhaps you are thinking, as you look at me, that I—you know . . . . but I must admit to you, that I received a mediocre education; means were lacking. You must

105

excuse me, I'm an outspoken man, and in short . . . ."

He did not finish his remark and waved his hand. I began to assure him, that he was in error, that I was very glad that we had met, and so forth, after which I remarked that, for the management of an estate, too intense culture was not necessary, apparently.

" Agreed,"—he replied:—" I agree with you. But nevertheless, a certain special inclination is requisite! One man will do God knows what, and it's all right! but I . . . . Permit me to inquire, are you from Peter [1] or from Moscow? "

" I am from Petersburg."

He emitted a long wreath of smoke through his nostrils.

" And I'm going to Moscow to enter the government service."

" Where do you intend to establish yourself? "

" That I don't know: as fortune favours. I must confess to you, that I'm afraid of the service: the first you know, you incur some responsibility. I have always lived in the country; I'm used to that, you know . . . . but there's no help for it . . . . necessity compels! Okh, hang that necessity! "

" On the other hand, you will reside in the capital."

" Yes, in the capital . . . . well, I don't know

[1] Abbreviation of St. Petersburg.—Translator.

what there is good there, in the capital. We shall see, perhaps it is good. . . . But I think that nothing can be better than the country."

"But is it impossible for you to live in the country any longer?"

He heaved a sigh.

"It is. The village is hardly mine any more."

"How is that?"

"Why, a kind man there—a neighbour has instituted . . . . a lawsuit . . . . . . there was a note of hand. . . . ." Poor Piótr Petróvitch passed his hand over his face, meditated, and shook his head.

"Well, never mind! . . . . But I must admit,"—he added, after a brief pause:—"I have no complaint to make of any one, I myself am to blame. I was fond of having my own way,—devil take it, I was fond of showing my independence!"

"Did you live in jolly style in the country?" —I asked him.

"Sir,"—he answered me, pausing between his words, and looking me straight in the eye,—"I had twelve leashes of greyhounds,—such greyhounds, I must tell you, are rare." (He pronounced this last word with a drawl.)—"They would shake the life out of a hare on the instant, and as for deer,—they were serpents, regular asps. But that's a thing of the past now, there's no use in lying about it. I used to hunt with a gun. I had a dog, Kontéska; a remarkable pointer, she took everything by her extremely fine scent. I used to approach the marsh, and say: ' Charge!' and she would n't hunt; even if you were to pass by with a dozen dogs,—you would waste your time, nothing would you find! but when she did begin,—you 'd simply be glad to die on the spot! . . . . And she was so polite in the house. Give her bread with your left hand and say:—' A Jew bit it,'—and she would n't take it, but give it to her with your right hand, and say: ' A young lady tasted it,'—and instantly she 'd take it and eat it. I had a pup of hers, a capital pup, and I wanted to take it to Moscow, but a friend begged it of me, along with my gun; says he: ' In Moscow, brother, you will have no use for them; everything will be quite different there, brother.' So I gave him the pup, and the gun too; everything remained there—behind, you know."

" But you might have hunted in Moscow also."

" No; what 's the use? I have n't known how to hold my ground, so now let me endure with patience. But here now, permit me rather to inquire, how is living in Moscow—dear? "

" No, not very."

" Not very? . . . . But tell me, please, the gipsies live in Moscow, don't they? "

" What gipsies? "

"Why, the ones who travel round to the fairs?"

"Yes, they live in Moscow. . . ."

"Well, that's good. I'm fond of gipsies,— damn it, I love them. . . . . ."

And Piótr Petróvitch's eyes sparkled with audacious jollity. But, all at once, he began to wriggle about on the bench, then grew thoughtful, drooped his head, and stretched out his empty glass to me.

"Give me some of your rum, pray,"—said he.

"But the tea is all gone."

"Never mind, I'll take it so, without tea. . . . . Ekh!"

Karatáeff laid his head on his hands, and propped his arms on the table. I gazed at him in silence, and waited for those emotional exclamations, probably, even, those tears, of which a man in a carouse is so lavish; but when he raised his head, the profoundly-melancholy expression of his face amazed me, I must confess.

"What is the matter with you?"

"Nothing, sir. . . . I have been recalling old times. There's an anecdote, sir. . . . I'd tell it to you, only I'm ashamed to disturb you. . . ."

"Pray, do not mention it!"

"Yes,"—he went on, with a sigh:—"things happen . . . however, for instance, to me also. Here now, if you like, I'll tell you the story. However, I don't know. . . ."

" Tell me, my dear Piótr Petróvitch." . . .

" Very well, although it 's rather . . . . Well, you see,"—he began:—" but really, I don't know . . . . . ."

" Come, enough of that, my dear Piótr Petróvitch."

" Well, as you like. So then, this is what happened to me, so to say. I was living in the village, sir. . . . . All at once, I took a fancy to a young girl. Akh, what a girl she was! . . . . beautiful, clever, and so good-natured! Her name was Matryóna, sir. And she was a simple lass,—that is to say, you understand, a serf, simply a slave, sir. And she was n't my girl, but the property of another,—and therein lay the misfortune. Well, and so I fell in love with her,— really, sir, the anecdote is of a sort,—well, here goes. So Matryóna began to entreat me to buy her from her mistress; and I was thinking of that same thing myself. . . . But her mistress was wealthy, a dreadful old woman; she lived about fifteen versts from me. Well, one fine day, as the saying is, I ordered my tróïka to be harnessed, —I had a pacer for a shaft-horse, a wonderful Asiatic beast, and his name was Lampurdos, by the way,—dressed myself in my best, and drove off to Matryóna's mistress. I arrived: 't was a big house, with wings, in a park. . . . . Matryóna was waiting for me at the turn of the road, and tried to speak to me, but merely kissed my hand and stepped aside. So then, I entered the anteroom, and inquired: ' Is the lady at home? ' . . . . And a footman as tall as that, says: 'What name shall I announce? ' Says I: ' My good fellow, announce that Squire Karatáeff has come to talk over a matter of business.' The lackey withdrew; I waited, and thought to myself: ' How will it turn out? I suppose the beast will demand a frightful price, in spite of the fact that she 's rich.' Well, at last, the footman returned, and said: ' Please come with me.' I followed him to the drawing-room. In an arm-chair sat a tiny sallow old woman, blinking her eyes. . . . ' What do you want? '—I thought it necessary first, you know, to declare that I came to make her acquaintance.—' You are mistaken, I am not the mistress of the house, I am a relation of hers. . . . What do you want? '—Thereupon I remarked to her, that I must speak with the mistress herself.—' Márya Ilínitchna is not receiving to-day; she is not well. . . . . What do you want? ' . . . . ' There 's no help for it,' said I to myself, ' I 'll explain the circumstances to her.' The old woman heard me to the end.—' Matryóna? what Matryóna?—Matryóna Feódoroff, the daughter of Kulikóff—Feódor Kulikóff's daughter? . . . . but how do you know her? ' ' Accidentally.'—' And is she acquainted with your intention? '—' She is.'—The old woman was silent for a while.—' I 'll give it to her, the

111

wretch! . . .'—I was amazed, I must admit.—
'What for, good gracious! . . . . I am ready to
pay a good sum for her, only please to designate
it.'—The old hag fairly frothed at the mouth.—
'Well, a pretty way you 've devised to astonish
people: much we care for your money! . . . .
but won't I give it to her, though! I 'll deal with
her. . . . I 'll thrash the folly out of her.'—The
old woman fell into a fit of coughing with rage.
'Is n't she well off with us, I 'd like to know?
Akh, she 's a devil, Lord forgive my sin!'—I
flared up, I must confess.—'Why do you make
threats against the poor girl? In what way is she
to blame?'—The old woman crossed herself.—
'Akh, O Lord, do you mean to say that I . . .'
—'But she does n't belong to you, you know!'
—'Well, Márya Ilínitchna knows all about that;
't is no business of yours, my good man; but just
wait, I 'll show that wretched Matryóna whose
slave she is.'—I must confess, that I came near
flinging myself on the cursed old woman, but I
remembered Matryóna, and dropped my hands.
It is impossible to tell you how timid I became;
I began to entreat the old woman. 'Take what
you will,' I said.—'But what do you want of
her?'—'I 've taken a fancy to her, mátushka;
put yourself in my place. . . . Permit me to kiss
your little hand.'—And I actually kissed the villain's hand!—'Well!' mumbled the old witch:—
'I 'll tell Márya Ilínitchna; it will be as she com-

mands; and do you drop in again a couple of days hence.'—I drove home in great perturbation. I had begun to divine that I had managed the business badly, that I had made a mistake in allowing my affection to be seen, but I had thought of it too late. A couple of days later I set off to call on the lady. I was shown into her study. There was a profusion of flowers, the decorations were fine; the lady herself was seated in such a curious easy-chair, with her head reclining on cushions; and the relative whom I had seen before was sitting there also; and, besides these, some young lady or other with white eyebrows and lashes, in a green gown, a wry-mouthed creature, a companion, probably. The old woman snuffled out: 'Please sit down.' I sat down. She began to question me, as to how old I was, and where I had served, and what I intended to do; and all this in a patronising, pompous way. I replied in detail. The old woman took a handkerchief from the table, and fanned and fanned herself with it. . . . 'Katerína Kárpovna has made a report to me concerning your intentions,' said she; 'she has reported to me,' said she; 'but I have made it a rule,' said she, 'not to release my people to go out to service. It is not seemly, and it is not proper in a respectable house: it is n't good form. I have already taken the proper measures,' said she, 'and there is no necessity for troubling you further.'—'It is no trouble, I assure you. . . . But

perhaps you need Matryóna Feódorovna?'—
'No,' said she, ' I don't need her.'—' Then why
will not you let me have her?'—' Because I don't
choose, because I don't choose to do it, and that's
all there is to be said. I have already made arrangements,' said she: ' she is to be sent to a village on the steppes.'—This was like a clap of
thunder to me. The old woman said a couple of
words in French to the green young lady: the latter left the room.—' I 'm a woman of strict principles,' said she, ' and my health is not strong. I
cannot endure being worried. You are still a
young man, and I am already an old woman, and
entitled to give you advice. Would not it be
better for you to settle down, to marry, to hunt
up a good match? Wealthy brides are rare, but a
poor girl, and one of good moral character, can be
found.'—Do you know, I stared at the old woman, and did n't understand a word of what she
was jabbering; I heard her saying something
about marriage, but the village on the steppes
kept ringing in my ears. ' Marry! Marry!' . . . .
what the devil! . . . ."

At this point the narrator suddenly halted, and
cast a glance at me.

" You 're not married, are you? "

" No."

" Well, certainly not, as a matter of course. I
could n't bear it:—' Why, good gracious, mátushka, what nonsense are you babbling? What

has marriage to do with it? I simply want to know, whether you will sell your maid Matryóna or not?'—The old woman began to groan.— 'Akh, he has worried me! Akh, order him to go away! akh! . . . .' The relative sprang to her assistance, and began to scream at me. And the old woman kept on moaning:—'How have I deserved this? . . . Am I no longer mistress in my own house? Akh, akh!' I seized my hat, and rushed out of the house like a madman.

"Perhaps," pursued the narrator, "you will condemn me for having become so attached to a girl of the lower classes: and I have no intention of defending myself. It was no fault of mine! If you will believe it, I had no peace day or night. . . . I tortured myself! 'Why have I ruined the unhappy girl?' I thought. As soon as I called to mind that she was herding the geese in a coarse, collarless smock, and ill-treated by her mistress's command, and the overseer, a peasant in tarred boots, was swearing at her and calling her names, the cold sweat would begin fairly to drip off me. Well, I could n't endure it: I found out to what village she had been sent, mounted my horse, and rode thither. I did not arrive until toward evening of the second day. Evidently, they had not expected such a caper on my part, and no orders had been given concerning me. I went straight to the overseer, like a neighbour; I entered the farm-yard, and behold, there sat Matryóna on the steps,

with her head propped on her hand. She was on
the point of crying out, but I shook my finger at
her, and pointed to the back-yard, to the fields. I
entered the cottage, chatted with the overseer,
told him a devilish lot of lies, took advantage
of a good opportunity, and went out to meet Matryóna. She, poor girl, fairly hung upon my
neck. She had grown pale, and thin, my dear
little dove. And, do you know, I said to her:
' Never mind, Matryóna, never mind, don't cry; '
—but my own tears were flowing all the while.
. . . Well, anyway, at last I felt ashamed; I said
to her:—' Matryóna, tears will not help: we must
act with decision, as the saying is; thou must flee
with me; that 's the way we must act.'—Matryóna
almost swooned. . . . ' How can I do that? why,
I shall be ruined, and they will persecute me
worse than ever! '—' Thou silly, who will find
thee? '—' They will find me, they will find me
without fail. I thank you, Piótr Petróvitch,—
so long as I live I shall never forget thy kindness,
but do thou leave me now; evidently, such is my
fate.'—' Ekh, Matryóna, Matryóna, I had
thought that thou wert a girl of firm character.'
—And, in fact, she had a lot of firmness . . . .
she had a soul, a soul of gold!—' Why shouldst
thou stay here? it will make no difference; thou
wilt be none the worse off. Come now, tell me:
hast thou tasted the overseer's fists, hey? '—Matryóna fairly boiled with wrath, and her lips be-

gan to quiver.—' But my family will be persecuted on my account.'—' Damn thy family. . . Will they exile it, pray?'—' Yes, they will certainly send my brother into exile.'—' And thy father?'—' Well, they will not exile my father; he is a very good tailor.'—' There now, seest thou; and thy brother will not be ruined by that.' —If you will believe me, I prevailed upon her by force; she tried to argue a while longer, saying: ' They will hold thee to account for it. . . .' ' But that 's no business of thine,' said I. . . . So I just carried her off . . . . not on that occasion, but on another: I came by night, in a cart—and carried her off."

" You carried her off? "

" I did. . . . Well, and so she settled down with me. My house was not large, my servants were few. My people, I will say it without circumlocution, respected me; they would n't have betrayed me for any sort of good fortune. I began to live like a fighting-cock. My dear little Matryóna got rested, and recovered her health; and I got so attached to her. . . And what a girl she was! she could sing, and dance, and play the guitar. . . . I did n't show her to the neighbours: they 'd have proclaimed the affair abroad the very first thing! But I had a friend, a bosom-friend, Panteléi Gornostáeff — perhaps you are acquainted with him? He simply adored her: he used to kiss her hand as though she had been a

117

well-born lady, he really did. And I must tell
you, that Gornostáeff was no mate for me: he
was an educated man, he had read Púshkin all
through; when he began to talk to Matryóna
and me, we would fairly prick up our ears.
He taught her to write, such an eccentric fellow
he was! And how I used to dress her,—better
than the Governor's wife, and that's all there is
to it; I had a fur-lined cloak of crimson velvet,
with a fur border, made for her. . . . . . And
how becoming that cloak was to her! A Moscow
mantua-maker madame made that fur cloak after
a new pattern, fitted in at the waist.[1] And how
wondrously beautiful Matryóna was! She used
to sit for hours at a time, staring at the floor, and
never moving an eyelash: and I would sit there
also, and gaze at her, and never could gaze my fill,
just as though I had never beheld her before.
. . . . She would smile, and my heart would
fairly quiver, as though some one had tickled it.
And then all of a sudden, she would set to laughing, and jesting, and dancing; she would embrace
me so warmly, so strongly, that my head would
grow dizzy. From morning till night, the only
thing I used to think about, was: 'How can I
give her pleasure?' And if you will believe me, I
used to give her presents simply for the sake of

[1] The ordinary Russian "shúba" is of the old-fashioned "circular" shape, reaching from the neck to the ground, fur-lined, and
with a long "shawl"-shaped fur collar, which can be drawn up
around the ears.—TRANSLATOR.

seeing how she, my darling, would rejoice, and blush all over with joy, and begin to try on my gift, and come to display herself to me in her new things, and kiss me. I don't know how her father, Kulík, ferreted out the business; the old man came to take a look at us, and began to cry. . . . Thus we lived for five months, and I had no objections to spending my whole life with her, but my fate is such an accursed one!"

Piótr Petróvitch paused.

"What happened?"—I asked him with interest.

He waved his hand.

"Everything went to the devil. And it was I that ruined her. Matryóna was excessively fond of sleigh-riding, and used to drive herself; she would don her fur cloak, and embroidered Torzhók [1] mittens, and do nothing but shout. We always drove in the evening, so that we might not meet any one, you know. So, once we picked out a magnificent day; very cold and clear, with no wind . . . and set off. Matryóna took the reins. So I looked to see where she was going. Could it be to Kukuévko, the village of her mistress? Exactly so, it was to Kukuévko. I said to her: 'Thou crazy girl, whither art thou going?' She glanced over her shoulder

---

[1] The leather wares made in Torzhók, not far from Moscow, are an imitation of the beautiful, many-hued and embroidered goods made at Kazán by the Tatárs. In comparison with the latter, they are coarse, and the embroidery in silks, gold, and silver is very perishable.—TRANSLATOR.

at me, and laughed. As much as to say: ' Let me show my daring! ' ' Ah! ' I thought: ' well, here goes! ' . . . . 'T was a nice thing to drive past the manor-house, was n't it? tell me yourself—was n't it nice? Well, we drove on. My pacer fairly floated along, and the trace-horses went like the wind, I can tell you,—and soon the church at Kukuévko came in sight; and behold an old green coach on runners is crawling along the road, and a footman is towering up on the footboard behind. . . . 'T was the lady, the lady driving! I was frightened, but how Matryóna slapped the reins on the horses' backs, and how we did dash straight at the coach! The coachman! He, you understand, saw that some wild phantom or other was flying to meet him,—and tried to turn out, you know, but turned too short, and overturned the coach into a snow-drift. The window was smashed, the lady shrieked: ' Aï, áï, áï! áï, áï, áï! ' the companion squealed: ' Stop, stop! ' but we drove past as fast as we could go. As I galloped on I thought: ' Harm will come of this; I ought n't to have allowed her to drive to Kukuévko.' And what do you think? the lady had recognised Matryóna, and had recognised me, the old thing, and she made a complaint against me: ' My fugitive serf-girl is living with nobleman Karatáeff; ' and thereupon she showed the proper gratitude.[1] And behold, the rural chief of

---

[1] That is, bribed in the proper quarter.—TRANSLATOR.

police comes to me; and this chief of police was a man I knew, Stepán Sergyéitch Kuzóvkin, a nice man; that is to say, in reality not a nice man. So he comes and says: thus and so, Piótr Petróvitch,—how came you to do this? . . . . 'T is a heavy responsibility, and the laws are clear on this point.—I said to him: ' Well, of course, you and I will talk this over, but won't you have a bite after your journey?' He consented to have a bite, but said: ' Justice demands, Piótr Petróvitch, judge for yourself.'—' It 's all right about justice, of course,'—said I: ' that 's understood . . . but see here, I have heard, that you have a black horse, so would n't you like to swap it for my Lampurdos? . . . . And I have n't got the girl Matryóna Feódorova in my house.'—' Well, Piótr Petróvitch,' says he; ' the girl is in your house, we are n't living in Switzerland, you know . . . . but I might swap my horse for your Lampurdos; I might take him now, if you like.' So I managed to get rid of him that time, somehow. But the old lady made a bigger fuss than before; ' I won't hesitate to spend ten thousand rubles,' said she. You see, as she looked at me, she had suddenly taken it into her head, to marry me to her green companion,—I found that out afterward; and that is why she made such a row. What whims those well-born ladies do take into their heads! . . . Out of boredom, I suppose. I was in a bad fix: I did not spare my

money, and I concealed Matryóna,—in vain!
They harassed me to death, they got me completely tied up in a snarl. I got into debt, I
lost my health. . . . So, one night I lay in
my bed and thought: 'O Lord my God, why
do I endure it? What am I to do, if I can't
renounce my love for her? . . . Well, I can't,
and that's all there is about it!'—and Matryóna
walks into my room. All this time I had been
hiding her at my farm, a couple of versts from
my house. I was frightened.—'What's the
matter? have they discovered thee there?'—'No,
Piótr Petróvitch,'—says she: 'no one is troubling
me at Búbnova; but can this continue long? My
heart,' says she, 'is breaking, Piótr Petróvitch;
I'm so sorry for you, my darling: as long as I
live I shall never forget your kindness, Piótr Petróvitch, but I have come now to bid you farewell.'—'What art thou saying, what art thou
saying, thou madwoman? . . . What dost thou
mean, what dost thou mean, by bidding me farewell?'—'Why, so . . I'll go and surrender myself.'—'But I'll lock thee up in the garret, thou
mad creature. . . . Hast thou taken it into thy
head to ruin me? dost thou wish to kill me, pray?'
—The girl said nothing, but stared at the floor.—
'Come, speak, speak!'—'I don't want to cause
you any more trouble, Piótr Petróvitch.'—Well,
it was no use talking to her. . . 'But knowest
thou, fool, knowest thou, thou cra . . . . crazy
woman. . . . .'"

PIÓTR PETRÓVITCH KARATÁEFF

And Piótr Petróvitch burst out sobbing bitterly.

" And, what do you think? "—he went on, smiting the table with his fist, and trying to frown, while the tears continued to stream down his flushed cheeks:—" the girl actually gave herself up,—she went and gave herself up. . . ."

" The horses are ready, sir! "—cried the superintendent solemnly, entering the room.

We both rose.

" And what did they do with Matryóna? "—I asked.

Karatáeff waved his hand.

A year after my meeting with Karatáeff, I happened to go to Moscow. One day, before dinner, I entered a café which is situated behind the Okhótny Ryády,[1]—an original, Moscow café. In the billiard-room athwart the billows of smoke, one caught fleeting glances of reddened faces, moustaches, crest-curls, old-fashioned hussar-jackets, and the newest-patterned coats. Gaunt old men in plain coats were reading the Russian newspapers. Waiters were flitting briskly about with trays, treading softly on the green carpets. Merchants were drinking tea with painful assiduity. All at once there emerged from the billiard-room a man who was somewhat dishevelled, and not quite steady on his legs. He thrust his hands into his pockets,

[1] Or, " game-market."—Translator

123

hung his head, and stared stupidly around him.

" Ba, ba, ba! Piótr Petróvitch! . . . . How are you? "

Piótr Petróvitch fairly hurled himself on my neck, and drew me aside with somewhat staggering steps, into a private room.

" Here now,"—he said, solicitously seating me in an easy-chair:—" Here you will be comfortable. Waiter, beer! No, I mean champagne! Well, I admit, that I was n't expecting, I was n't expecting. . . . Have you been in town long? are you here for long? Here, God has brought, as the saying is, the man . . ."

" But, do you remember . . . . "

" How could I fail to remember? how could I fail to remember? "—he hastily interrupted me: —" 't is an affair of the past . . . . an affair of the past. . . ."

" Well, what are you doing here, my dear Piótr Petróvitch? "

" I am living, as you are pleased to observe. Life is good here, the people are cordial. I have recovered my composure here."

And he sighed, and raised his eyes to heaven.

" Are you in the service? "

" No sir, I 'm not serving yet, but I 'm thinking of finding a position soon. And what 's the service? . . . . . People—that 's the principal thing. What fine people I have made acquaintance with here!" . . . .

A boy entered with a bottle of champagne on a black tray.

"Here, he's a fine man too . . . thou art a fine man, art thou not, Vásya? To thy health!"

The lad stood still for a moment, shaking his little head decorously, then smiled, and left the room.

"Yes, the people here are nice,"—went on Piótr Petróvitch:—"they have sentiment, they have soul. . . . I'll introduce you, shall I? Such splendid fellows. . . . They will all be delighted to know you. I must tell you. . . . Bobróff is dead, and that's a pity."

"What Bobróff?"

"Sergyéi Bobróff. He was a splendid man; he took care of me, an ignoramus, a steppe-dweller. And Panteléi Gornostáeff is dead too. All are dead, all!"

"Have you been living all the time in Moscow? Have you not made a trip to your village?"

"To the village . . . . they have sold my village."

"Sold it?"

"At *suction*.[1] It's a pity that you did not buy it!"

"What are you going to live on, Piótr Petróvitch?"

[1] Auction.—TRANSLATOR.

"Why, I shall not die of hunger. God will provide! If I have no money, I shall have friends. And what is money?—dust! Gold dust!"

He screwed up his eyes, fumbled in his pocket with his hand, and held out to me on his palm two fifteen-kopék pieces, and a ten-kopék piece.

"What's that? Dust, is n't it?" (And the money flew to the floor.) "But do you tell me, rather, have you read Polezháeff?"

"Yes."

"Have you seen Motcháloff in Hamlet?"

"No, I have not seen him."

"You haven't seen him, you have n't seen him. . ." (And Karatáeff's face turned pale, his eyes roved uneasily; faint convulsive twitches flitted across his lips.)

"Akh, Motcháloff, Motcháloff! 'To die, to sleep'"—he quoted, in a dull voice:

"No more; and by a sleep to say we end
   The heart-ache and the thousand natural shocks
   That flesh is heir to. . . . . 'T is a consummation
   Devoutly to be wished! To die,—to sleep. . . .

"'To sleep, to sleep!'"—he muttered, several times in succession.

"Tell me, please,"—I began; but he went on fervidly:

"For who would bear the whips and scorns of time,
   The oppressor's wrong, the proud man's contumely,

PIÓTR PETRÓVITCH KARATÁEFF

The pangs of dispriz'd love, the law's delay,
When he himself might his quietus make
With a bare bodkin? . . . . Nymph, in thy orisons
Be all my sins remembered!"

And he dropped his head on the table. He was
beginning to hiccough and to talk at random.
" ' And in one month,' " he enunciated, with
fresh force:

" A little month, or ere those shoes were old
With which she followed my poor father's body,
Like Niobe, all tears,—why, she, even she,—
O God! a beast, that wants discourse of reason,
Would have mourned longer. . . ."

He raised his glass of champagne to his lips,
but did not drink the wine, and continued:

" For Hecuba!
What's Hecuba to him, or he to Hecuba,
That he should weep for her? . . . .
Yet I . . . . a dull and muddy-mettled rascal, peak,
Like John-a-dreams! Who calls me villain?
Gives me the lie i' the throat?
'Swounds, I should take it; for it cannot be
But I am pigeon-livered, and lack gall
To make oppression bitter. . . ."

Karatáeff dropped his glass and clutched his
head. It seemed to me that I understood him.
" Well, never mind,"—he said at last:—" when

127

sorrow is asleep, wake it not. . . . Is n't that
true?" (And he began to laugh.)—" To your
health!"

" Shall you remain in Moscow?"—I asked
him.

" I shall die in Moscow!"

" Karatáeff,"—shouted some one in the adjoining room—" Karatáeff, where art thou?
come hither, my dear fe-ow!"[1]

" They are calling me,"—he said, rising heavily from his seat.—" Good-bye; drop in to see me
if you can, I live in * * *."

But on the following day, owing to unforeseen
circumstances, I was obliged to leave Moscow,
and never saw Piótr Petróvitch Karatáeff again.

[1] It is rather fashionable to pronounce *tchelovyék tche-a-ék.*
Thereby, also, the " hard *l* " is avoided, which is as difficult to pronounce, for some Russians (not to mention foreigners), as the *r* is
for many Englishmen and Americans.—TRANSLATOR.

VI

THE TRYST

I WAS sitting in a birch grove in autumn, about
the middle of September. A fine drizzling rain
had been descending ever since dawn, inter-
spersed at times with warm sunshine; the weather
was inconstant. Now the sky would be completely veiled in porous white clouds; again, all of
a sudden, it would clear up in spots for a moment,
and then, from behind the parted thunderclouds,
the clear and friendly azure would show itself,
like a beautiful eye. I sat, and gazed about me,
and listened. The leaves were rustling in a barely
audible manner overhead; from their sound alone
one could tell what season of the year it was. It
was not the cheerful, laughing rustle of springtime, not the soft whispering, not the long conversation of summer, not the cold and timid stammering of late autumn, but a barely audible,
dreamy chatter. A faint breeze swept feebly
across the tree-tops. The interior of the grove,
moist with the rain, kept changing incessantly, according to whether the sun shone forth, or was
covered with a cloud; now it was all illuminated,
as though everything in it were suddenly smiling:

129

the slender boles of the not too thickly set birches suddenly assumed the tender gleam of white silk, the small leaves which lay on the ground suddenly grew variegated and lighted up with the golden hue of ducats, and the handsome stalks of the tall, curly ferns, already stained with their autumnal hue, like the colour of over-ripe grapes, seemed fairly transparent, as they intertwined interminably and crossed one another before one's eyes; now, of a sudden, everything round about would turn slightly blue: the brilliant hues were extinguished for a moment, the birches stood there all white, devoid of reflections, white as newly fallen snow, which has not yet been touched by the sparkling rays of the winter sun; and the fine rain began stealthily, craftily, to sprinkle and whisper through the forest. The foliage on the trees was still almost entirely green, although it had faded perceptibly; only here and there stood one, some young tree, all scarlet, or all gold, and you should have seen how brilliantly it flamed up in the sun, when the rays gliding and changing, suddenly pierced through the thick network of the slender branches, only just washed clean by the glittering rain. Not a single bird was to be heard; they had all taken refuge, and fallen silent; only now and then did the jeering little voice of the tom-tit ring out like a tiny steel bell. Before I had come to a halt in this birch-forest I and my dog had traversed a grove of lofty aspens. I must confess that I am not particularly fond of that tree, the aspen, with its pale-lilac trunk, and greyish-green, metallic foliage, which it elevates as high aloft as possible, and spreads forth to the air in a trembling fan; I do not like the eternal rocking of its round, dirty leaves, awkwardly fastened to their long stems. It is a fine tree only on some summer evenings when, rising isolated amid a plot of low-growing bushes, it stands directly in the line of the glowing rays of the setting sun, and glistens and quivers from its root to its crest, all deluged with a uniform reddish-yellow stain,—or when, on a bright, windy day, it is all noisily rippling and lisping against the blue sky, and its every leaf, caught in the current, seems to want to wrench itself free, fly off and whirl away into the distance. But, on the whole, I do not like that tree, and therefore, without halting to rest in that grove, I wended my way to the little birch-coppice, nestled down under one small tree, whose boughs began close to the ground, and, consequently, could protect me from the rain, and after having admired the surrounding view, I sank into that untroubled and benignant slumber which is known to sportsmen alone.

I cannot tell how long I slept, but when I opened my eyes,—the whole interior of the forest was filled with sunlight, and in all directions, athwart the joyously rustling foliage, the bright-blue sky seemed to be sparkling: the clouds had vanished, dispersed by the sportive breeze; the weather had cleared, and in the atmosphere was perceptible that peculiar, dry chill which, filling the heart with a sort of sensation of alertness, almost always is the harbinger of a clear evening after a stormy day. I was preparing to rise to my feet, and try my luck again, when suddenly my eyes halted on a motionless human form. I took a more attentive look: it was a young peasant maiden. She was sitting twenty paces distant from me, with her head drooping thoughtfully, and both arms lying idly on her knees; on one of them, which was half bare, lay a thick bunch of field flowers, which went slipping softly down her plaid petticoat at each breath she drew. Her clean white chemise, unbuttoned at the throat and wrists, fell in short, soft folds about her figure: two rows of large yellow pearl-beads depended from her neck upon her breast. She was very comely. Her thick, fair hair, of a fine ash-blond hue, fell in two carefully brushed semi-circles from beneath a narrow, red band which was pulled down almost on her very brow, as white as ivory; the rest of her face was slightly sunburned to that golden tint which only a fine skin assumes. I could not see her eyes—she did not raise them but I did see her high, slender eyebrows, her long eyelashes; they were moist, and on one of her cheeks there glittered in the sunlight the dried

trace of a tear, that had stopped short close to her
lips, which had grown slightly pale. Her whole
little head was extremely charming; even her
rather thick and rounded nose did not spoil it. I
was particularly pleased with the expression of
her face: it was so simple and gentle, so sad and
so full of childish surprise at its own sadness.
She was evidently waiting for some one; something crackled faintly in the forest. She immediately raised her head and looked about her; in
the transparent shadow her eyes flashed swiftly
before me,—large, clear, timorous eyes, like those
of a doe. She listened for several moments, without taking her widely opened eyes from the spot
where the faint noise had resounded, sighed,
gently turned away her head, bent down still
lower than before, and began slowly to sort over
her flowers. Her eyelids reddened, her lips
moved bitterly, and a fresh tear rolled from beneath her thick eyelashes, halting and glittering
radiantly on her cheek. Quite a long time passed
in this manner; the poor girl did not stir,—only
now and then she moved her hands about and listened, listened still. . . . Again something made
a noise in the forest,—she gave a start. The noise
did not cease, grew more distinct, drew nearer; at
last brisk, decided footsteps made themselves
audible. She drew herself up, and seemed to be
frightened; her attentive glance wavered, with
expectation, apparently. A man's figure flitted

swiftly through the thicket. She glanced at it, suddenly flushed up, smiled joyously and happily, tried to rise to her feet, and immediately bent clear over once more, grew pale and confused,—and only raised her palpitating, almost beseeching glance to the approaching man when the latter had come to a halt by her side.

I gazed at him with interest from my ambush. I must confess that he did not produce a pleasant impression on me. From all the signs, he was the petted valet of a young, wealthy gentleman. His clothing betrayed pretensions to taste and foppish carelessness: he wore a short overcoat of bronze hue, probably the former property of his master, buttoned to the throat, a small pink neckerchief with lilac ends, and a black velvet cap, with gold galloon, pulled down to his very eyebrows. The round collar of his white shirt propped up his ears, and ruthlessly sawed his cheeks, and his starched cuffs covered the whole of his hands down to his red, crooked fingers, adorned with gold and silver rings with turquoise forget-me-nots. His fresh, rosy, bold face belonged to the category of visages which, so far as I have been able to observe, almost always irritate men and, unfortunately, very often please women. He was, obviously, trying to impart to his somewhat coarse features a scornful and bored expression; he kept incessantly screwing up his little milky-grey eyes, which were small enough

without that, knitting his brows, drawing down
the corners of his lips, constrainedly yawning,
and with careless, although not quite skilful ease
of manner he now adjusted with his hand his
sandy, dashingly upturned temple-curls, now
plucked at the small yellow hairs which stuck out
on his thick upper lip,—in a word, he put on intolerable airs. He began to put on airs as soon
as he caught sight of the young peasant girl who
was waiting for him; slowly, with a swaggering
stride, he approached her, stood for a moment,
shrugged his shoulders, thrust both hands into
the pockets of his coat, and, barely vouchsafing
the poor girl a fugitive and indifferent glance, he
dropped down on the ground.

"Well,"—he began, continuing to gaze off
somewhere to one side, dangling his foot and
yawning:—"hast thou been here long?"

The girl could not answer him at once.

"A long time, sir, Viktór Alexándrovitch,"—
she said at last, in a barely audible voice.

"Ah!" (He removed his cap, passed his hand
majestically over his thick, tightly curled hair,
which began almost at his very eyebrows, and
after glancing around him with dignity, he carefully covered his precious head again.) "Why,
I came pretty near forgetting all about it. And
then, there was the rain, you know!" (He
yawned again.)—"I have a lot of things to
do: I can't attend to them all, and he scolds

into the bargain. To-morrow we are going away. . . ."

" To-morrow? "—ejaculated the girl, and fixed a frightened glance on him.

" Yes, to-morrow. . . . Come, come, come, pray,"—he interposed hastily and with vexation, seeing that she was beginning to tremble, and had softly drooped her head:—" Pray, don't cry, Akulína. Thou knowest that I cannot endure that." (And he wrinkled up his stubby nose.)— " If thou dost, I 'll go away instantly. . . . . How stupid it is to whimper! "

" Well, I won't, I won't,"—hastily articulated Akulína, swallowing her tears with an effort.— " So you are going away to-morrow? "—she added after a short silence:—" When will God grant me to see you again, Viktór Alexándro-vitch? "

" We shall see each other again, we shall see each other again. If not next year, then later on. I think the master intends to enter the government service in Petersburg,"—he went on, uttering his words carelessly and somewhat through his nose:—" and perhaps we shall go abroad."

" You will forget me, Viktór Alexándro-vitch,"—said Akulína sadly.

" No, why should I? I will not forget thee: only, thou must be sensible, don't make a fool of thyself, heed thy father. . . . And I won't forget thee—no-o-o." (And he calmly stretched himself and yawned again.)

"Do not forget me, Viktór Alexándrovitch," she continued, in a tone of entreaty. "I think that I have loved you to such a degree, it always seems as though for you, I would . . . . you say, I must obey my father, Viktór Alexándrovitch. . . . But how am I to obey my father. . . . ."

"But why not?" (He uttered these words as though from his stomach, as he lay on his back, with his arms under his head.)

"But what do you mean, Viktór Alexándro-vitch . . . you know yourself. . . ."

She stopped short, Viktór toyed with the steel chain of his watch.

"Thou art not a stupid girl, Akulína,"—he began at last:—"therefore, don't talk nonsense. I desire thy welfare, dost understand me? Of course, thou art not stupid, not a regular peasant, so to speak; and thy mother also was not always a peasant. All the same, thou hast no education —so thou must obey when people give thee orders."

"But I'm afraid, Viktór Alexándrovitch."

"I-i, what nonsense, my dear creature! What hast thou to be afraid of? What's that thou hast there,"—he added, moving toward her:—"flow-ers?"

"Yes,"—replied Akulína, dejectedly. — "I have been plucking some wild tansy,"—she went on, after a brief pause:—"'T is good for the calves. And this here is a good remedy for scrofula. See, what a wonderfully beautiful flower! I have never seen such a beautiful flower in my life. Here are forget-me-nots, and here is a violet. . . . And this, here, I got for you,"— she added, drawing from beneath the yellow tansy a small bunch of blue corn-flowers, bound together with a slender blade of grass:—"Will you take them?"

Viktór languidly put out his hand, took the flowers, smelled of them carelessly, and began to twist them about in his fingers, staring pompously upward. Akulína glanced at him. . . . In her sorrowful gaze there was a great deal of devotion, of adoring submission to him. And she was afraid of him also, and did not dare to cry, and was bidding him farewell and gloating upon him for the last time; but he lay there, sprawling out like a sultan, and tolerated her adoration with magnanimous patience and condescension. I must confess, that I gazed with indignation at his red face, whereon, athwart the feignedly-scornful indifference, there peered forth satisfied, satiated self-conceit. Akulína was so fine at that moment: her whole soul opened confidingly, passionately before him, reached out to him, fawned upon him, and he . . . . he dropped the cornflowers on the grass, pulled a round monocle in a bronze setting from the side-pocket of his paletot, and began to stick it into his eye; but try as he would to hold it fast with his frowning brows, the monocle kept tumbling out and falling into his hand.

" What is that? "—inquired the amazed Aku-lína at last.

" A lorgnette,"—he replied pompously.

" What is it for? "

" To see better with."

" Pray let me see it."

Viktór frowned, but gave her the monocle.

" Look out, see that thou dost not break it."

" Never fear, I won't break it." (She raised it timidly to her eye.) " I can see nothing,"—she said innocently.

" Why, pucker up thine eye,"—he retorted in the tone of a displeased preceptor. (She screwed up the eye in front of which she was holding the glass.)

" Not that one, not that one, the other one! "—shouted Viktór, and without giving her a chance to repair her mistake, he snatched the lorgnette away from her.

Akulína blushed scarlet, smiled faintly, and turned away.

" Evidently, it is not suited to the like of me," —said she.

" I should say not! "

The poor girl made no reply, and sighed deeply.

"Akh, Viktór Alexándrovitch, what shall I do without you!"—she suddenly said. Viktór wiped the lorgnette with the tail of his coat, and put it back in his pocket.

"Yes, yes,"—he said at last:—"thou wilt really find it very hard at first." (He patted her condescendingly on the shoulder; she softly removed his hand from her shoulder, and kissed it timidly.)—"Well, yes, yes, thou really art a good girl,"—he went on, with a conceited smile; "but what can one do? Judge for thyself! the master and I cannot remain here; winter will soon be here, and the country in winter—thou knowest it thyself—is simply vile. 'T is quite another matter in Petersburg! There are simply such marvels there as thou, silly, canst not even imagine in thy dreams. Such houses, such streets, and society, culture—simply astounding! . . ." (Akulína listened to him with devouring attention, her lips slightly parted, like those of a child.)—"But what am I telling thee all this for?"—he added, turning over on the ground. "Of course, thou canst not understand!"

"Why not, Viktór Alexándrovitch? I have understood—I have understood everything."

"Did any one ever see such a girl!"

Akulína dropped her eyes.

"You did not use to talk to me formerly in that

way, Viktór Alexándrovitch,"—she said, without
raising her eyes.

" Formerly? . . . formerly! Just see there,
now! . . . . Formerly!"—he remarked, as
though vexed.

Both maintained silence for a while.

" But I must be off,"—said Viktór, and began
to raise himself on his elbow. . . . .

" Wait a little longer,"—articulated Akulína,
in a beseeching voice.

" What's the use of waiting? . . . I have already bade thee farewell, have n't I? "

" Wait,"—repeated Akulína.

Viktór stretched himself out again, and began
to whistle. Still Akulína never took her eyes
from him. I could perceive that she had grown
somewhat agitated: her lips were twitching, her
pale cheeks had taken on a faint flush. . . .

" Viktór Alexándrovitch,"—she said at last, in
a broken voice:—" 't is sinful of you . . . sinful
of you, Viktór Alexándrovitch: by heaven, it is! "

" What's sinful? "—he asked, knitting his
brows, and he half rose and turned toward her.

" 'T is sinful, Viktór Alexándrovitch. You
might at least speak a kind word to me at parting; you might at least say one little word to me,
an unhappy orphan. . . ."

" But what am I to say to thee? "

" I don't know; you know that better than I do,

Viktór Alexándrovitch. Here you are going away, and not a single word. . . How have I deserved such treatment? "

" What a queer creature thou art! What can I do? "

" You might say one little word. . . ."

" Come, thou 'rt wound up to say the same thing over and over,"—he said testily, and rose to his feet.

" Don't be angry, Viktór Alexándrovitch,"—she added hurriedly, hardly able to repress her tears.

" I 'm not angry, only thou art so stupid. . . . What is it thou wantest? I can't marry thee, can I? I can't, can I? Well, then, what is it thou dost want? What? " (He turned his face toward her, as though awaiting an answer, and spread his fingers far apart.)

" I want nothing . . . . . nothing,"—she replied, stammering, and barely venturing to stretch out to him her trembling arms:—" but yet, if you would say only one little word in farewell. . . ."

And the tears streamed down her face in a torrent.

" Well, there she goes! She 's begun to cry," said Viktór coldly, pulling his cap forward over his eyes.

" I want nothing,"—she went on, sobbing, and covering her face with both hands;—" but how do I stand now with my family, what is my position? and what will happen to me, what will become of me, unhappy one? They will marry off the poor deserted one to a man she does not love. . . . . Woe is me!"

" O, go on, go on,"—muttered Viktór in an undertone, shifting from foot to foot where he stood.

" And if he would say only one word, just one. . . . . such as: ' Akulína, I . . . . . ' "

Sudden sobs, which rent her breast, prevented her finishing her sentence—she fell face downward on the grass, and wept bitterly, bitterly. . . . Her whole body was convulsively agitated, the back of her neck fairly heaved. . . . . . Her long-suppressed woe had burst forth, at last, in a flood. Viktór stood over her, stood there a while, and shrugged his shoulders, then wheeled round, and marched off with long strides.

Several minutes elapsed. . . . . . She quieted down, raised her head, glanced around, and clasped her hands; she tried to run after him, but her limbs gave way under her—she fell on her knees. . . . . I could not restrain myself, and rushed to her; but no sooner had she glanced at me than strength from some source made its appearance,—she rose to her feet with a faint shriek, and vanished behind the trees, leaving her flowers scattered on the ground.

I stood there for a while, picked up the bunch of corn-flowers, and emerged from the grove into the fields. The sun hung low in the palely-clear sky, its rays, too, seemed to have grown pallid, somehow, and cold: they did not beam, they disseminated an even, almost watery light. Not more than half an hour remained before nightfall, and the sunset glow was only just beginning to kindle. A gusty breeze dashed swiftly to meet me across the yellow, dried-up stubble-field; small, warped leaves rose hastily before it, and darted past, across the road, along the edge of the woods; the side of the grove, turned toward the field like a wall, was all quivering and sparkling with a drizzling glitter, distinct but not brilliant; on the reddish turf, on the blades of grass, on the straws, everywhere around, gleamed and undulated the innumerable threads of autumnal spiders' webs. I halted. . . . I felt sad: athwart the cheerful though chilly smile of fading nature, the mournful terror of not far-distant winter seemed to be creeping up. High above me, cleaving the air heavily and sharply with its wings, a cautious raven flew past, cast a sidelong glance at me, soared aloft and, floating on outstretched wings, disappeared behind the forest, croaking spasmodically; a large flock of pigeons fluttered sharply from the threshing-floor and, suddenly rising in a cloud, eagerly dispersed over the fields —a sign of autumn! Some one was driving past behind the bare hill, his empty cart rumbling loudly. . . .

I returned home; but the image of poor Akulína did not leave my mind for a long time, and her corn-flowers, long since withered, I have preserved to this day. . . .

VII

DURING one of my excursions, I received an invitation to dine with a wealthy landed proprietor,
who was also a sportsman, Alexánder Mikhaílovitch G * * *. His large village was situated
five versts distant from the tiny hamlet where I
had settled down at that time. I donned my
dress-suit, without which I would not advise any
one to leave home, even on a hunting-expedition,
and set off for Alexánder Mikhaílovitch's house.
The dinner was appointed for six o'clock; I arrived at five, and found a large number of nobles,
in uniforms, civilian garb, and other arrays, already there. The host received me cordially, but
immediately ran off to the butler's pantry. He
was expecting an important dignitary and felt a
certain perturbation, which was entirely incom-
patible with his independent position in the
world and his wealth. Alexánder Mikhaílovitch had never married, and did not like women;
it was bachelor society which assembled at his
house. He lived on a grand scale, had augmented and refitted his ancestral mansion in magnificent style, imported every year from Moscow

fifteen thousand rubles' worth of wine, and, altogether, enjoyed the greatest respect. Alexánder Mikhaílovitch had long since resigned from the service, and aspired to no honours. . . . . . What, then, induced him to invite the dignitary to be his guest, and agitate himself from daybreak on the day of the ceremonious dinner? That is a point which remains shrouded in the gloom of obscurity, as a certain attorney of my acquaintance was wont to say when asked whether he accepted bribes from willing givers.

On parting from my host, I began to stroll through the rooms. Almost all the guests were entire strangers to me; a dozen men were already seated at the card-tables. Among the number of these devotees of preference were two military men with noble but somewhat worn countenances; several civilians in tight, tall stocks and with pendent, dyed moustaches, such as are possessed only by decided but well-intentioned persons (these well-intentioned persons were pompously gathering up their cards, and casting sidelong glances at those who approached them, but without turning their heads) ; and five or six officials of the district with rotund paunches, plump, perspiring hands, and discreetly-impassive feet (these gentlemen were talking in low tones, smiling benignantly on all sides, holding their cards tightly against their shirt-fronts, and, when they trumped, they did not bang the table, but, on the contrary, dropped their cards, with an undulating movement on the green cloth, and when they gathered in their tricks they produced a light, extremely courteous and decorous grating noise). The rest of the nobles were sitting on the divans and huddling in groups round the doors and windows; one landed proprietor, no longer young but of effeminate appearance, was standing in a corner, quaking and blushing, and twisting his watch-chain on his stomach with perturbation, although no one was paying any attention to him; other gentlemen, in round-tailed dress-coats and checked trousers, the work of a Moscow tailor, the perpetual member of the guild and master, Firs Kliúkhin, were chatting with unwonted ease of manner and alertness, freely turning their fat and bare napes; a young man of twenty, mole-eyed and fair-haired, clad in black from head to foot, was evidently intimidated, but smiled spitefully. . . .

I was beginning to be somewhat bored, however, when suddenly I was joined by a certain Voinítzyn, a young man who had not completed his studies, and who lived in Alexánder Mikhaílovitch's house in the capacity . . . . . it would be difficult to say in precisely what capacity. He was a capital shot, and knew how to train dogs. I had known him previously, in Moscow. He belonged to the category of young men who, at every examination, " played the dumb game,"—

that is to say, did not answer the professors' questions by a single word. These gentlemen were also called sidewhiskerites, by way of fine language. (This happened long ago, as you can easily see.) This is the way it was done: Voinítzyn, for example, was called up. Voinítzyn—who, up to that moment, had been sitting motionless and bolt upright on his bench, bathed from head to foot in boiling-hot perspiration, and rolling his eyes about slowly but stupidly—rose, hastily buttoned his undress uniform up to the throat, and stole sideways to the table of the examiners.—"Please take a ticket," the professor said to him, pleasantly. Voinítzyn stretched out his hand, and tremulously touched the package of tickets with his fingers.—"Be so good as not to pick and choose,"—remarked some irritable old man who had nothing to do with the matter, a professor from some other faculty, who had conceived a sudden hatred for the unlucky sidewhiskerite. Voinítzyn yielded to his fate, took a ticket, showed the number, and went off and took his seat near the window, while the man ahead of him answered his question. At the window, Voinítzyn never took his eyes from the ticket, unless it was to gaze about him slowly, as before, and otherwise he did not move a limb. But now the man ahead of him has answered his question, and the professors say to him: " Good, you may go," or even: " Good, sir, very good, sir," according to

his capacities. Then they call up Voinítzyn;—
Voinítzyn rises, and approaches the table with
firm steps.—" Read your ticket," they say to him.
Voinítzyn lifts the ticket to his very nose with
both hands, slowly reads it, and slowly lowers his
hands.—" Well, sir, please give the answer," languidly articulates the same professor, throwing
back his body, and folding his arms on his chest.
A profound silence reigns.—" What have you to
say? "—Voinítzyn maintains silence. He begins to get on the nerves of the old man who is
not concerned.—" Come, say something! "—My
Voinítzyn remains silent, just as though he had
expired. His closely-clipped nape rears itself up
in front of the curious glances of all his comrades.
The eyes of the meddlesome old man are ready to
pop out of his head: he has finally arrived at de-
testation of Voinítzyn.—" But this is strange,"
—remarks the other examiner:—" Why do you
stand there like a dumb man? come now, don't you
know? if you do, then speak."—" Allow me to
take another ticket," articulates the unlucky
wight dully. The professors exchange glances.
—" Well, do so,"—replies the head-examiner,
with a wave of the hand. Again Voinítzyn takes
a ticket, again he goes off to the window, again
he returns to the table, and again he maintains
silence like that of a dead man. The unconcerned
old man is ready to devour him alive. At last
they drive him off, and place a cipher against his

name. You think: " Now he will go away, at least?" Nothing of the sort! He returns to his place, sits there in the same impassive manner until the end of the examination, and as he takes his departure he exclaims: " Well, that was like a hot bath! what a tough job!"—And he roams about Moscow all that day, from time to time clutching at his head, and bitterly upbraiding his unhappy lot. As a matter of course, he does not touch a book, and the next morning the same story is repeated. So then, this Voinítzyn joined me. We chatted together about Moscow, about sport.

" Would n't you like to have me introduce you to the leading wit of these parts?"—he suddenly whispered to me.

" Pray do."

Voinítzyn led me to a man of short stature, with a lofty curled crest and a moustache, in a cinnamon-brown dress-coat and a flowered neckerchief. His bilious, mobile features really did exhale cleverness and malice. His lips curled incessantly in a fleeting, caustic smile; his small black eyes, which he kept screwed up, peered forth audaciously from beneath uneven lashes. By his side stood a landed proprietor, a broad, soft, sweet man,—a regular Sugar-Honey,—and with only one eye. He laughed in advance at the witticisms of the little man, and seemed to be fairly rapturous with delight. Voinítzyn presented me to the

151

wit, whose name was Piótr Petróvitch Lupíkhin. We made acquaintance, and exchanged the preliminary greetings.

"And allow me to introduce to you my best friend,"—said Lupíkhin suddenly, in a sharp voice, seizing the sweet proprietor by the hand.— "Come now, don't hang back, Kiríla Selifánitch,"—he added:—"nobody is going to bite you. Here, sir,"—he went on, while the disconcerted Kiríla Selifánitch bowed as awkwardly as though his paunch were falling off:—"Here, sir, I recommend him to you, sir, a splendid noble. He enjoyed excellent health up to the age of fifty, and all of a sudden took it into his head to put himself through a course of treatment for his eyes, in consequence of which he has lost the sight of one of them. Ever since then, he has been treating his peasants with like success. . . . . Well, and they, of course, with the same devotion . . . ."

"What a fellow he is!"—muttered Kiríla Selifánitch—and burst out laughing.

"Speak out, my friend—ekh, finish what you were about to say,"—interpolated Lupíkhin.— "Why, the first you know, you may be elected judge, and you will be elected, see if you are n't. Well, of course the assessors will do your thinking for you, I suppose; for, you know, 't is necessary, in case of need, to understand how to enunciate other people's ideas, at least. Perhaps the Governor will drop in;—he will ask: ' What makes the judge stammer?' Well, let us assume that they tell him: ' He has had a stroke of paralysis.'—' Then bleed him,' he will say. And that is unseemly in your position, you must admit yourself."

The sweet landed proprietor fairly roared with laughter.

" There, you see, he 's laughing,"—pursued Lupíkhin, with a vicious glance at Kiríla Selifánitch's heaving paunch.—" And why should n't he laugh? "—he added, addressing me:—" he 's full-fed, healthy, has no children, his serfs are not mortgaged, and he gives them medical treatment,—his wife is rather crack-brained." (Kiríla Selifánitch turned somewhat aside, as though he had not heard, and went on roaring with laughter.)—" I laugh also, and my wife eloped with a surveyor." (He grinned.)

" Why, did n't you know that? Certainly! She just took and ran away, and left a letter for me: ' My dear Piótr Petróvitch,' says she, ' excuse me: carried away by passion, I am departing with the friend of my heart. . . .' And the surveyor fascinated her simply because he did n't cut his finger-nails, and wore trousers like tights. You are surprised? Here 's a frank man, you say.—I-i, good heavens, we steppe-dwellers

speak the truth straight out. But let us step
aside. . . . . Why should we stand by the future
judge? . . . . ."

He took my arm, and we walked off to the
window.

" I bear the reputation of a wit here,"—he said
to me in the course of our conversation:—" don't
you believe it. I am simply an embittered man,
and I am swearing aloud: that is why I am so free
and easy. And, as a matter of fact, why should
I stand on ceremony? I don't care a copper for
anybody's opinion, and am not in quest of anything; I am spiteful,—what of that! A spiteful
man stands in no need of brains, at least. And
you would n't believe how refreshing it is. . . .
Here, now, for example,—here now, just look at
our host! Now why is he rushing about, for
mercy's sake, constantly looking at his watch,
smiling, perspiring, assuming a pompous mien,
torturing us with hunger? A pretty thing, truly,
a dignitary! There, there he is rushing about
again,—he has even begun to limp,—just look! "

And Lupíkhin laughed shrilly.

" 'T is a great pity that there are no ladies,"—
he went on, with a deep sigh:—" it is a bachelor
dinner,—and there 's no profit for the likes of us
in that. Look, look,"—he suddenly exclaimed:
—" yonder comes Prince Kozélsky—that tall
man with the beard, in yellow gloves. It is immediately evident that he has been abroad . . . .

and he always arrives so late. I 'll tell you one thing, though: he 's as stupid as a pair of merchant's horses; and you just ought to see how condescendingly he talks to men like me, how magnanimously he deigns to smile at the amiable attentions of our hungry wives and daughters! . . . . And he sometimes makes a joke, although he lives here only temporarily;—but what jokes! Precisely as though he were sawing at a hawser with a dull knife. He can't endure me. . . . I 'll go and make my bow to him."

And Lupíkhin hastened to meet the Prince.

" And yonder comes my personal foe,"—he said, suddenly returning to me:—" do you see that fat man, with the dark-brown face, and the brush on his head,—yonder,—the one who has his cap clutched in his hand, and is making his way along the wall, and darting glances on all sides, like a wolf? I sold him for four hundred rubles a horse which was worth one thousand rubles, and that dumb beast now has a perfect right to despise me; but he is so devoid of capacity for thinking, especially of a morning, before tea, or immediately after dinner, that if you say to him: ' Good morning,' he will reply: ' what, sir? ' And yonder comes the General," went on Lupíkhin:—" a civilian general on the retired list, a bankrupt general. He has a daughter made of beet-root sugar and a scrofula factory. . . . Excuse me, I did n't mean to say that . . . . well, you understand.

155

Ah! and the architect has got here! A German, and with a moustache, and does n't know his business,—astounding!—But why should he know his business? all he has to do is to take bribes, and set up as many columns and pillars as possible for our ancient nobility." [1]

Again Lupíkhin began to laugh violently. . . . But suddenly a breathless agitation spread all over the house. The dignitary had arrived. The host fairly flew headlong to the anteroom. Behind him scurried several devoted domestics and zealous guests. . . . The noisy conversation was converted into a soft, agreeable murmur, resembling the humming of bees in their native hive in springtime. The irrepressible wasp, Lupíkhin, and the magnificent drone, Kozélsky, alone did not lower their voices. . . . And now, at last, the queen-bee entered—the dignitary entered. Hearts flew to greet him, heavy seated bodies rose; even the landed proprietor who had bought Lupíkhin's horse cheap, even that proprietor thrust his chin into his chest. The dignitary preserved his dignity to perfection: nodding his head backward, as though bowing, he uttered a few words of approval, each one of which began with the letter *a*, enunciated with a drawl through the nose;—with indignation which reached the pitch of biting, he stared at

---

[1] A pun is here intended. *Stolb*, a pillar or post, *stolbovói dvoryanín* (column-noble), a nobleman of ancient family.—TRANSLATOR.

Prince Kozélsky's beard, and gave the ruined civil General with the factory and the daughter the forefinger of his left hand. After a few moments, during the course of which the dignitary had managed to remark twice that he was very glad he had not arrived late for dinner, the whole company wended their way to the dining-room, big-wigs at the head.

Is it necessary for me to describe to the reader how the dignitary was given the principal seat, between the civil General and the Marshal of Nobility for the Government, a man with a free and dignified expression of countenance, which thoroughly matched his starched shirt-front, his capacious waistcoat, and his circular snuff-box filled with French snuff;—how the host fussed and ran about, and bustled, and urged the guests to eat, bestowed a smile in passing on the dignitary's back, and, standing in one corner, like a school-boy, hurriedly swallowed a plate of soup, or a bit of roast beef;—how the butler served a fish an arshín and a half [1] in length, and with a nosegay in its mouth;—how the liveried servants, surly of aspect, gruffly plied each nobleman now with Malaga, now with dry Madeira, and how almost all the noblemen, especially the elderly ones, drank glass after glass, as though resigning themselves to a sense of duty:—how, in conclusion, bottles of champagne were cracked, and they

[1] Forty-two inches.—TRANSLATOR.

began to drink toasts to the health of various persons? All this is, probably, but too familiar to the reader. But what struck me as especially noteworthy was an anecdote, related by the dignitary himself amid universal joyous silence.

Some one—the ruined General I think it was, a man acquainted with the newest literature—alluded to the influence of women in general, and upon young men in particular.—" Yes, yes,"—put in the dignitary:—" that is true; young men should be kept under strict discipline, otherwise they are likely to go out of their heads over every petticoat." (A smile of childlike mirth flitted across the faces of all the guests; the gratitude of one landed proprietor even glistened in his glance.)—" For young men are foolísh." (The dignitary, probably with a view to increasing their importance, sometimes altered the generally-received accentuation, of words.)—"Now, there 's my son Iván, for instánce," he continued: " the fool is only twentý years of age, and all of a sudden he says to me: ' Dear little father, permit me to marry.' I say to him: ' Serve first, thou fool!' . . . . Well, then came despair, tears . . . . . but I 'm . . . you know . . . ." (The words " you know " the dignitary uttered with his belly rather than with his lips; then he remained silent a little while, and cast a majestic glance at his neighbour the General, at the same time elevating his eyebrows more than one might have expected from him. The civilian General bowed his head pleasantly somewhat on one side, and winked the eye which was turned toward the dignitary with extreme rapidity.)—"And what do you think," —began the dignitary again, "now he writes to me, saying: 'Thanks, father, for having taught the fool a lessón.' . . . . That's the way one must proceed."—All the guests entirely agreed with the narrator, as a matter of course, and seemed to brighten up as a result of the pleasure and instruction which they had received. . . . After dinner, the whole company rose and withdrew to the drawing-room with great but decorous uproar, as though it were permitted on this occasion. . . . . They sat down to play cards.

I managed to while away the evening, and having enjoined my coachman to have my calash ready at five o'clock on the following morning, I retired to rest. But it was my lot to make acquaintance on that same day with still another remarkable man.

In consequence of the multitude of guests who had arrived, no one had a bedroom to himself. In the small, greenish, and rather damp chamber to which Alexánder Mikhaílovitch's butler conducted me, there was already another guest, completely undressed. On catching sight of me, he briskly dived under the coverlet, covered himself up with it to his very nose, nestled about a little in the spongy feather-bed, and quieted down, peering forth keenly from beneath the round border of his cotton nightcap. I stepped up to the other bed (there were only two in the room), undressed, and lay down in the damp sheets. My neighbour turned over in his bed. . . . . . I wished him good night.

Half an hour elapsed. Despite my efforts, I could not get to sleep; useless and ill-defined thoughts followed one another in endless succession, persistently and monotonously, like the buckets of a pumping-machine.

" You are not sleepy, apparently,"—remarked my neighbour.

" As you see,"—I replied.—" And you 're not sleepy, either? "

" I 'm never sleepy."

" Why so? "

" Because I fall asleep I don't know why; I lie and lie, and then get to sleep."

" But why do you go to bed before you feel like sleeping? "

" Why, what would you have me do? "

I made no answer to my neighbour's question.

" I 'm surprised," he went on, after a brief pause:—" that there are no fleas here. I thought they were everywhere."

" You seem to regret them,"—I remarked.

" No, I don't regret them; but I like logical sequence in everything."

"You don't say so,"—I remarked to myself: "what words he uses!"

Again my neighbour was silent for a while.

"Would you like to make a bet with me?"—he suddenly said, in quite a loud voice.

"What about?"

I was beginning to find my neighbour amusing.

"H'm . . . . what about? Why, about this: I'm convinced that you take me for a fool."

"Good gracious,"—I murmured in amazement.

"For a steppe-dweller, an ignoramus.—Confess. . . ."

"I have not the pleasure of knowing you,"—I returned.—"How have you arrived at the conclusion? . . . ."

"How? Why, from the mere sound of your voice: you answer me so carelessly. . . . But I'm not in the least what you think. . . ."

"Permit me . . ."

"No, do *you* permit *me*. In the first place, I speak French quite as well as you do, and German even better; in the second place, I have spent three years abroad: I have lived eight months in Berlin alone. I have studied Hegel, my dear sir, I know Goethe by heart; more than that, I was for a long time in love with the daughter of a German professor, and married at home a consumptive young gentlewoman,—a bald, but very re-

markable individual. Consequently, I am a
berry from the same field as yourself; I'm not a
rustic steppe-dweller, as you suppose. . . . I also
am bitten with reflex action, and there's nothing
direct about me. . . ."

I raised my head, and looked at the eccentric
with redoubled attention. In the dim light of the
night-lamp I could barely distinguish his features.

" There now, you are staring at me,"—he went
on, adjusting his nightcap,—" and, probably, you
are asking yourself: ' How comes it that I did not
notice him to-day?' I will tell you why you did
not notice me:—because I do not raise my voice;
because I hide behind other people, stand behind
doors, converse with no one; because the butler, as
he passes me with a tray, elevates his elbow in advance on a level with my breast. . . . And
whence does all this proceed? From two causes:
in the first place, I am poor, and in the second, I
am resigned. . . . Speak the truth, you did n't
observe me, did you? "

" I really did not have the pleasure. . . ."

" Well, well, yes,"—he interrupted me:—" I
knew it."

He raised himself half-way, and folded his
arms; the long shadow of his nightcap flitted
from the wall to the ceiling.

" Come now, confess,"—he suddenly added,
casting a sidelong glance at me:—" I must seem

to you a great eccentric, an original, as they say,
or, perhaps, even something still worse; perhaps
you think that I pretend to be an eccentric?"

" I must repeat to you, once more, that I do not
know you. . ."

He cast down his eyes for a moment.

" Why I have so unexpectedly set to talking
with you,—with a man who is an entire stranger
to me,—the Lord—the Lord only knows!" (He
sighed.) " 'T is not in consequence of the af-
finity of our souls! Both you and I are respectable persons, egoists; you have nothing to do with
me, neither have I the slightest thing to do with
you; is n't that so? But neither of us is sleepy.
. . . Why not have a chat? I 'm in the mood, and
that rarely happens with me. I 'm timid, you see,
and not timid in virtue of the fact that I am a
provincial, without official rank, a poor man, but
in virtue of the fact that I am a frightfully conceited man. But sometimes, under the influence
of propitious circumstances, accidents, which I
am unable, however, either to define or foresee,
my timidity disappears completely, as on the
present occasion, for instance. You might set me
face to face with the Dalai-Lama himself now,—
and I 'd ask him for a pinch of snuff. But perhaps you want to go to sleep?"

" On the contrary,"—I hastily returned:—" I
find it very agreeable to chat with you."

" That is, I amuse you, you mean to say. . . .

So much the better. . . . So then, sir, I must inform you, that I am called an original in these parts; that is to say, I am so called by those from whose tongues my name chances, accidentally, to fall, along with other trifling things. ' No one is greatly concerned as to my fate.' . . . They think to wound me. . . . . O my God! if they only knew . . . why, I 'm perishing precisely because there is positively nothing original about me, nothing except such sallies as my present conversation with you, for example; but, you see, those sallies are n't worth a copper coin. That 's the very cheapest and most vulgar sort of originality."

He turned his face toward me and waved his hands.

" My dear sir! "—he exclaimed:—" My opinion is, that the originals are the only people who enjoy life on earth; they alone have the right to live. *Mon verre n'est pas grand, mais je bois dans mon verre,* some one has said.—You see,"—he added in an undertone:—" what pure French I speak. What care I if a man has a great and capacious head, and understands everything, knows a great deal, and keeps abreast of the times,—but has nothing special of his own! It merely makes one storehouse for commonplaces more in the world,—and who derives any satisfaction out of that? No, be stupid if you will, only do it in your own way! Have an odour of your own, that 's

what!—And do not imagine that my demands
with respect to that odour are great. . . . . .
God forbid! There's a mass of such originals: no
matter in what direction you look, you behold an
original; every living man is an original, but for
some reason I haven't fallen into their category! . . .

"And yet,"—he went on, after a brief pause:
—"what expectations I aroused in my youth!
what a lofty opinion I cherished of myself before
I went abroad, and during the early days after
my return thence! Well, while I was abroad, I
kept on the alert, I always made my way about
alone, as is fitting for a fellow like me, who understands everything, is up to everything; and in the
end, lo and behold,—he hasn't understood the
first thing! . . .

"An original, an original!"—he resumed,
shaking his head reproachfully. . . . "They call
me an original . . . . . as a matter of fact, it appears that there isn't a less original man in the
world than your most humble servant. I must
have been born in imitation of some one else. . . .
By heaven, I must! I exist as though in imitation of the writers I have studied, I exist in the
sweat of my brow; and I have studied, and fallen
in love, and married, in conclusion, just as though
it were not of my own volition, just as though I
were performing some duty, executing some lesson,—who can explain it!"

He tore the nightcap from his head and flung it on the bed.

" Shall I tell you the story of my life? "—he asked me in a spasmodic voice:—" or, rather, a few incidents of my life? "

" Pray do."

" Or—no, I had better tell you how I came to marry. For marriage is an important affair, the test-stone of every man; in it, as in a mirror, is reflected . . . . But that comparison is too hackneyed. . . . If you permit, I will take a pinch of snuff."

He pulled a snuff-box from under his pillow, opened it, and began to talk again, waving the open box.

" Put yourself in my position, my dear sir.— Judge for yourself, what profit,—come now, for mercy's sake, tell me,—what profit could I extract from Hegel's encyclopædia? Tell me, what has that encyclopædia in common with Russian life? And how would you have me apply it to our existence—and not that encyclopædia alone, but German philosophy in general . . . . I will say more—German science? "

He leaped up in his bed, and muttered in an undertone, viciously setting his teeth:

" Ah, that 's the point, that 's the point! . . . . . Then why didst thou trot off abroad? Why didst not thou stay at home, and study the life which surrounded thee on the spot? Thou wouldst have learned its requirements and its future, and thou wouldst have become clear concerning thine own vocation, so to speak. . . . But good gracious," —he continued, again altering his voice, as though defending himself and quailing:—" how is a man like me to inform himself about a thing concerning which not a single wiseacre has written anything in a book! I would be glad to take lessons from it, from that same Russian life,—but it maintains silence, my dear little dove. ' Understand me,' it says, 'as I am;' but that is beyond my power: give me the deductions, present to me the conclusion of the matter. . . . . The conclusion?— 'Here is the conclusion for thee,' people say: 'just listen to our Moscow folks—they 're nightingales, are n't they? '—And precisely therein lies the calamity, that they warble like Kursk nightingales, but don't talk like human beings. . . . . So I meditated and meditated,—you see, science is the same everywhere, apparently, and is the only genuine thing,—and took and set off, with God's aid, to foreign parts, to infidels. . . . What would you have,—I was besotted with youth, with pride. I was n't willing, you know, to swim in fat before my time, although 't is healthy, they say. However, the person who has not been endowed by nature with flesh, will never behold fat on his body!

" But I believe,"—he added, after reflecting a while,—" that I promised to narrate to you how

I came to get married. Listen, then. In the first place, I must inform you that my wife is no longer in the world; in the second place . . . . but in the second place, I perceive that I must tell you about my youth, otherwise you will not understand anything. . . . . You are sure you don't want to go to sleep?"

"No, I don't."

"Very good. Just listen . . . . how vulgarly Mr. Kantagriúkhin is snoring yonder, in the next room!—I am the son of poor parents,—parents, I say, because, in addition to a mother, there is a tradition that I had a father also. I do not remember him; they say that he was a man of limited capacity, had a huge nose and freckles, and took snuff up one nostril; in my mother's bedroom hung his portrait, in a red uniform with a black collar reaching up to his ears, and remarkably hideous. They used to lead me past it on my way to a whipping, and on such occasions my mother always pointed it out to me, with the remark: 'Thou wouldst have fared still worse at his hands.' You can imagine how greatly this encouraged me. I had neither brothers nor sisters; that is to say, to tell the truth, I did have a sort of wretched little brother, who was afflicted with the rickets, but he died very soon. . . . And why should the rickets perch in the Zhígry district of the Kursk government? But that is not the point. My mother busied herself over my

168

education with the headlong zeal of a landed proprietress of the steppes; she busied herself with it
from the very magnificent day of my birth until
I had attained the age of sixteen. . . . Do you
follow the thread of my story?"

"Certainly, proceed."

"Well, good. So then, when I had attained
the age of sixteen, my mother without delay took
and dismissed my French tutor and the German
Philipóvitch from the Greeks of Nyézhin:[1] she
took me to Moscow, entered me in the university,
and surrendered her soul to the Almighty, leaving
me in the hands of my own uncle, the pettifogger
Koltún-Babúr, a bird who was known to more
than the Zhígry district. This own uncle of
mine, the pettifogger Koltún-Babúr, robbed me
of my last penny, as is the custom. . . . But
again, that is not the point. I entered the university, to do my mother justice, tolerably well prepared; but the lack of originality was discernible in me even then. My childhood had differed
in no respect from the childhood of other youths:
I had grown up as stupid and drowsy as though
I had been under a feather-bed, and began just
as early to commit verses to memory, and to languish under the pretext of an inclination to
dreaminess . . . . . and all the rest of it. In
the university I did not travel along a new road:
I immediately fell into a circle. Times were

---

[1] A Greek colony in Little Russia.—TRANSLATOR.

different then. . . . . But perhaps you do not know what a circle is?—I remember that Schiller says somewhere:

> "Gefährlich ist's, den Leu zu wecken,
>   Und schrecklich is des Tigers Zahn,
>   Doch das schrecklichste der Schrecken—
>   Das ist der Mensch in seinem Wahn!

" He did not mean to say that, I assure you; he meant to say: 'Das is ein *circle* . . . . in der Stadt Moskau!' "

" But what is it that you find dreadful in a circle? "—I inquired.

My neighbour snatched up his nightcap, and pulled it down on his nose.

" What is it that I find dreadful? "—he shouted.—" Why, this: a circle—why, that is the perdition of all independent development; a circle is a hideous substitute for society, women, life; a circle. . . . O, but wait; I will tell you what a circle is! A circle is that sluggish and drowsy dwelling together, side by side, to which the significance and aspect of a sensible deed is attached; a circle substitutes arguments for conversation, trains men to fruitless jabbering, diverts you from solitary, beneficent work, infects you with the literary itch; it robs you, in short, of your freshness and virginal firmness of soul. A circle —why, it is staleness and boredom under the

name of brotherhood and friendship, a concate-
nation of misunderstandings and cavillings under
the pretext of frankness and sympathy; in a circle—thanks to the right of every friend to thrust
his unwashed fingers, at all seasons, at all hours,
straight into the interior of a comrade—no one
has a pure, untouched spot in his soul; in a circle,
men bow down before an empty, fine talker, a
conceited clever fellow, a premature old man;
they bear aloft in their arms the talentless scrib-
bler of verses, but with ' hidden ' thoughts; in a
circle, young fellows of seventeen discourse craftily and wisely of women, or talk with them just
as in a book,—and what things they talk about!
In a circle cunning eloquence flourishes; in a circle, men watch each other in a way not at all inferior to police officials. . . . O circle! thou art
not a circle: thou art an enchanted ring, in which
more than one honest man has gone to destruction! "

" Come, you are exaggerating, allow me to observe to you,"—I interrupted him.

My neighbour stared at me in silence.

" Perhaps,—the Lord knows,—perhaps I am.
But, you see, only one pleasure is left to fellows
like me—to exaggerate. So, sir, in this manner I spent four years in Moscow. I am not
able to describe to you, my dear sir, with what
rapidity, with what frightful rapidity, that time
passed; it even makes me sad and vexed to recall

it. 'T is as though you rose in the morning and
went coasting down hill on a sled. . . . . The
first you know, lo! you have reached the end; and
already it is evening; here 's the sleepy servant
pulling off your coat,—and you change your
dress, and wend your way to your friend, and set
to smoking a pipe, and drinking glasses of weak
tea, and discussing German philosophy, love, the
eternal sun of the spirit, and other remote objects.
But there also I met original, independent people; no matter how capricious one of them might
be, no matter how much he hid himself in a
corner, still nature would assert her rights; I
alone, unhappy wight, moulded myself like soft
wax, and my miserable nature did not display the
slightest resistance! In the meantime, I had
reached the age of one and twenty. I entered
into possession of my inheritance, or, to speak
more accurately, of that portion of my inheritance which my guardian had graciously seen fit
to leave me, gave a power of attorney to manage
all my hereditary estates to an emancipated house-
serf, Vasíly Kudryásheff, and went abroad to
Berlin. I remained abroad, as I have already
had the honour to inform you, three years. And
what came of that? There, abroad, also, I remained the same un-original being. In the first
place, there 's no disputing the fact, that I did not
make acquaintance with the actual Europe, with
European existence, not the least bit; I listened

to the German professors, and read German
books on the very spot of their birth . . . . .
that is all the difference there was. I led an isolated life, just as though I had been a monk; I
consorted with retired lieutenants who were oppressed, like myself, with a thirst for knowledge,
but were very dull of understanding, and not endowed with the gift of words; I frequented the
society of dull-witted families from Pénza and
other grain-producing governments; I lolled
in the cafés, read the newspapers, went to the
theatre in the evenings. I had little acquaintance with the natives of the country, I talked
with them in a constrained sort of way, and never
saw a single one of them at my own quarters,
with the exception of two or three intrusive
young fellows of Jewish extraction, who kept
incessantly running to me and borrowing money
from me,—luckily, *der Russe* was confiding. A
strange freak of chance at last took me into the
house of one of my professors; and this was the
way it came about: I went to him to enter myself
in his course, and the first I knew he suddenly invited me to spend the evening with him. This
professor had two daughters, twenty-seven years
of age, such buxom girls—God bless them!—such
magnificent noses, curls in papers, pale-blue eyes,
and red hands with pallid nails. One was named
Linchen, the other Minchen. I began to frequent
the professor's house. I must tell you that that

professor was not exactly stupid, but cracked as it were; he talked quite coherently on the lecture-platform, but at home he lisped, and kept his spectacles always on his forehead; moreover, he was an extremely learned man. . . . And what came of it? All of a sudden, I took it into my head that I had fallen in love with Linchen,—and for six whole months I thought so. I talked very little to her, it is true,—I chiefly stared at her; but I read aloud to her divers affecting compositions, pressed her hand on the sly, and of an evening meditated by her side, gazing intently at the moon, or simply into the air. Moreover, she did make such capital coffee! . . . . 'What more do I want?' I thought to myself. One thing troubled me: at the very moments of inexpressible bliss, as the saying is, I always had a pain in the lower part of my chest, for some reason or other, and an acute, cold chill coursed through my stomach. At last, I could endure such happiness no longer, and I fled. I spent two whole years abroad after that: I was in Italy, in Rome I stood in front of the ' Transfiguration,' in Florence in front of the ' Venus '; all at once, I went into exaggerated raptures, as though seized with a fit of ferocity; in the evenings I scribbled verses, and started a diary; in a word, I conducted myself there as everybody does. And yet, just see how easy it is to be original. I understand nothing about painting and sculpture, for example.

... I might simply have said that aloud . . . . .
no, impossible. I engage a cicerone, and run and
look at the frescoes. . . ."

Again he dropped his eyes, and again flung off
his nightcap.

" So, at last, I returned to my native land,"—
he went on, in a weary tone:—" I arrived in Moscow. In Moscow I underwent an amazing
change. Abroad I had chiefly held my tongue,
but here, all of a sudden, I began to talk with
unexpected boldness, and at the same time, conceived God knows what lofty opinion of myself. Indulgent people turned up, to whom I appeared something very like a genius; but I was
not able to maintain myself at the height of my
glory. One fine morning a calumny sprang into
existence with regard to me (who brought it forth
into the light of God, I know not: some old maid
of the male sex, it must have been,—there 's a lot
of such old maids in Moscow),—sprang into existence, and began to put forth shoots and runners, just as though it had been a strawberry-
plant. I got confused, tried to jump out of it,
to break asunder the adhesive threads,—but it
could n't be done. . . . . I went away. In that
case also, I proved myself an absurd man; I
ought to have quite quietly awaited the attack,
waited for this misfortune to run its course, just
as one awaits the end of nettlerash, and those
same indulgent persons would again have opened

their arms to me, those same ladies would again have smiled at my speeches. . . . . But there's the pity of it: I'm not an original man. Conscientiousness, you will be pleased to observe, suddenly awoke in me: for some reason, I became ashamed to chatter, chatter without ceasing, to chatter—yesterday on the Arbát, to-day on the Trubá, to-morrow at the Sivtzevóy-Vrázhek.[1] And forever about the selfsame thing. . . . And was it wanted? Just look at the genuine warriors in that career: that is a matter of no consequence to them; on the contrary, that is all they require; some of them will toil twenty years with their tongues, and always in the same direction. . . . That's what confidence in one's self and self-conceit will do for a man! And I had it, too,—self-conceit,—and it has not entirely quieted down even yet. . . . But the fatal point, I will repeat it once more, is, that I am not an original man, I stopped short in mid-career: nature should have allotted to me a great deal more conceit, or not given me any at all. But, at first, I really did have a pretty hard time: in addition to this, my trip abroad had completely exhausted my resources, and I did not wish to marry a merchant's widow, with a youthful but already flabby body, in the nature of jelly, and so I withdrew to my estate in the country. I think,"—added

[1] Squares and streets in Moscow.—TRANSLATOR.

my neighbour, casting another sidelong glance at me,—" that I may pass over in silence my first impressions of country life, allusions to the beauty of nature, the tranquil charm of solitude, and so forth. . . ."

" You may, you may,"—I replied.

" The more so,"—pursued the narrator,—" as all that is nonsense,—at least, so it seems to me. I got as bored in the country as a locked-up puppy, although I admit that, as I passed, for the first time, in springtime, on my homeward journey, through the familiar birch-grove, my head began to swim and my heart to beat with confused, sweet anticipation. But these sweet anticipations, as you yourself know, never are realised, but, on the contrary, other things come to pass, which you are not in the least expecting, such as: murrain, tax-arrears, sales at public auction, and so forth, and so forth. I made shift to live from day to day, with the assistance of the peasant overseer Yákoff, who had superseded the former manager, and proved, later on, to be as great a thief as he, if not even greater than he, and who poisoned my existence, into the bargain, with the odour of his tarred boots. . . . I one day called to mind a neighbouring family, with whom I was acquainted, consisting of the widow of a retired Colonel and her two daughters, ordered my drozhky harnessed, and drove off to my neighbours. That day must forever remain memorable to me; six months later, I married the Coloneless' second daughter. . . ."

The narrator hung his head, and raised his arms to heaven.

" And yet,"—he went on with fervour:—" I do not wish to inspire you with a bad opinion of my deceased wife. God forbid! She was the noblest, kindest creature, a loving creature, and capable of every sacrifice, although I must confess, between ourselves, if I had not had the misfortune to lose her, I probably should not have been in a position to chat with you to-day, for there still exists, in the cellar of my cherry-shed,[1] a beam on which I repeatedly made preparations to hang myself!

" Some pears,"—he began again, after a brief pause,—" must be allowed to lie for a certain time in the cellar, in order, as the saying is, to acquire their real savour; my deceased wife, evidently, also belonged to that sort of products of nature. Only now do I do her full justice. Only now, for example, do the memories of certain evenings, which I spent with her before the wedding, fail to arouse in me the slightest bitterness, but, on the contrary, affect me almost to tears. They were not wealthy people; their house, very old, of wood, but comfortable, stood

[1] In districts where the winter is too severe for unprotected cherry-trees, they are planted in a roughly-roofed, deep trench.— TRANSLATOR.

on a hill between a neglected park and an overgrown yard. At the foot of the hill flowed a
river, which was barely visible through the dense
foliage. A large veranda led from the house to
the garden; in front of the veranda flaunted a
long flower-bed, covered with roses; at each end
of the bed grew two acacias, which in their youth
had been interwoven in the form of a spiral by
the deceased owner. A little further off, in the
very thickest part of the neglected raspberry-plot,
which had run wild, stood an arbour, very artfully painted inside, but so aged and decrepit
outside, that it made one uncomfortable to look at
it. A glazed door led from the veranda into the
drawing-room; and in the drawing-room this is
what presented itself to the curious gaze of the
observer: in the corners, tiled stoves; a discordant
piano on the right, loaded down with manuscript
music; a divan, upholstered in faded sky-blue
material with whitish patterns; a circular table;
two étagères, with trifles of porcelain and glass
beads dating from the time of Katherine II; on
the wall, the familiar portrait of a fair-haired
young girl with a dove on her bosom and her eyes
rolled heavenward; on the table, a vase filled with
fresh roses. . . . . You see how minutely I describe. In that drawing-room and on that terrace
the entire tragicomedy of my love was enacted.
My neighbour's wife herself was a spiteful woman, with a permanent hoarseness of malice in

her throat,—a nagging and quarrelsome person; one of her daughters, Véra, was in no way different from ordinary young country gentlewomen; the other was Sófya,—and I fell in love with Sófya. The two sisters had still another room, their common bedroom, with two innocent little wooden beds, yellowish albums, mignonette, and portraits of their friends, male and female, drawn in pencil, and pretty badly done; among them one was especially noteworthy,—that of a gentleman with a remarkably energetic expression of countenance and a still more energetic signature, who in his youth had aroused incommensurable expectations, and had ended, like all the rest of us, in—nothing; with busts of Goethe and Schiller, with German books, withered wreaths, and other objects which had been preserved in commemoration. But I entered this room rarely and unwillingly: for some reason or other, my breathing was oppressed there. Moreover—strange to say! —I liked Sófya best of all when I was sitting with my back to her, or still more, probably, when I was thinking or meditating about her, especially in the evening, on the veranda. Then I gazed at the sunset glow, at the trees, at the tiny green leaves, which had already grown dark but were still distinctly discernible against the rosy sky; in the drawing-room, at the piano, sat Sófya, uninterruptedly playing some favourite, passionately pensive passage from Beethoven; the spiteful old woman snored regularly, as she sat on the divan; in the dining-room, illuminated by a flood of crimson light, Véra busied herself with the tea; the samovár hissed sportively, as though rejoicing over something; the cracknels broke with a merry snap, the teaspoons rattled resonantly against the cups; the canary-bird, which had been trilling ruthlessly all day long, had suddenly quieted down, and only now and then gave vent to a chirp, as though making an inquiry about something; sparse rain-drops fell from a light, transparent little cloud as it swept past. . . . And I sat and sat, and listened and listened, and my heart swelled, and again it seemed to me that I was in love. So, under the influence of an evening of this sort, I one day asked the old woman for her daughter's hand, and two months later I was married. It seemed to me that I loved her. . . . And even now, though it is time for me to know, yet, by heaven, I don't know even now whether I loved Sófya. She was a good-natured, clever, taciturn creature, with a warm heart; but, God knows why, whether from having lived so long in the country, or from some other causes, at the bottom of her soul (if there be such a thing as a bottom to the soul) she had a hidden wound, or, to express it better, she had a running sore, which nothing could heal, and neither she nor I was able to put a name to it. The existence of this wound I divined, of course, only long after the wedding.

And what efforts I made over her—all was to no avail! In my childhood I had a finch which the cat once held in her paws for a while: the finch was rescued and nursed, but it never recovered; it sulked, pined away, and ceased to sing. . . . The end of it was, that one night a mouse got into its open cage, and gnawed off its bill, in consequence of which, at last, it made up its mind to die. I know not what cat had held my wife in its claws, but she sulked and pined in exactly the same way as my unhappy finch. Sometimes it was evident that she herself wanted to shake her wings, to rejoice in the fresh air, in the sunshine, and at liberty; she would make the effort—and curl up in a ball! And yet she loved me: how many times did she assure me that she had nothing more to wish for,—whew, damn it!—and her eyes would darken the while. I thought to myself: ' Is n't there something in her past? ' I made inquiries: I found that there had been nothing. Well, so now then, judge for yourself: an original man would have shrugged his shoulders, heaved a couple of sighs, and taken to living in his own way; but I 'm not an original being, I began to stare at the rafters. My wife had become so thoroughly corroded with all the habits of an old maid,—Beethoven, nocturnal rambles, mignonette, correspondence with her friends, albums, and so forth,—that it was utterly impossible for her to get used to any other mode of life, especially to the life of the mistress of the house; and yet, it is ridiculous for a married woman to languish with a nameless woe, and sing in the evening: ' Wake thou her not at dawn!'

" So, sir, after this fashion we enjoyed felicity for three years; in the fourth year Sófya died in childbed with her first child,—and, strange to say, I seemed to have had a presentiment that she would not be capable of giving me a daughter or a son, a new inhabitant for the earth. I remember her funeral. It was in the spring. Our parish church is small and old, the ikonostásis has turned black, the walls are bare, the brick floor is broken in places; on each side of the choir is a large, ancient holy picture. The coffin was brought in, and placed in the very centre, in front of the Imperial Door,[1] draped in a faded pall, and three candlesticks were set around it. The service began. The decrepit lay-reader, with his little pigtail behind, girt low on the hips with a green girdle, mumbled mournfully in front of the folding reading-desk; the priest, also aged, with a kindly and sightless face, in a lilac cope with yellow patterns, did his own part of the service and the deacon's also. The fresh young foliage of the weeping birches fluttered and whispered to the full extent of the open windows; the fragrance of the grass was wafted in from out of

[1] The double central door in the ikonostásis (image-screen), which corresponds to the chancel-rail in the Western Church.— TRANSLATOR.

doors; the red flame of the wax candles paled
in the cheerful light of the spring day; the sparrows fairly filled the church with their twittering;
and now and then, up under the cupola, resounded
the ringing cry of a swallow which had flown in.
The reddish-brown heads of a few peasants,
who were zealously praying for the dead woman,
rose and fell in the golden dust of the sun's rays;
the smoke escaped from the orifice of the censer
in a slender, bluish stream. I looked at the dead
face of my wife. . . . My God! even death,
death itself, had not released her, had not healed
her wound: there was the same painful, timid,
dumb expression,—as though she were not at her
ease even in the grave. . . . My blood surged
bitterly within me. She was a good, good creature, but she did a good thing for herself when she
died!"

The narrator's cheeks reddened and his eyes
grew dim.

" Having, at last, got rid of the heavy depres-
sion which took possession of me after the death
of my wife,"—he began again,—" I conceived the
notion of taking to business, as the saying is. I
entered government service in the capital of the
Government,[1] but the huge rooms of the governmental establishment made my head ache, and
my eyes worked badly; and other causes presented themselves also, by the way. . . . . . I re-

---

[1] Corresponding to a State in the United States.—TRANSLATOR.

tired. I wanted to go to Moscow, but, in the
first place, I lacked the money; and, in the second
place . . . . I have already told you that I have
become resigned. This resignation came upon
me both suddenly and not suddenly. In spirit I
had long since become resigned, but my head still
refused to bend. I ascribed the modest frame of
my feelings and thoughts to the influence of
country life, of unhappiness. . . . On the other
hand, I had already long before noticed that almost all my neighbours, old and young, who had
been frightened at first by my learning, by my
trip abroad, and by the other opportunities of my
education, had not only succeeded in becoming
thoroughly accustomed to me, but had even begun to treat me, if not rudely, at least with sneer-
ing condescension, did not listen to me to the end
when I was arguing, and in speaking with me no
longer used the ' sir.' [1] I have also forgotten to
tell you that during the course of the first year
after my marriage I had tried my hand at literature, out of tedium, and had even sent an article
to a newspaper,—a story, if I mistake not; but
some time afterward I received a polite letter
from the editor, in which, among other things,
he said that while it could not be denied that I had
brains, it could be denied that I had talent, and in
literature talent was necessary. In addition to

[1] The addition of the letter *s* to words, here indicated, is not
precisely "sir" or "madam," but a courteous, lesser equivalent,
which must be rendered thus.—TRANSLATOR.

this, it came to my knowledge that a man from
Moscow, who chanced to be passing through,—an
extremely amiable young fellow, by the way,—
had referred to me in passing as an extinct and
empty man, at an evening party at the Governor's. But my semi-voluntary blindness still
continued: I did n't want to 'box my own ears,'
you know; at last, one fine morning, I opened my
eyes. This is the way it came about. The chief
of rural police dropped in to see me, with the purpose of calling my attention to a ruined bridge
on my domains, which I positively had not the
means of mending. As he washed down a bit of
dried sturgeon with a glass of vódka, this patronising guardian of order reproved me in a paternal way for my thoughtlessness, but entered into
my situation, and merely recommended me to
order my peasants to throw on a little manure,
lighted his pipe, and began to talk about the approaching elections. A certain Orbassánoff, an
empty swashbuckler, and a bribe-taker to boot,
was at that time a candidate for the honourable
post of Marshal of the Nobility for the Government. Moreover, he was not noteworthy either
for his wealth or for his distinction. I expressed
my opinion concerning him, and rather carelessly
at that: I must confess that I looked down upon
Mr. Orbassánoff. The chief of police looked at
me, tapped me affectionately on the shoulder, and
said good-naturedly:—' Ekh, Vasíly Vasílievitch,

HAMLET OF SHSHTCHÍGRY

't is not for you and me to judge of such persons;
—how can we? . . . . Let every one keep his
proper place.' [1]—' Why, good gracious! '—I retorted with vexation, ' what difference is there
between me and Mr. Orbassánoff? '—The chief
took his pipe out of his mouth, opened his
eyes very wide, and fairly burst with laughter.
—' Come, you funny man,'—he said at last,
through his tears: ' what a joke you have got off
. . . . . . ah! was n't that a good one! '—and he
never stopped making fun of me until he departed, now and then nudging me in the ribs with
his elbow and even addressing me as ' thou.' He
went away at last. That was the last drop: the
cup overflowed. I paced up and down the room
a few times, halted in front of the mirror, stared
for a long, long time at my disconcerted countenance, and, slowly sticking out my tongue, shook
my head with a bitter smile. The veil fell from
my eyes; I saw clearly, more clearly than I saw
my face in the mirror, what an empty, insignificant, and useless, unoriginal man I was! "

The narrator made a brief pause.

" In one of Voltaire's tragedies,"—he went on
dejectedly,—" a certain gentleman is delighted
that he has reached the extreme limits of ill luck.
Although there is nothing tragic in my fate, yet
I must confess that I have tasted something of

[1] In Russian, literally: " Let the cricket know his
hearth."—TRANSLATOR.

that sort. I have learned to know the venomous raptures of cold despair; I have learned by experience how sweet it is to lie, without haste, in bed for an entire morning and curse the day and hour of my birth;—I could not resign myself all at once. And, in fact, judge for yourself: my lack of money fettered me to my detested country-place; I was fit for nothing,—neither agriculture, nor the service, nor literature; I avoided the landed proprietors, books revolted me; for the dropsical and sickly-sentimental young ladies, who shook their curls and feverishly reiterated the word 'life,' I had ceased to be in the least attractive as soon as I ceased to chatter and go into ecstasies; I did not know how to isolate myself completely, neither could I do so. . . . I began to—what do you think?—I began to haunt my neighbours. As though intoxicated with scorn for myself, I purposely subjected myself to all sorts of petty humiliations. They passed me over at the table, they greeted me coldly and haughtily; at last, they took no notice whatever of me; they did not even allow me to mingle in the general conversation, and I myself used deliberately to back up from a corner some extremely stupid babbler, who at one time, in Moscow, would have kissed my feet, the hem of my cloak, in rapture. . . I did not even permit myself to think that I was surrendering myself to the bitter satisfaction of irony. . . . Good heavens, what is irony in solitude! This, sir, is the way I behaved for several years in succession, and the way I am behaving up to the present time. . . ."

"Why, this is outrageous," growled the sleepy voice of Mr. Kantagriúkhin, from the adjoining room:—"What fool has taken it into his head to prate by night?"

The narrator briskly dived down under his coverlet and, timidly peering out, shook his finger at me.

"Sh . . . . . sssssh!"—he whispered; and, as though apologising and bowing in the direction of Mr. Kantagriúkhin's voice, he said respectfully:—"I obey, sir; I obey, sir; excuse me, sir. . . . . It is permissible for him to sleep, he has a right to sleep,"—he went on again in a whisper: "he must gather fresh strength, well, if only in order that he may eat with his usual satisfaction to-morrow. We have no right to disturb him. Moreover, I think I have told you all I wished; probably, you would like to go to sleep also. I wish you a good night."

The narrator turned over with feverish haste, and buried his head in his pillows.

"Permit me at least to inquire,"—I asked:— "with whom have I the honour . . . ."

He raised his head alertly.

"No, for God's sake,"—he interrupted me:— "don't ask my name of me or of others. Let me remain for you an unknown being, Vasíly Vasílie-vitch, bruised by fate. Moreover, as an unoriginal man, I do not deserve to have a name of my own. . . . But if you absolutely insist upon giving me some appellation, then call me . . . . call me the Hamlet of Shshtchígry County. There are lots of such Hamlets in every county, but perhaps you have not encountered any others. . . . Herewith, farewell."

Again he buried himself in his feather-bed, and on the following morning, when they came to wake me, he was no longer in the room. He had departed at daybreak.

VIII

ONE hot summer day I was returning from the hunt in a peasant cart; Ermolái was dozing as he sat beside me, and bobbing his head forward. The slumbering hounds were jolting about like dead bodies under our feet. The coachman kept incessantly flicking the gadflies off the horses with his whip. The white dust floated in a light cloud after the cart. We drove into the bushes. The road became more full of pits, the wheels began to come in contact with the branches. Ermolái gave a start, and glanced around him. . . . "Eh!"—said he:—"why, there ought to be black-cock here. Let's alight."—We halted and entered the tract of second growth and bushes. My dog hit upon a covey of birds. I fired, and was beginning to reload my gun when, suddenly, behind me, a loud crash made itself heard, and, parting the bushes with his hands, a man on horse-back rode up to me.—"Pér-mit me to inquire,"—he said, in an arrogant voice, "by what right you are shooting here, m' d'r s'r." [1]

The stranger spoke with unusual rapidity, ab-

[1] His pronunciation is indicated as affected.—TRANSLATOR.

191

ruptly, and through his nose. I looked him in the face: never in my life had I beheld anything like him. Figure to yourself, dear readers, a tiny, fair-haired man with a little red snub-nose and a long red moustache. An octagonal Persian cap with a crimson cloth top covered his forehead to his very brows. He was clad in a long, threadbare, yellow Caucasian coat with black velveteen cartridge-sheaths on the breast and faded silver galloon on all the seams; across his shoulder hung his hunting-horn, a dagger projected from his belt. His emaciated, roman-nosed, sorrel horse staggered beneath him, like a drunken creature; two greyhounds, gaunt and wry-footed, pranced about between its legs. The face, the glance, the voice, every movement, the whole person of the stranger exhaled mad hardihood and boundless, unprecedented pride; his pale-blue, glassy eyes were shifty and squinting, like those of a tipsy man; he flung his head back, puffed out his cheeks, snorted and quivered all over, as though with excess of pride—for all the world like a turkey-cock. He repeated his question.

"I did not know that shooting here was forbidden,"—I replied.

"You are on my land here, my dear sir,"—he went on.

"Very well, I will go."

"But pér-mit me to inquire,"—he returned:

" have I the honour to explain myself with a noble? "

I mentioned my name.

" In that case, pray go on shooting. I am a noble myself, and am very glad to be of service to a noble. . . . . My name is Tchertop-khánoff. Pantaléi."

He bent forward, gave a whoop, lashed his horse on the neck with his whip, shook his head, dashed aside, and crushed the paw of one of his dogs. The dog began to whimper shrilly. Tcher-topkhánoff began to seethe and hiss, smote his horse on the head between the ears, sprang to the earth quicker than a flash of lightning, scru-tinised the dog's paw, spat on the wound, kicked the animal in the side with his foot to stop its out-cries, grasped the horse's forelock, and thrust his foot into the stirrup. The horse tossed its muzzle, elevated its tail, and darted sideways into the bushes; he went hopping after it on one leg, but vaulted into the saddle at last; he flourished his kazák whip like a man in a frenzy, blew a blaring blast on his horn, and galloped off. Before I could recover myself from this unexpected ap-parition of Tchertopkhánoff, suddenly, almost without a sound, a rather corpulent man of forty rode out of the bushes on a small, black nag. He drew up, removed from his head a green leather cap of military shape, and in a shrill, soft voice asked me whether I had seen a rider on a sorrel horse. I replied that I had.

" In what direction did they [1] deign to ride? " —he went on, in the same tone, and without putting on his cap.

" In that direction, sir."

" I am greatly obliged to you, sir."

He chirruped, jogged his feet against the horse's ribs, and rode off at a trot,—jog-trot,—in the direction indicated. I watched him until his peaked cap vanished among the boughs. This new stranger did not in the least resemble his predecessor, so far as his external appearance was concerned. His face, round and puffy as a ball, expressed bashfulness, good-nature, and gentle resignation; his nose, which was also round and puffy and speckled with blue veins, betrayed the sensualist. Not a single hair remained on his head in front; at the back, thin red hair stuck out; his small eyes, which seemed to have been cleft with a cutting sedge, blinked amiably; his red, lush lips smiled sweetly. He wore a surtout with a standing collar and brass buttons, extremely threadbare, but clean; above the yellow tops of his boots, his fat calves were visible.

" Who is that? "—I inquired of Ermolái.

" That? Nedopiúskin, Tíkhon Ivánitch. He lives with Tchertopkhánoff."

---

[1] The respectful form of " he " or " she," according to the context.—TRANSLATOR.

TCHERTOPKHÁNOFF

" What is he,—a poor man? "

" He is n't rich; but then, Tchertopkhánoff has n't a brass cent."

" Then why has he taken up his abode with him? "

" Why, they have struck up a friendship, you see. The friend never goes anywhere without his friend. . . . . 'T is a regular case of whithersoever the steed goes with his hoofs, thither also goes the crab with his claws. . . ."

We emerged from the bushes; all at once, the two huntsmen began to " give the view-halloo " alongside of us, and a huge grey hare rolled over the oats, which were already fairly tall. In their wake, the harriers and harehounds leaped out of the edge of the woods, and in the wake of the dogs forth flew Tchertopkhánoff himself. He was not shouting nor urging them on, nor hallooing; he was panting and gasping; from his gaping mouth abrupt, unintelligible sounds broke forth from time to time; he dashed onward, with protruding eyes, and flogging his unhappy horse frantically with his kazák whip. The harehounds " overshot "; . . . . . the hare squatted, turned sharply back on its track, and dashed past Ermolái into the bushes. . . . . The hounds swept by.—" L-l-l-look o-o-out, l-l-l-look o-o-out! " faltered the fainting sportsman, with an effort, as though stammering:—" look out, my good man! " Ermolái fired . . . . the wounded hare rolled like a spinning-top over the smooth, dry grass, gave a leap upward, and began to scream pitifully in the teeth of the dog which was rending him asunder; the harriers immediately dashed up.

Tchertopkhánoff flew· off his horse like a tumbler pigeon, jerked out his dagger, ran up, straddling his legs far apart, to the dogs, with wrathful exclamations wrested from them the tortured hare, and with his face all twisted awry, plunged his dagger up to the very hilt into the creature's throat . . . . plunged it in, and began to cackle. Tíkhon Ivánitch made his appearance on the edge of the woods. " Ho-ho-ho-ho-ho-ho-ho! " roared Tchertopkhánoff a second time. . . . " Ho-ho-ho-ho," repeated his comrade quietly.

" But, you know, it is n't the proper thing to hunt in the summer,"—I remarked, indicating the flattened oats to Tchertopkhánoff.

" 'T is my field,"—replied Tchertopkhánoff, barely breathing.

He ripped up the hare, disembowelled it, and distributed the paws to the dogs.

" Charge the cartridge to me, my dear fellow," —he said, according to the rules of sport, addressing Ermolái.—" And as for you, my dear sir," —he added in the same abrupt and cutting voice: —" I thank you."

He mounted his horse.

" Pér-mit me to inquire . . . I forgot about that . . . your name and surname."

Again I introduced myself.

"Very glad to make your acquaintance. If you happen to come my way, pray drop in to see me. . . . . But where's that Fómka, Tíkhon Ivánitch?"—he went on testily:—"the hare has been run down in his absence."

"His horse tumbled down under him," replied Tíkhon Ivánitch, with a smile.

"Tumbled down? Orbassán tumbled down! Phew, pshaw! . . . . . Where is he, where is he?"

"Yonder—the other side of the wood."

Tchertopkhánoff lashed his horse on the muzzle with his kazák whip,[1] and galloped off at a breakneck pace. Tíkhon Ivánitch made me a couple of bows,—one for himself, one on his comrade's account,—and again set off at a trot through the bushes.

These two gentlemen had strongly excited my curiosity. . . . What could unite in the bonds of indestructible friendship two beings so utterly different? I began to make inquiries. This is what I learned.

Tchertopkhánoff, Pantelái Eremyéitch, bore the reputation throughout the whole countryside of being a dangerous and crackbrained man, an arrogant man and bully of the worst sort. He

---

[1] This nagáika is a cruel—a deadly—implement. It consists of a short, thick handle, jointed to a stiff "lash" of nearly the same length (both of rawhide), terminating in a small, flat disk, also of rawhide.—TRANSLATOR.

had served for a very brief period in the army, and had retired from it, " in consequence of unpleasantnesses," with that rank concerning which there exists a wide-spread opinion that a "chicken is not a bird "—that is, too insignificant to be considered as rank at all. He was descended from an ancient house which had once been wealthy; his ancestors had lived luxuriously after the manner of the steppes; that is to say, they welcomed bidden and unbidden guests and fed them to satiety, as though for slaughter; provided strange coachmen with half a dozen bushels of oats for their tróïka horses; kept musicians, singers, buffoons and hounds; travelled to Moscow in the winter in their own ponderous ancient coaches; on festival days supplied the populace with liquor and home-made beer; and sometimes were without a penny for months at a stretch, and subsisted on horse-provender.[1] Panteléi Eremyéitch's father inherited the property in a ruined condition; he, in his turn, also " caroused," and, dying, left to his only son and heir, Panteléi, the mortgaged hamlet of Bezsónovo, with thirty-five souls of the male sex and seventy-six of the female sex, together with fourteen desyatínas and an eighth of inconvenient land in the Kolobród waste, to which, however, the deceased possessed no documentary proofs of his ownership. The deceased had ruined himself

[1] Oatmeal and cornmeal (which last is known in the south of Russia) would come under this head.—TRANSLATOR.

in a very strange manner, it must be confessed
—"domestic economy" had been his perdition.
According to his ideas, a nobleman ought not to
depend upon the merchants, the town-dwellers,
and such-like "brigands," as he expressed it; he
set up on his estate all sorts of handicrafts
and workshops: "'T is both more seemly and
cheaper,"—he was wont to say: "'t is domestic
economy!" He never got rid of that pernicious
idea to the end of his life; and it ruined him.
On the other hand, how he did enjoy himself!
He never denied himself a single whim. Among
other caprices, he once had constructed, according to his own designs, such a huge family carriage that, in spite of the vigorous efforts of
the peasants' horses, which had been impressed
from the entire village, along with their owners,
it tumbled down at the first declivity, and went
to pieces. Eremyéi Lúkitch (that was the
name of Panteléi's father) caused a monument
to be erected on the hill, but was not in the
least disconcerted. He also took it into his head
to build a church, on his own responsibility,
of course, without the aid of an architect. He
burned a whole forest to bake the bricks, he laid
an enormous foundation, as though for the cathe-
dral of a government capital, reared the walls,
and began to construct the arch for the cupola:
the cupola caved in. He rebuilt it,—again the
cupola fell; he did it a third time, and for the third

time the cupola fell to pieces. My Eremyéi Lúkitch reflected. " There 's something wrong," he
thought . . . . . " some damned witchcraft is
mixed up with it . . . ." and all of a sudden he
ordered that all the old peasant women in the
village should be flogged. The women were
flogged,—but the cupola refused to be constructed, nevertheless. He began to rebuild the
peasants' cottages on a new plan, and all at his
own expense; he built three cottages together
in a triangle, and in the centre he erected a pole
surmounted by a painted starling-house and a
flag. He was in the habit of devising a fresh
freak every day: now he made soup of burdock,
again he shaved off the tails of the horses to
make caps for his house-serfs, next he made
preparations to replace flax with nettles, or to
feed his pigs on mushrooms. . . . One day he
read in *The Moscow News* an article by a land-
owner of the Khárkhoff Government, named
Khryák-Khrupyórsky, concerning the advantages of morality in the life of the serfs, and on
the very next day he issued an order to all the
serfs that they should forthwith learn the Khárkhoff squire's article by heart. The serfs learned
the article; their noble master asked them: " Did
they understand what was written therein? " The
overseer replied: " How could they fail to understand? " About the same time he commanded all
his subjects, on the score of order and domestic

economy, to be numbered, and each one to have his number sewn on his collar. Each person, on meeting the master, used to call out: " Such-and-such a number is coming! " and the master would reply amiably: " Go thy way, and God protect thee! "

But, in spite of order and domestic economy, Eremyéi Lúkitch gradually got into very difficult straits: first he began to mortgage his estates, then he proceeded to sell them, and the last one, the ancestral nest, the large village with the unfinished church, was sold by the treasury, fortunately not during the lifetime of Eremyéi Lúkitch,—he could not have borne that blow,—but two weeks after his death. He managed to expire in his own house, in his own bed, surrounded by his own people, and under the supervision of his own medical man, but poor Panteléi inherited nothing except Bezsónovo.

Panteléi was already in the service, in the very thick of the above-mentioned "unpleasantnesses," when he heard of his father's death. He had recently attained the age of eighteen. From his very childhood, he had never quitted the parental roof, and under the guidance of his mother, an extremely amiable, but thoroughly dull-witted woman, Vasilísa Vasílievna, he had grown up a spoiled child, and a regular little country squire. She alone took charge of his education; Eremyéi Lúkitch, absorbed as he was in his experiments in domestic economy, had no time for that. To tell the truth, he did once chastise his son with his own hands for pronouncing the letter Rtzy,[1] artzy; but that day, Eremyéi Lúkitch was profoundly and secretly afflicted; his best hound had been killed against a tree. However, Vasilísa Vasílievna's anxieties in regard to the education of Pantiúsha were confined to torturing effort alone; in the sweat of her brow she hired for him as governor an ex-soldier, an Alsatian, a certain Birchhoff (and to the day of her death, she trembled like a leaf before him: " Well," she said to herself, " if he resigns—I am lost! What shall I do? Where shall I find another teacher? Even this one I lured away from a neighbour with the greatest difficulty! "). And Birchhoff, like the shrewd man he was, immediately took advantage of his exceptional position: he drank himself dead drunk, and slept from morning till night. At the conclusion of his " course of sciences," Panteléi entered the service. Vasilísa Vasílievna was no longer living. She had died six months previous to this important event, from fright; in her dreams she had beheld a vision of a white man riding a bear. Eremyéi Lúkitch speedily followed his better half.

Panteléi, at the first news of his illness, gal-

[1] The Slavonic name of the letter *R*. Russian children are taught a certain amount of Old Church Slavonic, to enable them to understand the services of the Church, which are conducted exclusively in that language.—TRANSLATOR.

loped home at breakneck speed, but did not find his parent alive. But what was the amazement of the respectful son, when he suddenly found himself converted from a wealthy heir into a pauper! Few are able to endure so abrupt a change. Panteléi grew unsociable and hard. From an honourable, lavish, amiable, though harebrained and hottempered fellow, he changed into an arrogant man and a bully, and ceased to hold intercourse with his neighbours,—he was ashamed before the wealthy, despised the poor, and behaved with unheard-of insolence to everybody—even to the constituted authorities; as much as to say: " I 'm a nobleman of ancient lineage." Once he came near shooting the commissary of rural police, who had entered his room with his cap on his head. The powers, of course, on their side, did not pardon his attitude, and, on occasion, made themselves felt; yet, all the same, he was feared, because he was a frightfully hot-tempered man, and at the second word proposed a duel with knives. At the slightest opposition, Tchertopkhánoff's eyes began to grow wild, his voice began to break. .... "Ah, va-va-va-va-va!" he stammered, "damn my head!" .... And bang it would go against the wall! And more than that, he was a clean man, and not mixed up in anything. Of course no one went to his house. .... And, nevertheless, his was a kind, even a great soul, in its way: he would not tolerate injustice or oppression even toward a stranger; he stood up for his peasants by every means in his power.—" What? " he said, frantically slapping his own head:—" touch my people, my people? Not while I am Tchertop-khánoff! . . . ."

Unlike Panteléi Eremyéitch, Tíkhon Ivánitch Nedopiúskin could not cherish pride in his extraction. His father had come of the petty free-holder class, and only by dint of forty years of service had he acquired nobility. Mr. Nedopiú-skin Senior had belonged to the category of people whom ill-luck pursues with an obduracy which resembles personal hatred. For the space of sixty whole years, from his very birth to his very death, the poor man had contended with all the poverty, infirmities, and calamities which are peculiar to petty people; he floundered like a fish on the ice, never had food or sleep enough, cringed, toiled, grieved, and languished, trembled over every kopék, actually suffered in the service, though innocent, and died, at last, in a garret or a cellar, without having succeeded in amassing either for himself or his children a bit of daily bread. Fate had shaken him as a dog shakes a hare in the chase. He had been a good and honest man, but had taken bribes—ranging from a twenty-kopék piece to two rubles, inclusive. Nedopiúskin had had a wife, a thin, consumptive woman; and he had had children: luckily, they had all died soon, with the exception of Tíkhon

and a daughter Mitrodóra, by profession a
" dandy of the merchant class," who, after many
sorrowful and ridiculous adventures, had married
a retired pettifogger. Mr. Nedopiúskin Senior
had managed, during his lifetime, to get Tíkhon
appointed as supernumerary official in a chancellery; but immediately after his parent's death,
Tíkhon resigned. The eternal trepidations, the
torturing battle with cold and hunger, the melancholy dejection of his mother, the toilsome, anxious despair of his father, the rough oppressions
of landlords and shopkeepers,—all this daily, un-
intermittent woe had bred in Tíkhon inexpressible timidity: at the very sight of his superior official he would begin to quake and turn faint, like
a captured bird. He abandoned the service. Indifferent, and perhaps derisive, nature imbues
people with various capacities and inclinations,
which are not at all in accordance with their position in society and with their means; with the care
and love peculiar to her, she had moulded Tíkhon,
the son of the poverty-stricken official, into a sensitive, indolent, soft, impressionable being, addicted exclusively to enjoyment, gifted with an
excessively delicate sense of smell and taste . . . .
had moulded him, carefully put on the finishing
touches, and had left her production to grow up
on sour cabbage and putrid fish. But he did grow
up, that product of hers, and began, as the saying
goes, to " live." Then the fun began. Fate,

which had unremittingly tormented Nedopiúskin Senior, began on his son: evidently, she had acquired a taste. But with Tíkhon she adopted a different course: she did not torture him,—she amused herself with him. She never once drove him to despair, never made him experience the mortifying torture of hunger, but she drove him all over Russia, from Velíky-Ustiúg to Tzárevo-Koksháisk, from one humiliating and ridiculous employment to another: now she promoted him to be "majordomo" to a vixenish and splenetic benefactress of noble birth; then appointed him at the head of the domestic chancellery of a mole-eyed nobleman with his hair clipped in the English fashion; then made him half-butler, half-jester to a master of the hounds. . . . . In a word, Fate forced poor Tíkhon to drain drop by drop, and to the last drop, the whole bitter and venomous potion of an inferior existence. He served, in his time, the ponderous caprice, the sleepy and spiteful tedium, of idle gentlefolk. . . . . How many times, alone in his chamber, dismissed at last with the words "God be with thee"[1] after a horde of guests had amused themselves with him to their fill, had he vowed, all flushed with shame, with cold tears of despair in his eyes, to run away secretly that very day, to try his luck in the town, to find himself some petty place, if only that of a copying-clerk; or,

[1] Equivalent to polite dismissal.—TRANSLATOR.

once for all, to die of hunger in the street. But, in the first place, God did not give him the strength for that; in the second place, timidity began to torment him; and, in the third place, in conclusion,—how was he to obtain a place for himself, whom was he to ask? " They won't give me one," the unhappy man would whisper, as he tossed dejectedly on his bed: " they won't give me one! " On the following day, he would begin to bear the yoke again. His position was all the more painful, in that nature had not troubled herself to endow him with even a small modicum of those capacities and gifts without which the part of jester is almost impossible. For example, he could not dance until he dropped with fatigue in a bear's skin worn wrong side out; neither could he play the buffoon and the courtier in the immediate vicinity of freely used dog-whips; when put out of doors naked at a temperature of twenty degrees below zero, he sometimes caught cold; his stomach could digest neither wine mixed with ink and other filth, nor toadstools and poison-mushrooms crumbled up in vinegar. The Lord knows what would have become of Tíkhon, if the last of his benefactors, a distiller who had acquired wealth, had not taken it into his head, in a jovial hour, to add a codicil to his will: " And to Zyóza (also called Tíkhon) Nedopiúskin I bequeath for eternal and hereditary possession my village of Bezselendyéevka, acquired by myself, together with all its dependencies." Several days later, the benefactor died of a stroke of paralysis, over a sterlet soup. There was a commotion; the officers of the law made a descent and affixed seals to the property in the regular form. The relatives assembled; the will was opened; they read it, and demanded Nedopiúskin. Nedopiúskin presented himself. The majority of the assembly were aware of the post which Tíkhon Ivánitch had occupied under his benefactor; deafening exclamations, jeering congratulations, were showered upon him on his appearance. " The landed proprietor, there he is, the new landed proprietor!"—yelled the other heirs.— " Well, now you know,"—put in one well-known jester and wit: " Now, really, you know, one may say . . . . . really, you know . . . . that . . . . is what is called . . . . that's . . . . . . the heir." And all fairly burst with laughter. For a long time, Nedopiúskin would not believe in his good fortune. They showed him the will,—he turned scarlet, screwed up his eyes, began to brandish his arms, and fell to weeping in torrents. The noisy laughter of the assembly changed into a thick and unanimous roar. The village of Bezselendyéevka consisted, in all, of two-and-twenty serfs; no one greatly begrudged it; therefore, why not have some sport out of it? One heir only, a man from Petersburg, a pompous man with a Grecian nose and the most noble ex-

pression of countenance, Rostisláff Adámitch
Schtoppel, could not endure it, moved up sideways to Nedopiúskin, and stared at him arrogantly over his shoulder. "So far as I can see,
my dear sir,"—he said, in a scornfully-careless
manner, "you have been living with the respected Feódor Feódorovitch in the capacity of
jester, or servant, so to speak?" The gentleman
from Petersburg expressed himself in insuffer-
ably clear, bold, and regular language. The flustered, agitated Nedopiúskin did not catch the
words of the strange gentleman, but all the others
immediately fell silent; the wit smiled condescendingly. Mr. Schtoppel rubbed his hands and
repeated his question. Nedopiúskin raised his
eyes in amazement, and opened his mouth. Rostisláff Adámitch narrowed his eyes venomously.

"I congratulate you, my dear sir, I congratulate you,"—he went on:—"truth to tell, not every
one would have consented to earrrrn his daily
bread in that manner; but *de gustibus non est dis-
putandum,* that is to say, every one to his taste.
. . . Isn't that so?"

Some one in the rear ranks gave a swift but decorous squeal of surprise and delight.

"Tell me,"—pursued Mr. Schtoppel, greatly
encouraged by the smiles of the assembly:—"to
which talent in particular are you indebted for
your good fortune? No, be not ashamed, speak
out; we are all of the family here, so to speak,

en famille. We are here *en famille,* are we not, gentlemen?"

The heir to whom Rostisláff Adámitch chanced to appeal with this question did not know French, unfortunately, and therefore confined himself to emitting a faint grunt of approval. On the other hand, another heir, a young man with yellowish blotches on his brow, made haste to put in: *"Voui, voui,* of course!"

"Perhaps,"—began Mr. Schtoppel again, "you can walk on your hands, with your feet elevated, so to speak, in the air?"

Nedopiúskin cast a sorrowful glance around him—all faces wore a spiteful smile, all eyes were covered with the moisture of satisfaction.

"Or, perchance, you can crow like a cock?"

A guffaw of laughter ran the round, and immediately ceased, quelled by expectation.

"Or, perchance, you can balance things on your nose. . . ."

"Stop!"—a sharp, loud voice suddenly interrupted Rostisláff Adámitch:—"are n't you ashamed to torment the poor man!"

All glanced round. At the door stood Tchertopkhánoff. In his quality of nephew thrice removed of the deceased distiller, he also had received a note of invitation to the family gathering. During the whole time of the reading, he— as always—had held himself haughtily apart from the rest.

" Stop! "—he repeated, throwing his head back arrogantly.

Mr. Schtoppel turned swiftly round, and, beholding a man poorly clad, not good-looking, he asked his neighbour in a low tone (caution is never amiss) :

" Who is that? "

" Tchertopkhánoff, a person of no importance," the latter replied in his ear.

Rostisláff Adámitch assumed an arrogant mien.

" How came you to be commander? "—he said through his nose, puckering up his eyes.—" What sort of a bird are you, permit me to inquire? "

Tchertopkhánoff flared up, like powder at a spark. Rage stopped his breath.

" Dz-dz-dz-dz,"—he hissed, like a choking man, and suddenly thundered out:

" Who am I? who am I? I am PIeléi Tchertopkhánoff, a noble of ancient lineage,—my great-great-grandfather's grandfather served the Tzar,—but who art thou? "

Rostisláff Adámitch turned pale, and retreated a pace. He had not anticipated such resistance.

" I am a bird, I—I a bird! .... Oo .. o! .... "

Tchertopkhánoff darted forward; Schtoppel sprang aside in great perturbation, the guests flew at the irritated squire.

" Exchange shots, exchange shots this very moment, across a handkerchief! "—shouted the thoroughly infuriated Panteléi:—" or thou must beg my pardon, and his . . . . . ."

" Beg his pardon, beg his pardon,"—murmured the startled heirs round about Schtoppel: " he 's a regular madman, you know,—quite ready to cut your throat."

" Excuse me, excuse me, I did not know,"—stammered Schtoppel:—" I did not know. . . . ."

" And do thou ask his pardon also! "—roared the irrepressible Pantelei.

" And do you pray excuse me also,"—added Rostisláff Adámitch, turning to Nedopiúskin, who was shaking as though with fever.

Tchertopkhánoff calmed down, went up to Tíkhon Ivánitch, took him by the hand, cast a challenging glance around, and, without meeting any one's eye, left the room in triumph, accompanied by the new owner of the village of Bezselendyéevka.

From that day forth, they never parted company again. (The village of Bezselendyéevka was only eight versts distant from Bezsónovo.) Nedopiúskin's unbounded gratitude speedily passed into servile adoration. The weak, soft, not altogether clean Tíkhon bowed down in the dust before the fearless and disinterested Pantelei. " 'T is no small matter," he sometimes thought to himself:—" he talks with the Governor, he looks him straight in the eye. . . . Christ is my witness, —he looks him in the eye, that he does! "

He admired him to the point of perplexity, to

the enfeeblement of his mental powers; he regarded him as a remarkable, a wise, a learned man. And, truth to tell, bad as Tchertopkhánoff's education had been, still, in comparison with that of Tíkhon, it might be considered brilliant. Tchertopkhánoff, it is true, read little in Russian, understood French imperfectly,—so imperfectly that one day, in reply to the question of a Swiss tutor: *"Vous parlez français, Monsieur?"* he answered: *" je ne* understand," and after reflecting a while, he added: *" pas ";*—but, nevertheless, he remembered that there had existed in the world a very witty writer, Voltaire, and also that Frederick the Great, King of Prussia, had distinguished himself in the military line. Among Russian writers he respected Derzhávin, but loved Márlinsky, and named his best dog Ammalat-Beg. . . .

A few days after my first encounter with the two friends, I set off for the hamlet of Bezsónovo, to call upon Panteléi Eremyéitch. His tiny house was visible from afar; it reared itself up on a bare spot, half a verst from the village, " in an exposed site," as the saying is, like a hawk hovering over ploughed fields. Tchertopkhánoff's entire manor consisted of four ancient log edifices of various sizes, namely: a wing, a stable, a carriage-house, and a bath-house.[1]

---

[1] The bath-house is always separated from the house, and consists generally of an anteroom and the main chamber, with shelves of different heights. The steam is generated by throwing cold

Each log-house stood apart by itself: neither fence round about nor gate was visible. My coachman halted in perplexity at the half-rotten and choked-up well. Near the carriage-house, several gaunt and shaggy hare-hounds were tearing a dead horse,—probably Orbassán; one of them raised his bloody muzzle, gave a hurried yelp, and began again to gnaw at the bared ribs. Beside the horse stood a young fellow of seventeen, with a bloated and sallow face, dressed as a page, and with bare feet: he was pompously watching the dogs, which were entrusted to his oversight, and now and then he lashed the most greedy of them with a long whip.

" Is the master at home? "—I asked.

" Why, the Lord only knows! "—replied the young fellow.—" Knock."

I sprang out of my drozhky and walked to the porch of the wing.

The dwelling of Mr. Tchertopkhánoff presented a very sorry aspect: the beams had turned black, and protruded themselves forward " in a paunch," the chimney had tumbled down, the corners were ruined with dampness, and were tottering, the tiny, dim, dark-blue windows gazed forth with indescribable sourness from beneath the shaggy roof, which sagged forward: some aged street-walkers have eyes like that. I

water on stones heated to a glow when a bath is wanted. Peter the Great, in some of his baths, appropriately used cannon-balls.— TRANSLATOR.

214

knocked; no one responded. But I heard these words sharply uttered on the other side of the door:

"A, B, V;[1] come now, you fool,"—said a hoarse voice;—"A, B, V, G. . . . . Not that way! G, D, E, E! . . . . Come now, you fool!"

I knocked again.

The same voice shouted:—"Come in,—who's there? . . . ."

I entered a bare little anteroom, and through the open door I descried Tchertopkhánoff himself. Clad in a dirty Bukhará dressing-gown and full trousers, with a red fez on his head, he was sitting at a table, gripping the muzzle of a young poodle with one hand, and with the other holding a bit of bread directly above his nose.

"Ah!"—he said with dignity, without stirring from his seat:—"I am very glad of your visit. Pray take a seat. I'm bothering over Vénzor[2] here, as you see. . . . Tíkhon Ivánitch,"—he added, raising his voice:—"please come hither. A visitor has arrived."

"Immediately, immediately,"—replied Tíkhon Ivánitch from the adjoining room.— "Másha, give me my neckerchief."

Tchertopkhánoff again turned his attention to Vénzor, and laid the bit of bread on his nose. I

[1] The Russian alphabet runs in the order here indicated.—TRANSLATOR.
[2] Probably intended for *Windsor*.—TRANSLATOR.

glanced about me. There was absolutely no furniture in the room, with the exception of a warped extension-table on thirteen legs of unequal length, and four dilapidated straw-seated chairs; the walls, which had been whitewashed long, long ago, with blue spots in the shape of stars, had peeled off in many places; between the windows hung a cracked and dimmed little mirror in a huge frame of imitation mahogany. In the corners stood Turkish pipes and guns; from the ceiling depended thick, black spiders' webs.

" A, B, V, G, D,"—enunciated Tchertopkhánoff slowly, then suddenly cried fiercely:—" E! E! E! . . . . What a stupid beast! . . . . E!"

But the ill-starred poodle only trembled, and could not make up his mind to open his mouth; he continued to sit there, with his tail painfully tucked between his legs, and, contorting his muzzle, blinked dejectedly and screwed up his eyes, as though he were saying to himself: " As you like, of course!"

" Come, eat, dost hear! Take!"—repeated the irrepressible squire.

" You have frightened him,"—I remarked.

" Well, then away with him!"

He gave him a kick. The poor animal rose quietly, dropped the bread from his nose, and went off, on tiptoe as it were, to the anteroom, deeply wounded. And, in fact, a strange man had arrived for the first time, and that was the way he was being treated!

The door from the adjoining room creaked cautiously, and Mr. Nedopiúskin entered, amiably bowing and smiling.

I rose and made my bow.

"Don't disturb yourself, don't disturb yourself,"—he stammered.

We took our seats. Tchertopkhánoff withdrew into the next room.

"Have you been long in our parts?"—said Nedopiúskin in a soft voice, discreetly coughing behind his hand, and, out of a sense of propriety, keeping his fingers in front of his lips.

"This is the second month."

"Just so, sir."

We were silent for a while.

"We are having fine weather just now,"—went on Nedopiúskin, and looked at me with gratitude, as though the weather depended upon me:—"the grain is thriving wonderfully, one may say."

I inclined my head, in token of assent. Again we were silent for a space.

"Pantaléi Eremyéitch ran down two grey hares yesterday,"—began Nedopiúskin again, with an effort, being obviously desirous of enlivening the conversation:—"Yes, sir, two extremely large grey hares."

"Has Mr. Tchertopkhánoff good dogs?"

"Very remarkable dogs, sir!"—returned Nedopiúskin, with pleasure:—"the best in the Government, I may say." (He moved up closer to me.) "But it's a fact, sir! Panteléi Eremyéitch is that sort of a man! No sooner does he wish for a thing—no sooner does he take a thing into his head—the first you know, there it is accomplished, everything is fairly seething, sir. Panteléi Eremyéitch, I must tell you . . . ."

Tchertopkhánoff entered the room. Nedopiúskin grinned, fell silent, and indicated him to me with his eyes, as much as to say: "There, convince yourself." We began to chat about hunting.

"Would you like to have me show you my leash of hounds?"—Tchertopkhánoff asked me, and, without waiting for an answer, he called Karp.

There entered the room a robust young fellow in a nankeen kaftan green in hue with a sky-blue collar and livery buttons.

"Order Fómka,"—said Tchertopkhánoff abruptly:—"to fetch in Ammalat and Sáïga (Gazelle), and in proper order, dost understand?"

Karp grinned to the full extent of his mouth, emitted a vague sound, and left the room. Fomá made his appearance, with his hair brushed, his belt drawn tight, booted, and with the dogs. I, out of propriety, admired the stupid animals (all hare-hounds are extremely stupid). Tchertopkhánoff spat straight into Ammalat's nostrils, which, however, apparently, did not afford the dog the slightest pleasure. Nedopiúskin caressed Ammalat from behind also. Again we began to chat. Tchertopkhánoff gradually grew thoroughly mild, and ceased to bear himself like a cock and to snort; the expression of his face underwent a change. He glanced at me and at Nedopiúskin.

"Eh!" — he suddenly exclaimed: — "Why should she sit there alone? Másha! hey there, Másha! come hither!"

Some one stirred in the adjoining room, but there was no reply.

"Má-a-asha," — repeated Tchertopkhánoff caressingly: — "Come hither. There's nothing wrong, have no fear."

The door opened softly, and I beheld a woman of twenty, tall and slender, with a swarthy gipsy face, yellowish-brown eyes, and hair as black as pitch; her large, white teeth fairly glittered from beneath her full red lips. She wore a white gown; a light blue shawl, fastened close around the throat with a golden pin, half covered her slender, high-bred hands.

"Here, let me commend her to your favour," —said Pantelĕi Eremyĕitch: — "she's not exactly my wife, but the same as a wife."

Másha flushed slightly and smiled in confusion. I made her a very low bow. She pleased me greatly. Her thin, aquiline nose, with its open, half-transparent nostrils, the bold line of her arching eyebrows, her pale, slightly sunken cheeks,—all the features of her face, expressed wayward passion and reckless daring. From beneath the coils of her hair, down upon her broad neck, ran two small tufts of shining little hairs—a token of good blood and of strength.

She walked to the window and sat down. I did not wish to heighten her confusion, and began to talk to Tchertopkhánoff. Másha turned her head slightly, and began to dart sidelong, stealthy, wild, swift glances at me. Her gaze flashed out like the sting of a serpent. Nedopiúskin sat down beside her and whispered something in her ear. She smiled again. When she smiled, she slightly wrinkled up her nose and elevated her upper lip, which imparted to her face an expression which was not exactly that of a cat, nor yet that of a lion. . . . .

" Oh yes, thou art a ' touch-me-not,' "—I thought, in my turn stealthily inspecting her willowy form, her sunken chest, and angular, agile movements.

" Well, now, Másha,"—asked Tchertopkhánoff:—" Must the visitor be treated to some sort of refreshments, hey? "

" We have some preserves,"—she replied.

" Well, fetch hither the preserves, and some

vódka too, by the way. And listen, Másha,"—he shouted after her:—" fetch thy guitar also."

" What 's the guitar for? I won't sing."

" Why not? "

" I don't feel like it."

" Eh, nonsense, thou wilt feel like it, if . . ."

" If what? "—asked Másha, swiftly contracting her brows.

" If thou art asked,"—Tchertopkhánoff completed his phrase, not without confusion.

" Ah! "

She left the room, speedily returned with the preserves and the vódka, and again seated herself by the window. The furrow was still visible on her forehead; both her eyebrows kept rising and falling, like the feelers of a wasp. . . . Have you observed, reader, what a vicious face the wasp has? " Well," I said to myself, " there 's going to be a thunderstorm." The conversation would not go. Nedopiúskin became absolutely dumb and smiled constrainedly; Tchertopkhánoff puffed, and flushed, and protruded his eyes; I was preparing to take my departure . . . . . when, suddenly, Másha rose to her feet, threw open the window with one movement, thrust out her head, and screamed angrily to a passing peasant-woman: " Aksínya! " The woman gave a start, tried to turn round, but slipped and fell heavily to the ground. Másha threw herself backward, and burst into a ringing laugh; Tchertopkhánoff also began to laugh; Nedopiúskin squealed with delight. We shook out our feathers. The thunderstorm had dissolved in one flash of lightning . . . . . the air had cleared.

Half an hour later, no one would have recognised us: we were chattering and frolicking like children. Másha was playing the maddest pranks of all, Tchertopkhánoff was fairly devouring her with his eyes. Her face had grown pale, her nostrils were dilated, her glance blazed and darkened at one and the same time. The savage was beginning to rise in her. Nedopiúskin waddled after her on his short, thick legs, like a drake after a duck. Even Vénzor crawled out from under the wall-bench in the anteroom, stood for a while on the threshold, gazed at us, and suddenly began to leap and bark. Másha fluttered out into the adjoining room, brought her guitar, flung the shawl from her shoulders, briskly took a seat, raised her head, and struck up a gipsy song. Her voice tinkled and quivered like a tiny cracked glass bell, it flared up and died away. . . . It produced a pleasing yet painful sensation in one's heart.—" Aï, burn away, spread out! " . . . Tchertopkhánoff began to dance. Másha writhed all over, like a piece of birch-bark in the fire; her slender fingers flew rapidly over the guitar, her swarthy neck heaved slowly under her necklace consisting of a double row of amber beads. Then, all of a sudden, she stopped short, nerely shrugged her shoulders, and fidgeted about on her seat, while Nedopiúskin wagged his head like a porcelain Chinaman;—then she began to warble again, like a madwoman, drawing up her figure and protruding her chest, and again Tchertopkhánoff began to squat down to the ground and leap up to the very ceiling,[1] spinning round like a peg-top and shouting: " Faster! " . . . .

" Faster, faster, faster, faster! "—chimed in Nedopiúskin, volubly.

Late at night I took my departure from Bez-sónovo. . . .

---

[1] These are figures, so to speak, in the favourite Russian dance. — TRANSLATOR.

THE END OF TCHERTOPKHÁNOFF

I

Two years after my visit, Panteléi Eremyéitch's calamities—precisely that, calamities — began. He had experienced unpleasantnesses, failures, and even misfortunes before that, but he had paid no attention to them, and had " reigned " as hitherto. The first calamity which overtook him was for him the most acute of all: Másha left him.

What it was that made her abandon his roof, to which, apparently, she had become so thoroughly accustomed, it would be difficult to say. Tchertopkhánoff, to the end of his days, cherished the conviction that the cause of Másha's treachery was a certain youthful neighbour, a retired captain of uhlans, nicknamed Yaff, who, according to Panteléi Eremyéitch's assertion, had fascinated her merely by incessantly twirling his moustache, using pomatum in excessive quantities, and smiling affectedly to a very decided degree; but we must assume, rather, that the roving gipsy blood which flowed in Másha's veins had asserted itself. At any rate, one fine summer evening, Másha took herself off from Tchertopkhánoff's house, after having made up a small bundle of some rags of clothing.

For three days before that she had sat in a corner, bent double and huddling closely against the wall, like a wounded fox,—and not a word would she utter to any one, but merely rolled her eyes about, and mused, and twitched her brows, and displayed her teeth in a faint grin, and moved her hands about as though she were wrapping herself up. This " quiet fit " had come over her on previous occasions, but had never lasted long; Tchertopkhánoff was aware of this,—and consequently was not worried himself, neither did he worry her. But when, on his return from his kennels,—where, according to the statement of his whipper-in, his last two greyhounds were " moulting,"—he met a maid-servant, who in a trembling voice announced to him that Márya Akínfievna had ordered her to present her compliments to him, and to say that she wished him everything that was good, but would never return to him again—Tchertopkhánoff, after spinning round a couple of times on the spot where he stood and emitting a hoarse roar, immediately dashed off in pursuit of the fugitive, catching up his pistol by the way.

He overtook her a couple of versts from his house, beside a birch coppice, on the highway leading to the county town. The sun hung low

above the horizon, and everything round about—
the trees, the grass, and the earth—suddenly
turned crimson.

" To Yaff! to Yaff!"—moaned Tchertopkhánoff, as soon as he espied Másha:—" to Yaff!"
—he repeated, as he rushed up to her, stumbling
at almost every step.

Másha halted and turned her face toward him.
She stood with her back to the light, and appeared
completely black, as though carved out of dark
wood. Only the whites of her eyes stood out like
silver almonds, while the eyes themselves—the
pupils—grew darker than ever.

She tossed her bundle aside, and folded her
arms.

" She has set off for Yaff, the good-for-
nothing hussy!"—repeated Tchertopkhánoff, at-
tempting to seize her by the shoulder;—but the
glance he encountered from her intimidated him,
and made him stop short on the spot.

" I have not started for Mr. Yaff, Panteléi
Eremyéitch,"—replied Másha in a quiet, even
tone:—" only, I cannot live with you any longer."

" Why canst not thou live with me? Why so?
Have I offended thee in any way?"

Másha shook her head.—" You have not offended me in any way, Panteléi Eremyéitch, only
I have begun to languish at your house. . . . I
thank you for the past, but stay I cannot—
no!"

Tchertopkhánoff was dumfounded; he even smote his lips with his hands, and gave a leap.

" How so ? Thou hast lived on and on, and hast experienced nothing but pleasure and tranquillity—and, all of a sudden, thou hast taken to pining! ' Herewith,' says she, ' I 'll abandon him! ' She takes and throws a kerchief on her head— and off she goes. She has received every respect, just as much as a born lady. . . ."

" I could have dispensed with that, at least,"— interrupted Másha.

" Why couldst thou have dispensed with it? From a gipsy stroller, thou hast got into the station of a born lady—yes: thou didst not care for it? Why not, thou base-born miscreant? Is that credible? There 's treachery concealed here,— treachery! "

Again he began to foam at the mouth.

" There is no treachery whatever in my thoughts, and there has been none,"—said Másha in her drawling, distinct voice;—" but I have already told you: I was seized with a pining."

"Másha!"—cried Tchertopkhánoff, and smote his breast with his clenched fist:—" come, stop it, enough, thou hast tortured me . . . . come, enough of this. And by God! only think what Tísha will say; thou mightest, at least, have pity on him! "

" Give my regards to Tíkhon Ivánitch, and tell him . . ."

Tchertopkhánoff brandished his arms.—" But no, thou art lying—thou wilt not go away! Yaff shall wait for thee in vain!"

" Mr. Yaff—" Másha made an effort to say. . . .

" '*Mis-ter* Yaff,' forsooth,"—Tchertopkhánoff mimicked her.—" He 's a sly dog, if ever there was one, a swindler—and he has the phiz of an ape."

For full half an hour did Tchertopkhánoff contend with Másha. Now he stepped up close to her, again he sprang away, now he brandished his hands at her, again he made her reverences to her girdle, weeping and cursing. . . .

" I can't,"—Másha kept reiterating:—" I 'm so dejected. . . . I 'm tortured with boredom."

Little by little her face assumed such an indifferent, almost sleepy expression, that Tchertopkhánoff asked her whether she had been drugged with stramonium.

" 'T is boredom,"—she said, for the tenth time.

" Well, now, what if I kill thee?"—he suddenly shouted, and pulled the pistol from his pocket.

Másha smiled; her face became animated.

" What then? Kill me, Panteléi Eremyéitch: as you please; but as for returning,—I simply won't do it."

" Thou wilt not return?"—Tchertopkhánoff cocked his pistol.

THE END OF TCHERTOPKHÁNOFF

" I will not, my dear little dove. I won't return as long as I live. My word is firm."

Tchertopkhánoff suddenly thrust the pistol into her hand, and squatted down on the ground.

" Well, then do *thou* kill *me!* without thee I do not wish to live. I have become abhorrent to thee,—and everything has become abhorrent to me."

Másha bent down, picked up her bundle, threw the pistol on the grass, with the muzzle turned away from Tchertopkhánoff, and moved up close to him.

" Ekh, my dear little dove, why dost thou grieve without cause? Dost not thou know us gipsy women? 'T is our character, our custom. If the yearning for departure begins to breed, and summons the soul to distant, foreign parts,— why remain? Do thou remember thy Másha,— such another friend thou wilt never find,—and I shall not forget thee, my falcón;—but my life and thine together is at an end!"

" I have loved thee, Másha,"—murmured Tchertopkhánoff into his fingers, wherewith he had covered his face. . .

" And I have loved thee, dear friend, Panteléi Eremyéitch!"

" I have loved thee, I do love thee madly, unboundedly,—and when I think now that thou art abandoning me thus, for no cause, without rhyme or reason, and art setting out to wander about the

MEMOIRS OF A SPORTSMAN

world,—well, then I begin to imagine that were I not an unhappy beggar, thou wouldst not have cast me off!"

Másha merely laughed at these words.

"Why, I was a penniless vagrant myself when thou didst take me in!"—she said, and gave Tchertopkhánoff a flourishing slap on the shoulder.

He sprang to his feet.

"Well, at least take some money from me,—how canst thou go off so, without a farthing? But best of all: kill me! I'm talking sense to thee: kill me on the spot!"

Again Másha shook her head.—"Kill thee? But what are people sent to Siberia for, my dear little dove?"

Tchertopkhánoff shuddered.—"So 't is only for that, out of fear of the galleys, that thou wilt not." . . . . . .

Again he fell prone on the grass.

Másha stood over him in silence.—"I'm sorry for thee, Panteléi Eremyéitch,"—she said, with a sigh:—"thou art a good man . . . . . but there's no help for it: farewell!"

She turned away, and took a couple of steps. Night had already begun to close in, and dim shadows were beginning to glide up from all quarters. Tchertopkhánoff rose briskly to his feet and grasped Másha by both elbows from behind.

" So thou art going, serpent? To Yaff ! "

" Farewell! "—repeated Másha significantly and sharply, wrenched herself free, and walked away.

Tchertopkhánoff stared after her, ran to the spot where the pistol lay, seized it, took aim, and fired. . . . But before he pulled the trigger he threw his hand upward; the bullet whistled past over Másha's head. She darted a glance at him over her shoulder, without pausing,—and proceeded on her way, swaying her hips as she walked, as though to provoke him.

He covered his face—and set off on a run. . . .

But before he had run fifty paces, he came to a sudden halt, as though rooted to the spot. A familiar, a too-familiar voice reached his ears. Másha was singing. " Life young, life charming," —she sang; every sound seemed prolonged in the evening air—wailing and resonant. Tchertopkhánoff lent an ear. The voice retreated further and further; now it died away, again it floated to him in a barely audible, but still burning wave. . . .

" She 's doing that to irritate me," thought Tchertopkhánoff; but immediately added, with a groan: " Okh, no! she is taking leave of me forever; "—and burst into a flood of tears.

On the following day, he presented himself at the quarters of Mr. Yaff, who, like a true man of the world, not liking the solitude of the country, had removed to the county town,—"nearer to the young ladies," as he expressed it. Tchertopkhánoff did not find Yaff; the latter, according to the statement of his valet, had set out for Moscow on the preceding day.

"Exactly so!"—exclaimed Tchertopkhánoff in a fury:—"it was a plot between them; she has eloped with him . . . . but wait a bit!"

He forced his way into the study of the young cavalry captain, despite the valet's opposition. In the study, over the divan, hung a portrait of the master of the house, in his uhlan uniform, painted in oils.—"Ah, there thou art, thou tailless ape!"—thundered Tchertopkhánoff, as he sprang upon the divan,—and smiting the tightly-stretched canvas with his fist, he broke a huge hole in it.

"Say to thy rascally master,"—he said, addressing the valet,—"that in default of his own disgusting phiz, nobleman Tchertopkhánoff has disfigured his painted phiz; and if he desires satisfaction from me, he knows where to find nobleman Tchertopkhánoff!—If he does not, I will find him! I'll hunt out the dastardly ape at the bottom of the sea!"

As he uttered these words, Tchertopkhánoff sprang from the divan and withdrew in triumph.

But Captain Yaff did not demand any satisfaction from him,—he did not even encounter him

anywhere,—and Tchertopkhánoff did not dream
of looking up his enemy, and no scandal resulted
from this affair. Másha herself soon afterward
disappeared without leaving a trace. Tchertopkhánoff would have liked to take to drink; he
" saw the error of his ways," however. But at
this point, a second calamity overtook him.

II

NAMELY: his bosom friend, Tíkhon Ivánitch Nedopiúskin, expired. The latter's health had begun to fail two years previous to his death: he had
begun to suffer from asthma, was incessantly
falling asleep, and, on waking, he was slow in
coming to himself: the county physician declared
that he had had slight strokes of apoplexy. During the three days which preceded the departure
of Másha,—those three days when she had been
" pining,"—Nedopiúskin had been lying in bed at
his own home in Bezselendyéevka: he had caught
a heavy cold. The shock of Másha's behaviour
was all the more unexpected to him: he was almost more deeply affected by it than even Tchertopkhánoff himself. Thanks to the gentleness
and timidity of his character, he displayed no
emotion, save tender sympathy for his friend, and
pained surprise . . . . but everything within
him broke and relaxed. " She has taken the soul
out of me," he whispered to himself, as he sat on

233

his favourite little couch covered with oiled cloth, and twiddled his fingers. Even when Tchertopkhánoff recovered, he, Nedopiúskin, did not recover,—and continued to feel that " there was a void within him."—" Right here,"—he was wont to say, pointing to the centre of his breast, above the stomach. He dragged on thus until the winter. His asthma was relieved by the first cold weather, but on the other hand, he was visited not by a small shock of apoplexy, but by a real one. He did not immediately lose consciousness; he could still recognise Tchertopkhánoff, and even to his friend's despairing cry: " How comes it that thou, Tísha, art leaving me without my permission, just like Másha? " replied with faltering tongue: — " But, P . . . . a . . . . léi E . . . e . . . yéitch . . . I al . . . ays . . . . have . . . . mind . . . . ed . . . . you . . ." This did not prevent his dying the same day, however, before the arrival of the county physician, for whom, at the sight of his corpse, which was barely cold, there was nothing left to do except, with melancholy consciousness of the transitoriness of all things earthly, to request " a little vódka and dried sturgeon." Tíkhon Ivánitch had bequeathed his property, as might have been expected, to his " most respected benefactor, Pantaléi Eremyéitch Tchertopkhánoff "; but it did not do his most respected benefactor much good, for it was speedily sold at public auction,—partly in order to defray the expenses of a mortuary monument, a statue, which Tchertopkhánoff— (evidently, a characteristic of his father's was making itself felt!)—had taken it into his head to erect over the ashes of his friend. This statue, which was intended to represent an angel in prayer, he had ordered from Moscow; but the commissioner who had been recommended to him, taking into consideration the fact that expert judges of sculpture are rare in the rural districts, had sent him, instead of the angel, a statue of the goddess Flora, which for many years had adorned one of the neglected parks in the vicinity of Moscow of the Empress Katherine II's day;—as he, the agent, had obtained the said statue—which was an elegant one, in the rococo taste, with plump little hands, curling locks, and a garland of roses around its bare bosom and curved figure —for nothing. Consequently, to this day, the mythological goddess stands, with one foot gracefully uplifted, over the grave of Tíkhon Ivánitch, and, with a genuine Pompadour-like grimace, surveys the calves and sheep, those inevitable visitors of our cemeteries, which roam round about her.

III

AFTER losing his faithful friend, Tchertopkhánoff again took to drink, and this time far more seriously. His affairs were completely on the downward path. There was nothing left to hunt, his last slender resources were exhausted, his last wretched serfs had fled. A reign of absolute isolation set in for Panteléi Eremyéitch: there was not a soul with whom he could exchange a word, much less any one to whom he could unburden his mind. The only thing in him which was not diminished was his pride. On the contrary: the worse his circumstances became, the more arrogant and haughty and unapproachable did he become. At last, he grew thoroughly wild. One consolation, one joy, alone remained to him: a marvellous grey saddle-horse of Don breed, which he had named Malek-Adel, and was, really, a remarkable animal.

He had acquired the horse in the following manner:

As he was passing one day, on horseback, through a neighbouring village, Tchertopkhánoff heard an uproar among the peasants, and the shouting of a crowd around the dram-shop. In the centre of this crowd, robust arms kept incessantly rising and falling.

"What's going on there?"—he inquired, in the imperious tone peculiar to him, of an old peasant-woman, who was standing on the threshold of her cottage.

Leaning against the lintel of the door, and seemingly in a doze, the woman was staring in the direction of the dram-shop. A tow-headed little boy in a calico shirt, with a small cypress-wood cross on his bare breast,[1] was sitting, with his feet wide apart and his little fists clenched, between her plaited bast-slippers; in the same place a small chicken was pecking at a crust of rye bread as hard as wood.

" The Lord only knows, dear little father,"— replied the old woman,—and, bending forward, she laid her dark, wrinkled hand on the head of the little boy: " I 've heard say that our lads are beating a Jew."

" A Jew? What Jew? "

" The Lord knows, dear little father. Some Jew or other made his appearance among us; and whence he came—who knows? Vásya, my little gentleman, come to mamma: 'ssh, 'ssh, thou good-for-nothing! "

The woman frightened off the chicken, and Vásya clutched hold of her plaid petticoat of homespun.

" And so, sir, they 're thrashing him yonder."

" Thrashing him? What for? "

" Why, I don't know, dear little father. For cause, it must be. And how could they fail to thrash him? For he crucified Christ, dear little father! "

Tchertopkhánoff gave a view-halloo, lashed his

[1] The cross placed there during the baptismal ceremony by the priest and worn during life. The material of the cross varies, naturally, according to circumstances.—TRANSLATOR.

horse with his kazák whip on the neck, dashed headlong straight into the crowd, and, having penetrated it, began with the said whip to deal blows to right and left, without discrimination, on the peasants, crying as he did so, in a very abrupt voice:—" Ta . . . . king the law . . . . into your own hands! Ta . . . . . king the law . . . . into your own hands! The law ought to chastise—but the un . . . hap . . . . py peo . . . . ple! The law! The law! the la . . . a . . . . aw! ! "

Two minutes had not elapsed before the whole crowd had dispersed in various directions; and on the ground, in front of the dram-shop, there appeared a small, thin, swarthy-visaged being in a nankeen kaftan, dishevelled and mauled. . . . . The pallid face, the eyes rolled up, the mouth agape . . . . What was it? the swoon of terror, or death itself.

" Why have you killed the Jew? "—shouted Tchertopkhánoff loudly, as he brandished his whip menacingly.

The throng buzzed faintly in reply. One peasant was clutching his shoulder, another his side, a third his nose.

" 'T was a hearty thrashing! " was heard from the rear ranks.

" With a kazák whip, too! " said another voice.

" Why have you killed the Jew? I ask you,

you damned Asiatics!"—repeated Tchertopkhá-noff.

At this point, the being who was lying on the ground sprang alertly to his feet, and running after Tchertopkhánoff, convulsively grasped the edge of his saddle.

A hearty laugh thundered through the throng.

"He's alive!" proceeded a voice once more from the rear ranks. "He's just like a cat!"

"Defend me, save me, Your Vell-Born!"—the unhappy Jew stammered, the while pressing himself, with his whole breast, against Tchertopkhá-noff's foot: "or they vill kill me, they vill kill me, Your Vell-Born!"

"What did they do that to you for?"—inquired Tchertopkhánoff.

"Vy, God ees my vitness, I cannot tell!—Zeir cattle begin to die . . . . and zey suspect me . . . . but, as God ees my vitness, I . . . ."

"Well, we'll look into that later on!"—interrupted Tchertopkhánoff—"but now, do you lay hold of my saddle, and follow me.—And as for you!"—he added, turning to the crowd,—"you know me? — I'm landed proprietor Panteléi Tchertopkhánoff, and I live in the village of Bez-sónovo,—well, and that means that you can complain of me whenever you see fit,—and of the Jew also, by the way!"

"Why should we complain?"—said a stately, grey-bearded peasant, a perfect patriarch of the olden days, in a low tone.—(He had not been worrying the Jew with the rest, by the way.)—"We know thy grace well, dear little father, Panteléi Eremyéitch; we are greatly indebted to thy grace for the lesson thou hast given us!"

"Why complain!"—joined in others:—"but we will have our will with that pagan! He shall not escape us!—We'll hunt him like a hare in the fields. . ."

Tchertopkhánoff twitched his moustache, snorted, and rode off at a foot-pace to his own village, accompanied by the Jew whom he had rescued from his oppressors, as he had formerly rescued Tíkhon Ivánitch.

IV

A few days later, Tchertopkhánoff's sole remaining page announced to him that some man or other had arrived on horseback, and wished to speak to him. Tchertopkhánoff went out on the porch, and beheld his acquaintance the little Jew, mounted on a fine horse of the Don, which was standing motionless and proudly in the middle of the court-yard.—The Jew wore no cap—he was holding it under his arm; he had not put his feet into the stirrups themselves, but into the stirrup-straps; the tattered tails of his kaftan hung down on each side of the saddle. On catching sight of Tchertopkhánoff he began to make a smacking noise with his lips and to twitch his elbows and jerk his legs about. But Tchertopkhánoff not only did not reply to his greeting, but even flew into a rage; he suddenly flared up all over: a scabby Jew had the audacity to sit on such a magnificent horse . . . . how indecent!

"Hey there, thou Ethiopian phiz!"—he shouted:—"dismount this instant, if thou dost not wish to be hauled off into the mud!"

The Jew immediately obeyed, tumbled in a heap out of the saddle like a sack, and holding the bridle with one hand, moved toward Tchertopkhánoff, smiling and bowing.

"What dost thou want?"—asked Panteléi Eremyéitch, with dignity.

"Your Vell-Born, please to look,—is n't dis a fine little horse?"—said the Jew, continuing to bow.

"H'm . . . . yes . . . . 't is a good horse. Where didst thou get it? Stole it, I suppose?"

"No, indeed I deed n't, Your Vell-Born!— I 'm an honest Jew, I deed n't steal it, but I got it for Your Vell-Born, really I deed! And vat trouble I have, vat trouble! And vat a horse eet ees! You can't find such anoder horse in all ze Don Proveence. See, Your Vell-Born, vat a horse eet ees! Blease to gome here! Whoa there . . . . . whoa . . . . . turn round, stand sideways!—And ve vill take off ze saddle.—Vat do you zink of heem, Your Vell-Born?"

" 'T is a good horse,"—repeated Tchertop-khánoff, with feigned indifference,—but his heart began fairly to thump in his breast. He was a passionate lover of " horse-flesh," and was a fine judge of it.

" But zhust inspect heem, Your Vell-Born! Stroke hees naick, hee, hee, hee! That 's right! "

Tchertopkhánoff, as though unwillingly, laid his hand on the horse's neck, administered a couple of pats, then ran his fingers down the animal's back, beginning with his forelock, and on reaching a certain place above the kidneys, he exerted a slight pressure on the spot, in expert fashion.—The steed instantly arched his back, and darting a sidelong glance round at Tchertop-khánoff from his haughty black eye, he snorted and shifted his forefeet.

The Jew burst out laughing, and clapped his hands softly.—" He recognises hees master, Your Vell-Born, hees master! "

" Come now, don't lie,"—interposed Tchertop-khánoff, testily.—" I have n't the means where-with to buy this horse of thee . . . and I have never yet accepted a gift from the Lord God Himself, much less from a Jew! "

" And how zhould I dare to gif you anyzing, good gracious! "—exclaimed the Jew:—" Buy it, Your Vell-Born . . . . and as for ze money, I vait for heem."

Tchertopkhánoff reflected.

" What wilt thou take? "—he said at last, through his teeth.

The Jew shrugged his shoulders.

" Vat I pay myzelf—two hundred rubles."

The horse was worth double,—probably even thrice that sum.

Tchertopkhánoff turned away, and yawned feverishly.

" And when dost thou want the money? " he asked, contracting his brows with an effort, and without looking at the Jew.

" Venever Your Vell-Born likes."

Tchertopkhánoff threw back his head, but did not raise his eyes.—" That 's not an answer. Talk sense, thou Herod's race!—Am I to run into debt to thee, pray? "

" Vell, zen, let us zay zo,"—said the Jew hastily,—" in seex monts . . . . ees eet a bargain? "

Tchertopkhánoff made no reply.

The Jew tried to get a look at his eyes.—" Do you agree? Vill you order ze horse to be taken to ze stable? "

"I don't want the saddle,"—articulated Tchertopkhánoff, abruptly.—" Take off the saddle— dost hear me? "

" Zertainly, zertainly, I vill take eet, I vill take eet,"—stammered the delighted Jew, and threw the saddle over his shoulder.

" And the money,"—went on Tchertopkhánoff . . . . " is to be paid six months hence.—And not

two hundred rubles, but two hundred and fifty.
Hold thy tongue! Two hundred and fifty, I tell
thee! Follow me."

Tchertopkhánoff still could not bring himself
to raise his eyes. Never had his pride suffered so.
—" Obviously, 't is a gift,"—he said to himself:
" this devil is offering it to me out of gratitude!"
And he would have liked both to embrace the
Jew and to murder him. . . .

" Your Vell-Born,"—began the Jew, gaining
courage, and displaying his teeth in a grin:—
" you ought, after ze Russian custom, to receive
heem from ze coat-tail to ze coat-tail." . . . .

" Well, here's a pretty thing thou hast taken
into thy head!—A Jew . . . . and Russian custom!—Hey, who's there? Take the horse, lead
him to the stable.—And give him some oats. I 'll
be there directly myself, and look him over. And
understand: his name is Malek-Adel!"

Tchertopkhánoff started to ascend the porch-
steps, but wheeled sharply round on his heels, and
running up to the Jew, he shook him warmly by
the hand.—The latter bent forward, and had already thrust out his lips—but Tchertopkhánoff
sprang back and, saying in an undertone: " Don't
tell anybody!" he disappeared through the door.

v

FROM that day forth, Malek-Adel became Tchertopkhánoff's chief business, his chief care, his

greatest joy in life. He came to love him as he
had not loved even Másha, he became more attached to him than to Nedopiúskin.—And what a
horse it was! Fire, regular fire, simply powder—
and stately as a boyár!—Indefatigable, with
great power of endurance, turn him whithersoever you would, he obeyed implicitly; and it cost
nothing to feed him: if there was nothing else, he
would eat the earth under his hoofs. When he
went at a foot-pace, his rider felt as though he
were being borne in arms; when he trotted,—as
though he were being rocked on the surge of the
sea; and when he galloped, the very wind could
not overtake him. He never got blown, for his
lungs were fine. His legs were of steel; and as
for stumbling—there was never even a hint of
such a thing! It was a mere nothing for him to
leap over a ditch or a paling. And what a clever
beast he was! He would run in answer to a call,
tossing back his head; order him to stand still, and
go away yourself—and he would not stir; as soon
as you started to return, he would whinny almost
inaudibly, as much as to say: " Here am I!"—
And he was afraid of nothing: he would find his
road in pitch-darkness, or in a blinding snow-
storm; and he would not let a stranger touch him
on any account whatsoever: he would bite him.
And let no dog sneak about him: he would smite
the dog instantly on the brow with his hoof,
whack! and that was the last of the dog.—He was
a spirited steed: you might flourish a whip

over him by way of display—but God preserve
the person who should touch him with it! But
what is the use of going into lengthy details?—
He was a perfect treasure, not a horse!

When Tchertopkhánoff undertook to describe
his Malek-Adel, he could not find words to do him
justice. And how he caressed and petted him!—
The creature's coat shone with the gleam of
silver—and not of old, but of new silver, which
has a dark gloss; pass your hand over it and it
was like velvet! The saddle, the horse-cloth, the
bit,—all his trappings were accurately adjusted,
and burnished to such a degree that you might
take a pencil and make sketches on them! Tchertopkhánoff—and what more can one say?—personally, with his own hands, plaited his pet's forelock, and washed its mane and tail with beer, and
even anointed its hoofs with salve. . . .

He used to mount Malek-Adel and ride off—
not to call on his neighbours,—for, as in the past,
he had no intercourse with them,—but across
their fields, past their manor-houses. . . . As
much as to say: "Admire from a distance, you
fools!" And if he heard that a hunt was on hand
anywhere,—that a wealthy gentleman was preparing to set off for remote fields,—he immediately betook himself thither, and pranced about
at a distance, on the horizon, astounding all be-
holders with the beauty and swiftness of his steed,
but permitting no one to approach close to him.

THE END OF TCHERTOPKHÁNOFF

On one occasion, a sportsman, accompanied by his whole suite, pursued him; perceiving that Tchertopkhánoff was escaping him, he began to shout at him at the top of his lungs, galloping at top-speed the while: " Hey, there! Listen! I 'll pay thee whatever thou askest for thy horse! I won't begrudge a thousand rubles! I 'll give my wife, my children! Take my last farthing! "

Tchertopkhánoff suddenly reined Malek-Adel up short. The sportsman dashed up to him.— " Dear little father! " he cried: " tell me, what wilt thou take? My own father! "

" If thou wert the Tzar,"—said Tchertopkhánoff, enunciating each word distinctly (and never in his life had he heard of Shakespeare),—" and if thou wert to give me thy whole kingdom for my horse,—I would n't accept it! "—So saying, he gave a guffaw, made Malek-Adel rear up on his hind legs, wheeled him round in the air, on his hind legs alone, just as though the animal had been a peg-top or a teetotum,—and off he flew! He fairly flashed in sparks over the stubble-field. And the sportsman (they say that he was a very wealthy prince) " dashed his cap on the ground," —and then flung himself, face down, on his cap! And there he lay for the space of half an hour.

And how could Tchertopkhánoff fail to prize his horse? Was it not thanks to him that he again became superior to all his neighbours—indubitably, definitively superior to all his neighbours?

247

VI

In the meanwhile, time passed, the term for payment drew near—and Tchertopkhánoff had not fifty rubles, much less two hundred and fifty. What was to be done, how was the situation to be redeemed?—" Never mind,"—he decided at last, " if the Jew will not show mercy, if he will not wait a little longer,—I 'll hand over to him my house and my land,—and I myself will ride off on the horse in some direction, at random! I 'll perish with hunger,—but Malek-Adel I will not surrender!" He became greatly agitated, and even grew pensive; but at this point Fate—for the first and last time—showed pity on him, smiled on him: some distant aunt, whose very name Tchertopkhánoff did not know, left him in her will what was a huge sum in his eyes—two thousand rubles!—And he received this money just in time, so to speak: the day before the Jew's arrival. Tchertopkhánoff nearly went out of his senses for joy—but the thought of vódka did not enter his head: he had not taken a drop into his mouth since the day Malek-Adel had come to him. He hastened to the stable, and kissed his friend on both sides of his muzzle above the nostrils, in the spot where a horse's skin is so soft.—" Now we shall not be parted!"—he cried, patting Malek-Adel's neck, beneath the well-combed mane. On his return to the house, he counted out and sealed up in a packet two hundred and fifty rubles. Then he mused, as he lay on his back and smoked his pipe, as to how he should dispose of the remaining money—in fact, as to what sort of hounds he should get,—genuine Kostromá hounds, and they must, without fail, be the red-spotted variety! He even had a chat with Per-físhka, to whom he promised a new kazák coat with yellow galloon on all the seams—and went to bed in the most blissful mood possible.

He had a bad dream: he thought he had ridden out to a hunt; only, not on Malek-Adel, but on some strange animal, in the nature of a camel; a white fox, white as snow, came running to meet him. . . . He tried to swing his whip, he tried to set the dogs on it—but in his hand, instead of a whip he found a wisp of bast,[1] and the fox kept trotting on in front of him, and sticking out its tongue at him in mockery. He sprang from his camel, stumbled, fell . . . . and fell straight into the arms of a gendarme, who summoned him to the Governor-General, in whom he recognised Yaff. . . .

Tchertopkhánoff awoke. The room was dark; the cocks had just crowed for the second time. . . .

Somewhere, far, far away, a horse was neighing.

---

[1] Bunches of shredded bast from the inner bark of the linden tree form the favorite bath-sponges.—TRANSLATOR.

Tchertopkhánoff raised his head. . . . . Again a faint, faint neighing was audible.

" That 's Malek-Adel neighing! "—he said to himself. . . . . " That 's his neigh! But why is it so far away? Good heavens! . . . It cannot be . . . ."

All at once, Tchertopkhánoff turned cold all over, leaped from his bed on the instant, found his boots, his clothing, by groping, dressed himself, and, snatching the key to the stable from beneath his pillow, he rushed out into the court-yard.

VII

THE stable was situated at the very end of the yard; one of its walls abutted on the open fields. Tchertopkhánoff did not immediately insert the key into the lock—his hands were trembling—and did not immediately turn the key. . . . He stood motionless, holding his breath, to see if anything were stirring behind the door. " Máleshka! Máletz! " he called in an undertone: deathly silence! Tchertopkhánoff involuntarily pulled out the key: the door creaked on its hinges, and opened. . . . That meant, that the door had not been locked. He stepped across the threshold and again called his horse—this time by his full name: " Malek-Adel! " But his faithful comrade did not respond, only a mouse rustled in the straw. Then Tchertopkhánoff flung himself into that one of three stalls in which Malek-Adel had been lodged. He went straight to that stall, although such darkness reigned all around that it was impossible to see a hand's-breadth in front of one. . . . It was empty! Tchertopkhánoff's head reeled; a bell seemed to be booming under his skull. He tried to say something—but merely hissed, and groping with his hands above, below, on all sides, panting, with knees bending under him, he made his way from one stall to the second . . . . to the third, which was filled with hay almost to the top, hit against one wall, then the other, fell, rolled heels over head, rose to his feet, and suddenly rushed headlong through the half-open door into the court-yard. . . .

" They have stolen him! Perfíshka! Perfíshka! They have stolen him! "—he roared, at the top of his lungs.

Perfíshka the page flew out of the garret in which he slept, topsy-turvy, clad in nothing but his shirt. . . .

The two crashed together like drunken men— the gentleman and his solitary servant—in the middle of the yard; they spun round like madmen in front of each other. The gentleman could not explain what the matter was; neither could the servant comprehend what was wanted of him.— " Alas! alas! "—stammered Tchertopkhánoff.— " Alas! alas! " the page repeated after him.—" A lantern! give me the lantern, light the lantern! A light! A light!" burst forth, at last, from Tcher-topkhánoff's exhausted breast. Perfíshka flew to the house.

But it was no easy matter to light the lantern, or to get a light: sulphur matches were consid-ered a rarity in Russia at that epoch; the last em-bers in the kitchen had long since died out; flint and steel were not speedily to be found, and worked badly. Gnashing his teeth, Tchertopkhá-noff snatched them from the hands of the panic-stricken Perfíshka, and began to strike a light himself; sparks showered forth in abundance, oaths and even groans showered forth in still greater abundance—but the tinder either did not take fire at all, or went out, despite the strenu-ous efforts of four inflated cheeks and lips! At last, at the end of five minutes, no sooner, the morsel of tallow candle was burning in the bot-tom of the broken lantern, and Tchertopkhá-noff, accompanied by Perfíshka, precipitated himself into the stable, elevated the lantern above his head, looked about him. . . . . Completely empty!

He rushed out into the yard, traversed it in all directions at a run—the horse was nowhere to be found! The wattled fence surrounding Pantélei Eremyéitch's manor had long since fallen to de-cay, and in many places it was bent over and hanging close to the ground. . . . Alongside the stable it had tumbled down completely for a

space more than two feet in width. Perfíshka
pointed out this place to Tchertopkhánoff.

"Master! look here: this was not so to-day.
Yonder, the posts are sticking out of the ground,
too; some one must have pulled them out."

Tchertopkhánoff dashed up with his lantern,
passed it along the ground. . . .

"Hoofs, hoofs, the prints of a horse's shoes,
prints, fresh prints!"—he muttered rapidly.—
"Here is where they led him through, here,
here!"

He instantly leaped over the hedge, and with
the cry: "Malek-Adel! Malek-Adel!" he ran
straight off across the fields.

Perfíshka remained standing in bewilderment
by the wattled fence. The bright circle cast by
the lantern speedily vanished from his eyes, swallowed up by the thick darkness of the starless and
moonless night.

Tchertopkhánoff's despairing cries resounded
with ever-increasing faintness. . . .

VIII

DAY was dawning when he returned home. He
no longer bore the semblance of a man: his entire
clothing was covered with mud, his face had assumed a strange and savage aspect, his eyes had
a morose and stupid look. In a hoarse whisper
he drove Perfíshka away from him, and locked

himself up in his own room. He could scarcely stand, so exhausted was he,—yet he did not go to bed, but sat down on a chair near the door, and clasped his head in his hands.

" They have stolen him! . . . . . stolen him! "

But how had the thief contrived to steal Malek-Adel by night from the fast-locked stable? Malek-Adel, who by day would not allow a stranger to come near him—to steal him without noise, without a sound? And how is it to be explained that not a single yard-dog barked? To tell the truth, there were only two of them, two young puppies, and even they had buried themselves in the ground, with cold and hunger—but notwithstanding. . . .

" And what am I to do now without Malek-Adel? " thought Tchertopkhánoff. " I have now been deprived of my last joy—it is time for me to die. Shall I buy another horse, seeing that I am now provided with money? But where am I to find another horse like that? "

"Panteléi Eremyéitch! Pantaléi Eremyéitch!"
—a timid call made itself audible outside the door.

Tchertopkhánoff sprang to his feet.

" Who is it? "—he shouted in an unnatural voice.

" 'T is I, your page, Perfíshka."

" What dost thou want? Has he been found, has he run home? "

" Not at all, sir, Panteléi Eremyéitch; but that little Jew who sold him . . . ."

" Well? "

" He has arrived."

"Ho-ho-ho-ho-ho-ho!"—Tchertopkhánoff guffawed with laughter,—and flung the door open with a bang.—" Drag him hither, drag him, drag him! "

At the sight of the savage, disordered figure of his " benefactor," which thus suddenly presented itself, the Jew, who was standing behind Perfíshka, made an attempt to take to his heels; but Tchertopkhánoff overtook him in two bounds, and seized him by the throat like a tiger.

" Ah! thou hast come for thy money! for thy money! "—he yelled hoarsely, as though *he* were being strangled, instead of *himself* doing the strangling; " thou hast stolen him by night, and by day hast come for thy money? Hey? Hey? "

" Have mercy, Yo . . ur Ve-ell-Bo-orn! " groaned the Jew.

" Tell me, where is my horse? What hast thou done with him? To whom hast thou disposed of him? Tell me, tell me, tell me! "

The Jew could no longer groan; even the expression of terror had vanished from his face, which had turned blue. His hands dropped and swung limply; his whole body, vehemently shaken by Tchertopkhánoff, swayed back and forth like a reed.

"I'll pay thee thy money, I'll pay thee thy money in full, to the uttermost kopék,"—yelled Tchertopkhánoff—"only I'll strangle thee, like the meanest of chickens, if thou dost not instantly tell me. . . ."

"But you have strangled him, master,"—remarked the page Perfíshka submissively.

Only then did Tchertopkhánoff come to his senses.

He relinquished his hold on the Jew's throat; the latter fell in a heap on the floor. Tchertopkhánoff picked him up, seated him on a bench, poured a glass of vódka down his throat—and restored him to consciousness. And having restored him to consciousness, he entered into conversation with him.

It appeared that the Jew had not the slightest comprehension as to the theft of Malek-Adel. And why should he steal the horse which he himself had obtained for "his most respected Panteléi Eremyéitch"?

Then Tchertopkhánoff led him to the stable.

Together they inspected the stall, the manger, the lock on the door; they rummaged in the hay, the straw, and then went into the yard; Tchertopkhánoff pointed out to the Jew the imprints of hoofs beside the wattled fence—and all at once smote himself on the thigh.

"Stop!"—he cried.—"Where didst thou buy the horse?"

" In Maloarkhángel district, at the Verkhosén-skoe horse-fair,"—replied the Jew.

" From whom? "

" From a kazák."

" Stay! Was that kazák a young man or an old one? "

" A sedate man, of middle age."

" And what was he like? How did he look? A sly rascal, I suppose."

" He must have been a rascal, Your Vell-Born."

" And what did that rascal say to you,—had he owned the horse long? "

" I remember that he said he had."

" Well, then, no one but himself could have stolen it! Judge for thyself, listen, stand here . . . . what 's thy name? "

The Jew gave a start, and turned his little black eyes on Tchertopkhánoff.

" What is *my* name? "

" Well, yes; what art thou called? "

" Moshel Leiba."

" Well, judge for thyself, Leiba, my friend,—thou art a clever man,—into whose hands, save those of his former master, would Malek-Adel have surrendered himself? For he saddled him, and bridled him, and took his blanket off him—yonder it lies on the hay! . . . . . He simply behaved as though he were at home! Malek-Adel would certainly have crushed under his hoofs any one who was not his master! He would have raised such an uproar that he would have thoroughly alarmed the whole village! Dost thou agree with me? "

" I do, I do, Your Vell-Born. . . ."

" Well, then, first of all, we must find that kazák! "

" But how are ve to find him, Your Vell-Born? I have never seen him except vun little time—and vere ees he now—and vat is hees name? Aï, vaï, vaï! "—added the Jew, dolefully shaking his ear-locks.

" Leiba! " — shouted Tchertopkhánoff suddenly,—" Leiba, look at me! I have lost my mind, I am not myself! . . . . I shall lay violent hands on myself, if thou wilt not help me! "

" But how can I? . . ."

" Come with me—and we will find that thief! "

" But vere zhall ve go? "

" Among the fairs, on the big highways, on the little highways, to the horse-thieves, the towns, the villages, the farms—everywhere, everywhere! And as for money, thou needst not worry: I have received an inheritance, brother! I 'll squander the last kopék—but I 'll get my friend. And the kazák, that villain, shall not escape us! Whithersoever he goes, thither will we go also! If he is under the earth—we, too, will go under the earth! If he goes to the devil—we 'll go to Satan too! "

THE END OF TCHERTOPKHÁNOFF

" Vell, but vy to Zatan? "—remarked the Jew,
—" ve can get along vizout heem."

" Leiba! " — interposed Tchertopkhánoff, —
" Leiba, although thou art a Jew, and thy faith
is accursed—yet thou hast a soul better than that
of many a Christian! Thou hast taken pity on
me! there is no use in my setting off alone, I cannot deal with this affair alone. I am hot-headed—
but thou hast a good head, a head of gold! That's
the way with thy race: it has attained to everything without science! Perhaps thou hast thy
doubts, and sayest to thyself: ' Whence has he the
money? ' Come into my room with me—I 'll show
thee all the money. Take it, take my cross, from
my neck—only give me Malek-Adel, give him to
me, give him to me! "

Tchertopkhánoff shook as though in fever: the
perspiration poured down his face in streams, and
mingling with his tears, became lost in his moustache. He pressed Leiba's hands, he entreated
him, he almost kissed him. . . He had got into a
transport. The Jew tried to reply, to convince
him that it was impossible for him to absent himself from his business. . . . . In vain! Tchertopkhánoff would not listen to anything. There was
no help for it: poor Leiba was forced to consent.

On the following day, Tchertopkhánoff, accompanied by Leiba, drove away from Bezsónovo
in a peasant-cart. The Jew wore a somewhat disconcerted aspect, clung to the rail with one hand,

and his whole wizened body jolted about on the quaking seat; the other hand he pressed to his breast, where lay a package of bank-notes, wrapped up in a bit of newspaper. Tchertopkhá-noff sat like a statue, merely turned his eyes about him, and took the air into his lungs in deep breaths; a dagger projected from his belt.

"Look out for thyself now, thou villain-separator!" he muttered, as they emerged upon the highway.

He had entrusted his house to Perfíshka, the page, and to the peasant who acted as his cook, a deaf old woman, whom he had taken under his protection out of compassion.

"I shall return to you on Malek-Adel,"—he shouted to them in farewell,—" or I shall not return at all!"

"Thou mightest, at least, marry me, I think!" —jested Perfíshka, nudging the old woman in the ribs with his elbow.—"Anyhow,—we shall never see the master again, and otherwise, thou wilt certainly expire with tedium!"

IX

A YEAR passed . . . . . a whole year: no news arrived of Panteléi Eremyéitch. The old woman died; Perfíshka himself was preparing to abandon the house and betake himself to the town, whither he was being lured by his cousin, who was living there as assistant to a hair-dresser,—when, suddenly, a rumour became current that the master was coming back! The deacon of the parish had received a letter from Panteléi Eremyéitch himself, in which the latter informed him of his intention to come to Bezsónovo, and requested him to notify his servants, in order that the proper reception might be made ready. These words Perfíshka understood in the sense that he must wipe off a little of the dust; he had not much faith in the accuracy of the news, however; but he was forced to the conviction that the deacon had told the truth when, a few days later, Panteléi Eremyéitch himself, in person, made his appearance in the court-yard of the manor-house, mounted on Malek-Adel.

Perfíshka rushed to his master, and, holding his stirrup, attempted to assist him in alighting from his horse; but the latter sprang off unaided, swept a triumphant glance around him, and exclaimed in a loud voice: " I said that I would find Malek-Adel, and I have found him, to the discomfiture of my enemies and of Fate itself!" Perfíshka advanced to kiss his hand, but Tchertopkhánoff paid no heed to his servant's zeal. Leading Malek-Adel after him by the bridle he wended his way with long strides to the stable. Perfíshka scrutinised his master with more attention—and quailed:—" Okh, how thin and old he has grown in the course of the year—and how stern and grim

his face has become!" Yet it would have seemed
fitting that Panteléi Eremyéitch should rejoice,
in view of the fact that he had accomplished his
object; and he did rejoice, as a matter of fact . . . .
and, nevertheless, Perfíshka quailed and even felt
afraid. Tchertopkhánoff placed the horse in his
former stall, slapped him gently on the crupper,
and said: " Now, then, thou art at home again!
Look out! . . . ." On that same day he hired
a trustworthy watchman, an untaxable, landless
peasant, established himself once more in his own
rooms, and began to live as of yore. . . .

But not altogether as of yore. . . . . Of this,
however, later on.

On the day following his return, Panteléi Eremyéitch summoned Perfíshka to his presence, and,
in the absence of any other companion, began to
narrate to him—without losing the sense of his
own dignity, of course, and in a bass voice—in
what manner he had succeeded in finding Malek-
Adel. While the story was in progress, Tchertopkhánoff sat with his face to the window, smoking the pipe of a long Turkish tchibúk, while
Perfíshka stood on the threshold of the door, with
his hands clasped behind him, and gazing respectfully at the back of his master's head, listened to
the story of how, after many fruitless efforts and
peregrinations, Panteléi Eremyéitch had, at last,
arrived at the fair in Rómny, alone, without the
Jew Leiba, who, through weakness of character,

had not held out and had deserted him; how, on the fifth day, when he was already on the point of departing, he had passed, for the last time, along the rows of carts, and had suddenly espied, among three other horses hitched to the canvas feed-trough—had espied Malek-Adel! How he had recognised him on the instant,—and how Malek-Adel had also recognised him, had begun to whinny and paw the earth with his hoof.—" And he was not with the kazák,"—pursued Tchertop-khánoff, still without turning his head, and in the same bass voice as before,—" but with a gipsy horse-dealer; naturally, I immediately seized on my horse, and tried to recover it by force; but the beast of a gipsy set up a howl, as though he were being scalded, and began to swear, in the hearing of the whole market-place, that he had bought the horse from another gipsy, and wanted to produce his witnesses. . . . I spat—and paid him money: devil take him! For me the chief thing, the precious thing, was that I had found my friend, and had recovered my spiritual peace. But, seest thou, I had grabbed a kazák, as the Jew Leiba put it, in the Karatchévoe district,—I had taken him for my thief,—and had smashed in his whole ugly phiz; but the kazák turned out to be the son of a priest, and was infamous enough to wring one hundred and twenty rubles from me. Well, money is a thing that can be acquired; but the principal point is, that Malek-Adel is with me once more! Now I am happy—I shall enjoy tranquillity. And here are thy instructions, Porfíry: just as soon as thou shalt behold a kazák in the neighbourhood—which God forbid!—run and fetch me my gun that very second, without uttering one word, and I shall know how to act!"

Thus spake Pantelei Eremyéitch Tchertopkhánoff; this was what his lips expressed; but he was not so tranquil at heart as he asserted.

Alas! in the depths of his soul he was not fully convinced that the horse he had brought home was really Malek-Adel.

X

A DIFFICULT time began for Pantelei Eremyéitch. Tranquillity was precisely the thing which he enjoyed least of all. Good days did come, it is true: the doubt which had assailed him seemed to him nonsense, he thrust from him the awkward thought as he would an importunate fly, and even laughed at himself; but he had his bad days also: the persistent thought began again to prey stealthily on his heart and to gnaw at it, like a mouse under the floor,—and he tormented himself keenly, and in secret. In the course of that memorable day on which he had found Malek-Adel, Tchertopkhánoff had felt only blissful joy . . . . but on the following morning, when, under the low penthouse of the posting-station, he began to saddle his treasure-trove, close to which he had passed the night—something stung him for the first time. . . . He merely shook his head—but the seed was sown. In the course of his homeward journey (it lasted for about a week), doubts awoke rarely within him: they became more powerful and distinct as soon as he had reached his Bezsónovo, as soon as he found himself in the place where the former, the indubitable Malek-Adel had dwelt. . . . On the road he had ridden mainly at a foot-pace, at a jog-trot, gazing about him on all sides, had smoked his tobacco from a short pipe, and had indulged in no meditations, unless it were to say to himself, " Whatever the Tchertopkhánoffs want, that they get! " and grin; but when he got home, it was quite a different matter. All this, of course, he kept to himself: his pride alone forbade his displaying his inward trepidation. He would have " rent asunder " any one who had even distantly hinted that Malek-Adel did not appear to be the former horse; he accepted congratulations on his " lucky find " from the few persons with whom he chanced to come in contact; but he did not seek these congratulations, and avoided intercourse with people more assiduously than ever—which is a bad sign! He was almost constantly putting Malek-Adel through his examination, if one may so express it; he would ride off on him to some extremely distant spot in the fields, and put him to the test; or he would creep stealthily into the stable, lock the door behind him, and, placing the horse's head before him, would gaze into his eyes, asking in a whisper: " Art thou he? Art thou he? Art thou he? . . . ." or he would stare at him in silence, and so intently, for whole hours at a stretch, now rejoicing and muttering: " Yes! 'T is he! Of course, 't is he! "—again perplexed and disconcerted.

And Tchertopkhánoff was perturbed not so much by the physical dissimilarity between *that* Malek-Adel and *this* one—it was not so very great: that one's mane and tail seemed to have been thinner, his ears more pointed, his cannon-bones shorter, and his eyes brighter,—moreover, that might only seem to be the case; but what troubled Tchertopkhánoff was, so to speak, the moral dissimilarity. *That* one had different habits, his whole moral nature was unlike. For example: *that* Malek-Adel had been wont to glance round and whinny slightly every time Tchertopkhánoff entered the stable; but *this* one went on munching his hay, as though nothing were happening—or dozed with drooping head. Neither of them stirred from the spot when their master sprang from the saddle; but *that* one, when he was called, immediately advanced toward the voice,—while *this* one continued to stand stock-still. *That* one galloped with equal swiftness, but jumped higher and further; *this* one had a more undulating gait when walking, but jolted more on a trot, and sometimes interfered with his shoes—that is to say, struck the hind shoe against the fore shoe; *that* one never had such a disgraceful trick—God forbid! *This* one, so it seemed to Tchertopkhánoff, was forever twisting his ears, —while with the *other* the contrary was the case: he would lay one ear back, and keep it so,—watching his master! *That* one, as soon as he saw that there was dirt around him, would immediately tap on the wall of his stall with his hind foot; but *this* one did not mind if the manure accumulated up to his very belly. *That* one, if he were placed head on to the wind, for example,—would immediately begin to inhale with all his lungs, and shake himself, but *this* one would simply snort; *that* one was disturbed by dampness foreboding rain—*this* one cared nothing for it. . . . *This* one was coarser, coarser! And *this* one had no charm, as *that* one had, and was hard-mouthed— there was no denying it! The other was a pleasing horse—while *this* one . . . .

This was the way things sometimes seemed to Tchertopkhánoff, and these reflections bred bitterness in him. On the other hand, there were times when he would launch his steed at full gallop over some unploughed field or make him leap to the very bottom of a ravine washed out by the rains and leap back again straight up the steep, and his heart would swoon within him for rapture, a thunderous halloo would burst from his lips, and he knew for a certainty that he had under him the genuine, indubitable Malek-Adel, for what other horse was capable of doing what this one did?

But even so, errors and calamities were not lacking. The prolonged search for Malek-Adel had cost Tchertopkhánoff a great deal of money: he no longer dreamed of the Kostromá hounds, and rode about the country-side in solitude, as of yore. And lo, one morning, about five versts from Bezsónovo, Tchertopkhánoff ran across that same princely hunting-train before which he had pranced in so dashing a manner a year and a half before. And this incident must needs happen: precisely as on that other day, so now, a grey hare leaped out in front of the hounds from under the hedge on the slope of a hill!

" Tallyho! tallyho! "—The whole hunt fairly dashed onward, and Tchertopkhánoff dashed on also—only not with them, but a couple of hundred paces to one side of them—precisely as on the former occasion. A tremendous gully intersected the declivity on a slant, and, rising higher and higher, gradually contracted, intercepting Tchertopkhánoff's road. At the point where he was obliged to leap it—and where he actually had leaped it eighteen months previously—it was still eight paces in width, and a couple of fathoms in depth. In anticipation of a triumph,—of a triumph so miraculously repeated,—Tchertopkhánoff began to cackle victoriously, brandishing his kazák whip; the huntsmen galloped on, never taking their eyes from the bold horseman,—his horse was flying forward like an arrow,—and now, the gully is right in front of his nose! Come, come, at a bound, as before! . . . .

But Malek-Adel balked abruptly, wheeled to the left, and galloped along the brink, jerk his head to the side as Tchertopkhánoff might, in the direction of the gully. . . .

The fact was, he had turned cowardly, he had no confidence in himself!

Then Tchertopkhánoff, all glowing with shame and wrath, almost in tears, dropped the reins and urged the horse straight ahead, up-hill, away, away from those sportsmen, if only that he might avoid hearing how they jeered at him, if only that he might escape as speedily as possible from their accursed eyes!

With flanks covered with stripes, all bathed in foam, Malek-Adel galloped home, and Tchertopkhánoff immediately locked himself up in his own room.

" No, it is not he, it is not my friend! That one would have broken his neck,—but he would not have betrayed me! "

XI

THE following incident definitively " finished " Tchertopkhánoff, as the saying is. Mounted on

Malek-Adel, he was one day making his way through the back-yards of the ecclesiastical settlement surrounding the church to whose parish the hamlet of Bezsónovo pertained. With his kazák cap pulled well down over his eyes, bending forward, and with both hands resting on the saddle-bow, he was slowly advancing; everything was cheerless and perturbed in his soul. All at once, some one called him by name.

He drew up his horse, raised his head, and beheld his correspondent the deacon. With a dark-brown three-cornered hat on his dark-brown locks plaited in a small pig-tail, arrayed in a kaftan of yellowish nankeen girt considerably lower than the waist with a fragment of sky-blue stuff, the servitor of the altar had come out to visit his " little granary," and, catching sight of Panteléi Eremyéitch, considered it his duty to express his respects to him,—and, incidentally, to get something out of him. It is a well-understood fact that ecclesiastical persons never enter into conversation with laymen without some ulterior motive of that sort.

But Tchertopkhánoff was in no mood to attend to the deacon; he barely returned his salutation, and, grumbling something through his teeth, he was already flourishing his kazák whip.

" But what a superb horse you have! "—the deacon hastened to add:—" really, you may congratulate yourself on it. Of a truth, you are a man of wonderful mind; simply, like unto a lion!"—The deacon was renowned for his eloquence—which greatly vexed the father-priest, whom Fate had not endowed with the gift of words: even vódka did not loosen his tongue.— "You have been deprived of one animal, through the machinations of evil-doers,"—went on the deacon,—" and, not in the least discouraged, but, on the contrary, relying still more firmly on Divine Providence, you have procured for yourself another quite as good, and even better, I think . . . . . . for . . . ."

"What nonsense art thou prating?"—broke in Tchertopkhánoff angrily: "What dost thou mean by another horse? This is the identical one: this is Malek-Adel. . . . I hunted him up. Thou art babbling at random. . . ."

"Eh! eh! eh! eh!"—ejaculated the deacon, with pauses between, and as though prolonging his words, running his fingers through his beard, and surveying Tchertopkhánoff with his bright, greedy eyes.—"What do you mean by that, sir? Your horse was stolen, if God gives me memory, a couple of weeks after the Feast of the Intercession [1] last year, and now we are at the end of November."

"Well, then, and what of that?"

The deacon still continued to play with his beard.—"It means that more than a year has

[1] October 1, O. S.; 14, N. S.—TRANSLATOR.

elapsed since that time, and your horse was then a dappled grey as he is now; he has even grown darker. How about that? Grey horses turn very white in one year."

Tchertopkhánoff shuddered . . . . it was just as though some one had pricked his heart with a spear. And, in fact, grey horses do change colour! How was it that so simple a thought had not entered his head up to that moment?

" Thou damned pig-tail![1] Get out! "—he yelled suddenly, his eyes flashing with fury—and instantly vanished from the sight of the astounded deacon.

Well! All was at an end!

Everything was really at an end now, everything had burst, the last card was trumped! Everything had crashed into ruin at that one phrase: " They turn white! "

Grey horses turn white!

Gallop, gallop, thou accursed one! Thou canst not gallop away from that word!

Tchertopkhánoff dashed home, and again locked himself up.

XII

THAT this wretched nag was not Malek-Adel; that not the slightest likeness existed between him and Malek-Adel; that any man who had the least

[1] Ecclesiastics in Russia all wear their hair long, and, as described in this story, often braid it to keep it out of the way, in private life. —TRANSLATOR.

sense must have perceived this at the very first
glance; that he, Panteléi Tchertopkhánoff, had
deceived himself in the most vulgar manner—no!
That he had deliberately, with premeditation
cheated himself, had lowered that haze over himself—there now remained not the faintest doubt!
Tchertopkhánoff paced back and forth in his
room, wheeling on his heels as he reached each
wall, exactly as a wild beast does in a cage. His
pride was suffering intolerably; but it was not
wounded pride alone which was harrying him:
despair had taken possession of him, fury was
choking him, the thirst for vengeance was kindled
within him. But against whom? On whom was
he to revenge himself? The Jew, Yaff, Másha,
the deacon, the thieving kazák, all his neighbours,
the whole world, himself in conclusion? His
mind became confused. His last card had been
trumped! (This comparison pleased him.) And
again he was the most insignificant, the most despised of men, a general laughing-stock, a ridiculous fool, a thorough-going idiot, an object of
derision to—the deacon! ! . . . He imagined that
he could picture clearly to himself how that vile
pig-tail would take to telling about the grey horse,
about the stupid gentleman. . . . O damn it! . . .
In vain did Tchertopkhánoff strive to suppress
the rising bile; in vain did he strive to convince
himself that that horse, ... although not
Malek-Adel, was every whit as good as he, and

might serve him for many years: he immediately repelled this thought with vehemence, as though it contained a fresh insult for *that* Malek-Adel toward whom he already, and without that, felt himself to blame. . . . . The idea! Like a blind man, like a dolt, he had placed that carrion, that jade, on a level with him, with Malek-Adel! And as for the service which that vile nag might still render him . . . . why, would he ever deign to mount it? Not for anything on earth! Never!! . . . . He would give it to a Tatár,[1] to the dogs to eat—that was all it was good for. . . . Yes! that would be best of all!

For more than two hours Tchertopkhánoff wandered about his room.

" Perfíshka! "—he suddenly issued his command. " Go to the dram-shop this very instant; bring hither a gallon and a half of vódka! Dost hear me? A gallon and a half of vódka, and be quick about it! Let the vódka be here instantly, and standing on my table! "

The vódka made its appearance without delay on Panteléi Eremyéitch's table, and he began to drink!

XIII

ANY one who had looked at Tchertopkhánoff then, any one who could have witnessed the grim viciousness wherewith he drained glass after glass,

[1] The Tatárs are extremely fond of horseflesh. In St. Petersburg and Moscow (where they pursue the avocations of old-clothes men and waiters) horse-meat shops exist for their benefit.—TRANSLATOR.

would certainly have felt an involuntary terror.
Night came; a tallow candle burned dimly on the
table. Tchertopkhánoff had ceased to rove from
corner to corner; he sat, all red in the face, with
dimmed eyes, which he sometimes lowered to the
floor, sometimes riveted persistently on the dark
window; he would rise to his feet, pour himself
out some vódka, drink it off, then sit down again,
again fix his eyes on one point, and never stir—
except that his breathing grew quick, and his face
more scarlet. It seemed as though some decision
were ripening within him, which daunted him,
but to which he was gradually accustoming himself; one and the same thought importunately and
unintermittently moved up ever closer and closer,
one and the same image delineated itself ever
more and more clearly ahead; and in his heart,
under the inflaming pressure of heavy intoxication, the irritation of wrath was replaced by a
feeling of fierceness, and a grin which boded no
good made its appearance on his lips.

" Well, all the same, 't is time! "—he said, in a
businesslike, almost bored tone:—" 't is time to
stop taking my ease! "

He drank off the last glass of the vódka, got
his pistol from under his bed,—the same pistol
from which he had fired at Másha,—loaded it, put
several percussion-caps in his pocket, " in case of
need," and set off for the stable.

The watchman started to run to him when he
began to open the door, but he shouted at him:

" It is I! Dost not thou see? Begone! " The
watchman withdrew a little to one side. " Go off
to thy bed! " Tchertopkhánoff shouted at him:
" there 's no need for thee to stand on guard
here! A fine wonder, what a treasure! " He entered the stable. Malek-Adel . . . . the false
Malek-Adel, was lying on the litter. Tchertopkhánoff gave him a kick, saying: " Get up, thou
crow! " Then he untied the halter from the manger, took off the blanket and flung it on the
ground, and roughly turning the obedient horse
round in the stall, he led it forth into the yard,
and from the yard into the open fields, to the intense amazement of the watchman, who could not
possibly comprehend where the master was going
by night with the bridleless horse in tow. He
was afraid to ask him, of course; so merely followed him with his eyes until he disappeared at
the turn of the road which led to the neighbouring forest.

XIV

TCHERTOPKHÁNOFF walked with huge strides,
neither halting nor looking behind him. Malek-
Adel—we shall call him by that name to the end—
followed submissively in his wake. The night
was fairly light; Tchertopkhánoff could distinguish the indented outline of the forest, which
rose blackly in front of him, like a dark blotch.
Thus embraced by the nocturnal chill, he cer-

tainly would have felt the intoxicating effects of the vódka he had drunk, had it not been . . . . had it not been for another, a more powerful intoxication, which had taken complete possession of him. His head grew heavy, the blood throbbed with a roar in his throat and ears, but he walked on firmly, and knew where he was going.

He had decided to kill Malek-Adel; all day long he had thought of nothing else. . . . . . Now he had reached a decision!

He proceeded to this deed, not precisely with composure, but with confidence, irrevocably, as a man proceeds who is obeying a sense of duty. It seemed to him a very " simple matter " to annihilate this pretender, he would thereby be quits with " everybody," would also punish himself for his stupidity, justify himself to his genuine friend, and demonstrate to the whole world (Tchertopkhánoff was greatly concerned about " the whole world ") that no one could jest with him. . . . But the principal thing was,—that he meant to annihilate himself along with the pretender, for what was there now left for him to live for? How all this had stowed itself away in his head, and why it seemed to him so simple, it is not easy, although it is not utterly impossible, to explain: wounded, solitary, without a single human soul who was near to him, without a copper farthing, and with his blood heated by liquor, to boot, he was in a condition bordering on insanity, and there can be no doubt that, in the most absurd freaks of insane people, there is a sort of logic and even right in their eyes. As to the right, Tchertopkhánoff was, at any rate, fully convinced; he did not hesitate, he made haste to execute the sentence on the criminal, without, however, clearly rendering himself an account as to whom, precisely, he was calling by that name. . . . Truth to tell, he had reflected very little on what he was about to do. " I must make an end of it—I must," was what he kept repeating to himself, dully and sternly: " I must make an end of it! "

And the innocent culprit trotted obediently behind him. . . . But there was no pity in Tchertopkhánoff's heart.

XV

NOT far from the edge of the forest, whither he was leading his horse, stretched a small ravine, half overgrown with oak bushes. Tchertopkhá-noff descended into it. . . . Malek-Adel stumbled and came near falling on him.

" Dost want to crush me, damn thee! "—shouted Tchertopkhánoff—and, as though defending himself, he jerked the pistol out of his pocket.

He no longer felt hardness, but that peculiar wooden rigidity of the emotions which is said to take possession of a man before the perpetration of a crime. But his own voice frightened him—so savagely did it resound beneath the canopy of the dark boughs, in the decaying and stifling dampness of the forest ravine! Moreover, in reply to his exclamation, some large bird or other suddenly began to rustle in the crest of the tree over his head. . . . Tchertopkhánoff shuddered. It was as though he had aroused a witness to his deed—and where? In this remote spot, where he should not have encountered a single living creature! . . .

" Begone, devil, to the four winds! "—he said through his teeth—and relinquishing Malek-Adel's bridle, he dealt him a flourishing blow on the shoulder with the butt of the pistol. Malek-Adel immediately turned back, scrambled out of the ravine . . . . and set off at a gallop. But the sound of his hoof-beats was not audible long. The rising wind interfered and shrouded all sounds.

Tchertopkhánoff, in his turn, slowly made his way out of the ravine, gained the edge of the forest, and trudged homeward. He was dissatisfied with himself: the heaviness which he felt in his head and in his heart diffused itself over all his limbs; he strode onward—angry, gloomy, dissatisfied, hungry, exactly as though some one had insulted him, had robbed him of his booty, his food. . . .

A suicide who has been prevented from carrying out his intentions is acquainted with such sensations.

All at once, something touched him from behind, on the shoulder. He glanced round. . . . Malek-Adel was standing in the middle of the road. He had followed his master, he had touched him with his muzzle, he had announced his presence. . . .

" Ah! " — screamed Tchertopkhánoff, — " so thou hast come thyself, of thine own accord, to thy death! Then take that! "

In the twinkling of an eye he pulled out his pistol, cocked it, placed the muzzle to Malek-Adel's forehead, and fired. . . .

The poor horse sprang to one side, reared up on his hind legs, leaped back half a score of paces, and suddenly fell heavily to the ground and began to rattle hoarsely in his throat, as he writhed convulsively on the ground. . . .

Tchertopkhánoff stopped up his ears with both hands and set off on a run. His knees gave way beneath him. Intoxication, and fury, and blind self-confidence—all deserted him on the instant. Nothing remained but a feeling of shame and disgust, and the consciousness, the indubitable consciousness, that this time he had done for himself also.

XVI

Six weeks later, Perfíshka the page considered it his duty to stop the commissary of rural police as the latter was passing Bezsónovo manor-house.

" What dost thou want? "—inquired the guardian of order.

" Please, Your Well-Born, come into our house,"—replied the page, with a low bow: " Panteléi Eremyéitch seems to be on the point of death; and so, I 'm afraid."

" What? He is dying? " questioned the commissary.

" Exactly so, sir. At first he drank vódka every day, but now, you see, he has taken to his bed, and has got very ill. I don't suppose he can understand anything now. He 's perfectly speechless."

The commissary alighted from his cart. — " Well, hast thou not been to summon the priest, at least? Has thy master made his confession? Has he received the Sacrament? "

" No, sir, he has not."

The commissary of police frowned.—" How comes that, my good fellow? Is that the proper way to behave—hey? Or dost not thou know . . . that the responsibility for it is very great—hey? "

" But I asked him the day before yesterday, and yesterday, too," put in the intimidated page, —" ' Do not you command me,' says I, ' Panteléi Eremyéitch, to run for the priest? '—' Hold thy tongue, fool,' says he. ' Don't meddle in what is n't thy business.' And to-day, when I began to report—he merely stared at me—and twitched his moustache."

"And has he drunk much vódka?"—asked the commissary.

" An awful lot!—But be so good, Your Well-Born, as to come to his room."

" Well, lead the way!"—growled the commissary, and followed Perfíshka.

An astonishing sight awaited him.

In the rear room of the house, dark and damp, on a miserable pallet, covered with a horse-blanket, with a shaggy kazák felt cloak in place of a pillow, lay Tchertopkhánoff, no longer pale, but of a yellowish-green hue, like a corpse, with eyes sunken beneath glossy lids, with a sharpened but still crimson nose above his dishevelled moustache. He was lying arrayed in his inevitable kazák coat, with the cartridge-cases on his breast, and full Circassian trousers. A kazák fur cap with a deep crimson top covered his forehead to his very eyebrows. In one hand Tchertopkhánoff held his kazák hunting-whip, in the other an embroidered tobacco-pouch, Másha's last gift. On the table by the bedside stood an empty liquor-bottle; and at the head of the bed, fastened to the wall with pins, two water-colour drawings were visible: one, so far as could be discerned, represented a fat man with a guitar in his hands—probably, Nedopiúskin; the other depicted a galloping horseman. . . . . The horse resembled those fabulous animals which children draw on walls and fences; but the carefully shaded dapples on its flanks and the cartridge-cases on the rider's breast, the pointed toes of his boots, and his huge moustache left no room for doubt: the sketch was intended to depict Panteléi Eremyéitch mounted on Malek-Adel.

The astonished commissary of police did not know what to do. Deathly silence reigned in the room. "Why, he has already expired," he said to himself, and, raising his voice, he said:—"Panteléi Eremyéitch! Hey there, Panteléi Eremyéitch!"

Then something remarkable took place. Tchertopkhánoff's eyes slowly opened, the extinguished pupils moved first to the right, then to the left, came to a rest on the visitor, and saw him. . . . Something glimmered in their dull whiteness, the semblance of a glance made its appearance in them;—the lips, already blue, gradually parted, and a hoarse, already sepulchral voice made itself heard.

"Panteléi Tchertopkhánoff, nobleman of ancient lineage, is dying; who can hinder him?—He is indebted to no one, he demands nothing. . . . Leave him, ye people! Begone!"

The hand which held the kazák whip made an effort to rise. . . . . In vain! The lips again adhered to each other, the eyes closed, and Tchertopkhánoff lay as before on his hard pallet, stretched out flat and with his feet drawn close together.

" Let me know when he is dead,"—whispered the commissary of police to Perfíshka, as he left the room;—" and I think thou mightest go for the priest now. Due order must be observed,—he must receive Holy Unction." [1]

That same day Perfíshka went for the priest; and on the following morning he had to notify the commissary of police that Panteléi Eremyé-itch had died that night.

At his funeral, his coffin was escorted by two men: Perfíshka, the page, and Moshel Leiba. The news of Tchertopkhánoff's demise had, in some manner, reached the Jew; and he had not failed to pay his last debt to his benefactor.

---

[1] This unction in the Eastern Catholic Church is not Extreme Unction in the sense of those words in the Roman Church, although it is generally administered before death. In the true spirit of James v, 14–15 it may be administered any number of times during life, when a person is ill and not expected to die. The full rite calls for seven priests, but one priest can administer it.—TRANS-LATOR.

X

LIVING HOLY RELICS

O native land of patient fortitude—
Land of the Russian folk art thou!
—F. Tiútcheff.

A French saying runs: " A dry fisherman and a wet sportsman are sorry sights." As I have no partiality for fishing, I am not able to judge of a fisherman's feelings in fine, clear weather, and to what degree the satisfaction afforded him in stormy weather by an abundant catch outweighs the unpleasantness of being wet. But for the sportsman rain is a veritable calamity. To precisely such a calamity were Eremyéi and I exposed during one of our excursions after wood·cock in the Byélovoe district. The rain had not ceased falling since daybreak. What did not we do to escape from it! We drew our rubber coats up almost over our heads, and stood under trees, so that there might be less dripping. . . . The waterproof coats let the water through in the most shameless manner, not to mention the fact that they interfered with our shooting; while, although at first it did not appear to drip under the trees, yet later on the moisture, which had been gradually accumulating on the foliage, suddenly broke through, every branch showered down on us water as though from a rain-spout, a chilly stream made its way under my neckerchief and trickled down my spine. . . . Well, this was " the last straw "! as Ermolái was wont to express himself.—" No, Piótr Petróvitch,"—he exclaimed at last. " This is unendurable! . . . . We cannot hunt to-day. The dogs' scent will be drowned out; the guns will miss fire. . . . Phew! What a mess! "

" What is to be done? "—I asked.

" Why, this.—Let us go to Alexyéevka. Perhaps you do not know that there is a farm there which belongs to your mother; it is eight versts from here. We can pass the night there, and to-morrow . . . ."

" We can return here? "

" No, not here. . . . I know some places the other side of Alexyéevka . . . . . much better places for woodcock."

I did not interrogate my faithful companion as to why he had not guided me straight to those places and that same day we reached my mother's farm, whose existence, I must confess, I had not hitherto suspected. At the farm there turned out to be a small, detached building, very old, but not inhabited, and therefore clean; in it I passed a fairly quiet night.

On the following morning I awoke very early. The sun had only just risen; there was not a single cloud in the sky; everything round about was glistening with a powerful double gleam: the gleam of the young morning rays, and of the heavy rain of the day before.—While my two-wheeled cart was being harnessed, I went off for a stroll in the small garden, which had formerly been a fruit orchard, and was now utterly run wild, surrounding the little wing on all sides with its fragrant, succulent thickets. Akh, how good it was in the open air, beneath the clear sky, where the larks were trilling, whence the silver notes of their ringing voices showered down! They had, probably, borne off drops of dew on their wings, and their songs seemed besprinkled with dew. I even took my hat from my head, and inhaled joyously, to the full extent of my lungs. . . . On the slope of a small ravine, close beside the wattled fence, a collection of beehives was visible; a narrow path led to it, winding in serpentine fashion between dense walls of tall steppe-grass and nettles, over which hung, brought God knows whence, the sharp-tipped stalks of dark-green hemp.

I wended my way along this path, and reached the beehives. Alongside them, stood a small shed with wattled walls,[1] a so-called *amshánik,* where coals are stored for winter use. I glanced in at the half-open door; it was dark, still, dry;

[1] In the centre and south of Russia, where wood is scarce, fences and walls are made of tree-boughs interwoven.—Translator.

there was an odour of mint and sweet-clover. In one corner a platform had been fitted, and on it, covered with a quilt, lay a tiny figure. . . . I was on the point of beating a retreat . . . .

" Master, hey, master! Piótr Petróvitch! "—I heard a voice, weak, slow, and hoarse, like the rustling of marsh sedges.

I stopped.

" Piótr Petróvitch! Come hither, please! "— repeated the voice. It was wafted to me from the corner with the platform which I had noticed.

I approached—and grew rigid with amazement. Before me lay a living human being; but what did it mean?

The head was completely dried up, all of one bronze hue,—precisely like a holy picture painted in ancient times; the nose was as narrow as the blade of a knife; the lips were hardly visible,— only the teeth and the eyes gleamed white, and from beneath the kerchief thin strands of yellow hair escaped upon the forehead. Two tiny hands, also bronze in colour, were moving by the chin, at the fold of the coverlet, the fingers like little sticks intertwining slowly. I looked more attentively: the face was not only not hideous, it was even beautiful,—but terrible, remarkable. And the face seemed all the more terrible to me, because I saw that a smile was striving . . . . striving to spread over it,—over its metallic cheeks,—and could not.

"Don't you recognise me, master?"—whispered the voice again; it seemed to evaporate from the barely-moving lips.—"But how should you!—I am Lukérya. . . . You remember, the one who used to lead the choral songs and dances at your mother's, at Spásskoe? . . . I was the leader of the singers, as well; don't you remember?"

"Lukérya!"—I exclaimed.—"Art thou she? Is it possible?"

"Yes, it is I, master,—I am Lukérya."

I did not know what to say, and stared like one stunned at that dark, motionless face with the clear and deathly eyes riveted upon me. Was it possible? That mummy was Lukérya, the greatest beauty among all our domestics,—tall, plump, white, and red,—the giggler, the dancer, the singer! Lukérya, the clever Lukérya, to whom all our young men had paid court, for whom I myself had sighed in secret,—I, a lad of sixteen!

"Good heavens, Lukérya,"—I said at last:— "what has happened to thee?"

"Why, such a calamity has befallen me! But do not look at me with aversion, master, do not loathe my misfortune,—sit down on that small tub yonder,—come nearer, or you will not be able to hear me. . . . I have become so loud-voiced, you see! . . . . Well, and how glad I am to see you! How comes it that you are in Alexyéevka?"

Lukérya spoke very softly and feebly, but without any breaks.

" Ermolái the hunter brought me hither. . But tell me . . . ."

" I am to tell you about my misfortune?—Certainly, master. It happened to me long since,—six or seven years ago. They had just betrothed me to Vasíly Polyakóff,—do you remember, he was such a stately, curly-haired fellow,—he used to serve in your mother's house as butler? But you were no longer in the country at that time; you had gone away to Moscow to study.—Vasíly and I were very much in love with each other; I thought of him continually; and it happened in the spring. So, one night . . . it was not long before dawn . . . and I could not sleep: the nightingale in the garden was singing with such wonderful sweetness! . . . . . I could bear it no longer, so I got up, and went out on the porch to listen to it. It warbled and warbled . . . and suddenly it seemed to me that some one was calling me in Vásya's voice, softly, so: ' Lúsha!' . . . . I glanced aside, and not being fully awake, you know, I made a misstep, straight from the landing, and flew down—bang! on the ground. And I did not appear to have hurt myself badly, for I soon rose and returned to my chamber. Only, it was as though something inside me—in my belly—had been broken. . . . Let me take breath . . . . . . for just a minute . . . . master."

Lukérya stopped speaking, and I stared at her in amazement. What particularly astounded me was, that she told her story almost cheerily, without any groans and sighs, without making the slightest complaint, and without any appeal for sympathy.

"From the moment of that accident,"—went on Lukérya,—"I began to wither, to pine away; I began to turn black; it became difficult for me to walk, and I had not full control of my legs; I could neither stand nor sit; I wanted to lie down all the time. I didn't feel like either eating or drinking: I grew worse and worse. Your mother, in her goodness, showed me to the doctors, and sent me to the hospital. But I obtained no relief. And not a single doctor could even tell what sort of malady I had. They did all sorts of things to me: they burned my back with red-hot irons, they laid me in cracked ice—but it did no good. At last, I got perfectly ossified. . . . . Then the gentlemen decided that it was useless to treat me any longer, and it wasn't fitting that a cripple should be kept in the gentry's manor-house . . . . . well, and so they transferred me hither,—I have relatives here. And so I live as you see."

Again Lukérya ceased speaking, and again she tried to smile.

"But thy condition is frightful!"—I ex-claimed . . . and, without knowing what more to say, I inquired:—" And what about Vasíly Polyakóff?"—It was a very stupid question.

Lukérya turned her eyes aside.

" What about Polyakóff?—He grieved and grieved,—and then he married another, a girl from Glínnoe. Do you know Glínnoe? It lies not far from us. Her name was Agraféna. He was very fond of me,—but he was a young man, you see,—he could not remain a bachelor. And how could I be his dear friend? But he has found for himself a good, kind wife,—and he has children. He lives there as manager to a neighbour; your mother gave him his passport, and he's doing very well, thank God!"

" And so thou liest here always like this?"—I put another question.

" And so I lie here like this, master, this is the seventh year. In summer I lie here in this wattled shed, and when cold weather comes on they carry me to the anteroom of the bath-house. There I lie."

" But who tends on thee? Does any one look after thee?"

" Why, there are kind people here also. They do not desert me. And I do not need much looking after. As for eating—I eat hardly anything, and as for water—yonder it is, in that jug: it always stands filled with pure spring water. I can reach the jug for myself: I can still use one of my hands. And then there is a little girl, an orphan; she always gives me what I need, thanks to her. She was here a little while ago. . . . . Did n't you meet her? She 's such a pretty, white little thing. She brings me flowers; I 'm very fond of them,—of flowers, I mean. We have no garden-flowers here,—there were some, but they have run out. But the wild flowers are nice too, you know; they smell even better than the garden-flowers. Take lilies of the valley, for instance . . . . what can be more agreeable!"

" Dost thou never feel bored or afraid, my poor Lukérya?"

" But what is one to do? I will not lie—at first I found it very tiresome; but afterward I got used to it, I grew patient,—'t is nothing, some people are still worse off."

" How so?"

" Why, one person has no shelter! Another is blind or deaf! But I, thank God, can see splendidly, and hear everything, everything. If a mole is burrowing underground, I hear it. And I can detect every odour, no matter how faint it is! If the buckwheat in the fields comes into bloom, or the linden in the garden,—it is not necessary to tell me about it: I am the first of all to perceive it, if only the breeze blows from that quarter. No, why anger God?—many people are worse off than I. Take this, for example: a healthy man can very easily fall into sin; but from me sin has departed of itself. A while ago,

Father Alexyéi undertook to give me the Sacrament, and he said: ' There 's no use in confessing thee: is it possible for thee to sin in thy condition?' —But I answered him:—' And how about sin of thought, bátiushka?' [1]—' Well,' says he, and begins to laugh, ' that 's no great sin.'

" And it must be that I am not very guilty of that same,—that mental sin,"—went on Lukérya, —" because I have trained myself so: not to think, and—most of all—not to remember. The time passes more quickly so."

I must confess that I was astonished.—" Thou art always entirely alone, Lukérya? Then how canst thou prevent thoughts from coming into thy head? Or dost thou sleep all the time? "

" Oï, no, master! I am not always able to sleep. Although I do not suffer great pain,— yet there is a gnawing there inside me, and in my bones also; it will not let me sleep as I should. No. . . . I just lie here by myself, and lie and lie—and don't think; I am conscious that I am alive, I breathe—and that is all. I see, I hear. The bees hum and drone among the hives; a pigeon alights on the roof and begins to coo; a mother-hen comes along with her chicks and begins to peck up the crumbs; or a sparrow or a butterfly flutters in—which pleases me very much. The year before last the swallows built themselves

---

[1] " Dear little father," literally; used in respectfully-affectionate address to a man of any rank, from the Emperor down, but especially the prerogative of the priesthood.—Translator.

a nest yonder in the corner, and raised their brood. How interesting it was! One would fly to the nest, alight on it, and feed the babies—and off it would go again. And lo, the other one would take its place. Sometimes the bird would not fly in, but merely dash across the open door—but the nestlings would immediately begin to squeak, and open their bills. . . . I watched for them the next year, but I was told that one of the sportsmen in the neighbourhood had shot them. And why did he covet them? For, altogether, a swallow is no bigger than a beetle. . . . How wicked you sportsmen are!"

" I do not shoot swallows,"—I hastened to remark.

" And then, once, what a good laugh I had!"—began Lukérya again.—" A hare ran in,—it really did! The dogs were chasing it, I suppose,—only it seemed just to roll in through the door! . . . . It squatted down quite close to me, and sat there for a long time,—and kept moving its nose and twitching its moustache, just like an officer! And it stared at me. It understood, probably, that I was not dangerous to it. At last it got up, went hop-hop to the door, glanced round on the threshold—and vanished from sight! It was so funny!"

Lukérya cast a glance at me . . . . as much as to ask: " Was n't it funny?" I laughed to please her. She bit her withered lips.

" Well, and in winter, I am not so well off, of

course: because it is dark; one hates to light a candle, and what's the use of it? Although I can read and write, and was always fond of reading, what is there for me to read? There are no books whatever here, and even if there were any, how could I hold a book? Father Alexyéi brought me a calendar to divert me, but saw that it was useless, so he took and carried it away again. But although it is dark, there is always something to listen to: a cricket will begin to chirp or a mouse to gnaw somewhere.—And under such circumstances it is a good thing not to think!

"And then I recite prayers,"—continued Lukérya, after resting a while.—"Only I don't know many of them,—of those same prayers. And why should I worry the Lord God? What can I ask of Him? He knows better than I do what I need. He has sent me a cross—which signifies that He loves me. We are commanded to understand it so. I repeat the Our Father, the Hail Mary, the acathistus [1] to the Virgin of Sorrows,—and then I go on lying here without any thought at all. And I don't mind it!"

A couple of minutes passed. I did not break the silence, and did not stir on the narrow tub which served me as a seat. The stiff, stony im-

---

[1] A service of hymns and prayers to the Saviour, the Virgin Mother, or a Saint. The congregation stands throughout.—TRANSLATOR.

mobility of the living, unhappy being who lay there before me had communicated itself to me: I also seemed to have become petrified.

"Hearken, Lukérya," — I said at last. — "Hearken to the proposition which I am about to make to thee. I will have thee taken to a hospital, to a good hospital in the town: wouldst thou like that? Perhaps they can cure thee—who knows? At any rate, thou wilt not be alone. . . ."

Lukérya contracted her brows almost imperceptibly.—"Okh, no, master,"—she said, in an anxious whisper,—"don't transfer me to the hospital, don't touch me. I shall only undergo more tortures there.—Cure me indeed! Why, a doctor once came here, and wanted to examine me. I begged him: 'Do not disturb me, for Christ's sake!' It was no use! He began to turn me about, he kneaded and bent my arms and legs, and says he: 'I'm doing this in the interests of science; that's what I'm a learned man in the service for! And thou,' says he, 'canst not oppose me, because I have been given an Order to wear on my neck for my labours, and I exert myself for the benefit of you fools!' He mauled me, and mauled me, and told me the name of my ailment, —such a hard name,—and then he went away. And all my bones ached for a whole week afterward. You say that I am alone, always alone. No, not always. People come to me. I am quiet, I do not disturb them. The young peasant girls drop in, and chatter; a pilgrim strays in, and begins to tell me about Jerusalem, about Kíeff, about the holy cities. And I am not afraid to be alone. I even like it better so, truly I do! . . . . Don't touch me, master, don't take me to the hospital. . . . . . I thank you,—you are kind,—only don't touch me, my dear little dove."

" Well, as thou wilt, as thou wilt, Lukérya. I meant it for thy good, seest thou. . . ."

" I know, master, that it was for my good. But, master dear, who can help another? Who can enter into this soul? A man must help himself! Now, you will not believe it—but I sometimes lie here alone like this . . . . . and it seems as though there were not another person in all the world except myself. I alone am living! And I feel as though something were blessing me. . . . Thoughts come to me—even wonderful thoughts."

" What dost thou think about at such times, Lukérya? "

" 'T is utterly impossible to tell thee that, master: it can't be explained. And one forgets it afterward, too. It is as though a little cloud descended, and spread abroad, and everything becomes so cool and pleasant,—but what has happened you can't understand. Only, I think to myself: ' If there were people about me, nothing of this sort would take place, and I should feel nothing, except my own misfortune.' "

LIVING HOLY RELICS

Lukérya drew breath with difficulty. Her lungs did not obey her, any more than the rest of her members.

"When I look at you, master,"—she began again,—"I feel very sorry for you. But you must not pity me too much, really! I'll tell you something, for example: sometimes, even now, I . . . . Of course, you remember what a merry girl I was in my day? A dashing maid! . . . So, do you know what? I sing songs even now."

"Songs? . . . . Thou?"

"Yes, songs, ancient ballads, choral songs,[1] Christmas carols, all sorts of songs! I knew a great many, you see, and have not forgotten them. Only I don't sing any dance-songs. It isn't fitting,—in my present condition."

"But how dost thou sing them . . . . . to thyself?"

"Both to myself and with my voice. I can't sing loudly, but they are audible, nevertheless. There now, I have told you that a little maid comes to me. She's a quick-witted orphan, you see. So I have taught her; she has already learned four songs from me. Don't you believe it? Wait,—in a minute I'll . . . ."

Lukérya mustered her forces. . . . The thought that this half-dead being was preparing

[1] The choral songs which accompany the games of the peasant girls. Many of these games consist of slow, circling movements.— TRANSLATOR.

299

to sing aroused in me involuntary terror. But before I could utter a word, a prolonged, barely audible, but pure and true sound trembled on my ears . . . . followed by a second, a third. Lukérya was singing " In the Meadows." She sang without altering the expression of her petrified countenance, even fixing her eyes in a stare. But so touchingly did that poor, forced little voice ring forth, like a wreath of undulating smoke, so greatly did her soul long to pour itself out . . . . that I no longer felt terror: unutterable pity gripped my heart.

" Okh, I cannot! "—she said suddenly,—" I have not the strength. . . . . It has given me great pleasure to see you."

She closed her eyes.

I laid my hand on her tiny, cold fingers. . . . She darted a glance at me—and her dark eyelids, fringed with golden lashes, as in an ancient statue, closed again. A moment later, they began to gleam in the semi-darkness. . . . . They were wet with tears.

As before, I did not stir.

" What a goose I am! "—said Lukérya suddenly, with unexpected force, and opening her eyes wide, she tried to wink the tears from them. —" Isn't it shameful? What ails me? 'T is a long time since anything of this sort happened with me . . . . not since the day when Vasíly Polyakóff came to me, last spring. As long as he

was sitting and talking with me, it was all right;
but when he went away, I just cried all by myself! I can't tell what made me do it! . . . .
Tears come easy to us women, you know. Master,"—added Lukérya,—" you have a handkerchief, I suppose. . . . Don't disdain to wipe my
eyes. . . ."

I hastened to comply with her request—and
left her the handkerchief. At first she tried to
refuse . . . . . saying: " Why should you make
me such a gift? " The handkerchief was a very
plain one, but clean and white. Then she seized
it in her feeble fingers, and did not relax them
again. Having become accustomed to the gloom
in which we both were, I could distinctly discern
her features, could even detect a faint flush which
flitted across the bronze of her face, could dis-
cover in that face—at least so it seemed to me—
traces of its former beauty.

" You were asking me, master,"—Lukérya
again began to speak,—" whether I sleep? As a
matter of fact, I sleep rarely; but when I do, I
have such fine dreams! I never see myself as ill:
in my dreams I am always so healthy and young.
. . . . One thing is unfortunate: I wake up, and
want to stretch myself well, and lo! I am as
though fettered all over. Once I had a wonderful dream! I 'll tell you about it, shall I?—Well
then, listen.—I seem to be standing in a field, and
all around is rye, so tall and ripe and golden! . . .

And I seem to have with me a small, reddish dog,
a very, very vicious beast—it is continually trying
to bite me. And there seems to be a reaping-hook
in my hands—not an ordinary hook, but exactly
like the moon when it resembles a reaping-hook.
And with that moon I am to reap the rye clean.
But I am greatly fatigued with the heat, and that
moon dazzles me, and languor comes upon me;
and all around corn-flowers are growing, and such
big ones! And they have turned their little heads
toward me. And I think to myself: ' I will pluck
those corn-flowers; Vásya has promised to come
—so I will first weave myself a wreath; I shall
have time to do the reaping.' I begin to pluck
corn-flowers, but they begin to melt away,—melt
away between my fingers,—I never saw anything
like it! And I cannot weave myself a wreath.
But, in the meantime, I hear some one coming
toward me, so close, and calling: ' Lúsha!
Lúsha!' . . . . . ' Aï,' thinks I to myself, ' woe
is me, I have n't got through the reaping! Nevertheless, I will place the moon on my head instead of the corn-flowers.' I put on the moon exactly like a kokóshnik,[1] and immediately I myself
began to beam all over, and lighted up the whole
field. And lo! over the very crests of the rye-
ears, there comes swiftly advancing toward me—
not Vásya, but Christ Himself! And how I

[1] The coronet-shaped head-dress of the peasant
maidens.—TRANSLATOR.

knew that it was Christ, I cannot tell.—He is not painted in that way,—but it was no one else but He! Beardless, tall, young, clad all in white,— only His girdle was of gold,—and He stretches out His hand to me.—'Fear not, my bride adorned for my coming,'—He says, 'follow me: thou shalt lead the chorals in my heavenly kingdom, and play the songs of paradise!'—And how I glue my lips to His hand!—My dog instantly falls at my feet . . . . but then we soared upward! He in front . . . . His wings spread out over all the sky, as long as those of a sea-gull,— and I after Him. And the little dog was forced to leave me. Only then did I understand that that dog was my malady, and that in the kingdom of heaven there will be no room for it."

Lukérya paused for a moment.

"And I saw something else in a dream,"—she began anew,—"or perhaps it was a vision— really, I do not know. It seemed to me that I am lying in this same wattled shed, and my dead parents come to me,—my father and my mother,— and bow low before me, but say nothing. And I ask them: 'Why do you do reverence to me, dear father and mother?'—'Because,'—they say to me, 'in that thou sufferest great torture in this world, thou hast not only lightened thine own soul, but hast removed from us also a great burden. And things have become much more propitious for us in the other world. Thou hast already finished with thine own sins; now thou art conquering our sins.' And having spoken thus, my parents did me reverence again—and became invisible; only the walls were visible. I was greatly perplexed afterward as to what had happened to me. I even told the priest about it in confession. But he thinks that it was not a vision, because only persons of the ecclesiastical profession have visions.

"And then, here is another dream I had,"—pursued Lukérya.—" I see myself sitting, apparently, on the highway, under a willow-tree, holding a peeled staff in my hand, with a wallet on my shoulders, and my head enveloped in a kerchief—a regular tramp! And I have to go somewhere very, very far off, on a pilgrimage. And tramps keep passing me; they are walking softly, as though unwillingly, and all in one direction; all their faces are dejected, and they all resemble one another greatly. And I see that a woman is winding in and out, darting about among them; and she is a whole head taller than all the rest, and she wears a peculiar garb, not like ours, not Russian. And she has a peculiar face, too,—a fasting, stern face. And all the others seem to draw away from her, and, all of a sudden, she wheels round, and makes straight toward me. She comes to a halt and gazes, and her eyes are like those of a falcon, yellow, large, and bright, very bright. And I ask her: ' Who art thou?'—And she says to me: 'I am thy death.' I suppose I ought to have felt afraid; but, on the contrary, I am glad, so very glad, and I cross myself! And the woman says to me: 'I am sorry for thee, Lukérya, but I cannot take thee with me.—Farewell!'—O Lord! how sad I became then! . . . . 'Take me,' I say, 'dear little mother, my dear little dove, take me!'—And my death turned round to me, and began to reprimand me. . . . . I understand that she is appointing me my hour, but so unintelligibly, indistinctly. . . . 'After the fast of St. Peter,' says she. . . Thereupon I awoke. . . . . I do have such wonderful dreams!"

Lukérya raised her eyes upward . . . . became pensive. . . .

"Only, this is my misfortune: it sometimes happens that a whole week will pass without my getting to sleep a single time. Last year a lady passed by, and saw me, and gave me a phial with medicine to prevent sleeplessness; she ordered me to take ten drops at a time. It helped me a great deal, and I slept; only the phial was emptied long ago. . . . Don't you know what medicine it was, and how I could get some?"

The passing lady had, evidently, given Lukérya opium. I promised to procure for her another such phial, and again could not help expressing aloud my amazement at her patience.

"Ekh, master!"—she returned.—"What

makes you say that? What do you mean by
patience? There was Simeon the Stylite, he had
great patience: he stood for thirty years on a pillar! And another saint ordered them to bury
him in the earth up to his very chest, and the ants
devoured his face. . . . And here is something
which a well-read person once told me: there was
a certain country, and Agarians [1] conquered that
country, and they tortured and slew all the inhabitants; and do what the inhabitants would, they
could not possibly free themselves. And then a
holy, chaste virgin woman made her appearance
among those inhabitants; she took a great sword,
put on armour eighty pounds in weight, went
against the Agarians, and drove them all beyond
the sea. Then, after she had driven them out, she
said to the people: ' Now do you burn me, for
such was my vow, that I would die a death by fire
for my people.'—And the Agarians took her and
burned her, and that people set themselves free,
from that time forth forever! That was a feat!
But what have I done! "

Thereupon, I marvelled inwardly, at the place
and the form which the legend of Jeanne d'Arc
had attained, and, after preserving silence for a
few moments, I asked Lukérya how old she was.

" Twenty-eight . . . . or nine. . . . I am not
yet thirty. But what is the use of reckoning

---

[1] In Russian, *Englishmen* is *Anglitchâne.* Lukérya says
Agaryâne.—TRANSLATOR.

the years! Here's something else I must tell
you. . . ."

Suddenly Lukérya gave a dull cough, and
groaned. . . .

"Thou art talking a great deal,"—I remarked
to her,—"it may injure thee."

"That is true,"—she whispered in a barely
audible tone,—"our conversation must end; but
never mind! Now, when you are gone I can
keep silent to my heart's content. At all events
I have eased my soul. . . ."

I began to take leave of her, repeated my
promise to send her the medicine, requested her to
think it over once more thoroughly, and tell me
whether she did not want something.

"I want nothing; I am content with everything, thank God!"—she articulated with a tremendous effort, but with emotion.—"May God
grant health to all men! And see here, master,
you ought to persuade your mother to reduce the
quit-rent of the peasants here a little, at least—
for they are very poor. They have not sufficient
land, they have no pasture-land. . . . . They
would pray to God for you if you did it. . . .
But I need nothing.—I am content with everything."

I gave Lukérya my word that I would comply
with her request, and was already at the door—
when she called to me again.

"Do you remember, master," she said,—and

something wonderful flitted through her eyes and over her lips,—"what magnificent hair I had? It reached my very knees,—you remember! For a long time, I could not bring myself to . . . . Such hair as it was!—But how could I comb it? In my condition!—So I cut it off. . . . Yes. . . . Well, good-bye, master! My strength is gone. . . ."

That same day, before I set out on my hunt, I had a conversation about Lukérya with the assistant manager of the farm. From him I learned that she was called in the village " The Living Holy Relics"; that no one ever beheld her uneasy: neither murmuring nor complaint was to be heard from her.—" She asks for nothing herself, but, on the contrary, she is thankful for everything; she 's the quietest of the quiet, I must say. She has been smitten by God,"—wound up the assistant manager,—" for her sins, it must be; but we don't go into that. And as for condemning her,—no, we do not condemn her. Leave her in peace! "

A few weeks later, I heard that Lukérya was dead. Death had come for her, after all . . . . and " after St. Peter's Day." The people narrated how, on the day of her death, she had heard uninterruptedly the chiming of bells, although it is reckoned more than five versts from Alex-

yéevka to the church, and it was a week-day.
Moreover, Lukérya had said that the ringing did
not proceed from the church, but " from up
above." Probably she had not dared to say
" from heaven."

XI

THE RATTLING

" I MUST tell you something,"—said Ermolái, **as** he entered my cottage: I had just eaten my dinner, and had lain down on the camp-bed, with a view to resting a little after a fairly successful, but fatiguing hunt for woodcock—it was about the tenth of July, and the heat was frightful. . . . " I must tell you something: we are completely out of bird-shot."

I sprang from the bed.

" Out of bird-shot? How is that? Why, we took about thirty pounds with us when we started from the village—a whole sackful! "

" That 's so; and it was a big sack: it ought to have been enough for a fortnight. But who knows! There may have been a hole in it; . . anyhow, there is n't any . . . . there 's enough left for about ten shots."

" What are we to do now? The very best places are ahead of us—we were promised six coveys for to-morrow. . . ."

" Send me to Túla.—It is n't far off: forty-five versts in all. I 'll fly like the wind and bring a whole pud [1] of bird-shot if you command me."

[1] About thirty-six pounds.—TRANSLATOR.

" But when wilt thou go? "

" Why, this very instant, if you like. What's the use of putting it off? Only, here's one thing: I must hire horses."

" What dost thou mean by hiring horses?—And what are our own for? "

" Our own can't be used.—The shaft-horse has gone lame . . . . awfully! "

" When did that happen? "

" Why, a little while ago,—the coachman took him to be shod. Well, and they shod him. He must have hit on a bad blacksmith.—Now the horse can't even step on that foot—his fore foot. So he carries it . . . . like a dog."

" What then? Have n't they removed the shoe, at least? "

" No, they have n't; but he certainly ought to have the shoe taken off. . . I think the nail must have been driven into the very flesh."

I ordered the coachman to be summoned. It turned out that Ermolái had told the truth: the shaft-horse really could not stand on his foot.—I immediately took measures for having the shoe removed and the horse placed on damp clay.

" Well? Do you order me to hire horses for Túla? "—Ermolái pressed me for an answer.

" Why, is it possible to find any horses in this remote wilderness? "—I exclaimed with involuntary irritation. . . .

The village in which we found ourselves was

out of the way, in the wilds; all its inhabitants appeared to be poverty-stricken; it was with difficulty that we had hunted up one cottage which, if not clean, was at least tolerably spacious.

" It is,"—replied Ermolái with his customary imperturbability. — " You have spoken truly about this village; only, in this same place there used to live one peasant.—Such a clever fellow! So rich! He had nine horses. He is dead, and his eldest son now administers everything. He 's a man—the stupidest of the stupid, but he has n't yet managed to get rid of all the paternal goods. —We 'll get some horses from him.—If you command, I will bring him here.—His brothers are lively lads, I 'm told . . . . nevertheless, he is their head."

" Why is that? "

" Because he 's the eldest!—That means,— Younger lads, obey! "—At this point, Ermolái expressed himself in strong and unprintable language about younger brothers in general.—" I 'll bring him. — He 's simple-minded. — You can make your own terms with him."

While Ermolái went in search of his " simple-minded " man, the idea occurred to me: " Would it not be better for me to go to Túla myself? " In the first place, taught by experience, I had not much confidence in Ermolái; I had once sent him to town to make some purchases, he had promised to execute my commissions in the space of one day

—and had disappeared for a whole week, had drunk up all the money, and had returned on foot, although he had set out in a racing-drozhky. In the second place, I was acquainted with a horse-dealer in Túla; I might buy from him a horse to take the place of the lame shaft-horse.

" That settles it! "—I thought.—" I 'll go myself; and I can sleep on the road—luckily, the tarantás is comfortable."

" I 've brought him! "—exclaimed Ermolái, a quarter of an hour later, tumbling into the cottage.—In his wake there entered a tall peasant, in a white shirt, blue trousers, and plaited linden-bark slippers,—a man with white eyelashes, bleareyed, with a small, red, wedge-shaped beard, a long, thick nose, and a gaping mouth. He really did look like a " weak-minded " person.

" Here, if you please,"—said Ermolái,—" he has horses, and he consents."

" This you see,—I . . . ." the peasant began in a husky voice and with a stutter, tossing back his thin hair, and fingering the rim of his cap, which he held in his hands.—" I, you see . . . . ."

" What is thy name? "—I inquired.

The peasant dropped his eyes and seemed to be meditating.—" What is my name, did you say? "

" Yes; what is thy name? "

" Why, my name will be Filoféi."

" Well, see here now, my good Filoféi; I hear

that thou hast horses.—Bring hither a tróïka,— we will hitch them to my tarantás,—it is a light one,—and do thou drive me to Túla. It is a moonlight night, the trip will be light and cool. What sort of a road have you thither? "

" Road? The road's all right.—It's twenty versts, all told, to the highway. There's one small stretch . . . . . which is bad; otherwise, it's all right."

" What is that bad stretch? "

" Why, the river must be forded."

" But are you going to Túla yourself? "—inquired Ermolái.

" Yes, I am."

" Well! "—said my faithful servitor, and shook his head.—" We-e-ell! "—he repeated, spat, and left the room.

The trip to Túla, evidently, no longer had any attractions; it had become for him an empty and uninteresting matter.

" Dost thou know the road well? "—I said, addressing Filoféi.

" Why shouldn't we know the road!—Only, you see, I can't go anyhow . . . . it's so sudden. . . . ."

It turned out that Ermolái, in hiring Filoféi, had announced to him that he had no doubt that he, the fool, would be paid . . . . . and nothing more! Filoféi, although he was a fool, according to Ermolái's statement, was not satisfied

314

with that announcement alone. He demanded from me fifty rubles,—a huge sum; I offered him ten rubles,—a low price.—We began to haggle; at first, Filoféi was obdurate—then he began to yield, but slowly. Ermolái, who came in for a minute, began to assure me that " this fool "— (" Evidently, he has taken a fancy to the word! " —commented Filoféi in an undertone)—" this fool does n't know the value of money "—and, incidentally, reminded me how, twenty years previously, the posting-station erected by my mother on a fine site, at the intersection of two highways, had sunk into utter decay, owing to the fact that the old house-serf, who had been placed there to manage the establishment, really did not know how to reckon money, and judged of it according to its quantity,—that is, he would give, for instance, a silver quarter-ruble for six copper five-kopék pieces, swearing roundly the while.

" Ekh, thou, Filoféi, art a regular Filoféi! "— ejaculated Ermolái at last,—and quitting the room in a rage, he banged the door behind him.

Filoféi made him no reply, as though conscious of the fact that to be named Filoféi was, in reality, not quite expedient, and that a man may be upbraided for it, although, properly speaking, the person to blame in the matter is the priest, who has not been as benignant to him as he should have been.

But, at last, we agreed upon twenty rubles.—
He went off to get the horses, and an hour later
led up five from which I was to make my choice.
The horses seemed to be pretty good, although
their manes and tails were tangled, and their bellies were big and taut as a drum.—With Filoféi
came two of his brothers, who bore not the slightest resemblance to him. Small, black-eyed, sharp-
nosed, they really did produce the impression of
being " lively lads "; they talked much and fast,
—" cackled," as Ermolái expressed it,—but rendered obedience to their elder brother.

They rolled the tarantás from beneath the shed,
and worked over it and the horses for an hour and
a half; now they loosened the rope traces, again
they hitched them up very tight! Both brothers
insisted upon harnessing the " roan " in the
shafts, because " you kin let that critter full-tilt
down hill "; [1]—but Filoféi decided in favour of
a very shaggy horse.—So the shaggy horse was
put in the shafts.

They stuffed the tarantás full of hay, and
thrust under the seat the lame horse's collar—in
case it should prove necessary to fit it to the
newly-purchased horse in Túla. . . . Filoféi,
who had contrived to run home and return thence
in a long, white peasant-coat which had belonged
to his father, a tall conical cap, and oiled boots,
clambered solemnly to the driver's box.—I took

[1] Russians drive at full speed down and up hills.—TRANSLATOR.

my seat, and looked at my watch:—it was a quarter past ten.—Ermolái did not even take leave of me, having set about thrashing his Valétka; Filoféi jerked the reins, shouted in an extremely shrill little voice: " Ekh, you tiny beasts! "—his brothers sprang up on each side, lashed the trace-horses under the belly, and the tarantás rolled off, and turned through the gate into the street. The shaggy horse made an attempt to dash to his place in the yard,—but Filoféi brought him to his senses by a few blows of his whip,—and we had soon left the village behind and were bowling along a tolerably level road, between dense thickets of nutbushes.

The night was calm and magnificent, the most convenient sort for driving.

At times, the breeze would rustle among the bushes, rocking the branches; at times it would die away completely: but here and there in the sky motionless silvery clouds were visible; the moon rode high, brilliantly illuminating the countryside.—I stretched myself out on the hay, and was already beginning to fall into a doze . . . . . when the " bad stretch " suddenly recurred to my memory, and I started up.

" How now, Filoféi? Is it far to the ford? "

" To the ford, you say? It will be about eight versts."

" ' Eight versts,' "—I thought to myself.— " We shall not get there under an hour.—I can

317

take a nap."—"Dost thou know the road well, Filoféi?"—I asked another question.

"Why, how could I help it, knowing the road? 'T is n't the first time I 've been over it."

He added something more, but I was no longer listening to him. . . . I was asleep.

WHAT aroused me was not my intention to awake precisely an hour later, as is often the case,—but a strange, though faint dragging through mud and gurgling directly under my ear.—I raised my head. . . .

What marvel was this?—I was lying, as before, in the tarantás; but around the tarantás,—and about fourteen inches—not more—from its rim, a watery expanse, lighted up by the moon, was dimpling and undulating in small, distinct ripples. I cast a glance ahead: on the box, with drooping head and bowed back, sat Filoféi, like a statue,—and further away still, over the purling water,—the curving line of the shaft-arch and the heads and backs of the horses were visible. —And everything was so motionless, so noiseless, —exactly as in the realm of enchantment: in a dream, a fantastic dream. . . . What did it mean?—I darted a glance backward from beneath the hood of the tarantás. . . . Why, we were in the very middle of the river . . . . the shores were more than thirty paces distant from us!

" Filoféi! "—I shouted.

" What? "—he replied.

" What dost thou mean by ' what '? Good gracious! Where are we? "

" In the river."

" I see that we are in the river.—But if we go on like this, we shall drown.—Dost mean to say that thou art traversing the ford in this manner? Hey?—Why, thou art fast asleep, Filoféi! Come, answer me! "

" I 've got a trifle astray,"—said my driver:— " I 've gone to one side, you know, more 's the pity; but now we must wait."

" What dost thou mean by ' must wait '?— What are we to wait for? "

" Why, here, let the shaggy horse look about him: wherever he turns, there the ford will be, you see, and we must drive in that direction."

I half sat up on the straw.—The head of the shaggy horse hung motionless over the water.— The only thing that could be seen by the clear light of the moon was, that one of its ears was moving backward and forward almost imperceptibly.

" Why, he 's fast asleep also, thy shaggy horse! "

" No,"—replied Filoféi:—" he 's sniffing the water now."

Again everything relapsed into silence, and, as

before, there was no sound save the purling of the water.—I also grew benumbed.

The moonlight, and the night, and the river, and we in it . . . .

" What 's that making such a hoarse sound? " —I asked Filoféi.

" That?—Ducklings in the reeds . . . . or snakes."

All at once the head of the shaft-horse began to shake, he pricked up his ears, he began to snort, and turned round. — " No-no-no-noo! " Filoféi suddenly roared at the top of his lungs, and, half-rising, he brandished his whip. The tarantás immediately moved from its stand, dashing forward at an angle across the current of the river—and advanced, quivering and swaying. . . . At first it seemed to me that we were sinking, plunging into the depths; but after two or three jolts and dives, the watery expanse seemed suddenly to grow shallower. . . . It kept sinking lower and lower, the tarantás kept rising higher and higher out of it,—lo! the wheels and the horses' tails had already made their appearance,—and now, with mighty and violent splashings, raising sheaves of diamonds,—no, not of diamonds, but of sapphires, which dispersed in the full gleam of the moon,—the horses dragged us cheerily and with a final effort on to the sandy shore, and proceeded along the road, up-hill, vying with each other in trotting along with their shining, wet hoofs.

"What will Filoféi say now?"—flashed through my mind: "'You see I was right!'—or something of that sort?" But he said nothing at all. Consequently, I did not consider it necessary to upbraid him for his lack of caution, and stretching myself out again upon the hay, I tried to get to sleep.

But I could not get to sleep, not because I was fatigued with hunting, and not because the trepidation I had undergone had driven slumber from me,—but probably because we were obliged to pass through very beautiful places. Now there were spacious, luxuriant, grassy water-meadows, with a multitude of small pools, lakes, brooks, creeks overgrown at their extremities with willows and vines, genuine Russian spots, beloved of the Russian folk, similar to those whither the heroes of our ancient epic songs [1] were wont to go to shoot white swans and grey ducks. The well-beaten road wound in a yellowish ribbon, the horses ran lightly—and I could not close an eye,—to such a degree was I admiring things! And all this glided past me so softly and sedately, beneath the friendly moon.—Even Filoféi was affected.

"Those are what are called among us the Saint-George meadows,"—he said, turning to me;—"and next come the Grand-Prince mea-

[1] See "The Epic Songs of Russia," by Isabel F. Hapgood. Charles Scribner's Sons.

dows; there are no other meadows like them in all
Russia. . . . . They are very beautiful!"—The
shaft-horse snorted and shook himself. . . .
" Lord bless thee!" . . . . . said Filoféi, staidly
and in an undertone.—" Are n't they beautiful!"
he repeated, with a sigh, and then indulged in a
prolonged groan. " The mowing-lands begin
pretty soon, now, and what a lot of hay they get
from them—an awful lot!—And there are quantities of fish in the creeks, too.—Such bream!"—
he added in a drawl. " In a word: there is no need
of dying from hunger!"

Suddenly he raised his hand.

" Ehva!—just look yonder! over yonder lake
. . . . is n't it a heron standing there? can it be
possible that it is catching fish by night? Ekh-ma!
't is a stump, not a heron. I was fooled that time!
but the moon always deceives."

Thus did we drive on and on. . . . But now
the meadows came to an end, small tracts of forest made their appearance, and tilled fields; a
hamlet on one side twinkled with two or three
lights,—not more than five versts remained to the
highway.—I fell asleep.

Again I did not wake of my own accord. This
time Filoféi's voice aroused me.

" Master . . . . hey, master!"

I raised myself on my elbow.—The tarantás
was standing still on a level spot, in the very middle of the highway; turned round toward me on

the box, full face, with his eyes widely opened
(I was even astonished, not having supposed that
he had such large eyes), Filoféi whispered significantly and mysteriously:

"There's a rattling! .... There's a rattling!"

"What's that thou 'rt saying?"

"I say there's a rattling!—Just bend down
and listen. Do you hear?"

I thrust my head out of the tarantás, and
held my breath:—and, in fact, I did hear somewhere in the distance, far away from us, a faint,
spasmodic rattling, as though of rumbling
wheels.

"Do you hear?"—repeated Filoféi.

"Well, yes,"—I replied. "Some equipage is
driving on the road."

"But you don't hear it . . . . . hist! There
it is . . . . harness-bells . . . . . and a whistle
too. . . . . Do you hear? Come, take off your
cap . . . . . you will hear more distinctly."

I did not take off my cap, but lent an ear.—
"Well, yes . . . . . perhaps I do.—But what
of that?"

Filoféi turned his face toward his horses.

"A peasant-cart is rolling swiftly . . . . .
unladen, the wheels have tires," he said, as he
gathered up his reins.—"It means, master, that
evil people are driving yonder; for here, in the vicinity of Túla, there's a lot of . . . . . . frolicking."

"What nonsense! Why dost thou assume that they must, infallibly, be wicked people?"

"I'm telling you truly.—With bells . . . . and in an unladen cart. . . . Who can it be?"

"Well, and is it very far to Túla still?"

"It must be a good fifteen versts, and there's not a sign of a dwelling."

"Well, then, drive on as rapidly as possible; we must make no delay."

Filoféi flourished his whip, and again the tarantás rolled on.

ALTHOUGH I did not believe Filoféi, still I could no longer sleep.—And what if, in reality . . . . ? An unpleasant sensation began to stir within me. —I sat up in the tarantás—up to that time I had been lying down—and began to gaze on all sides. While I had been asleep, a thin mist had gathered —not over the earth, but over the sky; it lay high up,—the moon hung in it like a whitish spot, as though veiled in crape. Everything had grown dull and confused, although below things were more visible.—All around lay flat, melancholy places; fields, and more fields, here and there a few bushes, ravines—and then more fields, and chiefly fallow land, with sparse, weedy grass. Empty . . . . dead! Not even a quail was calling.

We drove on for half an hour.—Filoféi was continually cracking his whip and chirruping

with his lips, but neither he nor I uttered a word.
Now we ascended a hillock. . . . . Filoféi
stopped the tróïka, and immediately said:

" There's a rattling . . . . . a rattling, master!"

Again I hung out of the tarantás; but I might
as well have remained under the hood, so clearly,
though distinctly, was there now borne to my ears
the sound of cart-wheels, men whistling, the jingling of the harness-bells, and the trampling of
horses' hoofs; I even fancied I heard singing and
laughter. The breeze, it is true, was blowing
from that quarter, but there was no doubt of the
fact that the unknown travellers had drawn
nearer to us by a whole verst—possibly, even, by
two versts.

Filoféi and I exchanged glances,—he merely
moved his cap from the back of his head over his
brow, and immediately, bending over the reins,
began to lash the horses. They set out at a gallop, but could not keep up the pace long, and
again dropped into a trot.—Filoféi continued to
belabour them. We must make our escape!

I could not account to myself for the fact that
this time I, who had not at first shared Filoféi's
suspicions, had suddenly acquired the conviction
that it was really evil-doers who were driving in
pursuit of us. . . . I had heard nothing new:
there were the same bells, there was the same
rattling sound of an unloaded cart, the same whis-

tling, the same confused uproar. . . . But I now no longer cherished any doubt. . Filoféi could not be mistaken!

And thus twenty more minutes passed. . . . In the course of these last twenty minutes, athwart the rattling and rumbling of our own equipage, we could hear another rattling, another rumbling. . . .

" Halt, Filoféi! "—I said: " it makes no difference—there can be but one end to this? "

Filoféi uttered a faint-hearted " Whoa! " The horses stopped instantly, as though delighted at the possibility of taking a rest!

Good heavens! the bells were simply roaring behind our backs, the cart was thundering on with a rattle, men were whistling, shouting, and singing, the horses were neighing and pounding the earth with their hoofs. . . .

They had overtaken us!

" Ca-la-mee-ty! "—said Filoféi brokenly, in an undertone—and, with an irresolute chirrup, he began to urge on his horses. But at the same moment, something seemed suddenly to give way with a crash and a roar and a groan,—and a very large, broad peasant-cart, drawn by three emaciated horses, overtook us abruptly, like a whirlwind, dashed past us, and immediately slowed down to a walk, blocking the road.

" A regular brigand trick! " — whispered Filoféi.

THE RATTLING

I must admit that my heart began to beat wildly. . . . I began to stare intently into the semi-gloom of the moonlight veiled in vapours. In the cart, in front of us, half-sitting, half-lying, were six men in shirts, with their peasant-coats wide open on the breast; two of them were bareheaded; huge feet in boots dangled, jolting, over the rail; hands rose and fell at random . . . . . bodies heaved to and fro. . . . . It was plain that the whole gang was drunk. Some were yelling hoarsely whatever happened to come into their heads; one was whistling in a very clear and piercing manner, another was swearing; on the driver's seat sat a sort of giant in a short, sheepskin coat, driving. They drove on at a foot-pace, as though paying no attention to us.

What was to be done? We drove after them, also at a foot-pace.

For a quarter of a verst we proceeded in this manner.—Anticipation was torturing. . . . . What chance was there of saving ourselves, defending ourselves! There were six of them: and I had not even a stick with me! Should we turn back on our course?—but they would immediately overtake us. I recalled a verse of Zhukóvsky (where he is speaking of the murder of Field-Marshal Kámensky):

" The despised axe of the brigand . . ."

If not that, they would strangle us with a filthy rope . . . . and fling us into the ditch . . . . . and there we might rattle in the throat and struggle like a hare in a snare. . . . .

Ekh, we were in a bad plight!

But they continued to drive at a walk, as before, and pay no attention to us.

" Filoféi! "—I whispered,—" pray try to turn more to the right. Endeavour to pass them."

Filoféi made the attempt,—and turned out to the right . . . . but they immediately drove to the right also; . . . . evidently, it was impossible to pass them.

Filoféi tried again: he turned out to the left. . . . . But they did not let him pass on that side, either. They even burst out laughing. Which meant, that they would not let us pass.

" Regular brigands! "—whispered Filoféi to me over his shoulder.

" But what are they waiting for? "—I asked, also in a whisper.

" Why, yonder—ahead, in the ravine, over the stream—is a small bridge. . . . They 're going to attack us there! They always do like that . . . . near a bridge. We 're done for, master! "—he added, with a sigh:—" it is n't likely that they will release us alive; because the principal thing with them is—to hide all traces.—I 'm sorry for one thing, master: my tróïka-team will be lost, and my brothers will not get it! "

THE RATTLING

I was surprised that Filoféi could worry about his horses at such a moment,—and I must confess that I did not think much of him just then. . . . . " Is it possible that they will kill us? " I kept re-iterating mentally.—" What for? I will give up to them everything I have about me. . . ."

And the bridge drew nearer and nearer, became more and more clearly visible.

Suddenly a sharp yell rang out, the tróïka in front of us seemed to soar into the air, dashed off, and having galloped to the bridge, came to an abrupt halt, as though rooted to the spot, a little to one side of the road. My heart fairly sank into my boots.

" Okh, brother Filoféi,"—said I:—" thou and I are driving to our death.—Forgive me, if I have destroyed thee."

" How is it thy fault, master! No one can escape his fate! Come on, shaggy, my faithful nag,"—said Filoféi, addressing the shaft-horse, —" go ahead, brother! Render us the last service! —All together now! . . . . . Lord, give us thy blessing! "

He launched his tróïka at a gentle trot.

We began to approach the bridge,—to approach that motionless, menacing cart. . . . All had grown silent in it, as though of set purpose. Not a sound was to be heard! Thus does the pike, the hawk, every beast of prey grow silent when its prey is approaching.—And now we came alongside the cart. . . . . Suddenly the giant in the short sheepskin coat gave a great leap from it, and dashed straight at us!

Not a word did he say to Filoféi, but the latter immediately drew rein. . . . The tarantás came to a standstill.

The giant laid his hands on the carriage-door— and bending forward his shaggy head, and grinning broadly, he uttered the following words in a quiet, even voice, with the accent of a factory-hand:

" Respected sir, we are on our way from an honourable carouse, from a wedding-feast; we have been marrying off our fine young fellow, you know; we have just put the young pair to bed; we lads are all young, reckless,—we 've drunk a lot,—but there was n't enough for us to get drunk on;—so, will not you do us a favour, will not you contribute to us just the least little bit of money,—so that we may buy a dram of liquor for each brother of us?—We would drink your health, we would remember Your Stateliness; [1]—but if you will not do us the favour,—well, then, we beg that you will not be angry."

" What 's the meaning of this? "—I said to

[1] *Stepénstvo,* the title given by the populace to respected persons of their own and of the burgher class. In Siberia, Orenburg, and the Caucasus, the title is applied to Asiatic sultans, murzas, petty princes, and elders, while it is decreed by law to the Kirghiz sultans. But Khans are called " Your High-Stateliness."—TRANSLATOR.

myself. . . . " Is it raillery? . . . . Is he jeering at me?"

The giant continued to stand there, with bowed head. At that instant the moon emerged from the mist, and illuminated his face. It was smiling, was that face—both with eyes and lips. And no menace was perceptible in it . . . . . only, it seemed to be all alert . . . . . and his teeth were so white, and so large. . .

" I will contribute with pleasure. . . . . Here, take this. . . ." I said hastily—and drawing my purse from my pocket, I took from it two silver rubles: at that time, silver money was still current in Russia.—" Here, if this is enough."

" We're very grateful! "—bawled the giant, in soldier fashion—and his thick fingers instantly snatched from me—not my whole purse—but only those two rubles. " We're very grateful! "—He shook back his hair, and ran to the cart.

" My lads! "—he shouted: " The gentleman-traveller contributes two rubles to us! "—They all instantly began to yell. . . . . The giant clambered to the box. . . .

" May you be happy! " . . .

The horses started off, the cart thundered up hill,—once more it flashed through the dark streak which separated earth from heaven, sank into it, and vanished.

And now the rattling, and the shouting, and the bells were no longer to be heard. . . .

Deathlike silence reigned.

Filoféi and I did not speedily recover ourselves.

" Akh, curse thee, what a jester thou art! "— said Filoféi at last—and taking off his cap, he began to cross himself.—" Really, he is a joker," —he added, and turned to me, all radiant with delight.—" But he must be a good man—really! —No-no-noo, my little ones! bestir yourselves!— You 're safe and sound! We 're all safe and sound!—That 's why he would n't let us pass; he was driving the horses. What a joker of a lad. — No-no-no-noo! — proceed, with God's blessing! "

I held my peace,—but I also felt relieved in soul. " We 're safe and sound! "—I repeated to myself, and stretched myself out on the hay.— " We got off cheaply! "

I even felt a little conscience-stricken at having recalled Zhukóvsky's lines.

All at once an idea occurred to me:

" Filoféi! "

" What? "

" Art thou married? "

" Yes."

" And hast thou children? "

" I have."

" How was it that thou didst not think of them?

THE RATTLING

Thou wert sorry about the horses—but not about thy wife and children?"

" But why should I feel sorry for them? They would n't have fallen into the hands of thieves, you see.—And I kept them in my thoughts all the while,—and I 'm keeping them there now . . . . so I am."—Filoféi stopped.—" Perhaps . . . . it was for their sakes that the Lord God had mercy on you and me."

" But supposing they were not brigands?"

" And how do we know?—Is it possible to crawl into another man's soul, I 'd like to know? —Another man's soul is . . . . darkness . . . everybody knows that. But 't is always better to have God's blessing.—No . . as for my family, I always . . . . Now-now-now, little ones, Go-d be with us!"

It was almost daybreak when we began to enter Túla. I was lying in the semi-forgetfulness of slumber. . . .

" Master,"—said Filoféi suddenly to me, " look yonder: there it stands, yonder by the dram-shop . . . . . their cart."

I raised my head . . . . it was they, in fact, and their cart, and their horses. On the threshold of the drinking-establishment the familiar giant in the short sheepskin coat suddenly made his appearance. " Sir!" he exclaimed, waving his cap, " We 're drinking up your money!—Well, and your coachman,"—he added, nodding his head toward Filoféi,—" I fancy that fellow was pretty well scared,—was n't he?"

" A very jolly fellow,"—remarked Filoféi, when we had driven about twenty fathoms from the dram-shop.

We arrived in Túla at last; I bought the birdshot, and wine and tea also, by the way,—and even took a horse from the horse-dealer.—At midday we set off on our return journey. As we drove past the spot where, for the first time, we had heard the rattling of the cart behind us, Filoféi, who had drunk considerable liquor in Túla, showed himself to be a very loquacious man,—he even narrated stories to me,—as we drove past that spot, Filoféi suddenly burst out laughing.

" But dost thou remember, master, how I kept saying to thee:' There 's a rattling ' . . . . ' there 's a rattling,' I said . . . . ' there 's a rattling!' "

He brandished his hand several times. . . . . These words struck him as very amusing.

That same evening we reached his village again.

I imparted our adventure to Ermolái. As he was sober, he expressed no sympathy, and merely grinned,—whether approvingly or reprovingly, is more than he himself knew, I suppose. But a couple of days later he informed me, with much satisfaction, that on that same night when Filoféi and I had driven to Túla,—and on that selfsame road,—a merchant had been robbed and murdered. At first I did not believe this news; but afterward I was compelled to: the commissary of rural police confirmed its veracity to me, as he galloped by to the inquest.—Was it not from that "wedding-feast" that our bold lads were returning, and was not he that "dashing young fellow" whom, according to the expression of the giant-jester, they had "put to bed"? I remained for five days longer in Filoféï's village.—And on every occasion that I chanced to meet him, I said to him:—"Hey! There's a rattling!"

"A jolly fellow,"—he replied to me every time, and began to laugh.

EPILOGUE

FOREST AND STEPPE

. . . . And backward, gradually, longing him to draw
Began; to the country, to the dusky park,
Whose lindens are so vast, so dense with shade,
And lilies of the valley are so virginally sweet,
Where globe-shaped willows from the dam
In serried ranks over the water bend,
Where grows the luxuriant oak upon the luxuriant mead,
Where hemp and nettle their perfume emit . . . .
Thither, thither away, to the abundant fields,
Where, like unto velvet black the earth lies duskily,
Where,—turn your eyes whichever way you will,—
The rye streams gently on in billows soft,
And from behind transparent, round, white clouds
A heavy ray of yellow light falls down
So beautifully . . . .

(From a poem consigned to the flames.)

PERCHANCE, the reader is already bored
with my memoirs; I hasten to reassure him
with the promise to confine myself to the frag-
ments which have been printed; but in taking my
leave of him, I cannot refrain from saying a few
words about hunting.

Hunting with gun and hound is very fine in
itself, *für sich,* as people used to say in days of
old; but, supposing you were not born a sportsman: nevertheless, you are a lover of nature; con-

EPILOGUE

sequently, you cannot but envy huntsmen like
us. . . . Listen.

Do you know, for example, what a delight it
is to sally forth in springtime before the dawn?
You step out on the porch. . . . In the dark-blue
sky stars are twinkling here and there; a damp
breeze sweeps past, from time to time, in light
gusts; the repressed, ill-defined whispering of the
night is audible; the trees are rustling, as they
stand enveloped in shadow. Now they lay a rug
in the peasant-cart, and place a box with the
samovár at your feet. The trace-horses fidget,
neigh, and shift coquettishly from foot to foot; a
pair of white geese, which have just waked up,
waddle silently and slowly across the road. Beyond the wattled hedge, in the garden, the watchman is snoring peacefully; every sound seems to
hang suspended in the chilly air,—to hang and
not pass on. Now you have taken your seat; the
horses have set off on the instant, the cart has
begun to rattle loudly . . . . you drive on and
on . . . . past the church, down-hill to the right,
across the dam. . . . . . The pond is barely beginning to smoke. You feel a little cold, you
cover up your face with the collar of your cloak;
you sink into a doze. The horses plash their hoofs
sonorously through puddles; the coachman begins to whistle. But now, you have got four
versts from home . . . . the rim of the sky is beginning to flush crimson; the daws scatter over

the birch-trees, flying awkwardly from tree to tree; the sparrows are chirping around the dark ricks. The air grows clearer, the road becomes visible, sleepy voices make themselves heard behind the gates. And in the meantime, the dawn is kindling; and lo, already golden streaks have flung themselves athwart the sky, the mists are swirling in the ravines; the larks are warbling loudly; the breeze which precedes the dawn has begun to blow,—and the crimson sun glides softly up. The light fairly gushes forth in a flood; your heart flutters within you, like a bird. All is bright, cheerful, agreeable! For a long distance round about everything is visible. There, behind the grove, lies a village; yonder, further away, is another, with a white church; yonder is a small birch-coppice, on the hill; behind it lies the marsh whither you are directing your course. . . . Faster, ye steeds, still faster! Advance at a smart trot! . . . . Only three versts remain, not more. The sun is rising swiftly; the sky is clear. . . . . The weather will be magnificent. A flock of sheep is advancing in a long line, from the village, to meet you. You have ascended the hill. . . . What a view! The river winds about for ten versts, gleaming dully blue through the mist; be yond it lie watery-green meadows; beyond the meadows are sloping hillocks; far away, lapwings are hovering and calling over the marsh; athwart the moist gleam diffused in the air, the distance stands forth clearly . . . . not as in summer. How boldly the bosom heaves, how swiftly the limbs move, how strong the whole man becomes, thus seized in the embrace of the fresh breath of the spring! . . .

And the summer—July—morning! Who, save the sportsman, has experienced the joy of wandering at dawn among the bushes? The trace of your footsteps leaves a green line on the dewy, whitened grass. You thrust aside the wet bushes, —you are fairly drenched with the warm perfume which has accumulated over night; the air is all impregnated with the fresh bitterness of wormwood, the honey of buckwheat and clover; far away, like a wall, stands an oak forest, glittering and crimsoning in the sun; it is still chilly, but the approaching heat can be felt. The head swims with the excess of perfume. There is no end to the thicket. . . . Here and there, perchance, in the distance, the ripening rye gleams yellow, and the narrow strips of buckwheat shine with a reddish glint. Now a cart creaks; a peasant is making his way along at a foot-pace, to put his horse in the shade as soon as possible. . . . You have exchanged greetings with him, and have gone on, when the ringing whine of the scythe resounds behind you. The sun rides higher and higher. The grass will soon be dry. It is already hot. One hour passes, then another. . . . The sky grows dark along the rim; the motionless air is blazing with stinging heat.—" Where can I get a drink, brother? "—you ask a mower.—" Yonder, in the ravine, is a well." You descend to the bottom of the ravine, through the dense hazel-bushes, all intertwined with tenacious grass. And, in fact, beneath the very cliff a spring is concealed; an oak-bush has eagerly thrown over the water its claw-like branches; great, silvery bubbles rise, dimpling, from the bottom covered with fine, velvety moss. You throw yourself down on the ground, you drink, but languor is beginning to stir within you. You are in the shade, you are inhaling the fragrant moisture, you are comfortable, while opposite you the bushes are getting red-hot, and seem to be turning yellow in the sun. But what is this? A breeze has suddenly flown up and dashed past; the surrounding air has quivered; is not that a clap of thunder? You emerge from the ravine . . . . what is yon leaden streak on the horizon? Is the sultry heat growing more intense? Is it a thunder-cloud coming up? . . . . But now comes a faint flash of lightning. . . . Eh, yes, it is a thunder-storm! The sun is still shining brilliantly round about you; it is still possible to hunt. But the cloud waxes: its front edge throws out a branch, it bends over into a vault. The grass, the bushes, everything round about has grown dark of a sudden. . . . Be quick! yonder, methinks, a hay-barn is visible . . . . be quick! . . . . . You have fled to it, have entered. . . . What rain! what lightning! Here and there the water has dripped through upon the fragrant hay. . . . But now the sun has broken forth again. The thunderstorm has passed over; you step out. Heavens, how merrily everything round about is sparkling, how fresh and thin the air is, what a strong scent of strawberries and mushrooms is abroad! . . .

But now evening is drawing on. The sunset glow has embraced half the sky in its conflagration. The sun is setting. The air close at hand seems somehow peculiarly translucent, like glass; far away a soft mist is spreading, and is warm in aspect; along with the dew a crimson glow falls upon the fields, so recently flooded with streams of liquid gold; long shadows have begun to run out from the trees, from the bushes, from the lofty ricks of hay. . . . The sun has set; a star has kindled and is trembling in the fiery sea of the sunset. . . . Now it waxes pale; the sky grows blue; separate shadows disappear; the air is permeated with vapour. 'T is time to go home to the village, to the cottage where you are to spend the night. Throwing your gun over your shoulder, you walk briskly on, in spite of the distance. . . . And, in the meantime, night has come; you can no longer see twenty paces in front of you; the dogs are barely visible as white spots in the gloom; yonder, above the black bushes, the rim of the sky is confusedly perceptible. . . . . .

EPILOGUE

What is that?—a fire? . . . . No, it is the moon rising. And yonder, down below, to the right, the tiny lights of a village are twinkling. . . . Now, at last, you reach your cottage. Through the tiny window you descry the table, covered with a white cloth, a burning candle,—supper. . . .

Or you order your racing-drozhky to be harnessed up, and set out in quest of hazel-hens. 'T is jolly to make your way along the narrow path, between two walls of lofty rye. The ears slap you gently in the face, the corn-flowers cling about your feet, the quail utter their calls all around you, your horse runs on in a lazy trot. And now here is the forest. Shade and silence. The stately aspens are whispering high overhead; the long, pendent branches of the birch-trees are barely stirring; a mighty oak stands, like a warrior, by the side of a handsome linden. You drive along the green pathway flecked with shadows; huge yellow flies hang motionless in the golden air and suddenly fly away; gnats circle in a column, gleaming brightly in the shadow, darkling in the sunlight; birds warble peacefully. The golden voice of the hedge-sparrow rings with innocent, loquacious joy; it fits in with the perfume of the lilies of the valley. Further, further yet, into the depths of the forest. . . . The forest grows dense. . . . Inexpressible tranquillity falls upon the soul; and all round is so dreamy and quiet! But now a breeze has sprung up, and

342

the crests of the trees have begun to ripple, like falling waves. Here and there tall blades of grass are springing up through last year's brown foliage; mushrooms stand apart beneath their caps. A hare suddenly leaps out, a dog dashes in pursuit with a ringing bark. . . .

And how fine is the same forest in late autumn, when the woodcock are flying! They do not harbour in the very densest parts: they must be sought along the edges. There is no wind, there is neither sun, nor light, nor shadow, nor movement, nor noise; the autumnal scent, akin to the smell of wine, is disseminated through the soft air; a thin mist stands far off above the yellow fields. The motionless sky gleams peacefully white between the brown, naked branches of the trees; here and there on the lindens hang the last golden leaves. The damp earth is springy under foot; the tall, dry grass-blades do not stir; long threads glisten on the whitened grass. The breast rises and falls in quiet breathing, and a strange disquietude descends upon the soul. You stroll along the skirt of the forest, you glance at your dog, and, meanwhile, beloved images, beloved faces, both dead and living, come to mind, impressions long since sunk to sleep unexpectedly wake up; your imagination flutters and soars like a bird, and everything moves along and stands before the eyes so clearly. The heart suddenly begins to quiver and throb, dashes passionately ahead, or is irrevocably submerged in memories. The whole of life unfolds lightly and swiftly, like a scroll; the man is in full possession of his past, his feelings, his whole soul. And nothing round about him hinders—there is no sun, no wind, no noise. . . .

And the clear, somewhat chilly autumnal day, which has been cold in early morning, when the birch, like a fabulous tree, all gold, is beautifully outlined against the pale-blue sky, when the low-hanging sun no longer warms, but shines more brilliantly than in summer, the small aspen grove is all glittering through and through, as though it found it a merry and easy thing to stand naked, the hoar-frost is still lying white on the bottom of the ravine, and the fresh breeze is softly stirring and driving along the fallen, withered leaves,—when blue waves dash gaily down the river, rocking the scattered geese in regular measure, and far away a mill is clattering, half-hidden by willows, and pigeons circle swiftly above it, flashing in motley hues through the bright air. . .

Beautiful also are the cloudy summer days, although the sportsman does not love them. On such days shooting is impossible: a bird, after fluttering up from under your very feet, instantly disappears in the whitish mist of the motionless haze. But how quiet, how inexpressibly quiet is everything around! Everything is awake, and everything is silent. You walk past a tree—it is not rustling; it is taking its ease. A long streak lies blackly before you, spread out evenly in the air, like a thin vapour. You take it for the forest hard by; you approach—the forest turns into a tall bed of wormwood on the grass-strip between the tilled fields. Above you, around you,—everywhere, lies the mist. . . . But now the breeze is beginning to stir lightly.—A scrap of pale-blue sky stands forth confusedly through the thinning, smoke-like vapour, a golden-yellow ray of sunlight suddenly breaks forth, begins to stream in a long flood, beats upon the fields, rests upon the grove,—and now, everything is again shrouded in clouds. For a long time does this conflict last; but how unutterably magnificent and clear does the day become, when the light at last triumphs, and the last waves of heated mist roll away and spread out like a table-cloth, or wreathe about and vanish in the deep, tenderly-radiant heights of heaven! . . .

But now you have betaken yourself to the remote fields, to the steppes. You have driven ten versts along country roads,—and here, at last, is the highway. For a long, long time, you drive past endless trains of freight-wagons, past tiny posting-stations with a hissing samovár under the shed, wide-open gates and a well, from one church-village to another, through boundless fields, along green hemp-patches. Magpies flutter from willow to willow; peasant women, with long rakes in their hands, roam about the fields; a wayfarer, in a threadbare nankeen kaftan, with a wallet on his back, trudges wearily along; the heavy carriage of a landed proprietor rolls smoothly toward you, drawn by six well-grown and broken-winded horses. From the window projects the corner of a pillow, and on the foot-board, clinging to a cord, sits a footman sideways, wrapped in a cloak, and mud-bespattered to the very eyebrows. Here is a wretched little county town, with wooden houses all askew, interminable fences, uninhabited stone buildings belonging to merchants, and an ancient bridge over a deep ravine. . . . Further, further! . . . . The steppe regions have begun. You cast a glance from the crest of a hill—what a view! Round, low hillocks, ploughed and planted to their very summits, spread out in broad waves; ravines overgrown with bushes wind about between them; small groves are scattered about, like long islands; from village to village run narrow paths; churches gleam white; between the sides of the cliffs a little river glitters, traversed in four places by dams; far away in the fields bustards stand up prominently in goose file; an ancient manor-house, with its offices, its fruit-orchard and thresh-ing-floor, is nestled down beside a tiny pond. But you drive further and further. The hills grow smaller and smaller, hardly a tree is to be seen. Here it is, at last,—the boundless, limitless steppe! . . .

And on a winter day to roam among the tall snow-drifts in search of hares, to inhale the keen, frosty air, involuntarily to narrow the eyes from the dazzling, fine glitter of the soft snow, to admire the green hue of the sky above the reddish forest! . . . . And the first spring days, when everything round about is glittering and falling; athwart the heavy steam of the melting snow there is already an odour of the warming earth; on the thawed spots, beneath the slanting rays of the sun, the larks are warbling with confidence; and, with merry noise and roar, the floods gather from ravine to ravine. . . .

But it is time to end. By the way,—I have mentioned the spring: in spring it is easy to part, in spring the happy long to rove afar. . . . Farewell, reader: I wish you permanent good fortune.